T0345563

The Search

The Search

SHAHEEN AKHTAR

Translated from the original Bengali by
ELLA DATTA

Edited by
SHABNAM NADIYA

zubaan

ZUBAAN
an imprint of Kali for Women
128B Shahpur Jat
1st floor
New Delhi 110 049
Email: contact@zubaanbooks.com
Website: www.zubaanbooks.com

First published by Zubaan, 2011

10 9 8 7 6 5 4 3 2 1

ISBN: 978 93 85932 29 8

Zubaan is an independent feminist publishing house based in New Delhi, India, with a strong academic and general list. It was set up as an imprint of the well known feminist house Kali for Women and carries forward Kali´s tradition of publishing world quality books to high editiorial and production standards. "Zubaan" means tongue, voice, language, speech in Hindustani. Zubaan is a non-profit publisher, working in the areas of the humanities social sciences, as well as in fiction, general non-fiction, and books for young adults that celebrate difference, diversity and equality, especially for and about the children of India and South Asia under its imprint Young Zubaan.

Typeset by Jojy Philip, New Delhi 110 015

Printed at Repro Knowledgecast Limited, Thane

To Ferdousi Priyobhashani
who opened the half-shut door, and drew me into the
inner chambers of the Muktujuddho

1

Acknowledgements

I am specially grateful to Dr Hameeda Hossain, Director of the Oral Histories Project on 1971, which inspired me to write the novel *Talaash*. I owe a debt of gratitude to innumerable unknown freedom fighters and many unnamed violated Biranganas.

I remember with gratitude Nilima Ibrahim, whose book *Ami Birangona Bolcchi* is the first chronicle of the unheard voices of Biranganas. I thank those who have been involved in the long and complex process of the English translation of *Talaash* – Firdous Azim, Manas Ray, Mofidul Hoque, Yasmine Kabir and Zahidur Rahim Anjan, who shared the joys and anxieties of the process. My special thanks go to Shabnam Nadiya and Mahmud Rahman for editing and preparing the manuscript. Many thanks to the translator Ella Datta and the publisher Urvashi Butalia.

ONE

I

The Maze of the Wetlands

Moments of her past surface in Mariam's mind like clumps of water hyacinth caught in the eddies of murky waters. This happens whenever someone asks about her life, or when Mariam, her mind and body becalmed like a still pond, recollects times gone by.

She was Mariam, Mary in other words. She remembers the moment: her body is stretched upwards, one hand reaching for the clothesline in the courtyard, the other hanging loosely by her side. One foot rests on a brick, the other is in the air—solid ground just three inches below. It is as if she is half suspended on the gallows, from where she watches Montu leave with tears in his eyes. Actually she does not see him. She hears the creak of the gate opening and knows that Montu has gone.

By the time she has fumbled along the rope, picked up the gamccha, blown her nose, wiped her eyes and looked up, Montu, her younger brother, has disappeared down the bend in the alley. Tears blur Mariam's vision. She is momentarily blinded. She does not see or hear anything—except for the metallic sound of the gate. She does not know it then but this unseen, unheard moment holds in its womb a terrible explosion. Montu is lost forever in its smoky eruption.

Mariam survives with her body squeezed and pounded like meat in a mortar and pestle or with a life which is portioned out like the sacrificial flesh of the qurbani. After that moment, her body is never her own. She can never lay claim to her life again.

It is not just in times of war but in times without conflict, in times of peace, that a woman's life is thought of as a four-wheeled vehicle, with the body as its driver. If the vehicle veers an inch away from the road paved with customs and rules, then it crashes into the rubbish heap. Life has fallen. She becomes a fallen woman.

Even now Mariam likes to think from time to time that she and Montu, having locked the house, are going out, carefully stepping on the untidy line of bricks through the water and the mud by the tubewell. Behind them is the empty house, ahead of them the village. At the time, city-dwellers were looking for safe havens, away from meetings, marches, slogans, police firings and the turmoil from the shifts in power play. It was the children who showed the way. The deep shade of the banyan tree, the quiet afternoon lull in the marketplace, the pleasant river bank in the evening, rows of boats with their sails aloft, and the distant fields bathed in moonlight – all these images in the pages of their drawing books echo dimly-lit memories. Many bundled up their belongings and left for those places. But some didn't. Others returned after a few days, irked by their own childishness.

Mariam forced Montu to return to their village home, but she stayed back, trying to cling desperately to life in a city rocked by turbulence. All her fears were centred around her adolescent younger brother who had picked up an iron rod and wanted to be among those who were creating history in the midst of the choppy waves of protest and repression.

Mariam had deprived him of that opportunity. Montu argued, refused to eat. Mariam was implacable. After many arguments and squabbles, the neo-rebel left the city with his newly sprouted moustache and beard, carrying within him the birth pangs of history. Mariam felt secure that even if there were skirmishes along the way, they would be between human beings. She was still afraid of ghosts and evil spirits like jinns and paris. She had not yet lost her faith in humans. In her conscious and subconscious being, the awareness of human violence was limited to head injuries.

If someone didn't hit him on the head first, then Montu would travel homewards in the bus through the first hours of the night. After that, before he would reach home, there was the Sundari marshland, about three miles long and two and a half miles wide. If people didn't cross it while daylight lasted then there was the danger of losing one's way or losing one's senses. Ghosts took hold of them, made them lock-jawed.

During the monsoon, the travellers had the boatmen for company. They ensured that no one got lost. Both the boatmen and those taking the ferry took turns at rowing, smoking a hukkah, swapping stories. Eventually the eerie darkness of the wetlands would disappear. The sky would lighten. The birds would begin to stir.

But as winter set in, the wetlands dried up and innumerable serpentine pathways wound their way through the heart of the marshes. Then the wetlands would seem like a map of hell. It was during such a period in the third week of March 1971 that Montu was completely alone in Sundari's marsh. Mary shivers with apprehension.

The hell that brother and sister had witnessed in the Sundari marsh just three years ago seemed to journey with them through the rest of their lives. It drove one of them to death and the other to become a victim of history.

Three years before the war broke out, Mariam was in her second year at college. Montu had just returned from his mathematics tuition in the late afternoon or early evening the day they got the news of the death of their Dadi.

Mother's letter instructed them to pray for their grandmother with two extra rakats of namaz. For she had been a nek-banda, a pious soul. *The Greatly Merciful has accepted the life of his dear insan while she was prostrate in shizda on her prayer mat. Montu, Mary – do not weep and wail needlessly. That will only increase the torments of the grave for your dear Dadi.*

Mariam and Monty did exactly what they had been told not to do in the letter. Returning from his private tuition, Montu did not even get a chance to put down his books and papers before he was told of his grandmother's death. Instantly, his pen fell from his hand and it was followed by his geometry box with its ruler and compass. Mariam stopped chanting the doa-darud. She clung to Montu and brother and sister cried their hearts out. They packed their bags as they shed tears and then, locking up the house, they ran towards the bus stand to catch the last bus.

At midnight when they reached the boggy Sundari's marsh, not only were there no human beings to greet them, there was also no familiar sound, nor even a sliver of light. Their feet made flapping noises in the dark silence as they walked over the bent stubbles of just-harvested paddy. Montu said to Mary in the frightened tone of a sailor on watch in mid-ocean who has lost his way, "Mary Bu, if we had a compass with us then we would have no fear of losing our way."

Mariam regretted that in the rush to get out, she had forgotten to bring even a flashlight. Just then she spied a flame nearby. The scientific-minded Montu said, "It's a will-o'-the-wisp. Here now, gone the next moment." Quite true! The flame flickered once again. One of them could see it, the other couldn't. This went on for a while and then finally both of them saw it at the same time. They also heard indistinct words whispered like the soft buzz of bees. "What if they're thieves or burglars, what if they attack us?" Montu paid no attention to Mary's fears. Although it had been only six months since he had begun smoking in secret, at that moment his craving for a smoke was intense. Afraid of being discovered by family elders, he had not brought his cigarettes and matchbox with him. There would most certainly be people around that fire. And if there were men, he deduced, there was bound to be cigarettes, or bidis or hukkahs, something with them. Montu's pace suddenly quickened. As he walked ahead, he said, "Mary Bu, speak some sense. What kind of wealth are we carrying that dacoits will attack us?"

But the more they advanced, the further the fire receded. When they got close to the spot, there was no trace of fire, the hum of conversation had disappeared. It was as if a swarm of bees seeking honey had flown away carrying a lantern. Brother and sister felt their bodies become leaden, their hearts palpitated with anxiety, their tongues turned stiff as planks. In the midst of this confusion, the thought flashed through Mariam's mind that this was the elusive aleya, the marsh-light. When she tried to say this to her brother, she found she had lost her voice. In their efforts to reach the fire, they had completely lost their orientation of east-west, north-south. All that was left to them was the ground under their feet and the sky above.

They sat down on the ground and tried to locate the polestar in the northern sky. The distant sky looked like a brilliantly woven, sumptuous Benarasi sari – the richly worked *zari* surface might have received appreciation at a wedding, but the sparkling silvery field of stars was a nightmare for them. Frustrated, they turned away from scanning the sky and looked down at the small pools of water that formed in Sundari's marsh at the onset of winter. There too they saw strips of the richly woven sari, torn reflections of the starry sky. Seeing those reflections and themselves walking topsy-turvy was enough to confuse them further. At a distance, the blue phosphorescent light seemed to mock them.

This was the chimera of Sundari's marsh which disoriented people and enticed them into a death trap. But Mary and Montu could not afford to be lured. They had to reach home at any cost. It was true that they wouldn't see their beloved Dadi there, but the garlic cloves planted on the grave would not have sprouted yet and the bamboo fencing surrounding it would still be intact.

Montu turned his eyes away from the alluring light and resolved that from then on he would no longer trust whatever he saw in the dark. He would have to move by trusting whatever he could not see. Three and a half years later he would take a similar decision without informing his companions.

The incident occurred in the dead of night when a bridge was being blown up near the border. The match had been lit on the safety fuses capping the circuits. All around them was the crackling noise of blazing flames. The other young men fled from the scene according to plan. Montu spotted a ray of light approaching from the opposite direction at the speed of a fast jeep. He was sceptical about the existence of that glimmer of light. And like the death-wish of a termite flying towards a flame, he ran towards the beam of light.

In Sundari's marsh, even when he saw the small piles of straw, Montu began to hallucinate that these were not piles of straw laid out in line but places set for a banquet of jinns. Immediately, he changed his route. Mariam, who was following a few steps behind, did not dismiss the idea that the straw might be signalling the possibility of a human settlement nearby. She yanked Montu back by his pullover. Montu groaned with a strangled voice. Mariam sensed the craziness in his behaviour. When she tried to force him, he began to ramble. In a thick, phlegm-laden voice he said, "Don't Mary Bu, don't you go that way. They'll twist your neck and bury you in the ground like Sundari."

Montu's body slewed, then crashed to the ground like the sawn trunk of a tree. Who was this Sundari, Mariam didn't know. Gradually, dawn broke. Mariam gently removed her brother's foaming face from her lap and stood beside the nearby swamp. She saw in the shadows of the fading stars and planets the reflection of a frightened woman. She did not recognize herself. Looking at the reflection, Mariam called soundlessly, "Sundari, Sundari." The reflection moved, a soft ripple on the surface of the water. As if the woman was shivering, awakeening to her call in the heart of the swamp after so many years.

Who was this woman? Had she killed herself, unable to bear the pain of unrequited love? Or did she die of starvation? Or perhaps she had been banished to Sundari's marsh because she was pregnant with an illegitimate child? And then she never went back to the village. She was lost forever amidst the marshlands, the haystacks, the reflections of innumerable stars. But the marsh that had been named after her spread a dark dread when shadows set in after sunset. It waylaid travellers, pushed them towards death.

Watching the reflection in the pool, Mariam felt herself becoming one with the other woman, Sundari, of the legend. The woman who did not live as a part of family or society, whose name was the only thing that lived on after her. At the close of that night, Mariam and Sundari – one wailed and the other laughed and their echoes reverberated in the vastness of space. It was impossible to distinguish who was laughing and who was crying.

And Montu, despite having his elder sister beside him, lost his way in Sundari's swamp and lost consciousness. He foamed at the mouth for two days and suffered a raging fever for a week. And just three years after this, he had to go to war, to give his blood to save men's lives, to defend this wetland, the haystacks, the aleya marsh-light, the homesteads and crops.

II

The Birth Story of Mariam Aka Mary

We'll give, give, give
our blood, our blood,
Brave Bangalis take up arms
Liberate Bangladesh

A long, serpentine procession crowds into the narrow lane in front of Mariam's house. The men are armed with iron rods, bamboo lathis, wooden oars, bed posts. Suddenly, two young boys rush out from the heart of the procession, panting. As soon as Mariam tells them, 'Montu has gone back to the village,' they hurry back and join the tail of the procession. At that very moment, a voice blares into the hand-held megaphone at the head of the procession, "*Tomar amar thikana* (Your address and mine…)." The response is immediate, "Padma, Meghna, Jamuna," a roar in unison, crashing all barriers.

Mariam stands like a solitary tree on the banks of the river, shaking helplessly as if in anticipation of a massive landslide. The movement that spelled liberation for all has meant imprisonment for her. All educational institutions are closed indefinitely. The law courts and commercial institutions are barely functioning. She has graduated but is sitting at home.

People will think her mad if she goes looking for a job in the middle of this turmoil. And in any case a job is not the solution to her present problems.

Mariam wishes that she had asked the two boys in for a little while at least. It was not so much that she wanted to know how the talks about their political future had progressed at the President Haven: should we participate in the National Assembly, or should we sacrifice whatever we have and go to war to demand our just rights? No, what she wanted was news of Abed.

She wanted to know if Abed would come today, Mariam had important matters to discuss with him. To obtain this information, and to inform him of this, she needed a messenger, anyone, known or unknown, human or even a bird. The situation was that perilous. Before March 25, Mary or Mariam's needs were no different from those of other girls of her age. She wanted a secure life with a husband and family. She wanted to be a mother.

By this time the procession has shaken up the lane and left it behind on its onward march. Mariam knows that this rally will end up at Paltan Maidan, like the others did. Just as rivers, tributaries and streams end up in the sea. She knows this, although she has never been a part of any procession from beginning to end.

In 1969, every day one rally or another would leave the Bakshi Bazar college where she was studying. Like bits of straw or flotsam, she and other students also got dragged out once or twice from the classroom or the college compound in the strong current of protest washing over the girl students. Once, Mariam's sandal strap broke when they reached the road in front of EPUET. The procession was supposed to go to Eden College. She limped along barefoot with all the other girls for a while. Then, just as they were nearing Palashi, she found the right moment to quietly escape. It was while she was getting her sandal repaired by a cobbler that she met Abed Jahangir, a resident student of S.M. Hall. Later, Abed would often say that if she had not run away from the procession that day, they would never have met. They would each have remained in their own orbit. From 1969 to 1971. Now Abed says, "Girls like you are going in for military training with dummy rifles. They are practising marching–left, right, left, right–under the blazing sun, shouting slogans at the top of their voices. And you, you can speak of nothing but marriage."

Why does Mariam talk of marriage anyway? Abed does not even wish to hear Mariam broach the subject. He avoids the woman as if she were a piece of trash.

Mariam leaps over the drain and reaches the head of the lane in a trice. By then the procession has reached the main road. Mariam stands still at the head of the lane, unable to decide whether to return or go out in search of Abed. She has been standing there from late afternoon to evening as long as she can remember. She stands there until the windows of the double-storied house in front open and a pair of eyes glints in the darkness. She stands numb, frozen. It seems as if she has been caught and held not by a pair of eyes, but within the range of a rifle barrel. A shot will ring out the instant she moves.

Mariam has not seen the person the eyes belong to. She sees only the eyes. She guesses that he is a man because the windows facing their home open and he stares at Mariam with a gaze as deadly as a gun only when Montu is absent. If a procession enters the lane at that moment, the windows immediately slam shut. Montu says that the man is either a thief or a murderer. He is probably one of the 325 prisoners who broke out of the Central Jail a few days ago. But he could also be a dalal, an agent. The owner of the house, the Haji Shaheb, has been a Muslim League man from the early days of British rule.

During the elections, Haji Shaheb drove away his son, a follower of the Awami League, along with his family. The first floor of the house remained empty for some months after that. Now, of course, ninety-nine per cent of the population supports the Awami League. So Haji Saheb does not want to rent out the first floor and bring in the enemy. Mariam thinks she will ask Haji Shaheb, 'The new tenant may be a dalal, a thief or murderer, but why does he stare at me with such an unblinking gaze?' She will demand punishment for his shamelessness.

But the women of Haji's house are in purdah. What if she has to return humiliated after having to listen to a sermon in response to her complaint? As it is, Haji Shaheb is furious with Montu. During the elections, Montu had painted the Awami League's boat symbol on Haji Shaheb's rough, unpainted wall. But then, she thinks, it was Montu who painted the symbol, not her. She has never punctured cycle-rickshaw tyres, never torched buses, never thrown brickbats at policemen.

But what if the Haji says, 'True you haven't done all this. But you're a college-educated, aware young woman. Tell me honestly, what do you want—a unified Pakistan or a nation partitioned through India's dalali, its nefarious agency?' If one looked at both ends of the Bengalis' weighing scales one could see a ninety-degree tilt. No matter how heavy the weights the Haji Shaheb added to his side, the scale would never be even with Montu's. That is why he is almost a prisoner in his own house now. And to bolster his resources, he has caught an owl and kept it on the first floor.

But where is Mariam at this moment? Is she inside or outside? From the entrance of the lane, her home and the main road are at equal distances. After Montu's departure, she has become neutral. The thought disturbs her, she feels afraid. It is a time when people are arming themselves with whatever they can lay their hands on. So Mariam struggles to pull out a post from the bamboo fencing near the gate in a bid to arm herself. The task is not easy. The worm-ridden bamboo seems to have struck roots. It will break but will not be pulled out. She gives up trying to free it and thinks of going inside the house. Instantly, she senses the rifle barrel-gaze boring into her back. She pulls herself together and drags at the post with all her strength. It breaks in the middle but she keeps hold of the upper portion, although the force of the movement makes her totter. As she regains her balance, the dense darkness of the first floor window is shattered by the sound of loud laughter. It's impossible to tell from the sound who is laughing. Even hyenas laugh like humans. Or humans like hyenas.

What can Mariam do with this fragment of bamboo? She needs a whole one to reach even the first floor window. But if she throws away this broken piece then she is quite defenceless. She is afraid that the window across the lane will seize not just her but their tiny house.

Fear flows in Mariam's blood.

It was after the Hindu-Muslim riots of 1964 and the Indo-Pak war of 1965, when Hindus were leaving for India in droves, that Abba, father of Mary and Montu, bought this piece of land in Rayer Bazar dirt cheap. Actually, he was never interested in acquiring land or property in the city. It was his brother-in-law, Golam Mostofa, his wife's eldest brother, who had become a millionaire buying and selling property owned by Hindus at the time of Partition.

It was Golam Mostofa who advised his sister's husband, who was a jotedar, a large landowner, to invest the money he'd earned selling the jute crop, in a property available in the city. He should consider the future of his children, Golam Mostofa told him. In any case, once his only son was educated, would he cling to the soil of the village and wield the plough?

Mary and Montu's Abba is a farmer. He is inseparably bound to the soil—soil that is rich and fertile. Initially, he was in two minds about buying land in the city. But afterwards, he became attached to this plot of land that was being strangled by the buildings surrounding it. The previous owner had left for India. The land he had left behind was now enemy property. The courts, at the time, were brimming with cases relating to this kind of real estate. Besides, he had never had faith in his brother-in-law's citified wheeling-dealing.

So, to stake his claim on this unfamiliar, barren piece of land, he brought two masons from his village, Fultali, and quickly built a two-roomed structure with a tin roof. The brick walls were without any lime-wash. In front of the house, there was an open yard similar to the ones in the village homes. There was a kitchen at one side and clumps of bamboo at the back.

In Fultali, there would have been a front room for outsiders to sit in, and a cowshed. Here the space was left vacant. In the middle of the yard, there was a tubewell and a bathing area enclosed in tin sheets. Inside, a plank of wood is in place like the steps on a riverbank. One could sit on it and pour water on the body. Placed next to the bamboo grove, the toilet was made with a bamboo frame. It was covered with bamboo matting on three sides and the entrance was hung with a hessian curtain. The boundary of the plot of land measuring four kattha was marked by a bamboo fence. The gate was made with heavy, black iron. On the gate, large, white letters proclaimed: "This property is owned by Kafiluddin Ahmed, Village Fultali, P. O. Saharparh".

For a long time there was no house number on the nameplate. A maulavi was brought from the village at Kafiluddin Ahmed's expense to secure the house by chanting spells and restraining evil spirits by bottling them up. He buried four bottles in the four corners of the house. This is how, by warding off the evil eye of both jinns and humans, Kafiluddin Ahmed of the village of Fultali became undisputed owner of the two-roomed house, built in a half-urban, half-rural manner.

That the house was not rented out and was left empty for a year was because he did not want strangers to live there in return for a few takas and become virtual owners of the property. The house might have continued to remain empty if Mariam had not done something unthinkingly, without anticipating its implications or its dangerous fallout.

Mariam was then in her in-between years, not too young, not too old. She was a student of Class Ten. Every year students from distant villages came to stay in their home to appear for the matriculation examination. The nearby town was just a mile away. The examination centre was in the two-storied high school and the tin shed that was the primary school.

That year they came as usual. During the gaps between the examinations, the boys tucked up their lungis and jumped into the pond to catch fish. At the end of the day they went to the village market and brought back the first mangoes of the season, as well as jackfruit with small juicy sections, biscuits, sweetmeats. It was not the custom to reimburse the hosts with cash for their hospitality. And so they tried to pay back in kind with these little gifts – catching fish, buying titbits from the market.

One of the examinees became interested in Mariam's studies right from the first day. Whenever he came into the inner quarters for a meal, he advised Mariam that it was not enough to do well in arithmetic and geometry; for top grades in mathematics, algebra was the thing to bank on.

The boy was a distant relative named Jashim. Jashimul Haque. On the last day of the examination, Jashimul Haque invited Mariam to accompany him to a movie. Abba was not at home. He was busy building the house in Dhaka. Without letting her mother know, Mariam went to the district town with Jashim to watch a film. She came home after three days. The boy got scared and abandoned her midway. He just vanished from the scene.

Initially, the people at home tried to get her married after the incident. In the village, scandal floats in the air faster than the fluff of cotton wool. When Mariam's parents realized that they could not arrange her marriage even if they spent huge sums of money, they thought of the house in the city.

Let Mariam go to the city and take up higher studies. Villagers don't remember anything for long, they forget. In a few years, they will forget this incident as well. Then there won't be any problems arranging a match for their daughter. Actually, this brainwave came from Kafiluddin Ahmed's brother-in-law Golam Mostofa. Having dealt in real estate for several years, he had learnt a bit about human psychology. What was most important was that he had tremendous self-confidence.

Mariam had by then matriculated and been placed in the first division. She got special credits in mathematics, having learnt the algebra formulas by heart. The house that had been built with the future of the only son in mind was thus opened up for the daughter. Montu went to Dhaka as a bonus: to guard his older sister.

Mary goes inside with the broken, worm-riddled bamboo in her hand. She had sent her protector, Montu, home to the village, just before the city was attacked, when even the birds were deserting their nests. Their house stands in the city with the appearance of the village. Mariam has been kept here for the last five years with the purpose of hoodwinking the scandalmongers of Fultali village. And then, taking advantage of their short memory, her marriage will be arranged. Mariam knows this; anyone who passes the threshold of the house would know. The house looks like a hostel. All the furniture it can boast of in the two rooms is made up of two beds, one clotheshorse, and two armless chairs on either side of the study table.

When Abed comes, he goes directly to the bed and sits on it instead of in a chair. Montu does not object. Montu had become a disciple of Abed's politics from day one. "Abed Bhai, was there really a conspiracy at Agartala? Is it true that Monem Khan is General Ayub Khan's nephew?" Abed the student leader is never impatient with Montu's silly questions. Instead, he is excited, all fired up. Instantly, his voice is raised to the skies, as if he is addressing thousands at Paltan Maidan. At such times, Mariam shuttles continuously between the room and the yard. She is apprehensive. On the one hand, she is concerned about Montu. His studies have almost been jettisoned after he was bitten by the politics bug. On the other, her eyes furiously scan the windows and balconies of the houses around them. The arrival of a third person in this house invariably stirs the inquisitiveness of others. Their eyes and ears are trained on this house at all times, like gun-barrels. Mariam has no way of preventing Abed's random arrivals and departures. She is nervous about him escaping from her. She has mortgaged herself to him and has reached a point of no return. In any case, how many times can one turn back?

Jashimul Haque had clasped her hand warmly when he had taken her to see an English movie at Mohua cinema. They had forgotten they were sitting in the rear stalls. A fellow villager had seen them holding hands and wolf-whistled. After that they had been too scared to go back home. For three days they had wandered in the streets. Then the boy ran away and left her stranded. Penniless, she managed to get home with great difficulty. That was the first return. If Jashim had had a job, they could have gone to court and had a love-marriage as a penalty for holding hands. Mary would not have had to return alone to the village. All this Jashim had told her in English. Mariam had been bowled over by his learning. In the fifteen years of her life she had not met a man as erudite as him. Mariam had believed what Jashimul Haque told her.

Coming home was the fall from paradise for this young girl. In the next year, she suddenly grew up. Even before she could understand the true nature of her feelings for a man—attraction or love—the feelings dried up. Now she is riddled with doubt about everything. The only thing she realizes now is that marriage is the only successful end to a woman's life, all else is false. What does it matter if her learned lover whispers sweet nothings to her? He doesn't have the balls to marry her. As a result, Jashimul Haque is promptly discarded from her heart, like an aborted foetus wrapped in blood-soaked rags and consigned to the trash-heap in shame and disgust.

Mariam arrived in Dhaka like a white swan who had shaken off the dirt stuck to her feathers after swimming in a scummy pond. The simile was Abed's. Apparently, this was the image that rose in his mind when he saw her for the first time, dressed for college. He told her this after hearing her story. But Mariam has other thoughts. Jashim was like a young sapling with potential, but she thinks of Abed as a young tree ready to bear fruit. One can climb and perch on it the moment one gets the opportunity. Then all the fruit is hers for the picking. Accordingly, in the two years between 1969 and 1970, Abed spins dreams for her and Mariam dreams.

At the time, the meetings and processions abounded in promises. If all the promises were collected in one place, they would have added up to dozens of mountains. The mountains would be made up of dreams of the deceived people. The people of this land suffered throughout their lives from a multitude of oppressions and deceptions. That it was the non-Bengali ruling elite who were the reason for their suffering was something that they had been hearing now and then ever since the Partition. Now the time had come for a hands-on confrontation. They felt the venomous attacks, even as they saw the posters of a giant serpent rising from the map of West Pakistan, arching over the huge landmass of India, and biting into their country. That's why political speeches today have the power of fables. The listeners can visualise how golden Bengal is being pillaged to pave the streets of West Pakistan with gold. Pakistan is no country, but a cow. Its front legs are planted in the east, the rear legs in the west. The Bengalis feed it daily with grass, while the West Pakistanis milk it. East Pakistan earns sixty per cent of the revenues but gets to spend only twenty-five per cent. West Pakistan gobbles up the rest. The per capita income is higher there but things cost less.

Election posters in 1970 showed detailed graphs and charts of unequal development and exploitation calculated down to the last penny. Mariam herself appears as the metaphor for the deprived motherland while Abed is its promising saviour. He sows the seeds of a dream of her salvation. He scatters them while they stroll down Fuller Road to Shaheed Minar, the martyrs' memorial, and along Curzon Hall to the wooden pier leading to the hanging restaurant on the lake in the Ramna Green. Abed has sat for his master's degree in sociology. The moment he gets a job, the seeds will sprout into a tree. The year of 1971 brings with it the smell of gunpowder. Mariam's dreams take wing and fly away. Now Abed speaks of nothing else but taking military training with dummy rifles.

The five years from 1965 to 1971 have muddied the waters and created powerful eddies. Mariam was then a young girl. Jashimul Haque had merely held her hand, and for that she had to leave her village and come to the city. But now her relationship with

Abed has rolled onto the bed. In the beginning, it was a peaceful relationship played out in the cool shade of the rain trees lining both sides of the avenue between S.M. Hall and EPUET, with the ground covered with leaves and flowers like a woven carpet. At first, their understanding of companionship and sharing remained limited to shelling peanuts and feeding each other.

Gradually, Dhaka turned into a political cauldron. Abed's studies were over. But in job interviews, the big bosses seem to think that they are the masters and the applicants their slaves. In those days, Dhaka University was truly an independent island outside the clutches of the Pakistani military junta. No laws, whether martial or not, were effective there. Abed has been an independent, autonomous resident of this place for several years now.

At the interview table, he wants to punch the nose of the employer as an answer to every question he asks. He gets into an even greater rage when he tries to suppress this urge. And then he decides, no more. He just won't accept kowtowing to the fat cats. He gets admitted to the library science course and extends his stay on this independent island. Earlier his political activities were limited to the occasional shouting of slogans while marching in processions and clapping from the rear ranks when President Ayub's effigy was being torched. During this phase, he shifts to the forefront of the processions, and sets fire to the effigy with his own hands. The independent islander is no longer happy with his tiny autonomous island.

He now feels the need to extend this domain by selecting the fat cats, the majority of them non-Bengalis, and exterminating them one by one, like lice. Abed becomes a busy man. His days of munching peanuts while walking down tree-shaded avenues are over. But he needs Mariam for other reasons. Through the ages, romance has gone hand in hand with heroism. The hero's excitement cannot be assuaged by merely pushing his hands under her white sari through her blouse in a curtained rickshaw. It was like carrying a flaming torch through the streets without setting anything on fire. He has the torch with him but he cannot light a flame. For that he has to possess the girl completely and that, in turn, means that he requires a bed for the purpose.

Mariam becomes bewildered at the fast pace of events. For the last few days, she feels herself melting behind the covered rickshaw, becoming moist with anticipation. She is scared but cannot resist. One afternoon, taking advantage of Montu's absence, Abed succeeds in bedding Mariam.

The same bed on which Abed had sat while giving Montu lessons in politics, has changed character in a trice. Mariam shivered with fear and excitement through the raging storm that overtook her. She was not sure whether it was right to do all this before marriage. Besides, Montu could have walked in any moment. This time Mariam experienced both fear and resistance. But Abed was not ready to listen. The whole act became very painful, perhaps because Mariam was resisting. Leaving the bed awash in blood, Abed descends as if exiting not a bed, but a stage in a theatre.

A new chapter in surrender began through this blood-letting. Mariam became pregnant. She cannot think of Abed as merely a lover at this point, she has to think of him as a husband. But Abed no longer thinks in terms of a job, a home, a wife and kids. His involvement has shifted to power, state, political movement. His conversation is dominated by these subjects. These thoughts obsess him even when Mariam clings to him in a desperate embrace during their brief bouts in bed, not willing to let him go in that intense moment of union.

Mariam and Abed's physical relationship is three months old. Abed is disoriented the first few weeks. When he is with Mariam his thoughts are dominated by the world outside and when he is away from her he thinks of her all the time. On the one hand, there is his country, on the other, his woman. The unnecessary clothing cloaking both of them has been removed. Two naked bodies before him are burning with feverish desire. He cannot find respite anywhere. Day and night, his sole companion is his body without a mind or a heart. Thus the presence of the body becomes manifest in bed and on the streets. Gradually, he removes his body from Mariam and reconciles his body with his mind in the world outside. The spread of this space is more than fifty-five thousand square miles, its potential huge. There the attraction of certain words and symbols – a flag with a bright red sun on a dark green field and a golden map in the centre, the national anthem, the word freedom – become irresistible.

One's wretchedness can no longer be accepted as merely a question of bad luck. The past will disappear into dust like magic. Whatever happens afterwards is nascent in the womb of the future. What lies between these poles is a battle. An unequal war – a pack of powerless people fighting against those who hold the reins of power. It is a battle of home-made bombs, firecrackers, iron rods, Molotov-cocktails, .22 bore rifles, spears, lathis against tanks, powerful cannons, rockets, airplanes and machine guns. The home-made weapons become potent in the hot palms of the rebels. The armed men do not know who prods them forward, incites them – the rebels or the weapons they hold in their hands. Both are desperate.

It is difficult to recognize Abed now. Mariam seldom meets him. Her time is spent in a strange trance from which she wakes up repeatedly with a jolt. There can be no return to her parents in Fultali. Before her is a life or death ordeal by fire.

The State is also facing an ordeal. Before leaving, Montu had said, "OK, Mary Bu, I'll go, but you have to go too. There's a war coming."

Mariam replied, "So what if there is a war? It will be fought by Abed and his kind."

Montu did not prolong the conversation. If his sister wanted to stay in Dhaka for a little longer, let her. When Kafiluddin Ahmed would come to fetch her, she would have to leave. So Montu leaves for their village home on the condition that he can take the radio with him.

Today, Montu is not at home, neither is the radio. On other days, a constant babel continued both inside and outside. In fact, even during curfew, there was always a procession or rally going through the narrow alley. Although they knew that firing was going on, people would deliberately break curfew and take out a procession only to be shot. One night during the curfew, Abed had come like a storm-tossed crow. Montu was astonished. He said, "Abed Bhai, so late at night? How did you get here?" Abed did not enter the room. Standing outside, he replied, "Just came to see how you were." And then he left without meeting Mariam. Today, there is no curfew and no Montu. Can't Abed come once? If he comes, then he wouldn't have to leave from the gate.

Mariam hears the rattle of the gate and steps outside. It must have been the wind or a trick of her hearing. As far as she can see, barring a stray dog, the alley is deserted. The dog has been tied to the lamppost outside the Haji Shaheb's house to keep watch. Mariam decides that she will wait for Abed outside. In case he comes, in case he turns back if he sees the gate locked. After all, there is no sound of human voices or even the radio inside. Mariam stands near the gate. At that very moment, the first floor window of Haji's house clatters open. It is the dead of night. The man seems to have become very bold. He is even clearing his throat to make his presence known. She quickly goes inside and slams the door shut.

That night, Mariam is restless. One moment she lies on the bed and the very next she sits up. She unties the strings of the mosquito net. A light breeze tickles the soles of her feet. The curtains flutter and slap against the windows. The street dog suddenly yelps. Its wail is echoed by another canine a couple of houses away. The dog in front of the Haji Shaheb's house leads the baying. It is picked up by hundreds of dogs very far away, ominously rending the night air with their moans and sending shivers down everyone's spine. In Fultali, dogs bayed like this when epidemics were about to strike. Mariam has heard that the dogs mourned the loss of humans.

This month, more than a hundred people have died as a result of the shootings. More will die if there is a war. Are the dogs howling for the dead, or are they signalling the imminent death of hordes of people if war breaks? The war marches down the deserted city streets, opens the gate of Mariam's house and sits on the threshold. It rests awhile and then crawls on all fours into the room. War dances around her bed. Will she die in the coming war even though she will not be fighting? Will Abed die or survive? Montu has left for the village. A night riddled with dread of the coming war weighs on Mariam like a heavy stone.

The next day the city is decorated with the red and green Joi Bangla flags. The red and green flags sporting the map of the new nation flutter from the rooftops of the houses lining the streets. The rickshaw, which Mariam has climbed into, has a six inch flag on a thin stick tied to the cycle bell with a length of string. It dances to the rhythm of the clinking bell. Although neither independence nor autonomy is the solution to Mariam's problem, her heart leaps in joy at the colourful flags. She gets off at the gate of S.M. Hall and buys two flags from a hawker for a taka. She thinks—here she is, holding the two-for-a-taka flags—freedom in her grasp without any bloodshed. She waves the flag of freedom and enters Abed's room.

Mariam has come to S.M. Hall to have a final showdown. But seeing Abed's annoyed face, the flags of free Bangladesh get crumpled in her clenched fists. Her plans fizzle out. She slumps down and sits in a corner of the bed. If Abed looked at her calmly, without getting angry, he would have seen an exhausted girl, who had not slept all night and, confused and anxious, had rushed to him for refuge. But he has no eyes for her distress.

It is March 23 today. Pakistan's Republic Day has been transformed into Bangladesh's day of resistance. In the morning, they had flown the flag of free Bangladesh at several embassies and the Hotel Intercontinental. But in Abed's heart, apprehension mounts. The flag, after all, is a bit of cloth, a mere rag. Raising or lowering it is a matter of minutes. On the other hand, a huge number of army generals and military officials are now in Dhaka with Bhutto and Yahya. Heavy armaments are also coming in from West Pakistan by sea. Days are being eaten up in the guise of "discussions" while all this was going on. Valuable days. Who will pay for them?

Inside the hostel room, there is a pile of bed posts, lathis, iron rods, brick dust, packets filled with explosives and other materials for making hand-bombs. He feels like throwing them all out. These are supposed to be their weapons of war! He needed to go to the house at Road 32 and demand of Sheikh Mujib directly, how long he thinks it will take to liberate Bangladesh by this non-cooperation movement. Could it be that he still can't give up his dream of becoming Pakistan's prime minister even after so much has happened? He is telling the people to make each home a fortress, keep the movement alive. But he himself is bargaining with Yahya and Bhutto at the President Bhavan, haggling as if buying fish.

Swinging his legs as he sits between Abed and Mariam, Abed's roommate Suman says dramatically, "Abed Bhai, no matter what the leaders do, for us there is no going back."

He may have said it in continuation of something that was being discussed before Mariam entered the room. But the situation had changed with her entrance. The two roommates take no notice of her arrival, bringing as she does a deeper problem and it did not look as if they are likely to. So Mariam quickly butts in responding to Suman's comment, "There's no going back for me either."

Only Abed understands the significance of her statement. He casts a sharp glance at her. Suman thinks she is talking in riddles. What could the girl have meant that could so anger their student leader? But Abed's angry glance pierces him as well. With all the dignity that he can muster, he leaves the room and walks out to the corridor outside.

"No room for retreat? What do you mean?" Abed shouts. There was a challenge in his voice, an invitation to fight. Mariam sounds like a piece of sodden wood. Choked with emotion, she cries, "Abed, you know very well what I am trying to say."

"No, I don't know and I don't want to know," Abed yells as he stands up, "whatever you have to say you better speak directly. Let's have it out once and for all." Mariam feels a shiver of fear. She says, "What do you mean once and for all?

Whatever had to happen has happened. I am not holding you responsible."

"Responsible? Why should I be responsible? It takes two hands to clap – was I the only one involved here?"

There is no way that one can discuss things with Abed today. He wants to see everything to its end – his relationship with Mariam, the liberation movement. He is aggressive, confrontational.

Mariam feels drained inside. What will she do when she leaves this dormitory? Where will she go? In a final attempt to entwine her life with Abed's like a creeper clinging to a tree, she proposes to take rifle training even though she is pregnant.

Her suggestion sets off an explosion. Abed sputters with rage, "Fight! You plan to fight? War is not child's play. Instead of going to the hospital, you've come here to join the war?"

"I won't go to the hospital," Mariam says, stubborn as a mule. When Abed tells her to return home, she refuses. She says that she is afraid to live there on her own. The man there not only stares at her through the window, but also tries to tell her things in gestures. She is trying to concoct more stories about the man's boldness and effrontery, when Abed screams, "Where is Montu? Why doesn't Montu smack him on the head?"

"Montu has gone home to the village. I persuaded him to go back. Nowadays you feel uneasy with Montu around."

Mariam's innuendo triggers Abed's memory. He remembers something, something irrelevant in the middle of all this movement and struggle. But something that cannot be so easily dismissed. The body will have its demands. Desire, so far submerged in an ocean of despair, slowly surfaces. He glances out of the open door towards the veranda outside. Suman is not there now. Abed comes forward, grabs Mariam's arm and pulls her towards him. He pushes his other hand in her blouse. The girl is unresponsive like a block of wood. She no longer feels the surge of a rising tide. After fingering her breasts a bit, Abed moves away annoyed. He says gravely, "The city is no longer safe. Mary, you had better go home to the village."

Can Mary go home in this condition? Has Abed gone off his head? Instead of getting angry, Mariam pleads with Abed for a fistful of charity. "Abed," she cries, "what about the baby?"

Abed looks around for the matchbox. He cannot remember where he kept it. He was supposed to have gotten a job after being interviewed. The likelihood of getting it has been squashed under the jackboot of repression. Does the girl want him to abase himself and sniff again that leathery smell? He is a new man now, new days ahead of him. Abed keeps striking the match to light up his cigarette. Pulling at his cigarette, he grabs Mariam and pulls her close.

Mariam has to leave things unsaid. The backlash of a tumultuous procession rips them apart. Abed regains his senses. He remembers that he is still oppressed, downtrodden. The enemy is advancing. There is a war looming. One has either to kill or be killed. Mary, he thinks, is like a leech. She is still clinging to him. No matter how much it hurts, how much it bleeds, she has to be shaken off and discarded.

At that very moment a huge crowd is marching in front of S.M. Hall like a stormy wind. The slogans have the intensity and sharpness of hail. The birds resting in the shirish trees flutter and fly away from their nests in all this uproar. Abed does not give Mariam time to pull herself together and neaten her sari. He grabs her by her shoulder and drags her to the corridor. He has an iron rod in his hand. Suman comes in running and collects a whole bundle of lathis. The rumour has spread that the Mujib-Yahya-Bhutto talks have broken down. The National Assembly meet scheduled for March 25, that is two days later, has once again been postponed.

The weapons piled in Abed's room vanish very quickly. The students are leaving their dormitories and running towards the road. Mariam, afraid of being crushed in the stampede, holds on blindly to something for support. It happens to be a cold, slippery iron rod. Abed races ahead, sees that his hands are empty and retraces his steps. He needs no force to snatch the rod from Mariam. Even so, being forced to come back becomes

a source of anger. Holding on to the rod with both hands, he
lets Mariam know in the midst of all the tumult, his decision
taken a few moments ago that he no longer wants her.

After that he feels the weapon is unnecessary, heavy and
excessive. He throws it away. He does not join the marching
crowds. He leaves the hostel empty of people and walks Mariam
to the road. He waits for a rickshaw under the tracery of rain
tree branches bordering the avenue. The huge wave of the
procession has receded. A faint trace of its clamour and roar
floats towards them as if from a deep, distant sea. Still, the
disturbed birds are too scared to return to their nests. There is
total emptiness all around. Not a soul, not a vehicle to be seen
anywhere. Abed and Mariam walk toward Palashi. The cobbler
sits on the footpath with all his tools just as he did on that first
day. Next to him stands an empty rickshaw. Mariam climbs into
the rickshaw ending the period of her life between 1969 and
1971 that was filled with such sweetness and sorrow.

Back home, Mariam's tears are not to lighten the burden of
her sorrow. After her heart becomes light as a feather, what then?
The aftermath is war. War means uncertainty. No one knows for
sure who will die and who will survive. Abed is on one side of
the two warring factions. According to the unchanging laws of
war, he has a fifty-fifty chance of killing or being killed. Let
us assume that he survives, is not killed. Their relationship has
ended before this life and death conflict can take shape. Mary
will become the mother of a child who has no father. This will
be her fate even if war does not happen. She takes a whole
strip of sleeping pills at one sitting. Thus, for the next two days
Wednesday and Thursday, she is oblivious to the war advancing
to her doorstep. During that time, Mary resumes her foetal form
in the process of being born anew.

For two days running, Kafiluddin Ahmed's brother-in-law
Golam Mostofa had sent people around to enquire about Mary
and Montu. The reason he did not come down himself to find
out about his nephew and niece was that he was busy saving his
skin. The possibility of beating the separatists into submission

or handing over power to them stood equally balanced. If the Bengali separatists come into power then it was likely that the Hindus will return from India and demand all the land, homesteads and other property they left behind. Although all the undeveloped land they had left behind now houses huge buildings, factories and offices, and private homes. Maktabs, Islamic primary schools, are being held in the fancy weekend villas. The signboard of a charity dispensary hangs on what used to be the crumbling walls of the Natmandir, the courtyard in front of the temple. Ponds, private homes and places of Hindu worship have been levelled out to cultivate rice and jute. It was through the agency of Golam Mostofa that, in accordance with the vision of the pro-Partition politicians, Hindustan had really been transformed into Pakistan. The visionaries who had nurtured these dreams are happily resting in their graves. But the time of reckoning has come. The person who has to answer questions is someone who has never harboured any dreams. To save his skin, Golam Mostofa joined the Awami League during the '70 election. No matter that his body was in the Awami League boat though, his mind remained occupied with the thoughts of the Pakistan that he had helped to build. He was no dreamer building castles in the air, he was a true artisan. Golam Mostofa had to remain in the boat for the two months of January and February. Because the Awami League had gained a majority by winning 167 seats out of a total of 313 of the National Assembly. They were the ones who had the rightful claim to form a government. This was more or less expected up till February. But in the afternoon of March 1, Yahya announced over the radio that the reconstituted National Assembly session, supposed to be held on March 3, had been postponed. Thousands reacted by rushing into the streets – just ascricket spectators invade the pitch. It was at this moment that Golam Mostofa jumped off the boat into the deep waters. And then, because of all the protest movements, he just could not reach the shore. All thoughts of his nephew and niece flew out of his mind and it wasn't until Wednesday that he remembered them. He summoned his three sons and asked them to enquire about their safety. Only the simple-minded Saju, the second son who had decided that he would marry no other girl but Mariam, took note of his father's orders. He even came up to the Haji Shaheb's house, but when he saw the dog, he lost his nerve and bolted. A sandal lying upturned within fifty yards of Mary-Montu's house bore testimony to his hasty retreat. When Golam Mostofa beat him up, he took no account of the boy's attempt to reach his cousins. Saju's only fault was that in his terror the poor thing had not noticed even in broad daylight that the dog was tied to the lamppost with a short length of string.

On Thursday evening, the uncle sent his assistant. On the way, the man heard many rumours of the army being deployed. The army was being led by General Tikka, the Butcher of Baluchistan. His bullets would not leave even a single leaf on the trees. He would raze the city to the ground. Suddenly one heard that soldiers wearing coarse, ochre uniforms were patrolling the streets. Golam Mostofa's assistant looks over his shoulders nervously, hesitates and then walks a little further. He finally reaches Pilkhana. But the moment he sees the gun post built with sandbags in front of the gate of the EPR Camp, he forgets all about his master's nephew and niece. To the terror of losing his job is added the concern for his own safety and survival. But if he survives, a job shouldn't be that difficult to find. Secure in this belief, he stands in front of Golam Mostofa and stammers that the boy and girl have left for their village home at mid-day, after the *zohr* prayers that day. Where did he get this information from? The assistant is unable to answer this question. After being scolded by the uncle, the assistant narrates in detail all the rumours that he has heard. Golam Mostofa's disturbed mind forgets the transgressions of his spoilt nephew and niece who have voted for the boat symbol and who have left the city without informing him. The rumours are like steps which he wants to climb to reach the shore that is the Pakistan of 24 years ago. But there are lots of obstacles on the way. The students and the people have cut down big trees and used them to build barricades on the roads. They have also dragged out the water reservoirs, sewerage pipes. They have filled up the gaps in the barricades with bricks. The army will have to clear these hurdles in order to enter the city.

Golam Mostofa is uneasy.

During this time, in her dreams Mariam starts bleeding within. But it happens bit by bit. It begins with the pulling out of her milk teeth. The blood clots, salty on the tongue, mix with her spittle as they come out. She opens her palms and shows the teeth to Montu. Montu sheds tears silently. Then brother and sister desperately search for a mouse hole to slip the tooth into. Montu recites, "Mouse, mouse, take my sister's ugly tooth and give her your beautiful one in return."

Then there's the surprise in Mother's eyes. The girl has started her periods so soon! The blood trickles out from where one urinates. Warmth drips from her body. Black, brown, pink blood clots stain her loose trousers. What disease is this, Mother? The cold curls under her feet, like dogs in winter. One must apply a hot compress at this time to one's lower abdomen to relieve the pain. The hurricane lamp is lit, its wick raised so that the fire flickering like a tongue can be seen through the glass chimney. A piece of cloth is scorched silently in Mother's hands as she heats it on the glass. The stream of blood overflows the drain, crosses the gate, floods the streets and gathers at the Paltan Maidan. There is a massive rally there. Abed gets on the stage. The crowd applauds. Mary gives birth. To a featureless, fatherless, blood clot.

The only reality then is the war. Close by, a bomb explodes very loudly. With the noise of the shattering glass of the window panes, Mariam breaks out of her curled, foetal position and falls to the ground. She is unable to move, unconscious. The solid darkness under the bed is inviting. With another bomb going off, she leaves the aborted foetus behind and leaps into the darkness.

At that moment, Dhaka is burning.

III

Operation Searchlight

March 25, Mukti has entered the long night of horrors. It is dark, and impenetrable like Behula's wedding chamber with its tiny, wax-sealed hole that opened with the hot, vengeful breath of Manasa, the snake goddess. The two women of different ages enter that moment through a similar aperture, the size of the point of a needle.

Mariam is lying unconscious under the bed. She has no recall of that night except for the noise of some explosions. But Mukti wants to envision the transformation of Mary aka Mariam. The war of twenty-eight years ago, that stripped Mariam of her previous identity and labelled her with the new tag of Birangana, the courageous one, provokes Mukti's curiosity. The new label proclaimed its importance for a while but served no useful purpose.

Twenty eight years – more than a quarter of a century. Mukti is also twenty-eight years old. At that very moment when the students and the populace were cutting down trees and dragging discarded water reservoirs to barricade Fuller Road, a mere hundred yards away, in the obstetric ward of the Medical College, Mukti was preparing to emerge from the darkness of her mother's womb. When she was born the next morning, there was not a soul beside her mother except an aged ayah. The lady doctor, after attaching a drip to induce labour, had left for home before Operation Searchlight commenced. That Mukti's birthday ended up on the morning of March 26 instead of March 25, was mainly due to the absence of the doctor, according to her mother. The rest of it was Allah's will. Although she had cursed the doctor that night as she was wracked by the birth pangs, later she forgave her. But she did not pardon Mukti's father. He came to the hospital only on March 27 when the curfew was lifted. By that time, all hell had broken loose outside.

The hospital beds had filled up with dying patients. There was hardly any space left even to walk in the corridors outside. People from the quarters and slums around the college had taken shelter in the corridors with their boxes and trunks. Mukti's Abba believed the Pakistani army had razed the hospital along with Jagannath Hall and the Shaheed Minar on March 25. When he saw his wife and the pretty little baby, he paled. A wife and daughter are burdensome in such times. Mukti's Abba was a young man. He had sired the child at the urging of his wife.

Mukti's mother saw her husband suddenly stand still at the threshold of the ward. His right foot remained outside the threshold for a while. He entered the room when he realized that his wife was gazing at him not just with her eyes but with all her senses. He did not even turn to look at his wife and child. He emptied the thermos patterned with bunches of grapes in the washbasin and put it inside his bag. This was to make sure that his burden grew no heavier. Then he ordered his convalescing wife to follow him with the baby. If they did not leave the city instantly, he would have to die along with the mother and child. He informed her that this was not something he wanted.

Apart from some additional trouble for her mother, the war was a time of hardship for both husband and wife. It was not a time of glory. From the hospital, they moved with only what they had on their backs and the little baby wrapped in rags. They stayed in other people's homes. There was an acute scarcity of baby milk. They had hardly any money in their pockets. They had had to feed the baby with rice water in the feeding bottle. In the middle of all this, Mukti's parents did not even realise when two baby teeth sprouted on Mukti's lower gums. The day the country became free, they removed the hospital rags from Mukti's body and let her roam fearless on the ground. Having moved from shelter to shelter, they were at the time with a distant aunt of Mukti's mother, householders who were comfortably off. Even through the war, they had huge piles of paddy spread around their courtyard. There were mouse holes in the midst of the paddy with little mounds of powdery soil surrounding the holes. The baby learnt to crawl, and then, quickly to sit and put a fistful of loose soil in her mouth before anyone could realize what she was doing. If Mukti's Amma and Abba looked upon the liberation of the country with a sense of wonder, then they thought Mukti's learning to crawl and eat the sacred soil of the free country on the very day of victory a miracle! After a very long time, they began to laugh together and clap their hands. And they named their nine-month-old daughter, Mukti, freedom. This was the only memento of their love for the liberation struggle, the daughter named after the bitter campaign.

Other than the name, Mukti bears no traces of the war, nor does she know much about it. It was not necessary to know about the war to land this job of conducting interviews for a survey. Knowledge about the liberation struggle can be problematic. It creates wrong impressions. The authorities told her repeatedly that instead of gathering prior information, it was more important to listen to those who have had first-hand experience of the war. By listening to them, she would get to learn the a to z of the war. That is what Mukti has been doing for the last two days. Mary aka Mariam has been speaking and Mukti's work has been to listen without comment. At this point in the narrative, the interviewee has lost consciousness from an overdose of sleeping pills and the miscarriage. The time she describes is midnight on March 25, 1971, just a few moments before Mukti's birth. It was a night filled with indescribable horrors. It was a dark night like the one when the venomous serpent bit Lakhindar in the mythical story. It was a night of deceit, betrayal and lack of symmetry. It was a night when military tanks and machine guns were ranged against the barricades of tree trunks and empty galvanized reservoirs of water. It was a night of confrontation between slogans and unending gunfire. It was a night of violence crushing non-cooperation. At the time Mukti's mother was gasping and gulping air. She was trying hard and drawing on all her reserves of strength to press down but she still could not give birth for lack of a doctor. Elsewhere Mary, in the process of aborting a fatherless child, slowly emerged from her foetal form.

The night advanced.

Twenty-eight years, two years shy of three decades. The records may not be mountain high, but scattered all over are sufficient documents and files relating to the war – books, musty-smelling newspapers in libraries. These are the inheritance of Mukti and her peers. But she has not read any of this. Her head is as blank as a sheet of white paper. Mariam is the first to make a mark on it. Like the first introduction to the alphabet, her interviews with Mariam initiate her into a new world of experience. Like an uncomprehending, sightless newborn creature who does not know how to tell food from junk, Mukti instinctively gropes for information on the night of March 25 among the books and papers she is looking at.

One of the novel features of the night is that the dramatis personae were also the audience. Annoyed by the insolence of the Bengalis, they attacked Dhaka from the north. A gentle spring breeze was wafting in from the south at the time. It was a wondrous night perfumed with flowers, a night for the call of the flute, a night for making love. Before dawn, Dhaka was reduced to a terrifying heap of rubble. At a safe distance from the city, the provincial capital was gathered in a place termed the second capital where those giving the orders were enjoying the ruthless acts of violence as if they were watching a film. No one was there to prevent them. Twenty-eight years after the war, to reconstruct the events of the night of March 25, Mukti selects that safe distance. She follows Pakistani Major Siddiq Salik's *Witness to Surrender*. In spite of taking inordinate care, the murderer leaves behind footprints. Even if the bloodstains are carefully wiped away while advancing, even if countless corpses are buried after digging up the ground with a bulldozer, they are eventually discovered. This truth was proved once again in the chapter *Operation Searchlight-I* written by the Major.

Mukti trails the footprints of the murderer.

On the night of March 25, a banner proclaiming 'Outdoor Operations Room' has been hung on the mowed lawn of the Second Capital. Rows of sofas and easy chairs are laid out on the grass. The audience take their seats one by one. Flasks of hot tea and coffee are stacked on the side tables so that the audience does not doze off to the melody of military music. A wireless set has been fixed on the back of a jeep. It will broadcast a running commentary on the war. The viewers are facing south, towards the city. The vista stretching to the horizon acts as a natural screen on which the action can be viewed. It is now dark, empty, peaceful. Those who cut huge trees and set up barricades on the city streets are now exhausted. Some of them have fallen asleep. The briefings at Sheikh Mujib's house at Road Number 32 are over. The leaders are going underground in the darkness of night. Their silent movements cannot be seen on the screen. Nor can Sheikh Mujibur Rahman be seen absentmindedly puffing at his pipe because the screen is darkened. It holds the inert image of the blacked-out, sleeping city in its heart.

In the Second Capital, the viewers are waiting impatiently for scenes of dreadful carnage. The attackers are armed, ready, restless. Their pleadings are coming over the wireless every minute. They are asking General Tikka Khan "the Imam" how long they have to wait with their weapons poised to attack. But the special Pakistan Airlines flight seems to be taking longer to reach Karachi airspace than it should. General Yahya is on board. Having left Dhaka in the dead of night, he is soaring at thirty thousand feet somewhere mid-way between Colombo and Karachi. This killing of time is very puzzling. The dramatis personae of history are ready with their greasepaint on but the curtain is not being raised. The General's personal safety and springing a sudden attack on the enemy are both equally essential. On the one hand, one has to play for time, on the other, snap one's fingers in its face. Ultimately, according to official records, the H-hour of attack was at one a.m. But in reality, it started rolling at least an hour and a half earlier.

The viewers at the Second Capital feel their lids sticking together in sleep in the soft, balmy breeze of spring. Sleep will come and go. But the viewers have to watch the battles, scene by scene. It is as big a responsibility as the actual fighting.

The blind king Dhritarashtra of the *Mahabharata* had to watch the whole battle of Kurukshetra. Sanjaya showed it to him—by recounting the deaths of his sons to the sightless father, by describing Krishna's tactical moves, the falsehoods by the Dharmaputra Yudhisthir, the apostle of truth, the young lad Abhimanyu's entry into the *chakravyuha*, the unbreachable battle formation. That war lasted eighteen days. It was an intricately woven tale of rise and decline, victory and defeat of the two sides. Those who won after the holocaust did not live happily ever after like the kings and queens of fairytales. A deep iron in the soul relentlessly corroded their self and drove them like herds of sheep to suicide, towards *mahaprasthan*, the path of eternal departure.

The audience of the night of March 25 were reckoning on one night only. Their side will kill, not be killed. They did not take into account the remaining nine months. That is why their observation of the battle was like watching a film show, without a speck of anxiety or fear. It was like being able to watch peacefully without worrying about falling asleep or even having to keep one's eyes open. Besides, just as Sanjaya had reported to Dhritarashtra on the details of the war between the Kauravas and the Pandavas, here there was the wireless set to do the job.

At about 11.30 p.m. at night, the screen shivers with the footfalls of the marching army. They are leaving the army camp and marching towards the city an hour and a half ahead of schedule. Their speed speaks of their confidence. It seems they're off to a friendly match, not a battle. There will be enemies there, but they are unarmed. The barricade at the Farmgate intersection now faces the soldiers. On the cinema screen can be seen massive tree trunks, the chassis of junked automobiles, abandoned steam rollers used for paving roads. No humans can be observed beyond the barricade. But startling the advancing soldiers, a loud slogan rises to confront them—Joi Bangla!

The viewers leap out of their seats like suddenly uncoiled springs. Their sleepiness vanishes instantly. Perhaps they think of their own safety. Because, officially, there is still an hour and a half left before the launch of Operation Searchlight. President Yahya is still in mid-air. They have to keep in mind his security till he lands on the sacred soil of Pakistan. Because one can't trust Indians. They can easily vow to exact revenge for the hijacking of a Fokker plane and its destruction in Lahore. Now, hearing the news of the attack on Dhaka, they can easily force the President's plane down like a kite whose string has been snapped. Or they may not ground the plane but destroy it and send the President to heaven. As it is, in the company of wine and women, he is close to heaven now anyway. Mistakenly, the viewers look up at the sky. And then they look at the screen in front of them. By that time, the weapons of destruction have started their work targeting the sloganeers. The automatic weapons whistle through the air. The screen is filled with smoke. The voices shouting 'Joi Bangla' are silenced with bullets. The slogans can no longer be heard. The harsh noise of guns dominates the pleasant spring air. The soldiers enter the city. The audience take their seats once again with coffee cups in their hands.

On the screen at that moment can be seen rocket launchers being fired to shatter the barricade at the entrance of Road 32. Nearby is a faded yellow building which looks greyish white on the screen. It is unprotected, without security guards. The army is marching towards it with all its heavy artillery, its tanks and accompanying paraphernalia. After the hurdles on the street, the four-feet high wall encircling the building blocks the advance of the soldiers. They cross it effortlessly. Rat-a-tat-tat-tat go the sten guns. The heavy thud of boots can be heard crossing the verandah and going up the stairs to the first floor. A locked door dominates the screen. The steel lock is blown to smithereens by the bullets. The door opens. Mujib comes out and asks, "Why are you shooting?"

A few minutes after the commando attack, the viewers at the Second Capital hear the wireless set crackling to life. A shaky, disembodied voice announces, "Big Bird in the cage... Others not in their nests... Over."

By that time General Yahya, President and Chief Martial Law Administrator, has safely landed at Karachi airport. Orders come over the wireless, "Sort them out." Sort them out and finish off the Bengalis. And with that single command the genocide begins.

The dark screen in front of the viewers turns red. The leaping tongues of flame reach skywards, wanting to touch the stars. The billowing smoke blocks the flames. There is a battle in the sky between fire and smoke for a while. Suddenly the fireworks of tracer bullets light up the sky, thrilling the viewers. There are brief intervals and then it continues, and the viewers are happy. It is as if some smart, dazzling commercials break the monotonous transmission of smoke and fire. The connoisseurs among the viewers cannot fail to appreciate them.

It is 2 a.m. The wireless set crackles to life again. Everybody runs towards it forgetting who should respond. But, ultimately, the man who drags the mouthpiece towards himself is the one who is officially responsible.

Dhritarashtra said "O Sanjay! My legion of soldiers is mighty, triumphant, nimble and in formation according to the just rules of war. They are healthy, dedicated, well-protected and armoured, adept at handling weapons, well-versed in strategy. The soldiers are not too old, nor too young, not too lean, nor too stout. They are bounden to us and ceaselessly perform their tasks according to our will. They are skilled in mounting, encompassing enemies, galloping, all manner of combat, entering and exiting formations, and their ability to handle elephants, horses and chariots is well-tested."

Words erupt from the wireless:

"The students of Iqbal Hall and Jagannath Hall are firing at us."

"What weapons do they have?"

".303 rifles."

"And you?"

"Rocket launchers, Romeo, Romeo (recoilless rifles), mortar and…"

"Nonsense! The Imam has ordered, use everything at once. Destroy them within two hours."

The office of *The People*, the English daily, is opposite the Hotel Intercontinental. The foreign journalists stand on the eleventh floor of the hotel watching jeeps armed with machine guns moving ahead on the street. The infantry follows. They are carrying rockets and similar weapons on their shoulders. The soldiers start firing all at once. They set fire to the newspaper press after destroying all the printing machinery.

On the wireless:

"What is the news about *The People*? Over."

"Two of our soldiers have been seriously injured. They have been sent to the CMH."

"How many casualties?"

"Difficult to say at this moment. There's a fire blazing there, it has been razed to the ground."

"We will probably never know how many Bengalis were in there."

The wireless reports the fall of the EPR Camp near Pilkhana at 2.30 a.m. Those who have been attacked were disarmed two days before. They were told that soon power would be transferred to the Sheikh. There is peace. So hand over your arms and relax. It was in the evening of March 25 that the Bengali EPR battalions first realized that they had been betrayed. By that time, there was a huge lock hanging on the armoury gates. At midnight, showers of bullets and shells whistled through the air towards the unarmed EPR members.

The screen is red with the image of the bloodied city. Even the sky over the city is crimson. The smoke has vanished. There are only blazing fires at different places. There is a reddish glow everywhere. The flames have taken over the screen. The skeletal, starving people who were running for their lives after the slums were set on fire cannot be seen on the screen. Nor does the screen show these people falling to the ground by the dozen, like little birds hit by pellets in mid-air. Suddenly the wireless falls silent. The human trash living in these slums have been transformed into garbage. Their attempt to escape was just an exception.

"Is there shooting at the university?"

"So many buildings, it's taking time to finish them off. The students are firing at us but we have suffered no casualties. Over."

"Big Brother (artillery support) will reach you very soon. Iqbal Hall, Liaqat Hall have fallen silent, am I correct?"

"Yes."

"Jolly good! Now listen. First, announce that curfew is being imposed. Then, tell them that all houses flying Bangladeshi flags will suffer consequences. Also announce that no black flag should be visible in the city. Announce kar do, it will have dreadful results. Anyone seen setting up barricades will be shot at sight. People from areas with barricades will be prosecuted. And the houses on either side, let me repeat, all houses left and right—just demolish them."

Some jeeps came slowly from the north and stopped near the Shaheed Minar. Lying all across the road are stout trunks from the banyan tree, discarded water tanks filled with bricks. The soldiers jump down from the vehicles. The boundary wall is to their left and in the centre is an iron gate. They break open the lock at one go. They race across the courtyard and climb the stairs, three steps at a time. They kick the door of the apartment with their boots. The curtains seem to tremble, echoing the palpitations in the hearts of the residents. They will be stilled by bullets the very next moment. The people will fall on their faces on the stairs, the landing or the neatly trimmed, green, grassy yard. The soldiers disappear from the screen at a fast pace. They leave behind some people on their last journey, floating in their own blood, begging for what would have been their last drop of water.

Around 3 a.m., the wireless begins to intone, "Rajarbagh captured...Ramna police station captured...Kamlapur rail station captured...TV/radio under control...exchange captured..."

"Why is there so much fire?"

"The police lines are burning."

"Good show!"

Towards dawn, at 4 a.m., the news of the fall of the university comes over the wireless at the Second Capital. The viewers leap with joy, as if the final goal has been scored in a football match.

The soldiers had just begun to enter Jagannath Hall, announcing all the while, "Surrender or you will be killed." They were midway through the slaughter. From the corners of rooms, crouching under the boundary walls, in the Colocasia fields and the servants' quarters, the students were yet to be dragged out and shot. Afterwards, there remained the task of scouring the place for corpses, piling them up in one place and counting the bodies. To do that, they rounded up the remaining students, sweepers, gardeners, electricians and guards. At one stage, the non-Bengali sweepers, gardeners, electricians start pleading with the military to save their own skins.

"No, Sahib, we are not Bengalis. We are paschimas, from the west. We are bhangis, latrine cleaners."

"So what are you doing here?"

"Sahib, we have come here to work. I have small children at home."

But it does not work. When their task of dragging the dead bodies is over, they are also lined up and shot. After the combing operation, only a very few remain alive to bear testimony. One man watched the slaughter while hiding in a manhole. When he came out after nineteen hours, he felt that everyone in the world was dead. He was the only survivor coming out from the netherworld of the sewers.

The northern wing of Jagannath Hall. Room number 29. Three students were brushfired, then grenades were thrown into the room. From that gory ruin, one person crawls out alive. But he looks more like a ghost than a human being.

Some twenty-five persons were rounded up on the terrace and shot at one go. Only one, a short man, survived although he was hit on the shoulder with a bullet. The bullet aimed at him flew over his head.

In a room, another man was shot in the leg. He pulled apart the window rods and jumped into a drain. Then he took cover under the thorny kul shrub and made his way into the pond. He submerged himself in the water, only his nostrils floating above the surface. Overhead, in the morning mist, scores of vultures and crows have spread their wings and are wheeling in the sky. A crow descends. He is about to peck at the nose. The man wags his tongue to drive off the crow.

A man exhausted by dragging the corpses of teachers, fellow students, roommates lay down to rest just before the brushfire. Suddenly, he is flooded by warm, gurgling blood like water from a spouting tap. He is covered by the flow of blood. After the soldiers leave, a professor living in a nearby quarter sees through the viewfinder of his camera, a strange-looking man rising from the heap of dead bodies and running through the smoke and mist. Those who shielded him with their blood would now beckon him in his lifetime – for even after levelling the land with a bulldozer, some hands could be seen above the mass grave.

"How many have been killed or injured at the university? Just give me the approximate number. Over"

"Around three hundred."

"Excellent. The Imam wants to know whether three hundred are dead or whether there are any wounded among them."

"I believe one thing only: that all three hundred are dead."

"I agree with you. It is an easy job. No questions asked,

nothing done. You don't have to give any explanations. I say again that you have performed well. For your excellent work, I repeat Shabash, Bravo. Main bahut khush hoon, I am very pleased. Over."

Dawn is breaking. The screen is empty. The movie session is over. The viewers will go back to their barracks to sleep. The Imam enters his air-conditioned room but soon returns to the open-air operation theatre. He rubs the blurred glass of his spectacles with his handkerchief. Smoke is billowing from the city. In the dawn azaan, the note of mournful lamentation can be heard. The Imam puts on his glasses. He thanks god, Khuda Meherban. Not one soul is living.

A stray street dog skulks through the smoke and, frightened, vanishes towards the city.

IV

Leaving Dhaka

There is a curfew on the morning of March 26. The people from the surrounding houses look out of their windows at the stray dog that was tied to the lamppost in front of the Haji Shaheb's house. It is dead but people are too scared to come out. Even at this hour, occasional gunshots can be heard here and there, the air is heavy with burning smoke. The assailants must be skulking somewhere nearby. Otherwise, how would the dog have died? The first martyr of the neighbourhood, the watchdog, lay on the road for the duration of one day and one night. In the morning, a white cat surveys the dead dog, daintily picking its way around it. A little later, the scrawny-necked hen from the doctor's house and her brood of chicks peck at the body. She then stretches her neck and cackles something to her brood. But hearing the loud noise of an exploding bomb, she gathers her flock around her and scampers off to the shelter of her house.

At noon, the doctor gathers courage and comes out to look at the dog. He diagnoses that the dog hasn't been shot, it has died from heart failure. Then the people in the neighbourhood climb up to their terraces and quickly bring down the flags of free Bangla. Some vault over the dead dog and visit each other in hurried steps. There's no saying who will survive and who will die, perhaps they have something urgent to tell their neighbours.

On the night of March 25, these people lay under beds or tables or wrapped in quilts against the shelter of the walls. They don't know yet what lies in store for them. The wailing dog who had been signalling the coming catastrophe for the last two days was now silent. In the absence of his leadership, the other dogs in the city have also become quiet. The phones are not working. The proclamation of military rule is being repeatedly broadcast on the radio. Instrumental music is being played during the intervals followed by repeated warnings that anyone venturing into the streets will be shot at sight. The day drags to an end filled with many apprehensions. At night, General Yahya's broadcast over the radio fills them with dread.

The man on the first floor of the Haji's house comes out noiselessly under cover of darkness. He glances up and down the street and dashes across the lane. Climbing the iron gate, he scales the wall and jumps into the yard. He does not make a sound. The ground is soft and muddy from the tubewell. He makes his way carefully across the uneven row of bricks in the yard and then leaps through the window to enter the room.

At first he cannot make out anything in the darkness. His nostrils are assailed by a stench. He slips on a blood clot and slithers forward a few yards. It is difficult to understand what the damp, sticky substance is. He looks to his right and sees nothing. He looks to his left and sees the empty bed. Where has the girl disappeared? He holds his breath and listens carefully. He detects a soft buzz from under the bed. Like the noise made by a careless fly trapped in a spider's web. The man crouches down. Under the bed he sees Mariam who has been deposited there by the disturbances of the night of March 25.

The man does not try to hold his finger beneath her nostrils or listen with his ear to her chest to make sure that she is not dead. He pulls her out from under the bed. The floor of the room is covered with splinters of broken glass and the strange, wet, sticky stuff. He pays no heed to this. He is so excited by now that he forgets about making no noise. But he has not opened the door. Maybe he finds the broken window panes more convenient. He brings in mugs full of water from the tubewell in the yard through the window. Mariam gets drenched with water but she does not regain consciousness. He wonders how long she has been unconscious – surely not before midnight, considering that she must have crawled under the bed by herself after the shooting started. The man counts the hours on his fingers and realizes that there are still two hours left to complete 24 hours. He gropes in the dark and walks into the kitchen. Matchbox, candles, kerosene lamps are all kept there. On the shelf near the stove there are containers of turmeric powder, salt and dry red chillies. He picks up the tin of red chillies and smiles to himself. A flash of memory pops into his mind suddenly with the speed of light. The wife is in a fit, lock-jawed. Two days go by and then three but her teeth are still clamped shut. The ojha is summoned to the house. In a shallow earthenware bowl he burns two or three bright red chillies in a fire made with chaff. The wife coughs, sneezes and opens her hibiscus red eyes which had been closed for the last three days along with her teeth. Then she goes off to her father's house. It was when he tried to force her to return that it turned into assault and murder.

Mariam opens her eyes like two curled blood red hibiscus unfurling their petals. The room is filled with smoke, a storm raised by burning chillies. In this red hot atmosphere, she sees someone going out through the billowing smoke. She does not feel reassured by the magic bottles buried in the corners of the house. At the same time, she does not lose consciousness in panic for fear of jinns and fairies. The sundari marshes are far from here. The ghosts have been replaced by men – men who have assaulted the city. The noise of gunshots nearby might have conveyed to her that the fighting was on and that she was alone in the house. She could have thought that she had a past from which she was now disconnected. Moreover the knowledge that the knots in her relationship with Abed had been ripped apart just before war had broken out could have saddened her. But none of these thoughts touches Mariam. She feels a slight pain in her lower abdomen. Even then she does not realise that her problem has vanished on its own. She only sees the strange man appearing through the smoke carrying a glass of water. The man lays her down on the bed, props her up with his arm and helps her to drink the water. Then he gently spreads a sheet over her body. As if all of this was a scene from a film. After the screen goes blank, Mariam closes her eyes in comfort.

On the morning of March 27, the man knocks at her door saying, "Come on, wake up sister, there are cars plying the roads." He leaves immediately without entering the house. Earlier he had hoodwinked the Haji and had leapt over the gate.

People have begun to leave Dhaka. There is no curfew from morning till afternoon. People are bundling up their belongings and carrying them on their backs or on their heads. Doors are locked up. Even if they can return some day, they have no hope of getting back the stuff they are leaving behind. But just at this moment, it is life which is most precious. Despite her weakened condition, Mariam joins the exodus. The man from the night before is walking with an enormous bundle on his head as he keeps an eye on her. The bundle contains stuff belonging to the Haji Shaheb. Haji Shaheb's personal servant drags the dead dog tied to a string—not to give it a funeral but to discard the impure creature outside the neighbourhood as per the Haji's orders. The Haji Shaheb asks Mariam, "Where's that brother of yours, what's his name, Montu or Jhontu?" On hearing that Montu had left for the village, he seems to curse under his breath. But he does not say anything to Mary.

When their group of fifteen to twenty people crossed the Buriganga river under the leadership of the Haji Shaheb, they saw a few corpses floating by. These were not in a hurry like the living. They were being carried gently by the rhythm of the little wavelets. Sometimes they got tangled in the clumps of aquatic plants or among the flotsam. From the distant sky a flock of vultures scans the scene with their telescopic eyes. Their wings are spread, the sharp beaks are shut tight as pincers, the talons curled up under the folds of the skin. Well below them are flying some carrion-hungry crows.

The sun has risen in the sky. The hot sandbanks are ahead. The group with which Mariam is travelling is going towards Keraniganj. The deceased wife of the Secretary of the Awami League's liberation struggle committee had her parental home in this area. The Haji Shaheb had played matchmaker at their wedding. The Secretary is still busy in the city looking after the office behind the barricades. The Haji Shaheb is no fool. He is taking a large group of people to the home of the in-laws of a marriage that he had arranged in the absence of the groom. The Secretary is now his political opposition. But at this moment all Bengalis are on the same side. And he is also an erstwhile leader of his mohalla. Hence, a lot of people are relying on him and moving ahead.

On the very first night, a cold war starts among the refugees sheltering at the war committee's Secretary's in-law's place. The owner of the house had refined airs. Before the war, he would listen to a request programme of film songs on an old three-band Pye radio. The instrument is now common property. Everyone fiddles with the knobs whenever they want. At night, they tune into the Swadhin Bangla Betar, the rebel radio station. The audience holds back its breath in sheer excitement and the Haji Shaheb's heart starts hammering. The declaration of independence is being made, "I, Major Zia, on behalf of our great national leader, the Bangabandhu, Sheikh Mujibur Rahman…"

By now it is clear that the war will not be one-sided. Who is this Major Zia? And on whose side is the Haji Shaheb after all? He had to leave Dhaka with his family to save their lives because Pakistani soldiers were killing Bengalis indiscriminately. He had thought that the army would be able to suppress the separatists within a few days and Pakistan would remain intact. But what if the other side also proclaimed freedom and led a counterattack? India, the life-long enemy, is just waiting to fish in muddied waters. The Haji Shaheb's attempts at leadership have backfired. He has entered the tiger's cage voluntarily.

The refugees are educated people from the city – know-it-alls. They sit in Keraniganj and quite accurately predict that if Dhaka falls then the war will spread throughout the country like a forest fire. But in spite of listening to the radio night and day, they still cannot say for sure whether the Bangabandhu has been imprisoned or has fled. These people are, in fact, blind though they have eyes, deaf even though they have ears.

Nervously, the Haji Shaheb says, "I think the Sheikh has been arrested and sent to an unknown destination." No one protests. The subject is sensitive. If the head is missing, what can one achieve with just the body? On March 27 and 28, the Haji Shaheb sings to the tune everyone else is singing. There is no way that he could tune into Radio Pakistan even stealthily to listen to the kind of news he wanted to hear.

On March 29, the Swadhin Bangla Biplobi radio station dishes up the rumour that Tikka Khan has been killed. The host, and all the others, look very pleased. They arrange for a feast that night. The Haji Shaheb realises that trouble is at his doorstep. He has been in politics from the time of the British Raj. He has witnessed communal riots between Hindus and Muslims. He has seen Bengali Muslims demand Pakistan and is now witnessing its break-up. He understands that the conviviality will not continue for long. The audience will become divided and there will be bloodshed from which he himself will not be able to escape.

It rains on the night of March 29. The Haji Shaheb says that Allah has sent this untimely yet inevitable rain to douse the fire. The burning city will once again be revived, just as has been recorded in Allah's Sacred Book that the world will once again be fertile after the great Flood. At dawn, he returns to Dhaka with his family, walking over wet earth. He takes with him the man who lived on the first floor of his house. Everyone in the group now knows that his name is Ramiz Sheikh. He is the right-hand man of the Haji Shaheb who gave him shelter in his time of trouble. Whether he goes under duress or out of gratitude, Ramiz Sheikh's thoughts remain at Keraniganj with Mariam who he had saved by burning chillies. And so like the Creator's rights on the world that He has created, Ramiz Sheikh had some kind of lien on the girl's life. Besides, if one gets punished for killing someone then why should one not reap the harvest for saving a life? Ramiz Sheikh carries the logic of the argument in his mind.

The rest of the group did not see in the night's rain any miracle by Allah. There seems to be no end to the shooting. They naturally set off towards their own village homes on foot. They cross waterways in small vessels without spending a penny. They walk on the narrow raised ridges separating the rice fields. They eat and sleep in the houses of strangers. During the day, villagers slice up green coconuts, trail them through the fields and feed them parched rice and jaggery, boiled eggs. The villagers see the city people, whether rich or poor, fleeing like lines of ants with their lives in their hands. They feel it is their duty to help with whatever they can afford.

Those who are leaving the city change course according to destination. The composition of the group changes continuously, people join and leave as they walk ahead. When Mariam crosses the turbulent Padma river on a boat that is carrying agricultural labourers from north Bengal to Barisal to harvest paddy, she finds that every person in her group is unknown to her. She finds herself eating rice on a burnt clay platter belonging to the boatmen. It is panta bhat, rice soaked overnight, which she eats with salt and burnt chilli. The fishing boats on the Padma are many and the boatmen are netting huge quantities of fish. At that time, the fish were not feeding on corpses and men had not excluded river fish from their diet. But the boatmen could not buy fish because of lack of money.

Two drops of salty tears flow down Mariam's cheeks and mix with the soaked rice that she eats.

V

Fall from Paradise

In the middle of April, Mariam's group leaves the turbulent Padma, the tarred road, the electric lines and the telephone towers far behind and takes shelter in an abandoned house in a village deep in the interior. The name of the house is Swargadham, paradise. There are lots of rooms in Swargadham, but no humans. The doors of the house are wide open. Clothes are drying in the sun in the front yard; even the fire in the hearth has not been doused. Mariam's group reaches the house immediately after the inmates have run away and before it could be looted, and they take possession. They become owners of the abandoned property and carefully inspect its advantages and drawbacks. The sacred tulsi plant in a corner of the yard and the image of the goddess Shitala in the bamboo grove allows them to deduce that the householders have fled to India and are not likely to come back in a hurry. They uproot the tulsi plant and push the Shitala image, along with the offerings of coconuts made to her, deep into the bamboo grove. Now no one will know that the house belonged to Hindus. They feel a certain sense of safety in erasing the signs of Hindu ownership. By this time a flock of poultry gathers in the yard from the undergrowth surrounding the house. There are a large number of bald chicks. The moment they enter the grounds, the hens cluck and look for places to lay eggs. And the single rooster struts around the yard, veranda and kitchen, puffing up its chest, keeping the hens under control. In the cattle shed, the red and the white cows moo loudly.

The rooms, the hearth, the clothes hung out to dry, the poultry, the cattle – all of these make these wanderers long to live once again as householders. They create a patchwork of family relationships. Even though she is staying with them, Mariam gets left out of this network of relationships. The group gets divided into sub-groups who oppose each other. The only common interface is the fear of military attack that can happen any time of the day or night and can happen without any prior notice. Even so, living under the shelter of a roof, they once again experience the old sense of values and subtle differences that occur in relationships.

Mrs Alauddin has left behind her husband's dead body in Dhaka. She is a widow with two daughters. Eight year-old twins who do not know the whereabouts of their parents have come under the protection of the group just three or four days back. They are now known as orphans. The childless couple, the Atiqs, have adopted the twins but in actuality are making them work like slaves. The Pakistan army lined up eleven male members of Malina Gupta's family including her husband, brother-in-law, father-in-law, son, and shot them. The line was crooked and uneven in height. The soldiers bullied them and beat them with batons in an attempt to make the line uniform. The moment before the brush firing, the line fell into disarray. The soldiers thought this was defiance and before leaving they doused the property with petrol and set fire to everything. Malina put her ornaments and money in a bag tied to her waist, grabbed her two children and fled. She is panic-stricken in case someone hands her over to either the army or dacoits. Her mind is not here anymore, it has flown to the security that awaits her beyond the border. She deliberates whether she should appear in her widow's garb at her brother and sister-in-law's place at

Krishnanagar or go to the refugee camp at Salt Lake. The rest of the time, she takes her two daughters under her wing and mutters to herself. The discord of the crooked and uneven line is never resolved.

Engineer Tayeb is an important official of WAPDA. His pregnant wife Swapna thinks that the reason he is not going back to rejoin work despite repeated announcements over the radio is Mary. On hearing the name, she had first thought that the girl was Christian. But then she could also be a Muslim. Because of Mary's coquettish nature, she is luring Swapna's husband astray. She has deserted her family and joined this group in order to entrap a man. Pregnant Swapna, whose unborn child is going to be murdered in her womb, confides to another married woman in the group. She says, "Atiq Bhabi if you trust a man you are finished. Can't these men drive her away from Swargadham if they want to? Alauddin Bhabi has no problems. You can only get a headache if you have a head. But she has a strong moral character. She suspects that Mary is a whore, and has stopped spending time with her."

Mariam is an old hand at this. She needs a cover very badly. These people will enter her past the moment they find a chink. Then she will lose even this shelter, which is neither too large nor too small but just right like a grave—which measures the space she occupies in the bed next to Mrs Alauddin and her children. There is no problem with food. Nobody is dependent on anyone else for food at Swargadham. The cows give milk. Laden with fruit, the trees in the garden are bent double like people bent over in prayer. The eggs are divided equally.

Mariam notices that no one has been calling her at mealtimes for two days now. Food is sent to her through the twins like offerings on a bell-metal platter. Is she a goddess or a witch? She notices that even Alauddin Bhabi avoids her, just like everyone else. She rarely talks to Mary during the day, but now in the darkness of night she is tossing and turning. The night shows no signs of ending. The two four-posters at Swargadham are in the possession of the two married couples, where waves of pleasure and delight are washing over them. The pleasures that she was entitled to even six weeks back when her husband was alive now pierce her through the closed doors and windows. At such moments, she usually wakes Mariam. She tries to distract herself from what is happening in the other rooms by conversing loudly with her. The woman who is an enemy during the day becomes a friend at night. Now Mrs Alauddin feels embarrassed. No sound comes from her throat when she tries to call Mariam, she cannot speak. But she pities the girl. She realizes that she has been too unfair during the day. Who knows where Mariam's parents and loved ones are. She, at least, has her two children with her. People are blinded by daylight. These thoughts come to Mrs Alauddin only at night, when she is lying alone on her bed of thorns, when her daytime friends are transformed into enemies behind closed doors.

The inmates of Swargadham forget that even if the cows yield pails full of milk, and the hens lay eggs, and the trees bear fruit, it is actually a time of war. Swargadham is actually an illusion, an imagined place or a dream of their war-troubled minds which will disappear the moment they wake up. Even if it is a reality, heavenly pleasures do not last long on this earth. The price of these pleasures is also very high. The freedom that Mariam enjoys because of her isolation from the group gives rise to questions. The questions grow as the days pass. Her hidden past suddenly explodes and in an unexpected way. Rameez Sheikh startles everybody and appears at Swargadham one day. What happens then has already happened in Mariam's life, albeit with a slight difference.

Pregnant Swapna is the happiest at the arrival of Rameez Sheikh because she has no faith in her husband. As the time of delivery approaches, her husband behaves oddly and seems indifferent to her. Malina Gupta reacts differently to the arrival. On the night that Rameez Sheikh comes, she ties her possessions securely in her drawstring bag and leaves the shelter with her two daughters. Mrs Alauddin and Atiq Bhabi warmly greet Rameez Sheikh. Like Swapna, they also have their special reasons for welcoming him. They have their natural born and adoptive children, but in such a large group, there are effectively only two able-bodied males. And the two males have become bone lazy in the comfortable environment of Swargadham. Looking at them, at Atiq Mian and Tayeb Shaheb, the women had almost forgotten that men in this country were fighting the Pak army in the jungles and the wetlands. No matter what announcements Swadhin Bangla Betar, the underground radio station, makes, the radio is, after all, a machine. There is no way of verifying its claims. The gun-toting Rameez Sheikh is a flesh and blood man. In case there is trouble, this wide-shouldered, stocky, impassive, rustic man will be there to ward it off.

Tayeb Shaheb and Atiq Mian are annoyed at the women gushing. They see Rameez Sheikh as coming to partake of their fortune in Swargadham in which they, as males, have so far been the only stakeholders. Everyone in the group knows that they are attracted to Mariam. There is even a secret rivalry between them in this regard, which becomes manifest when they play cards. According to the rules, if one wins, the other will lose. They break this daily and the card game ends in shouting and arguments. Mariam remains steady in her own place. As married men they face many hurdles in their attempt to seduce Mariam, hurdles which Rameez Sheikh does not face. The man is a little wild and mulish and moves around with his rifle on his shoulder the whole day. One does not need anything more if such a thing as a rifle is at hand. One can do whatever one wants. Atiq Mian and Tayeb Shaheb have no idea what they can do if the control of Swargadham, including that of the unmarried young woman, goes into the hands of such a man. This problem appears bigger to them than a probable attack by the military.

Mariam is bewildered to see the whole of Swargadham ranged either for or against Rameez Sheikh. She does not know whether this stranger is her enemy or her friend. For a day and a night after March 25, Mariam was unconscious. That time is an unfathomable dark abyss. Beyond the abyss, Rameez Sheikh is an object of terror as he hangs upside down like a bat within his window. On this side of the abyss, he is a saviour, emerging like a ferishta, an angel, through the billowing smoke. Even now Mariam has not been able to bridge the gap between this side and that side. She does not have this doubt about the other people of Swargadham though. They are absolutely like the people of Fultali village before the war. Their frowns, reproaches and faces distorted with revulsion float quickly to this side of the March 25 abyss. The women of Swargadham are loud and harsh in their condemnation, the men ogle – things she had witnessed after the Mahua cinema hall incident at Fultali. The rictus of disapproval seems deathless. Meanwhile, Montu is lost, Abed is missing, Kafiluddin's family gets smaller, Golam Mostofa sits on the shore and basks in the sun, the Haji Shaheb turns into a patriot, and Rameez Sheikh becomes confused and disoriented between the slogans Pakistan Zindabad and Joi Bangla.

The ten years when the alienation between the Pakistanis, of being Bengalis or non-Bengalis, grew, Rameez Sheikh had been in prison. He is not clear why the war broke out and who is killing whom even though March and April have gone by and it is now May. What little knowledge he has of politics comes from the Haji Shaheb. That is why, when he is excited, he shouts Pakistan Zindabad and stutters when saying Joi Bangla. His tongue becomes stiff.

Rameez Sheikh thinks weapons are superfluous when one can kill a person by strangling them. But he does not let go of the rifle on his shoulder. He is enamoured of its power. He caresses the smooth butt now and then, polishes it with oil. He thinks of the collaborator Peace Committee people as patriots. As far as he knows, their duty is to serve the Pakistani soldiers by supplying them with women and chickens. The Haji Shaheb is a patriotic citizen. He has become a member of the Peace Committee after his return to Dhaka from Keraniganj. He kept Rameez Sheikh by his side. Like a fisherman throwing a net, Rameez Sheikh had had instructions for rounding up women and chickens from different neighbourhoods every day. Now there is a dearth of these in the city.

The free run that the chickens enjoy and the abundance of women at Swargadham worry Rameez Sheikh. If he does have to become a patriot, he will deliver even the young girls and the little chicks that are here to the army. But he won't hand over Mary. Not even if the army people insist. He has saved the girl by burning chillies; now the rest of her life is in his hands. That is why he broke away from the Haji's snare and groped his way to Swargadham.

Although Atiq Mian and Tayeb Shaheb do not know Rameez Sheikh's past, some incongruity in his behaviour does not escape their eyes. They wait for the Mukti Fauj, the freedom fighters. A group of bare-foot, lungi-clad men carrying Sten guns on their shoulders will knock on the door some evening under cover of darkness and ask for shelter and food for the night. Atiq Mian and Tayeb Shaheb will fully cooperate with the liberation army according to the instructions given by the Swadhin Bangla radio station. But they will first inform them of Rameez Sheikh's stiff, stuttering Joi Bangla slogan, and they will point to the gun with the smooth butt, which in a time of war is not being used to kill the enemy, but is being toted around without purpose.

The day passes, night comes. No one comes knocking to ask for shelter and food. Instead a coded letter between the freedom fighters comes by mistake to Swargadham. Atiq Mian and Tayeb Shaheb tremble in fear. Two particular lines of the letter make their hearts freeze: "We have been sending so many chicken and eggs, why are you not using them? What is the matter?… I repeat, the punishment for traitors is death." From the moment they receive the letter, the two are scared. They now think that Rameez Sheikh is a freedom fighter in disguise. He is corresponding about them under cover. They begin to think that they are being charged with eating up eggs instead of utilising them for a better purpose – a new kind of betrayal for which the penalty is death.

Then there are the women. They are the majority and they are all toadying up to Rameez Sheikh. Swargadham is an isolated island. The man seemed to arrive there by navigating a small scull through stormy seas. He has brought with him a gun, a pair of iron-hued shoulders and a devil-may-care attitude. If one adds up all the distinctive features, that is how legends are born. The women offer him the same adulation that they would a heroic freedom fighter. And for the hero they allocate double the rations and a comfortable bed.

What they should have thought of, and do not, happens a few days later. Swargadham faces a shortage of food. The bare branches of trees shorn of fruit shoot upwards. The udders of the cows shrink. The hens move around with empty egg-sacs. They look lost because they have not been able to sit on eggs for hatching. They go berserk when they see the empty cages. They get fed up with laying eggs and run wild. The first victim of this scarcity is Mariam. The women stop her food. The two men also have a hand in it, because their frustrated attraction for Mariam has, by now, turned into fury. Besides, they are determined to retain control of Swargadham, even if it means keeping on the good side of the women.

At first Rameez Sheikh feeds Mariam from his own plate, but he does not tolerate this injustice for long. How can he accept the fact that she should die of starvation when he has saved her life? A raging storm breaks out in Swargadham. The women change their position and with the help of the men depose Rameez Sheikh from his pedestal. They tell each other that Mariam and Rameez Sheikh are having an affair. It's indecent before the consummation of the wedding night. The rumour takes on the shape of truth and nobody demands proof. It's a time of war. There is no law, the courts are not functioning. The highest punishment that can be given to the pair is expulsion from Swargadham.

Sharing Rameez Sheikh's food with him, Mariam realises that the person who is giving her protection in all her difficulties is none other than Rameez Sheikh. Who is he – her mother, father, brother, sister, husband, friend? Such questions are irrelevant. He can be any of these or no one at all. There is no one here now, neither Abed, nor Montu, neither the Kafiluddin family, nor her friends, who would faint at seeing Rameez Sheikh by her side. He is a convicted murderer who has escaped from prison. He had served ten years in jail. Mariam does not know what Rameez Sheikh's identity will be in independent Bangladesh when the war is over. Life now is reckoned just by the day. All needs are reduced to two meals a day, a bed for the night, a safe shelter. And only this man can give it to her.

Mariam tempts Rameez Sheikh to taste the forbidden fruit of paradise. She says, a crore of people have left their homes and sought refuge in India. Abandoned homes like Swargadham should be easy to find if one looked. There won't be anyone there to humiliate them.

Rameez Sheikh cannot ignore Mariam's arguments. He thinks she is very learned and intelligent. His own knowledge is limited to the alphabet. And yet they are being forced to flee not from the fear of snakes or other dangers but two worthless men and a pack of women. But the person who has given the advice is close to him. So in spite of owning a weapon, he relinquishes control of Swargadham without a fight.

The role of men in Mariam's life is double-edged. Whether it is in times of war or peace, they bring a streak of bad luck along with good luck. They emerge from the mist garbed in the robe of dreams.

Jashimul Haque had been a good student, he could speak in English. Mariam had paid a high price to learn from him that to score better marks in maths, one must know algebra by heart. When she first met Abed, one of her sandals was torn and she could have been described as handicapped. For a girl who goes to the movies and returns home after three days, the prospect of marriage becomes difficult. Abed is an independent inhabitant of the university. One can stand up holding on to him. One can even walk with his help, without falling flat on one's face. But the haze disappears, the dreams take a beating. The night of March 25 comes. Despite the dog giving advance signals of impending trouble, Mariam has to take cover under the bed. Rameez Sheikh appears like Robinson Crusoe on a deserted island called Swargadham. There are no humans at Swargadham, all are beasts of prey. Outside, the murdering, raping soldiers are camping. They have taken control of roads, jute fields, houses, shops, markets. Mariam sees before her a pair of iron-hued shoulders, a rifle and a man's devoted love for her – for which there is no substitute during times of war.

Leaving Swargadham behind, Adam and Eve are confronted with a scorched, dangerous, murderous world. They take with them the dream of a similar house that they have left behind. There they will be the only man and woman. The sliver of moon in the sky glances at them from afar. The very next moment it hides behind the clouds in fear. Deep, thunderous thuds break out from the heart of heaven. The ashen leaves shiver in intense dread. But the two leave for an unknown destination without any apprehension.

The night is not quite over yet. There has been a shower of rain a little earlier. Two files of soldiers advance on the muddy road toward Swargadham. Their ghostly shadows are reflected in the pools of water collected by the sides of the road. This is the third month of war. There is no lack of preparation. Killing, looting and rape, with the beat of the march, the earth trembles in its end-of-night sleep. It disrupts the rhythm of the dawn songbirds, and they fly away helter-skelter.

There were no guards at the gates of paradise. The soldiers march down the road which is exactly opposite the one down which Mariam and Rameez Sheikh have escaped. Swargadham is empty. The inmates heard the sound of marching boots and fled. Instead of entering the chicken run, the rogue chickens roost on tree branches. From their perch they hear Swapna's moans during her birth pangs. No midwife comes for her. A few days earlier, she had said, "Atiq Bhabi, you are doomed if you trust men." How true her words become in her life. The soldiers search each room. In sheer rage, they destroy the matresses still warm from the bodies of the recently escaped sleepers. But they do not fire a shot. They tear open Swapna's swollen abdomen with the point of a bayonet. In the cowshed the two cows are still tied to their stakes. They do not hurt the animals but pull them outside by the rope tied round their necks. The gains from the operation are two cows along with two calves (alive) and a dead woman and child. But they are not satisfied with the results. They set fire to the rooms at Swargadham. The heat from the flame scorches the hens. They begin to cluck loudly. In the dark one cannot see their jostling. The soldiers are apprehensive, as if a group of Mukti Fauj soldiers have cocked their light machine guns to automatic and were holding them over their heads. Quickly they lie on the ground and position themselves. The first round of firing goes over the head of the birds. When the clucking and crowing get louder, the soldiers point to the branches of the trees and fire. The rogue hens do not surrender. They begin to fly, light as they are with their empty egg sacs. The soldiers are obstinate and continue to fire till the cackling stops. That day, in the battle of Swargadham, the soldiers had no humans as opponents. What they had was a flock of chickens which had turned wild because they could not sit on the eggs they had laid and hatch chicks.

VI

It is Now the Third Month of War

Mukti, who interviewed Mariam twenty eight years after the war, circled the night of the fall of Swargadham with a thick yellow marker and made a note in the margin of her notebook: 'the beginning of doom?' The question remained in her report. Because it wasn't as if to her the question was complex and the answer simple. It might seem to some that Mariam's misfortune began that day at the Mahua cinema hall where a young man appearing for his matriculation examination got carried away while watching an on-screen love scene and clutched her hand. Or one could think of the moment, two days before the war, when she stood on the brick near the tubewell after having sent Montu home. The moment that Mariam herself had identified as the moment when her run of bad luck began. But perhaps it was neither of these. Perhaps, Mariam's life is a sum total of all these. Mukti also thinks that Mary, also known as Mariam, is merely an example. The real cause of her misfortune are her reproductive organs - needed for continuing the family line and hence the need for chastity- which were reserved for the legalised use of a single male. These became unprotected the year of the war. The enemy's phallus entered them; his sperm moved towards the ovary. The foetuses began to mature rapidly.

Even after special orders were given for an abortion, the chastity of the female body could not be restored.

All this of course happened later.

It is the third month of war. Mariam does not yet know how far the village of Fultali is or whether she will ever be able to reach there at all. Along with Rameez Sheikh, she searches for a house similar to Swargadham: abandoned, without a soul, but full of riches. There are one or two empty rooms in the settlements they pass through, but these are impoverished, unfit for habitation. There are no doors or windows or fencing, and the thatched roofs hang askew. Weeds and vegetation grow wild around the homesteads, jackals howl near the ponds even during the day, owls swing on the beams of the house, and the path to the house is so slimy with moss that one can break one's limbs trying to walk on it. But still Mariam and Rameez Sheikh do not abandon hope. War does not only take with both hands, it gives as well. Otherwise, how had they found Swargadham? But they do not wish to face unnecessary problems on their journey. So they avoid people as much as they can. But even if they walk past some house by mistake, the householder calls out, "who goes there?" It's an unnecessary waste of time trying to disentangle themselves by making this excuse or that. The cultivated fields are safer in comparison. Those who work in the fields during wartime do so out of dire need. They have little time for irrelevant chatter. But once in a while, a straw-hatted head followed by the rest of the man springs up from the distant paddy fields and shouts, "Where are you going, where are you from, eh?" After he repeats his question twice, it does not look good to keep quiet. Rameez Sheikh asks him the name of the village. The farmer points to the horizon with his scythe that looks like the crescent moon of Eid and hollers, "That village is Radhanagar. The military set it ablaze and burned it to ashes. The next village is Notungaon. You might find people still living there."

The names Notungaon and Radhanagar sound familiar. Some thirty years ago, Mariam's aunt, Sahar Banu, her father's sister, was married into the Munshi family of Radhanagar. Just about a year after her marriage, she died of smallpox. Mary has never seen her. If she played hookey from school or did not want to study, Kafiluddin Ahmed would talk to her with sadness about his little sister Sahar Banu. Sahar Banu was supposed to have been good at her studies. When she came for the firani, her return visit to her parental home, after her marriage, and then went back to her in-laws, she took a trunkful of books with her. But for that whole year, she did not even get a chance to open the trunk! After her death, her in-laws kept all her clothes, her jewellery, and returned the locked trunk of books to her parents at Fultali. At the time, it was not the custom for the young women of the Radhanagar Munshi family to study.

Now, as they walk along the northern boundary of Radhanagar, there is nothing but mounds of ash everywhere. Not a soul in sight. The Pakistani army has torched all the houses. After this desolate place, there is another village which the farmer in the paddy field called Notungaon. There must be people living there, having two meals a day, sleeping in their beds at night.

They reach Notungaon after walking for a while. But the people there are restless. They are indeed living in their village but are ready to flee at any time. When they see the rifle on Rameez Sheikh's shoulder, they scurry away like rats. Whether he is a Razakar or a freedom fighter, he will not bring them any comfort. Just two days ago, the Pakistani army scented the presence of the Mukti Fauj in the next village and burnt it down like a cremation ground. And they themselves are sick of the marauding of the Razakars. So far, Rameez Sheikh has juggled a space for himself between these extremes. He began explaining loudly to everyone he met that he was neither a Razakar nor a Mukti.

Then a teenaged boy, keen to join the fight and tote a gun, emerges from the darkness and grabs the rifle with a, "So brother, why keep the rifle with you? Give it to me, I will use it."

Neither Mariam, nor Rameez Sheikh is prepared for such a special welcome. Although the weapon has been of no use to them so far, it has helped to identify Rameez Sheikh as both a Mukti soldier and as a Razakar. Rameez Sheikh, by now, is quite adept with both slogans, Pakistan Zindabad and Joi Bangla. But he is still not quite sure when to shout which. Perhaps he could have learnt, if he had had nine months to do so. But this is only the third month of war.

Even if they lose the weapon, Rameez Sheikh and Mariam get a meal and shelter for the night in the Choudhury household at Notungaon. After that the women of the village take over Mariam's life and Rameez Sheikh is armed with a lathi and sent out on sentry duty with half a dozen young men. Armed with diverse weapons – guns, spears, lathis, choppers, the men of Notungaon shout as if they are venturing out to grab land that surfaces from the shifting course of the river. Or as if preparing to catch a petty thief out to steal ripe paddy from the fields. Rameez Sheikh smiles quietly to himself. The villagers are so stupid, he thinks. Guarding the village against the Pakistani soldiers with such crude weapons! He feels quite smart among these half dozen vigilantes. He forgets his sorrow at losing his rifle. Sitting on the ridge separating the cultivated fields, he pulls at his gurgling hukkah and wants to talk of many things.

The half dozen guards listen without demur to Rameez Sheikh's story of rounding up women and chickens in the city to supply the Pakistani soldiers. But they are not prepared to accept that the Haji Shaheb is a patriotic citizen. They say that the man is a traitor and if the Muktis catch him, they will bury him alive. Why? Rameez Sheikh gapes dumbly without understanding. He knows that it's a bad thing forcing or luring women to hand them over to the army. Once, he had even asked the Haji Shaheb why he did this. But that Haji guy is a pious man, who won't take a single step without the sanction of religion. He explained, "Look, son, East Pakistan is now enemy territory and women are the *Ganimate Maal*, the spoils of war. The holy book of Allah speaks of enjoying them in the fields of war." Then his bearded face looms over Rameez Sheikh's face. After all, he had exchanged Rameez Sheikh's prison uniform for a set of his own clothes in the dark of night, made a bed for him in the empty bed of the son he had driven out – the man could have no secrets

from the one who gave him shelter. For two consecutive days he
interrogated the convict and found out almost everything about
the prisoner's crime. Once he discovered that the man had been
serving a prison sentence for murder, he realised instantly that
this man would be his faithful follower in this untrustworthy
world. Too scared to let his crime become public knowledge,
he would spend the rest of his life like a chained dog at his feet.
He won't even whine by mistake. But now it is wartime. He
consoles himself that if the dog wants to question him, better to
answer or he might run away. The spittle from the Haji Shaheb's
lowered face spatters on Rameez Sheikh's face. He grinds his
teeth, trying to curb his anger and says, "So listen you son of a
bitch, could you stay without your wife, huh? You tried to force
her to come with you – h-heh! Tell me, how can they stay? Their
wives and children are thousands of miles away. How can they
do without women, huh?" And then Rameez Sheikh's patron,
who is old enough to be his father, gave in to rage and grabbed
hold of his member and balls through his lungi and gave them a
good twist. Even as Rameez Sheikh saw stars, he heard the Haji
saying, "As if you're the only one with a rod! Huh!"

If the Haji is now punished as these vigilantes predict, what
will happen to him? Just because his wife refused to leave her
father's house, he had gripped her throat and held fast till her last
soft, fluttering breath gasped through her tongue and expired
between his palms. During cross-examination in the court, his
advocate pleaded to the court with folded hands, "Your honour,
my client is innocent, he did not know that just a bit of fun
and games would kill his wedded wife, the love of his life. My
client, huzoor, was devoted to his wife, he couldn't sleep when
his wife was staying at her parents' home. Having lost sleep for
nights on end, he became a nervous wreck." This was not a
cold-blooded murder. There was no other motive in it except
an excess of passion. This was proved in court. So, instead of
sentencing him to death, the honourable court gave Rameez
Sheikh life imprisonment. Rameez Sheikh escaped from prison
after serving only a couple of years. He knew that this would

not be considered a major crime during wartime, nor would the murder of his wife. No court would bother to sit for such trials. One does not even have to lavish money on advocates and solicitors nor mortgage one's home to bear the legal expenses. So many people are dying without reason, no one keeps a record of who is killing whom. And these fools are saying that if the Mukti forces get hold of the Haji Shaheb, they will bury him alive for supplying women and chickens to the army! Rameez Sheikh is amused. But he does not laugh.

The vigilantes of Notungaon, who are standing guard against the army with teta and spears in hand, are now annoyed with Rameez Sheikh. Just imagine, if during such a critical time one has to explain who is a hypocritical traitor and who is a real patriot! Where has this prize idiot come from? The ass could not follow the simple logic that the scoundrel Haji is now in the city busy with Razakar activities and if the Muktis get him they will just bury him alive. Who could explain this to him? The six vigilantes glance at each other in the dark. Suddenly one of them loses his cool and shouts, "Your Haji Shaheb is like Mir Jafar—an ungrateful traitor. He sold the country to the British, do you remember that?" Immediately, someone else laments, "Indeed, he sold the country, he did not stand and fight. In the mango groves of Palashi, he stood frozen like a wooden puppet, that scoundrel commander-in-chief." By equating Haji Shaheb with Mir Jafar, they feel somewhat relieved. They are also pleased with their cleverness. Which leaves the patriot, Siraj-ud-daula.

Every year, the jatra or play on Nawab Siraj-ud-daula is staged in the grounds of the Notungaon school. The jatra-troupe, the Nabaratna Opera, arrives from the Bhati area. They dig up the grounds, fix the tent pegs and erect a canopy. Starting late at night under the light of the magnesium vapour hajak-lamp, the jatra goes on till the morning. And even then, the performance does not end. When the rays of the early morning sun filter through the gaps in the canopy and crawl onto the stage the audience begins to leave for home even as they curse the theatre troupe. The next day they throng the school grounds once again to see the rest. They buy tickets and enter the canopy with the money earned by the sweat of their brow. They wait impatiently for the spine-tingling scene of Siraj-ud-daula's entrance to the Durbar, where the nakib, a court official, proclaims with a flourish on the trumpet, "Nawab Mansur-ul-mulk Siraj-ud-daula Shahkuli Khan Mirza Muhammad Hayawat Jung Bahadur-r-r." Their chests swell with pride at the mention of the Nawab. They would have felt more proud had his string of titles been longer, their chests would have doubled in girth. Their own small, insignificant names vanish like steam into the atmosphere. Once when he was delivering the dialogue, "See, the storm clouds of destiny have darkened the skies of Bangla," his moustache glued on with bel tree gum came unstuck and hung down the side of his face. But the audience did not laugh or whistle. They were transported and held captive by the play of light and darkness in the conspiracy-riddled palace of Murshidabad. Siraj-ud-daula's crisis is their own—of life or death, victory or defeat. Perhaps theirs is a crisis more acute than Siraj-ud-daula's. Because Siraj had not known, but they do, that he will be defeated in battle, lose his kingdom, that the young, tragic Siraj-ud-daula, the last Nawab of Bengal will be brutally murdered. They also know that nights will go by, but the play won't be over. They won't have to witness the inevitable death scene of the Nawab in stony silence and with profound sorrow. Besides, in this act of the jatra he is still alive. He is swaying between trust and distrust. Present in the Durbar are Mir Jafar, Rajballav, Jagat Seth, Rai Durlabh, Umichand, and the East India Company agent, Watts. Below the stage, the drums are beating a thunderous tattoo that echoes in the hearts of the audience. Pulling the slack moustache back in position, the Nawab says with the same vibrato in his voice, "There is a tracery of blood on the green expanses of Bangla. The bright sun of this country's good fortune is about to set. Only the sorrowing mother sits at the head of her sleeping children—counting the hours before the dark of night ends. Who will give her hope? Who will reassure her? Who will speak to her the heartening words of a reawakening? Rise, O Mother, rise.

Wipe away your tears. You have seven crore children, Hindus and Muslims. With our lives, we will defend this venture. We will lay down our lives."

Huge clouds are massing in the sky. The world at night is filled with an inky darkness. The enemy camps are nearby. A pack of jackals howls through the night, counting out the hours. The owl perches on treetops, its hooting signalling ill omens. The six vigilantes seem to be standing in the darkness of Palashi's fields. They are armed with teta, spears, machetes. Their determination to pursue their goals till death can be seen shining on their faces. They will defend their country from the foreign enemy with the last drop of their blood. They love their country. They are Mir Mardan and Mohanlal, the loyal followers of Nawab Siraj-ud-daula.

Rameez Sheikh fidgets at such noble sentiments of patriotism and enthusiasm for martyrdom. He thinks these Notungaon villagers are strange. They are haunted by Siraj-ud-daula, stricken to stone by the sorrow of a king of the distant past whom they have never seen or known. They no longer demonstrate mulishness. Each one has a pleasing appearance like a ferishta. But in their hearts, they have a single resolve, that they will lay down their lives for their land, they will destroy the foreign enemies and kill the Mir Jafars. Rameez Sheikh feels a twinge of fear. Where is the end to these killings and retaliation? Are these cold-blooded or hot-headed murders? If the court does sit in judgment one day after the war, who will judge them and under which law?

The world is a strange place. Spurred by greed, the foreigners are bound to come. There will always be a patriot within the country—either Siraj-ud-daula or Sheikh Mujib. And the Mir Jafars will also be hanging around nearby, trailing their shadows. As if it's a well-scripted play with the characters following a set pattern. No one can remain outside this scheme—no one who does not want to kill or get killed. The same play has been staged for so many hundreds of years and the protagonists are playing their predictable roles. On whose side is Rameez Sheikh—the

Haji Shaheb's or that of the six vigilantes? It is clear to him now that the Haji Shaheb is no patriot. He is Mir Jafar. But in that war, it was Siraj-ud-daula who was defeated, and Mir Jafar, who was not a patriot, ascended the throne of Bengal.

Rameez Sheikh does not want to die. He was lucky to have escaped the hangman's noose despite being accused of murder. During the five long months that he waited to hear the sentence, he had realised deep down in his being that life was not a trivial thing. Every night Azrael, the Angel of Death, would don the guise of his wife and come and sit outside his prison bars. She would croon wedding songs to him. And then when the prison guard called out the last watch, she would get up and disappear slowly. After he received his life sentence, the wife never came again. Probably because she was hurt.

As they watch, the place is transformed into Palashi and the time is no longer 1971, but 1757, two hundred and fourteen years ago. The vigilantes of Notungaon do not remain simple guards but become Siraj-ud-daula's trusted followers. They walk and talk in a trance, like jatra performers. The crude home-made weapons turn into swords in their hands. In moments of excitement, they pull the swords out of the scabbards and hold the bare blades over their heads. Rameez Sheikh is frightened. Although, he has not yet been able to decide which side he's on, he thinks that these men have already placed him in Mir Jafar's side. He would not have felt so helpless if he had still had his rifle. Where did that boy disappear after grabbing his weapon? Has he run away? He was nowhere to be seen afterwards.

There are so many dangers at every single step; he should have stayed back with the Haji Shaheb. Even though people curse Mir Jafar, after all it is the Mir Jafars who win the wars and Siraj-ud-daula's side gets trampled. He has left the winning side and gambled with his life for a woman. He's learnt nothing from his ten years in prison. His parents died while he was in jail, practically without food or medical treatment. During the last few days of their lives the penniless old couple went begging from house to house for a fistful of rice. No one gave them alms.

Everyone in the village, rich and poor alike, enjoyed the death from starvation of the impoverished parents of a murderer son. Rameez Sheikh wonders, if the Haji Shaheb had not given him protection, where could he have gone for shelter in his prisoner's garb, who would have held out a helping hand? How would the world that had turned away his innocent parents treat him? And yet, surprisingly, that rich, distant relative, at whose threshold he had nervously stood once, feet bare, wearing shorts and a torn shirt, holding onto his mother's hand, had recognised him instantly despite his bearded face and prison clothes. And he had not turned him away. When he had heard everything, he had welcomed Rameez Sheikh even more warmly. Other than once twisting his balls in anger, what harm had the Haji ever done to him that he left his protection without a word? If there is any disloyal traitor in this country, it is he.

In the last few days, Rameez Sheikh has found it difficult to understand Mariam's moods. An educated girl, she left Swargadham clinging to him like a girl rejecting her family bonds. They spent two days walking the roads. And when they finally reached a shelter, she discarded him like a bundle of soiled clothes. Is this justice? She could have told the people of Notungaon that this man has not eaten or slept for two days. Don't take him on guard duty, let him rest the night. But no. Not only did she not say this, she acted as if she didn't know him – and she walked off to the inner quarters along with the women. If he can walk out alive from this theatrical setting, he will certainly teach that snooty woman a lesson or two. But very likely that opportunity will never come in Rameez Sheikh's life.

Nawab Siraj-ud-daula's play is fast gathering momentum and moving towards its climax. The condition of the six performers is critical. The Nawab's troops have lost in Palashi, Mir Jafar is in Clive's camp. The time for playing hide-and-seek is over and done with. Everything is clear as daylight, one can easily recognise friend or foe. The British soldiers are advancing fast to arrest the Nawab. Only Golam Hossein, his constant companion, remains by his side. He does not leave the Nawab.

Nor will another person—Aaleya. Since there are no women among the vigilantes, they have omitted the character altogether. No matter how often the Nawab repeats, "There is no way out, Golam Hossein, no way out," it is Golam Hossein who is his last resort. And the Nawab knows it. Golam Hossein is pushing Siraj-ud-daula to rush back to the capital, commandeer an army and fight again. Although the broken-hearted Nawab is speaking nineteen to the dozen, he is filled with lassitude and unable to move. Golam Hossein is stubborn as a mule. He tries to incite the Nawab subtly, "Your Majesty, we will fight again. We will again put together an army. If not in this life, in lives to come, we will remove this stain on the Bengalis." The Nawab may have become unbalanced but he is canny. He grinds out, "But won't the likes of Mir Jafar, Jagat Seth, Rajballav, Rai Durlav, Yar Latif and Umichand be born again as well, Golam Hossein?"

So what is the solution? The bewildered eyes of the six vigilantes rest upon Rameez Sheikh. In the blink of an eye, they traverse the many years in between and go far back in time. The Mir Jafars and the Jagat Seths are born again and again in Bangla, to help subjugate the land under the crushing boots of the enemy. He is right here before them—this new incarnation of a traitor. Unless the enemy is completely exterminated the Bengalis will never be free. The vigilantes quickly march towards Rameez Sheikh. They swear an oath that they will avenge the shame of Bangla and Bengalis from two hundred years ago, and they pounce on the faithful follower of the Haji Shaheb.

Before he can understand what's going on, Rameez Sheikh finds himself surrounded by the enemy. Their weapons flash before his face in the dark. He has no preparation to deal with this as he was no co-conspirator of Mir Jafar's. Still, he thwarts the first slash of the chopper with the palm of his hand. Two fingers drop to the ground. Even if Rameez Sheikh does not want to be, he is a protagonist in this play. So he knows that the end is terrible. Close by is the British camp where Mir Jafar can be found. If he can make it there, he will be saved. Rameez Sheikh feels the strength of a demon possess him. He fights single-handedly against the six and breaks through the enemy barrier. Then, bleeding and wounded, he runs towards the enemy camp, the compatriots of Mir Jafar of 1971. He is chased by the six vigilantes. They are still focused on their performance in the play. The act which they could not watch even after buying tickets night after night because dawn would break, that unwitnessed scene is now being enacted by them. The story goes that after defeat in the battle of Palashi, the Nawab went back to Murshidabad. The patriot Mohanlal remained in the battlefield; he fought the British with the last drop of his blood. History repeats itself unerringly once more. And its witness is a cloudy night in Bangla.

Just two days earlier, the military encamped in the small thana town next to Notungaon. Mallikpur. Already, the villagers have left their homes. The military rape the women and grab the young men and bring them to the camp. According to the reports of the patriots, there are no young men left in the neighbouring villages. The soldiers feel secure with this state of affairs and they go off to sleep after ordering a sentry to guard the camp. But sleep does not come to those who love their land. And where will they sleep? They are patriots only in name. In reality, they have no land. If they go home, they will be caught by the Mukti fighters. They have been given leave for tonight from the camp. So they walk along the village paths stealthily like hunters in the wild. And luckily, they get their prey. They catch a fifteen or sixteen year old boy with a rifle and lash his hands behind his back. They bring him before the sentry and say in pidgin Urdu, "Here is a Mukti. We caught him with great difficulty." The camp comes alive. "Got a Mukti, got a Mukti." The young boy understands nothing. He had become the owner of the rifle that very evening. He had left home without dinner in search of Mukti fighters to learn where the trigger was on the gun, and how to fire a shot. On the way these people have captured him by mistake. But like them, he is also searching for the Mukti fighters. Before he can say all this, the sentry clubs him unconscious. They carry him away and put him in the lockup and they take position. The soldiers think this boy must be the advance guard, the main force must be following. They are coming to attack the camp. The soldiers don't have to wait too long for the main force. When Rameez Sheikh runs in bleeding, they imprison him. Behind him, the army of Nawab Siraj-ud-daula himself comes. The spears, tetas, choppers in their hands flash like lightning in the darkness. In the distant sky, the clouds rumble in accompaniment. The soldiers don't wait. The vigilantes who had thought that like Mohanlal, they would fight against the foreign soldiers to the last drop of their blood, find their chests riddled with machine gun shots. Like the play of the Nabaratna Opera, their battle also remains unfinished, waiting for the next night.

In the enemy camp, Rameez Sheikh's welcome was beyond imagination. First, he is given a thrashing by the followers and disciples of Mir Jafar the traitor. They beat him whichever way they can, with rods, kicks, punches. After that the men leave him in the lockup with his hands and feet tied, half-dead. How the rest of the night went by, Rameez Sheikh could not say. In between the comings and goings of his consciousness he would see the large eyes of the teenager burning in the night. In the morning, from that faraway past floats the court official's long-drawn cry, "Nawab Mansur-ul-mulk, Siraj-ud-daula, Shahkuli Khan, Mirza Muhammad Hayawat Jung, Bahadur p-r-e-s-e-n-t." The iron gates of the prison open with a clang and Rameez Sheikh understands that it is time for him to go to the Durbar. He is dragged to a standing position by two men. And then he is pushed to a veranda skirting a longish room. A Razakar is sitting next to a Pathan Havildar. The Razakar holds one side of his moustache and pulls it out. Rameez Sheikh cannot do anything. Because, his hands are tied at the back, he cannot even restore it like the actor in Nabaratna Opera. Even though his mouth is open, his tongue lacks the strength to deliver dialogue at this critical moment.

Inside the room, the Durbar is in session. A clean, crisply-clad major sits in judgment. A man enters the Durbar from somewhere, pulling a broken trunk. Some others rush in behind him. They are the plaintiffs, Rameez Sheikh the defendant. This is the second time that a court is sitting on Rameez Sheikh's case. In the first instance, he was the murderer, now he thinks he is going to be killed. One plaintiff points to him and says, "Huzoor, Your Honour, this man murdered my uncle Lal Mohammed." Then he throws open the broken trunk, "See Huzoor, this man has looted my house." The next plaintiff's name is Chan Mian, Member. He falls at the major's feet and screams, "On March 1, this man stabbed me with a knife in my stomach. You judge the case. I was almost disembowelled. Luckily, I was saved." The third man is Maulana Tofazzel. "Sir, this man has snatched away my gun." Saying this, the Maulana slaps him hard. The hanging moustache flies on impact and lands in the major's lap. He jumps up from his chair and says, "You people get out right now. I'll take care of this guy."

Now begins the interrogation. Told that the six dead vigilantes were the soldiers of Nawab Siraj-ud-daula, the major signals his personal attendant. The man first seats Rameez Sheikh on a chair, then ties both his legs and hangs him upside down from a beam in the ceiling. When he says the same thing even while suspended, the major orders the attendant, "Take him away. Prepare this Nawab of Bangla, Bihar, Orissa well." The moment they cross the doorway and the attendant gets ready to give him the treatment, the order comes once again, softly, "Bring him back tomorrow."

When he returns from the Major's room, he cannot see the young boy in the lockup. On the wall is written in blood, "Don't cry Mother, I am your Khudiram." The sentry informs him, "The little kiddy has been packed off to Bangladesh. And what difference does it make that you are a Nawab, you will be treated the same way."

The next day the Durbar is in session again. The interrogation is about to start. Just then, the telephone rings. The major picks up the receiver and shouts, "Ghurliye." From early morning, the Mukti Bahini have been fighting in Ghurulia, Notungaon,

Daudnagar, Khidirpur. On the wall behind hangs a map of the war. The major takes it off the wall and brings it to his table to see where Notungaon is, where is Daudnagar, where lies Khidirpur and where is Ghurulia. Even as the major is about to finish reading the map, the district Peace Committee's vice-president Hossein Ali rushes in on his fifty cc motor cycle. "Sir, Sir, there's an attack, there's an attack," he shouts. Rameez Sheikh does not know this man, has not seen him ever. But he understands from his manner that he belongs to traitor Mir Jafar's side. At the moment, he is a patriotic citizen who has rushed to the foreign enemy with news of the war. The Major Sahib leaves Rameez Sheikh and charges towards the patriotic vice-president of the Peace Committee, waving his pistol. He says, "Son of a pig, why did you shout? Now everyone will know all about it. I'll shoot you."

The man sees the pistol before his nose, and shuts up immediately. But Rameez Sheikh faces a dilemma. If this is the condition of the patriots, then with what hope are they doing their Mirjafari, their treacherous acts? They will never be able to ascend the throne. The lion's share of the beating that Rameez Sheikh has got is from these men. Meanwhile, the major has quickly readied his squad. He is the hero of the battle. The patriotic citizen acts as his guide. The soldiers are jumping into the vehicles. When he tries to stand up, Rameez Sheikh finds that the chair also gets up with him. His hands are tied firmly to the arms of the chair with thick ropes, which cannot be bitten through. So he walks towards the door with the chair. The major starts the engine and calls his attendant, "Bring this sister-fucker again tomorrow." The order given, he drives towards the battlefield.

Rameez Sheikh can tell from inside his prison that Major Sahib returns from battle triumphant. The courtyard in front is hellishly noisy with the clacking of poultry, the mooing of cows, and the bleating of goats. In the darkness, the lock of the prison door opens with a clang and some five men come flying in and stumble on him. Immediately, they vomit. One cannot make out in the dark if the lockup cell is being flooded with blood or vomit. The men are here inside, one can hear the poultry outside, but where are the women? If Notungaon has been attacked, then Mariam is bound to have been captured. But the idea does not worry Rameez Sheikh as it did earlier. Now everybody is lamenting, "Ya Nafasi, Oh my soul, alas my soul." The first thing is to save one's own life and then one can think of others.

At midnight, in the middle of the stench of blood, excreta, vomit, Rameez Sheikh wakes up to the aroma of cooking meat. A banquet is going on to celebrate the victory. The delectable aroma wafts in and churns his stomach. Ah! He wonders what meat it is with such a heavenly aroma. Two nights have passed since the light khichari at the Choudhury house and he has not had a morsel since then. He begins to feel the pangs of hunger for the first time and feeling a craving for meat, Rameez Sheikh starts vomiting.

The next day, there is once again the farce of the interrogation. On Rameez Sheikh's way to and from the interrogation room, the scene is changing constantly. The prison has extended from the lockup cell to the schoolhouse nearby. The major's Durbar is held in the room where the headmaster used to sit once. In the glass cupboards of the room, the bundles of answer papers by students have been removed to make way for the invisible files related to the accused prisoners. While the Durbar is in session, the major's personal attendant, following orders, opens the cupboard but does not find even a slip of paper in the empty shelves. He closes the cupboard and acts out a charade of placing something on the table but actually it is nothing. The major smiles. On the wall behind him hangs a photograph of a serious-looking Muhammad Ali Jinnah. On the roof flies the Pakistani flag of a crescent moon and a star.

Near the southern boundary of the school grounds under the gulmohur tree sat the square Shaheed Minar, the martyr's memorial. Now the man wearing a loose black robe who sits on the broken cement platform from dawn to night is a butcher named Naimuddin. He receives twenty taka per human throat.

He gets up repeatedly and goes to the sepoys to negotiate. This is exactly what he used to do with the traders before the war, to get a major share of the cows at the haat, the weekly market. One day, before going to the durbar, butcher Naimuddin had given Rameez Sheikh a bidi to smoke. Because his hands were tied, he pulled at the bidi furiously as Naimuddin held it for him with fingers reeking with the stench of stale blood. When the place would be taken over by the Indians, Naimuddin shed his black robe, but he could not hide his identity too long under a Mujib jacket. Before the Mukti fighters ripped him in two by grabbing his legs and pulling them apart, Naimuddin the butcher had begged to smoke a bidi.

Right now, Major Sahib is being afforded immense pleasure from recording the same statements from Rameez Sheikh by stringing up Rameez Sheikh, feet downwards at first and then hanging him upside down. In between, he is getting to watch Nabaratna Opera's play on Siraj-ud-daula without buying a ticket, a bonus for the Major during these joyless wartime days. Moreover, at his request, Rameez Sheikh acts out the role of the imprisoned Nawab every day while the Major twirls his moustache thinking himself to be the British army chief. On the other hand, the thrashing that Rameez Sheikh gets from the patriotic citizens is for real and not play-acting.

Rameez Sheikh, acting out his role at the durbar daily, slowly assumes the identity of the Nawab. The patriotic Nawab Siraj-ud-daula. He accepts with dignity the jokes at his expense, the sarcasm, the torture and the injustice at the hands of the enemy soldiers and traitors. He begins to think of himself as Nawab Siraj-ud-daula whom the enemy had captured at Bhagabangola and brought to Murshidabad. He is the one whose torn shoes and throne of thorns could not shake his regal bearing. In the dead of night, when on one side can be heard the wails and moans of women, and on the other side, by the river bank, the scrapping of dogs and jackals over the share of the corpses, the imprisoned Nawab sits in his cell and plots the battle strategy for the coming day. He is joined by the six dead vigilantes who materialise from the surrounding darkness. They correctly identify Rameez Sheikh crouched in one corner of the Nawab's poor, shabby, crowded quarters. The Nawab welcomes them. He makes place for them by pushing away the dirty plates and the excreta. Written in blood on the wall where they sit in a cluster are the words, "Mother, please do not cry. I am your Khudiram." Looking at the graffiti on the wall, one vigilante says, "The number of Khudirams is increasing like the swelling flood waters." In the course of conversation, the subject of untimely floods in the area comes up. The place where the Siraj-ud-daula play was enacted is now under ten cubits of water. There is nothing to be gained by regularly guarding the village anymore. The Mukti forces have also arrived. They position themselves under cover of the jute fields. The women of the village ferry meals to them in banana-plant rafts. Sometimes the hunting is good, sometimes not. Whenever they hear the sputtering of a mechanised boat nearby, they open fire with their Sten guns. Once the ammunition is finished, they flee the area in their boats through the rear of the village. From the other side, the Pakistani soldiers enter and beat up people, take them prisoner, burn their houses and destroy the village. "We cannot let this go on for long," says one former guard and takes Rameez Sheikh's fingerless palm in his hands. One by one they caress the empty place and kiss it with deep emotion. Rameez Sheikh also pats their bullet-riddled chests and backs. They want to know when the Nawab will once again attack the enemy camp; when they will be able to return once again to the land of their birth, Bangla. One of them says poetically like Golam Hossein, "Loving Bangla, we have come to love Bangla's Nawab." Chained and shackled Rameez Sheikh stands up on shaky legs. Jangling music is heard. The Nawab says in a trembling, emotional voice, "Golam Hossein, I have not loved Bangla as much as you. But why does Bangla constantly come to my mind today more than my own sad, troubled state?"

There is pin-drop silence in the Nawab's hut. The meeting time is also over. When two sepoys open the cell door to take the Nawab to the major's durbar, the dead vigilantes scurry away with their ripped and torn bodies. But Rameez Sheikh's trance-like state, where he thinks he is still the Nawab, lingers. He accompanies the sepoys to the school grounds. And then suddenly, he runs towards the two-storied school building, shouting, "Aleya, Aleya." What Rameez Sheikh thinks of as running with all his might appears to Mariam, looking out of the first floor window, like a hobbled rooster's tiny hops. All this – Rameez Sheikh's sighting of Mariam, his shouts for Aleya and his stumbling towards her – happens in an instant. Mariam is bewildered. The idiot has to be stopped somehow or he will be shot dead. But the room is locked from outside. Also, she suddenly remembers that apart from her scanty underwear, she is wearing no clothes.

Meanwhile, Rameez Sheikh is still running when he feels a shove at his back and with it a twinge of pain like the prick of a needle. Not a sharp pain, but very powerful. In an instant, Rameez Sheikh breaks out of his role as Nawab and returns to his old identity. There he is an insignificant subject who had been sentenced to life imprisonment for murdering his wife and who after ten years, breaks out of prison in these troubled times. Rameez Sheikh sees his wife dressed up as a bride blocking his way at an arm's length. The woman does not move even when he shouts for her to move away. She runs along with her murderer husband maintaining the distance of an arm's length. But their way is no longer straight and smooth. It suddenly curves near the headmaster's room, passes the two-storied school building, and leaves below the Pakistani flag and the gulmohur tree, going upwards.

VII

Chastity, Sari and Underwear

After twenty-eight years of war, the fact serves as a clue. For Mukti it is an important finding that at the Pakistani military camp, Mariam was clad only in her underclothes and not a single other garment. This is the first time that a similarity, however small, has been found between Mariam and the Biranganas, the heroic women. It will definitely help to make her report more credible. In 1971, the Pakistani soldiers stripped the imprisoned women of their saris, they did not allow them to wear any unstitched clothing. There were many explanations for this action. Jaitun Bibi of Notungaon told Mukti, "We heard that where the Pakistani soldiers had come from, the women did not wear saris. They covered their bodies with Mussalmani kurtas. Saris were considered a Hindu dress." Shahrukh, a college student said, "Don't you realize, the sari is the Bengali woman's adornment, a thousand year-old heritage for Bengalis. For their part, the Pakis hated Bengalis. So they burned the saris and all other garments that were the adornment of Bengali women, along with the Bangladeshi flag during that year of war." There was another reason recorded and this was that some women, afraid of losing their chastity, used the sari as a noose and hanged themselves in many Pakistani army camps and military stations. The soldiers, therefore, disrobed them and deprived them of their right to suicide.

True or false, the event later became a matter of shame for Bengalis. The thousand-year old tradition of the sari and chastity, nurtured by the women and borne through generations was lost at one go during that year of war. Mukti made a brief mention of this in her report as the most important reason for the sacrifice of the Biranganas, on a national scale.

After this Mariam's tale is free of complexities, clear and crisp for a while. Indistinguishable from the stories of other Biranganas. The mess that was created following the arrival of Rameez Sheikh was resolved at this point. It was lucky that it was the Pakistani soldiers who shot him and that he was not killed by the freedom fighters. If the opposite had happened, Mukti did not know how she would explain the development. After three months of war, the man who could not distinguish between the two slogans – Joi Bangla and Pakistan Zindabad – had a fifty-fifty chance of death at the hands of the Pakistani army and the Mukti Bahini. Then of course, one learnt from Mohammed Shamsuddoha's memoirs of being imprisoned in '71 that before his death Rameez Sheikh had become a nationalist, albeit because of mental derangement. Shamsuddoha was captured by the Razakars, Sten gun in hand, while he was about to destroy a bridge. The Razakar commander grabbed his weapon and produced him before the martial law court. Although a Bengali, Shamsuddoha is a *mohajer,* a refugee. After the 1947 Partition, he had fled India with his parents and come to East Pakistan. Since then the family of this Razakar commander had been after them. Repeatedly, he made statements in Urdu that these people had come to take over his lands. Shamsuddoha escaped the death traps set by the martial law court, the FIO (Field Intelligence Office), and MPs (military police) and was sent to prison around October. On December 7, 1971, the Muktijoddhas broke open the prison locks and freed him.

For quite some time after his arrest in June, Mr Shamsuddoha shared prison space with Rameez Sheikh at the lockup in

Mallikpur police station. He had a close encounter with this strange man. In his book, *71-er Bandi Jiban,* (Prison Life in '71), he raised a significant question that went in favour of Rameez Sheikh. He wrote, "It was not unexpected for Rameez Sheikh to lose his mind due to excessive torture. Otherwise, why should an ordinary peasant, without rhyme or reason, begin to think of himself as Nawab Siraj-ud-daula?" Besides this, in an interview, Mariam has described in detail, how the man shouted "Aleya, Aleya" and ran towards her, pushing aside the soldiers' gun barrels as one would clear water hyacinths in a pond. Would any sane person, anyone other than a lunatic, show such daring and run forward knowing that death is inevitable?

After being shot in the back, Rameez Sheikh's pace accelerated. He was no longer hobbling like a rooster with bound legs. The rope tying his legs had broken and his running was transformed into the leaps of a deer chased by a tiger. Mariam told Mukti that the man seemed to have sworn on his life that he would not stumble and fall. For a while, he circled the school grounds, like an airplane gathering speed on the runway before taking off. At the last moment, his feet no longer touched ground and he even made a low rumbling sound like a plane. Before dying, he had threatened the Pakistani soldiers. But Mariam could not hear what he actually said. Because at that very moment, several guns were fired together with a deafening noise. The field was covered with black smoke. That is why Mariam cannot say for certain whether Rameez Sheikh's final journey ended with a run or a flight.

Fear and anxiety drove Mariam into a state of hysteria. She told Mukti during the interview that she was distressed most by seeing the man run towards her. It is true that she moved away from the window because at the time, she was wearing only a bra and a little rag that acted as a fig leaf. And after that the matter slipped her mind, because the whole thing was unimaginably frightening. Mariam tells Mukti, "It was not just that they made us wear rags or raped us, for me each kick of the boot, each prod of the bayonet, each cigarette burn was equally dreadful. None of it was normal. Not one was less than the others. The Bengali nation only wants to know how many times we were raped day and night. They do not consider the other tortures as tortures."

Mariam grieved for Rameez Sheikh many years after the war. This was when she realized that the men of liberated Bangladesh would use her body which had been used by the enemy in the very same way. That no one would think of her as his dear one. She consoled herself with the thought that at least there was one man in the world who had invited death by running towards her. But Mariam could not know in advance that Rameez Sheikh would have such an indirect role in her life. Both of them were prisoners then. One could not help the other.

Mariam says, "It is my bad luck, my fate." Otherwise, why should she be captured in a village which was just a day's journey from her own home? The distance they calculated by reckoning the time taken to travel to her aunt Sahar Banu's in-law's village and back.

Sahar Banu was married, thirty years before the war, to a family in Radhanagar, a village near Notungaon. It was during the British rule. The roads were then infested with dacoits. That is why Kafiluddin's deceased father, Salimuddin, would put his daughter in a palanquin carried by trusted palanquin bearers before sunrise. They would call out "uhoom na, uhoom na," to mark the pace, and reach the gates of the Munshi household right after the period for the afternoon prayers, when the sun was about to set in the western sky. The bearers never walk, they always run. By that count, if Mariam walked, she would have reached home latest by ten at night. Accordingly, she started the next day following the disappearance of Rameez Sheikh and the six vigilantes. But the roads are not safe in times of war; the elders of Notungaon did not approve of a woman's setting off for her home alone. At the time, the military vehicles were whizzing madly along the highways. The bridges were closely guarded by the Razakars and the Mujahids. Each village had a check-post. The elders advised her to wait for a few more days for the situation to improve and immediately went to the mosque to have prayers read for the absent villagers and for an end to the troubles. The next day, the six corpses of the vigilantes were found and immediately lamentations started in each house like the mourning for the deaths at the battle of Karbala. And even before they had completed the rituals for burial, the military had entered the village.

Jaitun Bibi says, "It was as if the girl had called in the Khan soldiers." Because, the war was three months old by then and although the military had ravaged the neighbouring villages and towns, Notungaon had been left unscathed. The moment Mariam arrived, things began happening. And yet, on hearing that a girl from the city had arrived in the Chowdhury house, Jaitun Bibi had crossed the canal in those troubled times and had gone to see her that very night. So what if she was a city girl? There was a softness about her. Her face was as beauteous as the moon. She also spoke gently. In the course of conversation, it transpired that the girl's Fupu or aunt was married into the Munshi family of Radhanagar, the year before smallpox struck. That was also the year of Jaitun Bibi's marriage. She had still been a new bride then. When smallpox was spreading like pestilence in village after village, her elder brother had come to take her to her father's home. Her eldest son was just a month old then. Her mother-in-law would not let her go. She had a single diktat. "If you wish, you can go with your brother. But you'll have to leave my grandson behind." Elder brother was quite strong-minded, but he shed tears as he left for his home, alone.

Jaitun Bibi's heart melts as she remembers past sorrows. She returns home praying for the girl, that she is kept safe and not ravished by the Khan soldiers. Subsequently, disaster struck her own life. One of the vigilantes was the eldest son of her husband's co-wife. She had brought him up with great love and care. When he was buried, he seemed to take a part of her life with him. That is why, when they heard that the Khans were coming, Jaitun Bibi and her husband's other wife could not leave the house. They hid behind the karamcha shrub at the near of the house. At the time the Khans were advancing like locusts on the district board road. Now, they could be seen in front of Aziz Khalifa's house and before you could blink your eyes, you saw them near the betel leaf plantations, fruit orchards and bamboo groves belonging to the Hindu households. At the time one could see nothing but their dark bums. And then huge tongues of flame leapt up on the other side. They were dowsing the Hindu homes with petrol and setting them on fire. On the way to the Hindu houses, the invaders called out the people to loot and pillage. Jaitun Bibi and the co-wife watched people running helter skelter with the loot from the cover of the karamcha shrub. Then came the sharp cracks of gunshots. That day the Pakistani soldiers dragged from the woods Balai, a sadhu and his two disciples. They dragged them across the fields, stood them in a row and shot them down at one go.

Earlier as he watched the violence escalate, Balai sadhu had wanted to escape along with his disciples. And yet when his relatives left for India and wanted to take him along, he said, "You go if you want to. Why do you have to drag me with you? I believe in the one god. The Khans won't kill me." The soldiers did not remain in the village for long. After burning down homes, murdering men and women in broad daylight, they went back the way they had come. During their return march, Jaitun Bibi saw that they were dragging with them Tuki, the domestic help in the Chowdhury household, Jogen Bayen's eldest daughter Bindubala, and Mariam along the district board road.

At the time Mariam was oblivious of who saw her and who did not. She became numb and a darkness filled her senses. When the soldiers entered the gates, the women of the Chowdhury family locked themselves in a room and started reciting verses from the Quran under their breaths. But the children shut up in the room began wailing. They could not be hushed even after their mouths were covered with cloth. The Khans, after burning the Hindu homes and killing Hindus, were running amok. The door fell off its hinges with a single kick and fell open. There were only women and children in the room. The men had fled. When the women were asked to come out, they started screaming and shouting and trying to hide in the corners. They didn't understand the language of the Khans. The children had stopped yelling by then. Another round of loud crying was to be heard when the women were hit with rifle butts and shoved out of the room. Some of them were even then reciting their prayers loudly. Mariam was wearing a salwar-kameez with a wide cotton dupatta. She veiled her face by covering her head with the dupatta and pulling it forward. But as she came out, in the middle of all the pushing and jostling by the women, her beautiful face came uncovered. In the courtyard, she saw five or six soldiers standing. They did not take part in the operation. Perhaps they were standing outside issuing orders. One of them noticed her before she could cover herself again. He leapt on her like a cheetah. Mariam says, "I don't know what happened to me after that. I could not understand, could not feel a thing. I was captured by the army. What would they do to me, would they kill me, or what? I did not know a thing, I was senseless."

Mariam does not know how she walked miles in this condition to Mallikpur. Since they were walking down village roads, at every turn and twist of the way, there must have been human habitations, they must have crossed canals and water bodies, the cultivated fields must have had knee-high jute saplings and paddy seedlings, and yet Mariam did not notice any of these. Only when they hit the tarred road going to town did she feel that her feet were scorched and realized that she was not wearing sandals. She also noticed fingers clamped on her arm like a vice. When she raised her eyes, she saw thick reddish moustaches. The moustachioed man was gripping her arm even when they climbed the stairs to the first floor. He released her arm only when he threw her into the room. Mariam found herself flying across the room and falling on some benches.

"Benches? Where did benches come from?"

"The place where I was first kept was a schoolroom."

"Was there a ceiling fan in the room?"

"Was there? No, there was not. Or, perhaps there was. Did they have fans in schoolrooms in those days?"

"Please try and remember. It's important."

"No, I can't remember. But even if there was no fan, there must have been a hook on the ceiling. Why?"

"Were you wearing your dupatta? The large cotton dupatta?"

"Yes. I was wearing a kameez, so there must have been a dupatta. At that time, there were similar kameezes, but they were a little tighter, a little shorter."

"Do you remember the food? What sort of food did you eat?"

"They gave us dal and possibly, rice. Sometimes, they gave us a small piece of meat."

"Rotis?"

"Yes, yes. They gave us rotis mostly. But we had infections down there. There was always fever and one had no appetite."

"Did they give you glasses for drinking water?"

"The things you say, glasses for drinking water! The school sweeper brought us an earthenware platter and a vessel of water which would be replenished every couple of days. One had to drink that water, as well as use it for washing after pissing and shitting. There were no bathrooms. It was a schoolroom after all. Right at the rear, there were some latrines for students. How we spent those days! We couldn't bathe, not a single time."

"Didn't you smell bad? Body odours?"

"Yes, one did smell. Haven't you noticed that bloodstains on your clothes leave a distinct smell? But the situation forced us to live like that. There was no alternative. Can one explain all this? Is there a language to describe this experience? What language shall I use?"

"But tell me, was there a fan in the room? And if not a fan, was there a hook in the ceiling?"

"There could possibly have been a hook but who then bothered to notice and remember? All I could think of was how to survive those terrible things."

"Surprising: there was a hook in the ceiling, and you had a long dupatta with you."

"What's so surprising about that?"

"In those days many women committed suicide in a situation like that."

"Oh! But, I did not think about suicide. I used to think about living. I thought of suicide after the war. Uh-uh. There was another thing I remember. There was a window in the room which was partially broken. It was through that window that I saw Rameez Sheikh running one day."

"When you saw him, were you wearing the salwar-kameez and dupatta?"

"No. The military had torn them off our bodies. When the sweeper came to collect the waste from the room, he bundled them up as rags and took them away. Days passed but I did not get back the clothes. That is why when I first saw Rameez Sheikh running towards me, I moved away from the window."

"Weren't you wearing anything then?"

"Oh, yes. I was wearing a bra and a bit of torn rag."

Mukti breathes a sigh of relief. The long, large dupatta does not correspond with the information in the books. Especially for a woman, who may not have had a fan in her room, but certainly a hook from which she could hang herself by tying a noose with her long scarf. Suicide was scripted for such a woman after having lost her chastity. The nation, at least, had nurtured such a wish. In such a scenario, the sweeper taking away Mariam's clothes, not only released Mariam from her duty of committing suicide but also granted Mukti a measure of relief. But what were Tuki, the Chowdhury family's domestic help, and Bindubala, Jogen Bayen's eldest daughter, wearing? Mariam gives an ambiguous answer, "Possibly, a sari. Village women wore saris along with an underskirt and a blouse. However, the maid Tuki was perhaps wearing only a sari." Later, Tuki said the same thing to Mukti, but put it differently. "Who would buy me a blouse and petticoat? I was wearing only a sari, a printed sari. Abba bought it for me for Eid from the Khidirpur market. In all my years, I've not worn a salwar-kameez."

Mariam did not know even then where they were being held, what was being done to them. She could only hear screams, but could not identify who was crying where. Was it in the next room, or the room after that? There was no dearth of rooms in a school. Before the war, many classes from six to ten would be bundled together in a room. From these, suddenly, the sound of sobbing and moaning would waft in. That is how she understood that there were other girls nearby and it was not impossible for Tuki and Bindubala to be there as well. Therefore they were not dead, but alive.

The day Mariam was transported from Mallikpur, there was no way of knowing whether it was night or day, whether the two girls were with her or not, whether they were wearing saris or not. Because, they were brought out of the room blindfolded. They stood there for a while like blind owls. Then the military kicked them on their asses and pushed them into a vehicle. Then came the order, "Lower your heads" and the engine of the vehicle revved up. That the vehicle was a truck and they were crouching in its open rear portion, they realized only when they felt a shower of rain on their backs. Someone like Tuki whispered in Mariam's ears, "It's an open truck. I'll die of shame. Everyone on the road can see us."

The truck trundled along an uneven, rutted road. For a long time, only the rumbling of the engine could be heard. Suddenly there was the noise of a cheering crowd which drowned out the noise of the engine. Who were these people, during this time of war? With nothing else to cover herself, Mariam hid her face with her hands. Clad only in underclothes, her body cringed in a corner of the truck like a beaten animal. It was not strangers that she feared, but people who she knew. Mariam sees through her blinded eyes her scantily clad body in an open truck being driven in front of Mahua cinema. Jashimul Haque is in the audience at the cinema hall that day. He was Mariam's first lover with whom she went to see a movie, where love blossomed. Then in the span of three days they parted. He may have been smoking a cigarette under the huge hoarding with other cinema-goers after the show was over and seeing a truckload of naked women had clapped and whistled along with the others. Such a scene cannot be witnessed even in the English movies marked 'for adults only' for which tickets have to be purchased on the black market.

As she remembers that time, sweat tattoos Mariam's forehead. Her head bows in shame, her gaze focusing on her toes. But suddenly the idea comes to her that no one will go to see a film during the war. It seems to come to her from the open sky. Mariam looks directly at Mukti and says, "Otherwise, where did it come from at that moment when, for all we knew, we might have been facing death?" Perhaps to cover their shame, rain poured in torrents from the sky, a massive downpour that seemed like a deluge. The truck braked instantly. The soldiers jumped down and threw huge sheets of tarpaulin, black as a bat's wing, over them. "It was because our eyes were blindfolded that we were thinking like that, I think," Mariam says after considering it a bit. Because each one of them had thought that the truck was driving by their homes. And those who were clapping or giving wolf whistles were people known to them, perhaps even ex-lovers. Those thoughts were like a blind man's stick with which they touched the future that awaited them with the ridicule and castigation of everyone including strangers and dear ones. Not even a hundred tarpaulin sheets could be protection against these.

There is no end to this journey. It is not a road but a labyrinth, confusing like the wetlands of Sundari. And Montu is with her. With her eyes blindfolded under the tarpaulin, Mary thinks that it has been an eternity that brother and sister have been trying to find their way back home. But in the maze of the wetlands, they can never find the right path. Montu is foolish as always – even during this time of war. He never did unravel the mystery of the Sundari marshes and enter the world of adults. War enters the life of this young boy before he even finds answers to his childhood questions. He goes to war.

VIII

The Warrior

"What! Are you afraid?"

"No, no, Sir." Montu puffs out his chest and answers Major Sharma. The major walks on towards the next fighter standing in line. Today is their first operation. They will enter their own country, now occupied by the enemy, armed with light machine guns, grenades and rifles. Having checked out each young man, the major is now giving a speech. Montu does not expel his breath. He struggles hard to hold on to it, so that when the Major is speaking, he can see among the many young men his expanded chest. And this effort takes a lot of Montu's attention. The Major is inciting the fighters. Montu repeats the Major's words in his mother tongue, "Young people, have courage, be brave. One cannot free one's country without a war. The enemy is playing havoc with the land of your birth. They are killing your people like cats and dogs. The honour of your mothers and sisters is at stake."

On Montu's small, hairless chest, at the time, there was the tremor of an earthquake. His breath, held back with difficulty, surges and knocks at his chest and is, at last, pushed out through his nose. April has followed March and is almost over and still there's no news of Mary. Mother wakes up at midnight and paces the house. She cannot sleep. No one is allowed to weep loudly at home. Father tries hard to keep everything under cover. "Not even a dog or a cat now remains in Dhaka." Hearing such words from people who have fled the city, the villagers visit their house and want to know, "Where is Mary? Has she come home or is she still in Dhaka?" For a long time, Mother has fielded such questions with the answer, "She is with my younger brother. Please pray for her, she is very precious to me." The neighbours then say, "We pray for your daughter. We hope Allah keeps her safe and well." But events take a different turn when her younger brother Golam Mostofa comes to the village with his entire family. Everything is clear as daylight then. The people don't need to come home and ask about Mary. And Mother has no more explanations to give. She can only shed tears in secret. The girl is lost forever – her darling daughter.

"Take revenge," Montu hears Major Sharma's excited voice saying. The speech is nearing its end. The major says, "Don't be afraid. We are with you. We will help you with whatever you need. One day your country will definitely be independent. This is as it should be. Good luck, sons. Joi Bangla."

The same night, Montu's group crosses the border and embarks on an expedition to capture a Razakar. Not finding the Razakar at home, they capture his pony and bring it to the camp. The man used to mount this animal during the rice harvest and go begging. On their way back, they throw four out of the five grenades in their hands at the beggar's courtyard and start running. Only one of the grenades bursts with a huge explosion. They are running and the animal trots with them. They don't have the courage to remain for a moment on the land of their birth. In their mad hurry, they even forget to remove the pins from the grenades. They stop only after they cross the border and step into India. And then it suddenly strikes them that they are thieves, horse thieves. The first operation of their lives they've conducted like thieves.

"Is this the way we will fight and liberate our country?" scolds the platoon commander. The boys who participated in the operation ask themselves the same question. But they are happy to have been able to return alive to the camp. Not a single one of them was lost. They had not known that their own country could be so frightening. Living in the training camp in India, they had looked forward to the time when they would escape mosquito and leech bites, when they would not have to do physical training on half rations, when they would enter their country as full-fledged fighters, fully armed. In the meantime, the sun has burned their complexions to a coppery hue, a tracery of blue veins has covered their muscles, a bushy undergrowth of whiskers has sprouted on their faces for want of shaving. The heart underneath the altered appearance is also changing. They are itching to plunge into the war.

At first, they were disappointed at the scarcity of weapons. The Pakistani forces had tanks, machine guns, and state-of-the-art weapons of destruction. How long will they take to fight against these with rifles, grenades, Sten guns in order to free the country? They grew depressed that they could not use an ordinary grenade. They also notice that the fire of revenge has slowly died down leaving only ashy remains. But the battlefield does not tolerate despondence and disorder. You have to go there either to kill or be killed. There is no alternative. Sometimes they want to run away when they hear such harsh words from the platoon commander. The old days hold on to their shirtsleeves and pull them back to the past. There they find themselves again in the boring, exhausting life of studying and learning by rote while preparing for examinations. Or, as deeply embarrassed young men, caught writing love letters. Everyone in the group has experienced deceit and rejection. Sometimes life is so hard that they feel they have no choice but to commit suicide. But faced with war, all these old sorrows vanish into thin air. The monotonous past becomes resplendent with different colours and inviolable like a dream.

The seasonal rains are upon them with full force. As it is, the freedom fighters are nocturnal in their movements and then there is the torrential rain. The time of the 'operation' is fixed during one such rainy night. They wrap the grenades in gamchhas and tie them around their waists. They wear dark shirts that are indistinguishable in the inky night. They sling rifles and Sten guns on their shoulders. They lift the lower edge of their lungi and knot it around their waists to make it a knee-length garment. They leave the camp after tying a piece of polythene over their heads. The enemy clings like leeches to the sides of the damp bunkers. They don't leave their dugouts. Montu's group takes advantage and walks forward, getting soaked to the skin in their country under siege. Although they have not encountered the real enemy and do not know when the country will be liberated, each step they tread on the grassy, slushy land seems to them to have been earned by their own merit. They even think that they are the only shareholders of this Bangla sky massed with clouds, and the inky dark night is their companion, and theirs alone. They have exchanged their attachment to life for a share of all this when they crossed the Indo-Bangladesh border. They will not forfeit these rights even if they die. This staking of a claim is more powerful than weapons. It spurs them to kill the enemy and inspires them to become martyrs.

The problem arises when often, during the night operations, the target is not found at home. Somehow he gets prior information and flees. But Montu and his companions never return empty-handed. They drag cattle or goats from the sheds back to the camp in the hope that the meat will tickle their palates which are fed up with tasting the same food. They sit in the courtyard and make a bundle of odds and ends from the house to take along. They don't know what purpose the stuff will serve in the battlefield but they loot and plunder all the same either because of greed or to punish the enemy agents, or perhaps they do it to cover the feelings of shame and defeat at having to return empty-handed.

On the return journey, an inexpressible fear pursues Montu. Waiting ahead of him is the mysterious wetland of the night from whose maze he can never find his way back home. He constantly changes his place among the two columns of marching freedom fighters. He wants to hide behind the piles of loot. Then suddenly he realizes that he has fallen behind everyone. There is a vacuum behind him, ahead lies darkness. Only a few sparks of light are visible. A strangled cry issues from his throat, which his mates call fear-song, the music of terror. To help him overcome this fear, the group leader ordered the killing of the enemy agent, but Montu groaned the same way that night while returning from that mission.

Montu steps ahead with pride after receiving group leader Sharif Bhai's orders. It is the first time in his life that he has been given such an important assignment, a task that befits his wishes. There was a measure of compulsion when he had to come to the city with his sister while still at school. No one had asked him, "What would you like Montu, do you want to go to the city or would you like to remain in the village?" Montu in the city had been like the tiny fledglings he brought out of nests from the holes in tree trunks, trembling in his small palms. How many nights had he wet the pillow with his tears. There he was a puppet in his sister's hands—a slave to her wishes. At last, when he got involved with meetings and demonstrations and he began to think of the heated city as his own, his sister Mariam forced him to go back to the village. No one in the family had taken account of his growing up. Not even outsiders. Here he is training to be a freedom fighter, and his fellow trainees do not take him seriously. Sometimes they tease him saying, "Fraidy Montu, don't dare to wet the bed at night." Only commander Sharif Bhai gave him his due respect. Handing over the gun, he asked, "Can you do it?"

"I can, Sharif Bhai, I can," Montu nods and picks up the weapon. Just three yards from him glimmer a few sparks of light. These do not scare Montu—they are will-o'-the-wisps, they have no existence in the real world. They create an illusion and draw travellers onto the wrong track, making them go round and round endlessly and killing them eventually. "One-two-three," Sharif Bhai's voice floats across as if from a long distance. It seems he is giving an order in someone else's voice, "Montu, ready, open fire. The punishment for a traitor is death." Rat-a-tat-tat! A burst of fire flashes from Montu's Sten gun like loud laughter. The bullets fly and hit the man tied to a tree – strike his chest, throat, beard. Instantly, the strapping man falls to the ground and like a tiny bird struggles awhile and then becomes inert. Before he dies, he asks for a drink of water, parting his lips just like a bird. Montu is the hero that night. Sharif Bhai personally lights a Charminar cigarette for him. On the way back, he pats his back and tells him not to fall back but to walk alongside. But after a while, Montu's game of hide-and-seek begins. And then as usual, the groaning fear-song makes itself heard.

No matter what they boast, not everyone in the group is brave. This discovery was made on the day they were winding up camp and returning from India. Before this, they were infiltrators. They quickly crossed the border of another country, conducted their attacks as soon as they entered and then returned under cover of the night. Such an act is called infiltration in the language of war. It is an illegal act. As long as war is not announced formally, India cannot send people inside Pakistani territory to fight. Besides, Montu and the others have been trained to fight a guerrilla war in their country. One cannot see the results of such warfare directly, but harassing the enemy with acts of sabotage and destruction can also be called war. This will create difficulties for the enemy forces. They will be annoyed, feel nervous. They will get exhausted.

The boys are not happy with Major Sharma's long speech. They express their reservations with low-key grumbling. They object to this strategy of playing safe. When will their country become free? It is not possible for the major to explain the strategy in detail. It is, after all, a state secret. He gets annoyed with the boys. It seems they have no idea of how the world operates. They sit in India and dream of liberating their country after killing a couple of enemy agents at night. He leaves the camp after advising them to buy a two-band radio. The advice is treated as an order.

The radio is bought but no one has the time or inclination

to listen to it. They have to dismantle the camp while there is still daylight. They have to search for a safe shelter. Montu and his group members are dropped along with their luggage in two trucks at some suitable place near the border. They feel like refugees. The only difference is that the refugees are going towards India while they are going towards the land under enemy occupation. It is a rare scene. Many people from the neighbouring villages come running with their children to see them. They behave just as they would when a circus comes to town. A spark of amusement in their faces. The little boys are the most daring. They break into peals of laughter while being chased away. The very next moment, they come back on tiptoe to touch the metallic barrels of the guns. The fighters feel like elephants fallen into a dung heap, they're in a deep mess. If the beggar's pony was with them at least, they would face less harassment. The horse is a symbol of aristocracy, even if it belongs to a beggar. When they were breaking camp, someone made the argument that cavalries are commonly used in war, so the pony could also be used for fighting. By that time, some of the boys had become experts at riding the pony. But Sharif Bhai did not agree. Instead, he gave an hour-long speech, "You should realize guerrilla warfare is not direct confrontation. You have to conduct it silently, covertly, without alerting the enemy to our presence. To do that, we have to go barefoot through the water and slush, get sores between our toes. The soles of our feet will get riddled with holes from the bites of water insects. They'll start looking like sieves. When a co-fighter gets shot, it's time to confront the enemy by throwing a grenade…"

Sharif Bhai has this one bad habit. He always ends his speeches with reference to Majibar. Is Majibar the symbol of their heroism or their miscalculation? Now when they enter their country with all their bundles, they have to cross his grave. No one agrees to this. But this is the only way to re-enter the country. That is why they disperse among the curious crowds and wait for nightfall. After night comes, they take cover in the darkness and cross the scary area where the first casualty, the first murdered freedom fighter Majibar, lies in eternal sleep.

Majibar had been sent with two young men to Madhyamgram to do a recce of the temporary army camp. It was not night but afternoon and there was bright sunlight. Even so, they were supposed to seek an opportunity and explode a couple of grenades there. They gripped their Sten guns, lowered their heads and ran fifty yards into the enemy camp crouching low before the sentry became aware of anything. Immediately they began firing bullets like a shower of rain. The two young men fled and took shelter behind the jute fields. Majibar, however, took his position and pressed the trigger of his Sten gun. Just after two rounds of brush fire, the magazine was empty. Instead of escaping behind the jute fields, he stood there opening the pin of the grenade. Then he ran forward like an athlete throwing a spear and hurled the grenade and in turn was shot at. He became still like a freeze frame. The people in the neighbouring villages ran away when they heard gunshots. They stopped in their tracks when they saw the body of the freedom fighter suspended in mid-air in an athletic pose. They stood stock-still in their places till the next round of firing began.

The residents of Madhyamgram complain to Mukti twenty-nine years after the war that the liberation statues are not being crafted properly in the city. They demand a stone sculpture that is leaping in the air with raised arms and with no stakes in the soil of Bangla. But why? Mukti's question keeps them quiet for a while. Then they say, hesitantly, that in reality they had seen such a martyred freedom fighter whose memory is triggered off every time they see a tall jute plant. Because he could have hidden in the jute fields instead of fighting. But he did not do that because he was not a human being, but a ferishta. Besides, they say that this business of demands and receipts is in the realm of human affairs. Man does not give up his claim even after death. This last they say to Mukti after showing her the mother of a martyr from the village. An octogenarian woman, she begs for a living after losing her grown-up son. She has not given up her son's claims on the Bangla soil. She is carrying them with her and will continue to do so till she goes to her grave.

But the residents of Madhyamgram have no pride in the living freedom fighters as they have not seen them fight. Some of the villagers seem a little hesitant in talking about this. "Why? Have they given up their claims?" They tell Mukti, "No, no. It is not that." It is not just an issue of claims and dues. The account of the lives of the living freedom fighters in the last twenty-nine years is just like any other person's in society. It is no different. They have aged like everyone else. They have fathered children, some have become grandparents. Immediately after the war, they had a shining image and wielded enormous clout. Looking at them you felt that although they were children of the village, they had fought to liberate the country, they were the pride of the village, heroic freedom fighters – but now the shine has worn off and old memories are no longer stirred. They have seen themselves, been witness to their own rise and fall. A few of them have earned huge amounts of money as dealers. But the money's gone the way it came. They could not enjoy it. Meanwhile, the area commander's home, made with cement meant for relief, remains undamaged. He has changed sides with each change in government and now he is the owner of two petrol pumps and cold storage facilities. He does not live in the village but comes down before elections to solicit votes. Each time he has a different symbol. But for others, when the government changes, the police come and drag them to the police station, beat and torture them. There is no end to the oppression. The only consolation is that some criminal cases of murder and other wrongful acts continue to crop up in the village. Serving prison sentences, appearing in courts has become an everyday affair. The villagers tell Mukti that she should have come to the village earlier. Because now it is difficult to identify who is a freedom fighter and who is a Razakar. When a government comes to power, it sifts them. It so happens that a man who was a Razakar becomes a freedom fighter, and the person who really was a freedom fighter gets scratched out of the government list with one stroke of the pen. Everything has become so confused now. The only person with a clear mind in this topsy-turvy state of affairs is the landless peasant Aminul.

Aminul Islam tells Mukti, "Oh my! That year it rained and rained. The night was so dark that one could not see the palm of one's hands. I could hear from my hut that they were splashing through the water behind my hut. I took a peek at them but did not dare to talk." One night Aminul took courage and flashed a torch. And guess what happened? They immediately pulled him out of his room with his hands up. Someone hit him, someone else wanted to tie him up. But that day the Mukti fighters had an important operation. They took Aminul along and from his home they got down to the rice fields, walked through them, crossed the wetland into the next village. As a result, Aminul became friends with the Mukti forces, they shared their lives. Mukti gets to know from him that the grave in Madhyamgram is not Montu's but Majibar's, the Mukti fighter with the raised arms. Aminul dug Majibar's grave himself. The leader of the group, Sharif Bhai was shot in the leg and lay unconscious in the hideout on the day of Montu's last operation. He could not fight again. His leg had to be amputated. The freedom fighter who gave the news of Montu's death, albeit late, was called Sarfaraz Hossein. He had been sent to India at the time to collect arms or rations. It would be from him that Mariam got the incorrect information about Montu's grave in the month of August, 1975.

Aminul remembers clearly the day of death of Majibar, the freedom fighter with the raised arms. It was a Wednesday, the day of the weekly market. He was struggling to tie the legs of a pair of egg-laying hens, to sell in the market. "Why did you want to sell hens which lay eggs?" Aminul loses track at Mukti's question. Then he says with annoyance, "First listen to what I have to say, whether it is true or false, and then you can make your investigations if you want to."

Desperate need spoils character. He is also getting on in years. His memory is faltering. If anyone interrupts, everything gets confused in his mind like the other villagers. "In '71 however"

Aminul says, "I was very strong and well-built. Looking at me people would say be careful. My parents would try to hide me. My uncles would say watch out that Pakistani forces do not come and catch you. It was a very serious situation. The war had started. People were leaving the city and swarming into the country."

"What did you do then?"

"I was the Mukti soldiers' guide, showing them the way."

"No, no. I am not asking that. When I asked what you did, I meant what was your occupation then?"

"During the war, I used to live with my parents. I used to work on the land. Abba was very poor. Father and son, we used to work on other people's land. I used to help Abba in his farm work. I used to catch fish. At the time of rice or jute sowing, I would buy from the traders and would sell it at the weekly market. Abba would say, Aminul be a little careful."

"Then you became guide to the Mukti Fauj."

After becoming a guide, Aminul pointed out the important spots to the Mukti soldiers, did a recce before an operation, found out the role of various people in the villages nearby – whether they were for or against the Mukti forces, the movements of the army, he collected all this information. All this work had to be done at night. In the morning, when you returned home and got ready to sleep, the hens started cackling after laying eggs. Aminul got hassled with all kinds of disturbances at home and outside. That Wednesday, ignoring his mother's pleading, he began tying the legs of the birds when the firing started. At first he thought, the army was entering the village while firing their guns. But what was the noise in return? By that time, Aminul was able to recognize the different sound of exploding mortar shells, the intermittent sounds made by the brush fire of automatic weapons, the single shot of the rifle. He realized that he could not delay finding out what was happening any longer. He released the hens and quickly climbed the tallest areca nut tree standing in the corner of the courtyard.

From the top of the areca nut tree, Aminul could see the people at home running for their lives. The pair of hens tied together by their legs hopped behind them. The noise of shooting had by then stopped. But there was no end to the running and jumping around by the people. From the tree, he saw small puffs of smoke on the paved front yard of the Union Parishad office. An attack by the Mukti Fauj on the enemy camp in broad daylight! Whatever it may be, it had stirred up a hornet's nest. Now one had to flee before they stung. He climbed down the tree and ran to join the procession of escaping villagers.

After dusk, when the four Pakistani soldiers and seven Razakars had left, Aminul slowly walked towards the camp. On the way, he heard news of the death of one of the Mukti Fauj. The pedestrians were talking among themselves about how even after death the man was standing with his arms upraised. When he arrived at the place, he saw an ordinary corpse, covered with a red gamchha. A small oil lamp was burning above his head and some seven or eight fellow-fighters were sitting around the body. They were nervous but in their faces and eyes burned the desire for revenge. Although the idea of martyrdom inspired them, they just could not accept the reality that one of them had become a martyr. After things became a bit more normal, they proposed that the body be taken to the base camp in India and buried there with military honours. But the authorities on the other side rejected the proposal. They got very upset with that. The hostility of the past revived. They said that India was their enemy just a little while back, now it was their friend because they were fighting against its enemy, Pakistan. Aminul was shuddering with apprehension. True, the four Pakistani soldiers and the seven Razakars had left the place alarmed, but there was every possibility of their return in full force with lots of ammunition. It was not right to sit in mourning in enemy-occupied territory. The one who was gone, was gone. One had to think of the security of the other freedom fighters. On his own initiative, he began to dig a grave with spades and shovels. At that very moment, Montu left the clutch of freedom fighters and walked towards him. Standing on clods of earth, he requested a cigarette from the gravedigger. When Aminul plucked out a bidi from behind his ear and handed it to him, he said it was the first time he had seen anyone digging a grave. The gravedigger was amazed. Continuing to wield his spade, he asked, "What are you saying, Mia?" Montu listened to the swish of the spade cutting into the ground, he peered into the darkness of the hole and quickly stepped back scared. He muttered that he did not like people put in holes. It gave him a claustrophobic feeling. Aminul could not see the boy's face in the darkness. But he realised that the boy was afraid. Maybe to drive away his fear, he pulled at the bidi a few times and finished it without giving Aminul a turn. Aminul informs Mukti, twenty-nine years after the war, "Look at Khoda's *kudrat,* his wonder. The boy did not go into a grave. The Khans did a vanishing trick with his corpse."

After Montu's group set up camp in an abandoned house surrounded by a jungle on this side, Aminul went to live with them, leaving his home and family behind. The reason was that instead of the two hens, the local band of Razakars was now harassing him. The military also seemed poised to capture him. They entered the village and asked each one, "Mukti Fauz kahan hai, where is the Mukti Fauj?" The uncles at home also had one piece of advice, "Listen to us, Aminul, you be careful." Could one remain at home after all this? After hearing everything, group leader Sharif Bhai said, "Aminul, it is very nice that you want to stay with us, but you will have to take arms training. Only then can you fight the enemy." Although, Sharif Bhai was soft-hearted, he was a terrific soldier. Morning and evening, he personally supervised Aminul's training at the Aurpara school grounds. The arms were only 303 rifles and grenades. But Aminul's heart would quake when he was asked to charge with a grenade.

"This training that you were taking, didn't the military hear the noise?"

She keeps interrupting. Somewhat annoyed, Aminul Islam nonetheless tries to describe the locality to Mukti. He says, "Of course, they heard the sounds, but the army had no way of getting there. It was a backward area. Aurpara High School was like an island. All around us the area was flooded by the rains. I used to practise there with 303 rifles. This was the best training I had. I fought the war with this."

And Montu had a Sten gun, with which he went into operation. Aminul Islam went with a 303 rifle. They were doing everything together then – eating, sitting around, sleeping. At moments of leisure, they even played cards together. "But the boy was a little afraid. He would often whimper in his sleep." Aminul says with deep regret, "I used to think of him as a younger brother, born of the same mother. He was very young. There was a deep sorrow in his heart, but he never disclosed it to us. But then, who did not suffer grief at the time. Everyone had left home, family, parents to go to war. Someone's father had become a martyr, someone's sister could not be found, someone's wife had been abducted by the military – it was like that."

In the group Montu had a bad reputation – everyone said he was nervous and scared. Along with being afraid himself, he would bewilder the other men in the group as well. On two occasions, the group had lost its way and faced danger because of him. Going out on night operations, he saw things that others didn't see, heard things that others didn't hear. This seeing and hearing was infectious. Even Sharif Bhai began to believe him when he spoke. Then there would be a scramble to change the route. Once they fell into a Pakistani ambush because of this. If nothing else, guerrilla fighters are adept at flight. That night, they came back to the camp somehow after having swum through lakes and water bodies, soaking their ammunition, shedding their lungis. The loss was terrible. It took three or four days for them to dry their weapons and ammunition and to recover. So they had to cancel two important operations.

Montu was punished for destroying the confidence of the young men by being detailed to work in the mess. This was humiliating for him. It was not as if he did not want to fight, he wanted to very much. He had played a crucial role in some of the operations. It was unfair to deprive him in this way. He went on hunger strike. Sharif Bhai was very kind. In his place anyone else would have court martialled him for the crime of breaking military discipline. Sharif Bhai only made him take an oath. If he saw some strange glimmer of light or heard ghostly whispers, he would not speak of it to others. He would keep it to himself. Montu went a step further. Moved by the generosity of the group leader, he promised that if he heard of or saw strange occurrences, he would refuse to believe them. This last promise sealed Montu's doom.

Montu left the mess and went to war. It was not a war between kings but a guerrilla fight. No one beat drums, blew trumpets or let off fireworks. There was no spectacle involved in the conduct of this war, no pomp and panoply to overwhelm onlookers. There were no elephants, no horses. But Montu's heart beat like a drum. Excited, he walked ahead of everyone else dreaming of doing something incredible to show people. Aminul pulled at his Sten gun strap and said, "Why are you acting mad, Mian. I tell you such courage is not good." Montu did not pay heed to his words. He continued to act as before. What had happened to Montu? Why was he acting like a starving man? They were going on a perilous operation. The bridge of Aillarganj ahead of them made of iron railings, wooden platforms and a dozen pillars and named after a British government official, Elliott, had a Razakar camp at its head. They had to expel the Razakars and take possession of the bridge. Then, if they had time, they had to blow it up. Sharif Bhai was not part of this operation. He was in the hideout with a broken leg. In his absence, the leadership had come to the second-in-command, Matin Patwari. He was terrific and stubborn. Only Allah knew how this operation would end.

Aminul's duty was on the south bank of the canal. There were some hijal trees there sending down sprays of red flowers. They had to take cover behind the hijal trees and open fire. The fighting started very soon. Aminul says, "That day our group leader was Matin Bhai, Matin Patwari. He was very daring. He told me, watch out Aminul. Die but don't retreat. Everyone try to go forward from whatever position you are in. There's water ahead and you can't move forward because of that. And if you leave the cover of the trees, you will get hit by bullets. So I did not leave the stand of trees. I stood on one side and continued to fire. Many people on my right, on my left and ahead of me were also firing. Then a whistle was blown indicating that the battle was over. The Razakar troops had fled. We cheered and gave the Joi Bangla slogan. Then we went forward."

Operation successful. It was midnight. There were still a few hours left for dawn. The real work then began – breaking up the wooden bridge. Montu and Milan Poddar had been positioned on the other side of the bridge facing the highway. They were given charge of looking after everyone's security. Then leaving the rest of the men on land, Matin Bhai took four fighters and descended into the waters of the canal. Aminul was in the canal. They had just fixed explosives to the pillars when Montu's companion, Milan Poddar, spotted two soldiers walking down the sandbanks of the river. Immediately, the Mukti fighters began scurrying away and those who were in the canal dove underwater. Although his co-fighters had fled, Montu stood there rock-solid. Milan realised that it was an optical illusion and came back and said, "I became afraid, Montu, weren't you scared?" Montu did not answer him. He still had his Sten gun aimed in the direction of the sandbanks and remained stuck to his position which was not only exceptional, but also unnatural.

Then everyone got down to their assigned duties. The safety fuse caps had been lit without any problems. The planks of the wooden bridge were burning with a crackle. Those above pulled Montu and Milan back from their positions. Now was the time to run. Just then a bright slanting ray of light advanced, pointing towards them. Everyone was fleeing. But where was Montu? There were just a few moments left before the explosion. And the vehicle was also fast approaching. Aminul turned his head and what he saw appears to him incredible even now. In his own words, after the seven wonders of the world, this was the eighth wonder. Aminul was still so close that when the bridge came crashing down with a huge clatter and a bright flash, he was thrown to the ground from his standing position. And he felt as if the ground under him was heaving him upwards. But what Aminul turned his head and saw just before the explosion was an incomparable scene. Montu was at the time wearing a lungi and a sleeveless Sando vest, a Sten gun on his shoulders. In the dim light of the burning safety fuse his ghostly silhouette first appeared on the edge of the bridge. Then he saw the shadow cross the flaming bridge and the bushy undergrowth on the other side and like a tiny insect Montu was leaping into the glaring headlights of the army jeep. At the time Montu's Sten gun had not taken aim.

IX

Anuradha's Diary

Mariam first read that Montu was missing in February 1972 in the pages of a magazine advertising lost, untraced people. At the time, she was in a hospital bed in a women's rehabilitation centre. Among a sheaf of photographs reporting the warm welcome accorded to Senator Kennedy in various places in liberated Bangladesh, there was a bunch of photographs and announcements about missing people. A black and white photograph of Montu taken during his school life was published there. Below it was written Saifuddin Ahmed, Montu, Age 20. Before this Mariam had glanced through newspapers and magazines in her hospital bed but had not really read them. The letters in the words looked like a tangled mess and the lines climbed on each other and seemed to blow a whistle and move towards an unknown direction: they had no meaning for Mariam. The laughter and tears, the reunions of the new country, did not seem to touch her. The old photographs of a martyr's family exhausted her. The stories of eagerness and dedication on the part of foreign volunteers, she bundled up like trash and threw under her bed. All this din and excitement over a pile of debris and destruction was not for her, she wanted no part in it.

That day, the moment she saw the announcement about Montu being untraced, she read it at one go. But it took her a little while to comprehend its import. Her heartbeat accelerated. She looked at the familiar photograph once again – Montu's well-oiled hair neatly combed, his forehead moist so that if you touched it with your finger it would get stuck on the sticky oily surface. The flashbulb of the camera could not capture the astonishment in the pained eyes of the young person who had been transported to the city from the soil of Fultali village. The lips were firmly closed, trying desperately to keep a lid on the hurt and pique that he felt. He was determined not to give vent to his feelings despite the photographer at the studio telling him repeatedly to relax and breathe out, be easy, like an x-ray machine operator. Mariam had scolded her brother angrily that day after they came out of the studio. She had said, "You really are a country bumpkin. Will any school in the city admit you after seeing a photograph like this? It's just been a waste of money."

Today that photograph of Montu where he refused to obey instructions to relax and breathe easy is part of a news report headlined "Those who have not returned yet" – he is now included in the daily list of lost people. The printed letters which had so far seemed jumbled become clear. Montu has been absent from home since the end of April 1971. The only communication was a hand-delivered note written while he was at the training camp in India. Since then there has been no news. The parents, the two younger sisters await him eagerly. They keep putting in requests that if any kind person has information they should immediately contact the address given below. Father: Kafiluddin Ahmed, Fultali, P.O. Saharparh.

This is the home address for lost Montu. Father-mother, the younger twin sisters Ratna and Chhanda live there. They are alive. Montu has been missing since April last year. Mariam is not present in all of this. No parents or younger sisters wait eagerly for her return. Even if they do, it is not mentioned in the advertisement. But she is alive, and according to the doctor, recovering quite fast. At the rehabilitation centre, they repeatedly ask her for her address, just in case relatives come to take her back. Some of the girls have already returned home after recovery, although their numbers are very few. When they come for her address, Mariam turns her back to them and faces the wall. She does not utter a sound. After reading the advertisement, her mind is filled with one thought, Montu remains untraced. The question haunts her: can a missing person return two months after independence? Will Montu come back?

The white wall of the hospital shifts from her gaze. Instead, she sees a room in semi-darkness. There, under a dim bulb, a thin, short man is reading the future. His voice, however, is rich and resonant. It sounds as if it is coming from someone else, "With a long lifeline marked on the palm no one can be lost forever unless there is some major reneging on a promise." Montu sits depressed, leaning back on the damp mouldering wall in the office of "Professor Q M Talukdar, an expert in astrology and a palmist of Asian-renown". Montu's little palm trembles like a tiny nestling clutched in the stone-ringed paw of the professor. Mariam sits at a little distance. She is anxious about her relationship with Abed. She could not come alone to this narrow alley and so she dragged her brother along. Getting Montu's palm read was a bonus. In the damp office of the astrologer, she did not remember the pledge that she had broken in childhood. Now she is reminded of it.

Mary was then seven and Montu five. They had just been shifted from Abba and Amma's bed to the next room. Two neat beds were made up side by side for brother and sister. Montu had no major illness then, just a slight temperature. But it was not getting cured by the medicines prescribed by Naresh doctor of Fultali bazaar. The sister had shed tears silently in the darkened room and had vowed to Allah that when Montu got well, she would light four annas' worth of candles at the Chhapra Mosque. Somehow she kept postponing the lighting of the candles and finally forgot all about it. Indeed, when he recovered, they resumed their usual quarrels and fisticuffs. If one hit the other one and ran away, the one who had been hit cursed, "You will die a leper." It is true that when Mary and Montu grew up, they did not harbour any death wish against each other, but neither did they pray for each other's long life in Allah's durbar. Perhaps they would have read these prayers if they had lived long and grown old together. But long before that time the war started.

Montu is now missing, Mary in a hospital bed. She feels deeply hurt that her parents do not acknowledge her existence, in spite of the fact that she also denied their existence and would not allow her case history to be recorded at the time of registration in the rehabilitation centre. But there is a sharp difference between these two attitudes. Her parents denied the existence of their child, but she was merely obscuring her past. Indeed, she can no longer live with that past identity. This was the prediction of Anuradha Sarkar, who used to crouch behind the wall of the torture chamber and eavesdrop. Anuradha could predict the future without reading one's palm.

They were imprisoned in a longish room. Mariam still does not know its exact location, because they were blindfolded when any of them was brought in or taken out. Mariam noticed the day she entered that the windows were boarded up. And all the gates, apart from the main gate, were locked. There was hardly any illumination in the huge room. Whatever light entered was from the ventilators near the ceiling. Some women wrapped in blankets moved around the room like zombies. They could not be distinguished from each other; they had no separate identities, or names.

The girl who eavesdropped near the wall whispered to Mariam one day, "Just suppose my name is Anuradha Sarkar." Mariam was astonished to see her eyes from so close. Her acutely myopic eyes looked cloudy and she looked like a fish without her glasses. When she smiled quietly, Mariam thought that she looked even more strange and unreal. The Pakistani soldiers uprooted this first year student of B.M. College and brought her to the confines of the four walls. Her glasses were broken during a scuffle on the first day. But even if they had not broken, what purpose would they have served here? But Anuradha told Mariam that if she had pen and paper, she would keep a prison diary like Anne Frank.

The day the youngest among them was shot by the military just outside the door, Anuradha beckoned to Mariam from the edge of the wall. The wall was damp. For the last few days, the girl had been spitting blood while coughing. Perhaps she had TB. But to shoot her down just for that? Inside the large room, the women were afraid to stir. In the middle of all this, Anuradha began her game of eavesdropping and then she would begin recording what she heard in her invisible diary. When Mariam went towards Anuradha, she whispered, "Put your ears to the wall, Mary. Can you hear anything?" Mariam shook her head. Anuradha said, "Hold your ear firmly against the wall. You will be able to hear. Shut the other ear with your hand. What can you hear?" Holding up her index finger, Mariam asked Anuradha to be quiet. After a while, she could hear the steady drizzle of rain. She may have anticipated hearing something impossible and so she answered dismissively, "Oh! Rain."

Anuradha narrowed her eyes and creased her brows, "Yes. Rain." Mariam listened attentively. Anuradha began taking notes in the invisible pages of her diary without a pen. "The monsoon has come. The freedom fighters had thought that the soldiers would not be able to move easily in the mud and slush. They would squirm like worms. Their assessment was completely wrong. The soldiers are reaching inaccessible places in the interior with their speedboats and they are razing them to the ground. After a few days, this room will be filled with village girls. If we are five now, by month end we will be ten."

And that was exactly what happened. One of the new women was called Shobha Rani. She was caught in the heavy rains as she hid in the forest behind her house. It was not even six months since Shobha Rani had been married. During this time she lost her husband. Whenever she got the opportunity, she spewed out the story of her torture like vomit and wept copiously. Shobha Rani was dragged from her hiding place and raped by two soldiers. Close to where she was being raped was a bamboo frame on which she raised pumpkins. It grew on her husband's property. She had prepared the earth with care and planted the seed herself before the war began. Even before running away to hide for fear of the army, she cleaned out the weeds and watered the climber with pots of water brought from the pond. She and her husband Bimal Das carefully trained the young shoots to climb the frame. All through wartime, the pumpkins flourished. They were overrun with yellow flowers and bore fruit. The military and the Razakars did not even give them the respite of picking the fruit and cooking it so that the whole family could enjoy a meal. But that day, one of the soldiers plucked a large pumpkin and offered it to her as payment for rape. Out of sheer loathing, Shobha Rani did not take it. As punishment, they took her, smeared with blood and grass and mud from the yard and sent her to the camp. Before sending her there, they shot her husband dead under the bamboo frame of the pumpkin. At the time, her old mother-in-law, Surobala leaped and struggled like a decapitated hen in front of their house, bound and gagged.

Slowly, the times were getting tougher. The happy, smiling girl named Jaba died on the spot after a gang rape. She breathed her last even as the last soldier was still mounted on her. After that a whole day had passed and night had fallen, but no one came to remove the dead body. Jaba, who had blossomed like a flower and was their constant companion, bloated and rotted under a blanket. During that time, Anuradha continued to note in her invisible diary: "There is no visible enemy before the invaders now. Those who are there hide in jute fields and attack unexpectedly under cover of the night; they plan ambushes on highways and waterways. Living in fear of the unseen enemy, the Pakistani soldiers are losing their reason. They are directionless. Under pressure in this way, they will lose their confidence and will be unable to fight. They will remember their homes. They will want to go back to their happy, safe, luxurious lives of golf clubs, tennis balls, ghee-basted *tengri* kebabs. That is why the authorities have lifted all restrictions. The soldiers can loot, murder, rape as freely as they like. These acts fuel the tempo of the war." Anuradha lost track in the middle of her running commentary. Suddenly, the present was whisked away and got stuck on the pages of some faded album. One found some black-and-white pictures there, which on some rainy day, the people of today are poring over.

Perhaps, after the war, some investigators will search these rooms. But looking at the shreds of lungis and vests or the remains of bones, they will not be able to make out whether men or women were confined here. At that time, Anuradha pulled her tangled hair to her face and predicted, "This hair will bear testimony in the future."

And that is what happened. After the liberation, long hair was discovered in the underground bunkers and the barracks. Mother Teresa arrived at the army base in December or January. She, of course, had in her mind the prevention of the Christian sin of abortion and a directionless plan of sending these yet unborn children to foreign lands for adoption. The Mother did not see any women there. She had to return to Kolkata having seen thick tresses, torn petticoats and other such garbage.

Once Anuradha stopped eavesdropping and made an odd proposal to Mariam. She said, "Let's smell the walls." The nose instead of the ears. Why? Mariam refused. From the other end of the room, Shobha Rani came running. Weakened by starvation, she panted. Her breath was shallow. Rubbing her nose to the wall, she said breathlessly, "Oh God! It smells of pumpkin." Shobha Rani was pregnant. Even as she said this, she vomited out pieces of pumpkin although for the last one month there had been no pumpkin on the menu. After Shobha Rani, it was once again Mariam's turn. She sniffed at the wall. It smelled of damp bricks, cement and sand. "Press your nose against the wall," Anuradha said excitedly. "It's wonderful, the sweet smell of shiuli flower mixed with the smoky scent of morning dew." Sitting over the mess of her vomit, Shobha Rani muttered, "Mother Durga has left Kailash and is soon coming." At the time she could not recall Indira Gandhi's face.

Autumn had come and soon the weather would turn cool. How long would they have to live like this? Anuradha said, "Just as soldiers cannot fight a war when they lose their confidence, so with us. We won't survive if we lose our will power."

Mariam lets out a long sigh. She had such a lust for life and now she does not know whether she is alive or dead. What hopes she had nurtured. How she had discussed her future. Mukti stirs in her seat. It was a different time, she thinks. It was an age of optimism, shorn of complexities, unidirectional. The prevailing ideas, for instance, were one country, one nation, one leader and one slogan. People were ready to lay down their lives in order to be able to shout the slogan, "Joi Bangla." They believed that anything could be earned by paying with blood. Even singers and musicians celebrated the idea of blood sacrifice. They sang, "If the flower of life blossoms in blood/then let it do so." In that reckless time of optimism, Anuradha had faith in eternal life.

Anuradha had wanted future generations to know and remember their torture and oppression, and remember too who had oppressed them and why. In the research project that Mukti and her peers had undertaken, there was a proposal for a possible trial of war crimes. This had not been part of Anuradha's vision. Because that was the year 1971. It took another two decades for women to demand such a trial and it was brought forth by women in another country, forty-five years after the war had ended there. The plaintiffs were known as comfort women, or sex slaves. They were women who were forced to offer sexual services to men during the war. After the war was over, these women were like dead fish – neither family nor society had any use for them. It was another story enacted in the eastern end of the world, in Japan, the land of the rising sun. It was a story of the sun king Emperor Hirohito, considered to be God's representative, and his imperialist expansion.

The people of that country immersed in the abstractions of Buddhism and Shintoism, finally found a living god in their emperor himself. He is as powerful as God is believed to be, the Japanese address him as God. His palace is a temple and their day begins by offering prayers to him. War is a way of demonstrating the power of the living god. The war began in Manchuria in 1932 and ended thirteen years later in 1945 at Burma, now known as Myanmar. Like destiny, the Japanese soldiers carried with them the imprisoned women of the Pacific Islands along with the comfort stations. These women cooked for them, washed their dirty clothes, gave them sexual pleasure like their wives or the geishas. In return, the soldiers would slash their genitals, cut off their breasts, bite off their nipples, get them aborted, infect them with gonorrhoea and syphilis, shoot them, put them in submarines and drown them in the deep sea. In August, 1945, Hiroshima and Nagasaki were bombed within three days of each other. Having been defeated, Emperor Hirohito relinquished his divine position and came down to earth. On August 15, he addressed his devoted subjects and said, "I am no longer God. I am human."

The Japanese citizens broke down and wept, not because the atom bomb had been dropped on Hiroshima and Nagasaki, not because they had lost the war, but because they had lost their long-standing object of worship. Since 1991, the same God has been stood in the dock as the accused. The comfort women resurrected the deity from his royal tomb. The god in human form is the perpetrator of shocking acts like rape and the establishment of comfort stations. They want him to be tried along with high-ranking officials and generals. They want him to publicly apologize and pay compensation. He has to pay not only for the wrongs done between 1932 and 1945 but also pay for all the losses incurred by the women after the war.

Listening to Mukti recount stories of war crime trials, after several years Mariam is reminded of a woman called Shyamali – Shyamali Rahman. After the liberation war, Shyamali Rahman did not wait for war crime trials but took the law into her own hands. Yet in Mariam's reckoning she was the only woman who was released alive from their incarceration while the fighting was continuing. This development shook Anuradha the most. Soaring in the sphere of deathlessness, she came to ground like a bird with broken wings. And from then on she began thinking that wars end, this war will also end. But they would never be able to go back to their old identities, never regain their former addresses. Their place would be in the whorehouses of their own land and in foreign lands.

A few years after the war was over, Mariam met Shyamali again in front of the Pakistan embassy. She was hanging around the place with a rusty kitchen knife stuck in her waist. Her feet were swollen like those of a pregnant woman. She was wearing a dirty sari, her hair was piled up untidily on her head and her breath smelled of liquor. The moment she saw Mariam, she took her by the hand and dragged her to the other side of the road. She showed her the knife hidden within the pleats of her sari. With this she would kill men.

"Who?"

Pakistani army officer Shahadat, who had promised Shyamali marriage but in the end did not keep his promise. Meanwhile, her younger son Bulu died from lack of treatment and nursing.

There were so many stories submerged in those times, so many of stories of torture. Even if one wanted to speak of them, it became difficult to articulate. Words are like the leaves of a tree, once detached from the tree they can never return. Better not to open the can of worms. But Mukti asks her, "If some of you from that time sit together and talk among yourselves, and there are no outsiders anywhere around, would it be possible to speak freely then?"

Mariam does not know if it is possible or not. But listening to Mukti, she smiles. If Anuradha had heard of this strange proposal, she would have named it in her literary language – a conference of the oppressed.

X

A Conference of the Survivors

Shyamali Rahman, who would die of liver cirrhosis by the time she was thirty-five, used to say, "The Pak army caught me by mistake from the drugstore where I had gone to buy medicine after work. My younger son was ill."

"One can understand your son's illness. But did women work in offices at the time of war?"

Shyamali worked in an office during the war. It was called Moon Jute Mill. The boss was a Punjabi. She was a Bengali telephone operator. She had gone to her office even on the day of her capture. But she had left after locking up the telephone at least an hour before closing time. She had to go beyond the city limits across the railroad tracks to a quiet semi-rural area called Taltala. There her two sons were cared for by her widowed mother. The younger son Bulu was ill.. At the entrance of the mill, the Bihari gateman was powdering a wad of tobacco in his palm to stuff into his mouth. He asked her, "Where are you going, Didi?"

"Me? I am going to buy medicine."

Things were bad in the city that day. Random arrests were being made. A top leader of the Peace Committee had been killed in broad daylight. There was a sari-clad person among the assailants. But Shyamali had no choice but to buy the medicine for her son. She had just entered the medicine shop and taken out the prescription. Before the Bihari pharmacy assistant even had the time to look at it, a group of army personnel stormed into the shop. She was determined to buy medicine for her son and the army would not let her. Some words were exchanged. She was asked where she worked, whether she knew any officers in the army, who her friends were. Even though she had answered all the questions, she felt a pistol barrel at her back. She just had time to scribble a couple of lines at the back of the prescription and give it to the pharmacy assistant to deliver it. And then the military hustled her into the jeep.

Bindubala, daughter of Jogen Bainya, who was captured on the same day as Mariam from Notungaon, and who was renamed Laili Begum in February 1972 when she married the freedom fighter Nazar Ali says, "Our house was half a mile from the main road. It was a village home so there was thick vegetation all around. All we could see through the trees was billowing smoke, raging fire. We could hear rifle shots and see people fleeing. Baba tells Ma to take the kids and hide elsewhere. Ma says, I'm not going anywhere leaving you at home. So all of us went. We were very poor. After walking a little while, Ma said to me, Bindu run back and bring the rice left behind in the gamla. The kiddies won't survive if they don't eat." Bindubala ran through the flames like a circus artiste. She just about had time to pour the dal into the rice. Before she could run back with the vessel, a soldier grabbed her.

"Didn't you struggle with them?"

Bindubala had a long plait. The previous night, her old grandmother had oiled her hair and braided it tightly like a rope. The soldiers caught hold of her braid and she gripped the bamboo post propping the roof. Bindubala says, "You can't struggle with them. They broke the post and threw me on the ground and dragged me. On the main road, the Razakars carrying rifles walked ahead and the military walked behind. I was in the middle."

"What were you wearing at the time?"

"I was wearing a brown printed sari. The end of it was torn in two while I was dragged. I wasn't wearing a blouse. Whether I had a petticoat or not, oh! It was all so long ago, I really don't remember."

Freedom fighter Parul, whose name was to be included in the list of freedom fighters during one regime but dropped after scrutiny by another regime, says, "I was caught in direct battle. It was a Friday night. We were caught with all our arms and ammunition. How could we escape leaving all that behind? And where could we escape? All the lakes, reservoirs, cultivated fields were flooded with monsoon rains. We had nowhere to go."

"What's the proof that you were a freedom fighter? Can you fire a rifle?"

"Yes, I can. Do you want to see? We used to stretch our chests and hold the .303 rifles like this. Before firing, one has to load the chamber with bullets, then hold up the rifle, fix the target with your eye and fire. The left hand will hold up the middle of the rifle while the right hand will hold the trigger."

After being brought to the camp, one of the Razakars handed her a rifle and said, "Take this. Show us how you fought with us. Show us how you shoot."

"So you fired a shot?"

"Yes. After I fired the shot, the Razakar said, good God, this woman won't stop. She'll be finishing everyone off, finish all our kith and kin."

Shyamali says, "I did not know anything—whether anyone was going to India or whether anyone was getting trained there or whether a liberation army was being created. I knew nothing. I was busy with my own battles." The reason was that after her divorce Shyamali was in one place while her sons were elsewhere. The war began at such a strange moment.

There was trouble in the area that Shyamali lived in even before the war. There was tension and riots between the Bengalis and Biharis all the time. If one of them killed the other one day, the other retaliated the next. Looting, arson, factory strikes never ceased. There were bloody conflicts between the Bengalis and Biharis during the phase of non-cooperation. There were corpses everywhere. The roads were slippery with blood. Boats could not ply the river. The poles used to navigate the boats would get stuck among the dead bodies. That is why, following the army assault on March 25, the Bengalis in the locality were a little late in escaping.

The day the military broke the barricades and entered the city, Shyamali began running over the dead bodies. Everyone who was on the run had his or her family. She was the only exception. The woman had nothing now—no job, no money, no husband. She was destitute like a beggar on the street. Even then, she tried to stay in a house through April by being nice to the men of the refugee group. Such behaviour put the women against her.

Mariam recalled her own situation at Swargadham.

Freedom fighter Parul says, "My situation was different. We were separated into groups and had to stay with our brother-fighters. We couldn't stay at the same place for more than one night. Until I was captured, I wasn't safe at any moment—safe with my honour or my life. Because we were constantly worrying about which way danger would be coming from, when we will be captured and by whom, who will harm us. We spent so many days submerged in water—whole nights were spent in water. It wasn't winter then, it was the warm season, the month of Bhadra."

"You didn't face any problems while you stayed with your brothers-in-arms?"

"No, at the time nothing like that happened. Men and women fought the enemy shoulder to shoulder. Problems arose after the war. When fellow-freedom fighter Sharafat lied to me and took me to a whorehouse to sell me off."

"What terrible humiliation." Shyamali cries without stopping. The people in that house would not serve her any food. They had taken away the bedding on which she slept on the floor at night. It was better to die than go through this. But she says, "I love life." So it was important for her to recover her old life.

There she had a job. At the end of the month she received a salary. She could do her own shopping with that money. The boys felt happy if she bought them some sweets and toys. If one has money, whatever people say behind one's back, nobody dares to say anything to one's face.

"Apa, what happened after this? Did you go back to work?"

"God, what strength of spirit!"

"But how could she do it? Was it not betrayal of the country in its moment of trouble?"

"What kind of a person is she, looking for her own comfort and pleasure?"

There is a buzz in the room like that of stinging bees. Shyamali is scared, Mariam worried. She remembers Abed's patriotism and selfishness. The chairperson of the conference knocks on the table, "Quiet. This is not the time to sit in judgment. No one here has that right. Please let her speak first. After the speaker has finished, everyone will have an opportunity to state her opinion. Each one will get a minute."

Only a minute? Can one condense nine months of war experience into one minute? No one was happy with the idea. So the one minute is extended to two minutes for the listeners. Interventions from the others will also be allowed. Questions will be allowed. Because no one here is an intellectual. Memories are weakened by all the torture. No one can wait with their questions till Shyamali finishes speaking. The upshot of it all is that the conference continues in the same fashion. Shyamali is asked to go on. It was not a good idea to hide anything. That might distort history.

Shyamali's office was an office only in name. During the war, her real work started after office hours. Each day a different army officer would drive in. The boss fixed the schedule. One day it would be the commander of the naval force, another day a major would come from the circuit house, the next day it would be the turn of the colonel of the martial law court. That is how it went. But there could be upsets in the schedule at the last moment. If the commander wanted her services for two days in a row, then the major's name would be scratched off with one stroke of the pen. Gradually the contours of her life were changing. Daily an officer, depending on whose turn it was, would come to the office to pick her up in luxurious cars. The passengers in those cars would move through the city markets as effortlessly as fish in water. They would ask in Urdu, "What kind of clothes are you wearing?" Beautiful silk saris, perfumes, lipsticks, watches would come through the car window. One did not have to climb down and enter the shops. Nor was there any talk of payment.

Bindubala says, "In the village, the military would raid homes and drag off someone's goat, or hen, or cow. They would loot shops and take rice, lentils, oil. The Razakars would cook them in the dak bungalow."

"Did they offer you the food?"

"They gave us a handful of rice only once during the day."

"What did they give with the rice?"

"They would give us the bones of the chickens that the soldiers and the Razakars looted."

"Did they give you water?"

"If we asked for water, they would fill green coconut shells with piss and if we wanted to piss they would fill the green coconut with water and bring it in."

"Did they give you clothes?"

"No. At that time I used to be completely naked." Bindubala pressed her lips trying to stop her tears. "Even now, at night, I dream that they are coming across the lakes and the marshes."

Tuki, who had been a domestic help in the Sarkar household and was captured on the same day as Mariam from Notungaon, who left her job in the garment business twenty years after the war and began breeding poultry in the Rayer Bazar house, says, "Apa, as it is I have had bad memories. It's become worse with the relentless military torture. I can't remember where they took me and what they did to me. I was eighteen at the time. A woman can become a mother at that age. I had a baby there." Tuki's baby was still-born. She wrapped the baby in a piece of sacking from the floor and put it in the corner of the room. That very day the military opened the door and entered the room. Tuki says, "The moment they entered they wanted to touch me. They were advancing with some scheme for torture." So she quickly pushed the bundle towards them. They left the room with the bundle but the room remained soiled. There was a stench from Tuki's body. "I had to clean the room but I had nothing – no pots and pans, no broom and bucket, no rags or cloth," Tuki says ruefully. "I existed there somehow. I ate when they gave me something to eat, starved when they didn't. I lived there like a mad woman."

Shyamali's treatment was different. When the army officers brought her to the guest house, after extorting the saris and cosmetics from the shops for her, her eyes were not blindfolded. They had nothing to fear from the woman. She had come to work during wartime. She was a needy woman, a divorcee. Her community did not see her in a good light. If she left her job, she would die on the streets for want of food and a roof over her head. It would be foolish to opt for death in this fashion. Shyamali did not want to die. Besides in her heart of hearts, she had a liberal outlook. Even so she stiffened with fear and anxiety at the prospect of having sex with a different man every day at gunpoint. Some men took her to bed while holding a pistol to her breast. Others begin with sweet talk. "How old are you, sixteen?" They flirted, "Look at you. Such sexy lips, tender breasts. Come play with me." Some thought that if they could ply her with whisky then sex would be easier and more fun. Then it was just alcohol and women. Liquor was poured into two glasses, a little more in one, a little less in the other. The glass that held more had to be refilled constantly. The drink would be finished as they talked of their wives and families and cursed Yahya, Bhutto, Sheikh Mujib. The glass in front of Shyamali would remain as it was. "Drink, drink," she would be urged. First he would force open her lips with his hands and pour the drink into her mouth. The eyes of the man forcing her were red, his speech slurred. If Shyamali continued to protest, he would upend the glass and pour the liquor over her private parts. A few minutes between inhuman shouts and loud laughter, everything became dark.

Mariam shivers in acute panic while remembering. The army officer who sat dozing on the red sofa was called Major Ishtiaque. The Major had been drinking all evening. At midnight, the hall room was unlocked and Mariam was brought out and flung at the feet of a drunk. Before this, the soldier who had been instructed to bring her had raped her twice in the car, sodomising her once. The car had entered the courtyard of the circuit house even as he was about to perform a third time. Mariam's body was filthy with dirt and sweat, her hair was a tangled mess. With her entry, the dining room was filled with a foul smell. The major's batman placed a dish of lobsters on the table and quickly summoned a sweeper woman. She pushed Mariam into the bathroom. But to shut the door during the bath was forbidden. The sweeper woman took off her torn lungi and top. By the time Mariam had showered and come out wrapped in a towel, the table had been laid for dinner. There were red lobsters fried in ghee, roasted chicken and pulao, as well as a jug filled with fruit juice. How long, she thought, she had not eaten good food. She started having cramps from hunger. She had been allowed to sit on a chair after her bath but she had no opportunity to serve herself with food. The rich dishes on the table revolved like numbers in a game of Housie. When they finally stopped before her, she saw that the dishes and the jug were empty. Only the lobsters' claws remained. Major Ishtiaque roared with drunken laughter.

"Do you smoke?"

His huge paw held a packet of Dunhills. But unlike the dishes on the table, the packet was neither restless, nor empty. Mariam was startled. If, instead of a cigarette, he had offered her a pistol, perhaps she would have been less disturbed. It was as if it was peace time, not war, and her future office boss had offered her a Dunhill by mistake. Quickly Mariam replied, "No. No thank you Sir." The major was pleased. Dropping the cigarette packet, he advanced towards her and asked, "Do you know English?"

Without waiting for an answer, he removed the towel wrapped around her, picked her up and walked towards the bedroom. Instead of charming Mariam, his unexpected action frightened her. Her knees started knocking. She had liked Jashimul Haque because the boy knew English. That had happened in a distant village where no one spoke English. The major was whispering in her ears, "I want to talk to you. I have to talk to someone. Such a bloody war. If I can't talk, I'll die." As he spoke to her, he suddenly noticed the shaking knees of the young woman, which she could not control. "What happened?" Seeing his annoyance, Mariam narrated all that had happened to her in the car. The major's face transformed into a fierce expression, which was what Mariam had anticipated. "*Sala* Noor Khan, that son of a pig." The major rushed towards the telephone perhaps to reprimand Noor Khan but he could not be reached. He turned round to see that Mariam was standing on the bed. "Bloody whore," he shouted. Then he came and slapped her so hard that her tortured, weakened body flew out of the open door like a fallen leaf and got stuck to the veranda railings. If the railings had not been tall, then her dead body would have been lying in the courtyard of the circuit house the next day.

Parul says, "There were many dead bodies that I buried myself. The military had killed them by torture. They'd bring us spades and shovels in the darkness of night. We would dig a hole and drag three or four bodies and bury them in the same grave. They were young girls. They were about my age or perhaps younger. The whole cantonment area should be ploughed. One could find a lot of corpses there."

"Were the army keeping watch when you dug the graves?"

"Yes, they would be hovering around. They would be chatting and joking. At night, they would drink and smoke."

Bindubala says, "If they came drunk, the Razakars would push them into our rooms and vanish. There were four or five of us women in this room made of tin sheets and planks. This is where they tortured us in full view of everyone. There were no curtains, nor did they make any distinctions."

"How many would enter the room together?"

"Four or five of them would come in together. They would threaten us that if we didn't listen to them they would kill us and throw us into the river. When I remember those times, my blood freezes."

"Did you understand what they spoke? I, for instance, do not understand a word of Urdu."

"We did not understand what they were saying, we would stand around like idiots."

Shyamali Rahman, who after liberation slowly became an alcoholic and for the sake of money and liquor or just a few pegs of whisky would haunt the Gulshan locality under cover of darkness and sleep with white men, says, "At that time, the officers could not make me drink a sip even by forcing me. It drove them mad with rage..."

It would be midnight by the time the officers debauched her body and forced liquor down her throat. Some of the daring officers would drop her home in their car. But most of them were not willing to leave the bed after they finished with her. One of them, fed up with Shyamali's tears and pleading, phoned someone from the bed, "Hullo, Shaukat Jung, do hurry. I have a guest. She needs a lift, yaar." In five minutes, the sycophantic, non-Bengali businessman had arrived with his car. He didn't talk to Shyamali on the way. But when he dropped her off at her door, he hissed like a snake, "I knew you as a nice woman. When did you join this line?" Shyamali knew that the man would also make a dirty offer, but a couple of days later. All the civilian men would use the same language to make the proposition, "You see, er, my wife does not..." Shyamali says, "When I remember these things, a fire rages in my brain."

The next day, the boss locked the office and demanded his dues. If she objected, he would write out a cheque beforehand and put it on the table. "You're nothing but a whore." At first, Shyamali loathed touching the money. Then she realized that it made no difference whether she took the money or not. And the expenses had spiralled. Relatives would come to her surreptitiously and ask for money. The very same people would malign her behind her back. Shyamali's body had become public property. So everyone had a right to her money. The drivers and peons in the office freely made passes at her – they pawed her, squeezed her breasts, offered to sleep with her.

Those who are women of the household, whether during war or peace, could never understand the essence of such a life. The chairperson thinks that this experience of sleeping with several men in the course of a single night is unique to the participants of this conference. But they had been prisoners then. Shyamali had not been a prisoner. Why didn't she escape from the office?

Shyamali said that when an army officer, after knowing her past, had proposed marriage, why should she have run away, he would have married her soon enough. The conference room burst into loud laughter when they heard her. The chairperson keeps quiet. In other words, she endorses the mocking laughter. But the girl was a prisoner then, so how would she get married?

Well, she was a prisoner because of a misunderstanding. She was mistakenly arrested by the Pakistani soldiers. After the interrogation and torture at the cantonment, they could not elicit any information from her. She had to remain confined till the note that she had sent to the army officer through the Bihari pharmacy assistant reached him.

And what was the guarantee that the army officer would marry her?

At the time, Shyamali had been hundred per cent sure that he would. She had proof. The man would address her mother Khodeja Begum as Ammi and would pick up her two sons in his arms. He would pinch their cheeks and say, "How sweet!" Just a week before her arrest, the younger son had pissed and wet the officer's uniform. Shyamali was scared stiff. "Shame on you, Bulu, what have you done!" But the man had been laughing like a child. How innocent was that laughter.

Freedom fighter Parul agrees with her. "All of them were not alike. The day I was captured, my body was bleeding from bayonet wounds. His name began with an R. Rauf, Abdur Rauf. I got to know because someone called him by that name. He felt me all over and then bought an ointment and applied it on my body. While he was doing this he spoke to me of many things but I did not understand what he was saying because I am an ignorant woman."

"Why should I be pressurized to lie?" This is not a statement in court. Even so, Shyamali vows, "I will speak the truth and nothing but the truth." The officer dropped in at the house one evening. He said, "I'm feeling stressed. Let's go out somewhere." They went out for a drive and then he said, "Let us stop somewhere for a cup of tea." Shyamali answered, "No tea for me. I'll have coffee." After having coffee at the Al-Eslam restaurant, the officer said, "This place isn't safe. The Mukti Fauz could attack. Do you want to come with me to my guest house?" "Okay. Let us go," Shyamali answered. The officer smiled and said, "I won't force you if you don't want to go." "No, no. Let's go." The chairperson shakes her head in apprehension. The audience gets absorbed in the story. A tryst is a tryst. After all he did not use force and rape her. But all wars come to an end. This one would too. What would Shyamali do then?

Bindubala counts the months on her fingers. She says, "Before the war ended, say sometime in June, they captured me. Then after three months around October/November, our brothers the Muktijoddhas, the guerrilla forces, freed me." At the time Bindubala and her fellow inmates did not have a shred of cloth on them. The guerrilla fighters scouted around the neighbourhood and brought clothes for them to wear. From there, the imprisoned women left for their homes. But Bindubala had no place to go. By then Jogen Bainya had taken his family to the refugee camps in India. The Muktijoddhas were then in constant touch with India. There would be daily exchanges, comings and goings, interactions. They said, "Come Bindu, we will take you to India." Bindubala dug her heels in. She was ready to go anywhere, but not to India.

"Why?"

"If I went to India, then people would say, the military captured you, they tortured you, why have you now come to India? So I didn't agree. I told the Muktijoddha brothers, this country, this land is my mother. This land is everything I have. If I have to die, I will die here. I told them that I fought one kind of war, now I want to fight another war. And so I joined them"

Tuki says, "I smeared the walls of the room in which they imprisoned me for four months with my blood."

"Why?"

"Because, they were signs – signs of our torture. The bloodstains that the Mukti Fauj found in that room were my blood."

Meanwhile, the letter that Shyamali had written took two days to reach from the medicine shop to the army officer Shahadat. It took another two days for him to get the release order. Her prison life came to a sudden end in four days.

XI

Future Plans

The day Shyamali was released, Anuradha could not sleep the entire night. Mariam dreamt of walking naked through the streets of an unknown city. Shobha Rani dreamt that she was driving around with Bimal Das in a car. It was a white car, their own. After hearing her descriptions, Mariam said that her dream car was a Volkswagen.

The day was October 25, 1971. It was a Monday. *Time* magazine had a sensational news item: every single one of the 563 women held in Dhaka's military cantonment was pregnant. They had crossed the time when the pregnancies could be terminated. Kafiluddin Ahmed was shattered when he heard the news from his brother-in-law Golam Mostofa. In the house at Maghbazar, he got up from the sofa and collapsed on the floor. From where he sat, Golam Mostofa's feet were just an arm's length away. Kafiluddin had reached Dhaka yesterday having taken five days to travel from Fultali, a journey that normally should have taken only a day. His aim was to coax and cajole his brother-in-law, who was younger than him, to get his daughter released. Golam Mostofa did not speak but shook his head, and with every shake, his feet would swing from side to side in front of Kafiluddin's face. Is it credible, can one possibly believe that the man who wielded so much clout in neighbouring mouzas like Fultali, Ballavpur, Nabinagar, Komalkandi and many other nearby areas was less than a fly or a mosquito in Dhaka?

Golam Mostofa smiled at such a description. He said, "Dulabhai, only your Allah knows what you think of me." But both were convinced that the girl had disappeared from Dhaka; if she was not dead then she was in the army camp. Residence in the army camp meant that she was now pregnant and the safe term for termination of pregnancy was over.

Even though they were not in the Dhaka army camp, the three women lying under one blanket – Mariam, Anuradha and Shobha Rani – were all pregnant. Among them only Shobha Rani had crossed the safe period for having an abortion. But unlike Kafiluddin Ahmed and Golam Mostofa, she was not at all worried about this. Poised between life and death through the stressful period of imprisonment, she had savoured the movement of the foetus in her womb. "Mary Didi, Anuradha Didi, just place your hands here. I can't tell you how much the baby kicks. My husband was also a very angry person."

Shobha Rani's childish prattle entered Anuradha's ear and exited through the other ear. She was very absent-minded. Something had gone wrong somewhere. So many women were dying from grief, illness, torture, or being shot, that one could not keep count. No one could even make a sound. Anuradha suddenly felt that to live was even more valuable than immortality. She who had held the diaries of Anne Frank as her inspiration, now found other examples before her eyes. Shyamali opted for a shortcut in her desire to live. She received instant results. Would they get such opportunities? Time was fast running out. From the sound of firings outside one could make out that the war was no longer one-sided. Very soon the country would be free. On Shobha Rani's belly lay Anuradha's hand. It was detached, left there at Shobha Rani's request. She said "There will be a big battle very soon. India is advancing."

Shobha Rani sat up hurriedly. And Mariam asked with a child-like innocence, "How do you know, Anuradha?"

"How? Because roads are resurfacing and the waters are receding. India's preparations are more or less complete. The Indian soldiers will have no trouble in moving with their tanks and heavy weapons. The people will help them wholeheartedly."

Mariam's blood froze as she listened to Anuradha. She thought of something else. Excitedly she tells Mukti, "That independence will not be a gift from the heavens, that there will be hard-fought battles with tanks, guns, airplanes, this thought had not occurred to us clearly. We were only occupied with how to cope with the military torture and oppression. Just think of it. There you were caught in a locked room and over your head fighter planes were buzzing like bees."

True, the scene appears to be like falling into a rat hole and dying. "But then when you saw so many women dying before your eyes, did you not give a thought to the possibility of your own death?" Mukti asks.

Mariam answers, "Yes, we thought about it, but not in this manner. Not in this helpless, captive state. Also we did not want to die of bombings from our own side."

For the women prisoners of war, one's own side and the enemy were big issues then. Post-liberation the dividing line got erased and everyone became an adversary. Anuradha's prediction was made a month before the formal war engagement between India and Pakistan. It was only then that Mariam got to understand that the real fight would be between India and Pakistan and the Muktijoddhas would give support from the sidelines. By then she had been imprisoned for five months. It was impossible for her to know that Mrs Indira Gandhi had left Brussels and was on her way to Vienna. She was no longer feeling the pressure of ten million refugees. She was flying from one country to another and then to another to present her case. Her plea was clear. At a press conference in Brussels, she stated, "There was no room for arriving at an understanding between India and Pakistan on the East Pakistan question." This meant that an Indo-Pak war was imminent. The country was about to be liberated.

Mariam was disoriented and fearful of bombings. Anuradha was annoyed and said, "Say you did not die from the bombings, but continued to live. The country became independent. What would you do then? Where would you go?"

Shobha Rani butted into the conversation and said, "I will go to my father-in-law's house." The foetus in her womb grew like swelling pumpkins on the frame, it grew despite the hatred, humiliation and hunger. This was an instance of the failure of the Pakistani project of exterminating Hindus. The soldiers slaughtered the husband and impregnated the wife. In the independent country, Shobha Rani would become the mother of a male child. A house would rise once again on the desolated property. Once again a conch shell would be blown, deities worshipped once again with incense and joss sticks, flowers and leaves. Once again, on the cowdung-smeared courtyard, the future Hindu descendants of this family would crawl. The process of extermination that the Pakistanis had started on the night of Operation Searchlight, where lungis were lifted and the uncircumcised genitals were separately lined up and shot, from those same bloodlines would be born Shobha Rani's child, who would be fatherless certainly but not entirely without an identity.

While Shobha Rani was absorbed in the dreams of her future, Mariam began her journey from Fultali village and walked out with her head lowered from the cluster of rain trees near S.M. Hall. She lost all the shelter she had even before the war had begun. After that, her experience of life as an uprooted person and a prisoner was shared by millions of people. She had lost sight of her personal problems in that huge upheaval. But she was pregnant then just as she was pregnant now. If the country became free while she was in this condition, where would she go? To whom could she return?

Anuradha had not finished having her say. She said, "Do you think our countrymen will greet us with garlands? No, Mary, nothing like that has happened in the history of the world. When the war ends, the men are acclaimed as heroes and the women are described as fallen. Just you watch, they will turn us into whores."

What unlucky words. This woman spoke of things not written about in religious texts. Shobha Rani felt annoyed. It was by the infinite grace of God that she had conceived. And the child was growing in her womb, so let the ill wishers go to blazes. If this had not happened, she would have had to spend the rest of her life alone with the slur of a barren widow. There would be nobody left to light the evening lamp in the home of her husband's forefathers. The religious books say that women surrendered themselves to the gods while praying for a son. Shobha Rani was a chaste Sati by the same rule that made Satyavati, Kunti, Draupadi chaste Satis. Why should she become a prostitute who had left the shelter of her family? Casually she lifted Anuradha's hand from her stomach and put it down.

But Anuradha's words scared Mariam. If it was a sin to have held Jashimul Haque's hand those many years ago, how would all this be seen? She did not know a thing about all those who raped her day after day—their names, addresses, family, education, marital status. All the men looked similar, their behaviour did not vary much. How many men were they—a hundred, fifty, a score—but they all summed up into one abstract male. Out of all these men, she remembered only the appearance of the army officer seated on a red sofa and called Ishtiaque. Although he had been drunk, the man had wanted to tell her about his misfortunes.

Anuradha said, "A man does not get drunk only from alcohol. War is the biggest intoxicant."

"That may be."

"Then why were you scared that day? You should have listened to what the man had to say."

"What would I have gained by listening to him?"

"How can you say that you would have gained nothing? You could have secured your future by listening to him."

"Is that at all possible? Especially at a time of war? And when the man belongs to the enemy side?"

"What do you think of the Shyamali business?"

"I think it is a betrayal."

"Whose betrayal?"

"Of one's country."

"What country? The country which treats our dishonour and torture by the enemy as a mark of its shame and will either hide us or force us into prostitution, betrayal of that country?"

Anuradha's words stuck in Mariam's heart like fish-hooks. The pain made her writhe. If this was what life was all about, then how would it all end? Anuradha continued to mull over her words. She said, "Mary, if you went to Pakistan with Major Ishtiaque, it would not be treachery."

"What would it be?"

"It would be revenge."

XII

Intermission

After winning the war in 1972, when Pakistani prisoners of war were leaving this country for India, I learnt that some thirty or forty raped women were leaving with them. Immediately, I appealed to the military attaché of the Indian embassy Brigadier Ashok Vohra and the person appointed by the Bangladesh authorities, Noorul Momen Khan (Deceased), whom we knew as Mihir. They considered my application sympathetically and allowed me to interview these women. Naushaba Sharafi, a teacher at Dhaka University, Dr Sharifa Khatun and I went to the army camp and had a shattering experience.

Nilima Ibrahim, *Ami Birangana Bolchi*
(I am a Birangana Speaking)

"Revenge. Against whom?" One of the lady social workers asked, surprised. And yet the women volunteers had entered the barracks announcing, "Please do not go away. We want to do something. We have come to help you." Instead of accepting the help with outstretched hands, it sparked off a flash. The girl in front asked angrily, "You want to know revenge against whom? Against golden Bangla and its golden young sons and…"

"Enough! You don't have to elaborate. What an awful choice of words – revenge!" Nervously, the lady stepped back in a hurry. There was terrible anarchy all round at the time. Amid all this, a father had come to take back his daughter. She refused to go with him. Seeing this, one of the social workers intervened, "Fine. If you don't want to accompany your father, come home with me."

"Why should I go to your home?" This girl was even more aggressive, ready to quarrel in a trice. She yelled, "Are we animals in a zoo? You want to open your door to visitors who will come to gawk at us and you can collect the kudos?"

"So what if I take kudos, would it inconvenience you?" It was now the turn of the social worker to lose her temper. "What will you do in Pakistan? You will just be sold off to whorehouses there!"

"If we are sold, we will be sold. What's that to you?" This retort came from another girl.

"My goodness. Who are these girls?" A social worker replies to Mukti's question and says that there were all kinds of women: rich, poor, educated, illiterate.

"But we misunderstood the situation. Because it was the first time we experienced a war in our lives." She goes on to tell Mukti, "Even when I sit alone today, I keep thinking that although they knew that they may be sold off there or exploited in the flesh trade, still they had preferred to go to Pakistan rather than remain here."

That day, when they received the news, some fathers and brothers rushed to the cantonment. Particularly fathers. Seeing the stubborn stance adopted by their daughters, they shed tears and went home. There were a few husbands as well. They came not to take back their wives but to give them saris. This was their last ritual act of maintenance of their wives in marriage.

"Are there any official documents relating to the exodus of all these women that happened right before your eyes?"

"There should be, if they're not all destroyed."

"Where can one find them? Which ministry's responsibility was it?"

"Possibly it fell under the jurisdiction of department of relief and rehabilitation."

"Could it possibly be social welfare? Which is now the department of women?"

"Another source could be Mr Ashok Vohra, who was then perhaps military attaché at the Indian High Commission."

"Yes, there could be some records in India."

"It is a matter of great shame that these documents cannot be found in our country and we have to go to a foreign country to search for them."

Mukti returns to Mariam. She asks, "Ultimately, you didn't go to Pakistan? Why did you remain behind?"

The question sounds as if despite having a ticket in hand, a passenger is dragged back by force midway.

Mariam's face becomes distorted with distress caused by the awkwardness of the question. She pushes her trembling hands through the pleats of her sari and gropes around her lower abdomen for something. Because the problem is not hers but her womb's, the organ that is being squeezed by her fingers.

The women had the status of war prisoners then. They had established relationships with the attacking soldiers – of so-called marriage or companionship. One set of criminals would join another set of criminals and travel by train through India and thence to Pakistan. The tangle of relationships became so confused that it appeared to have no connection with the nine months of rape, torture and murder. Of course, by that time everything had turned upside down. Pak soldiers were prisoners in the Dhaka army base. And the Indians were proudly stamping around. In the underground bunkers and torture chambers of the army base, there were even then swarms of horseflies settling on the dried, clotted blood on the walls. On the floors and walls, there were blackish marks like bruises left by fat and flesh. Here and there were piles of women's bangles and long hair. The rotting flesh had not separated from the bones. Suddenly, everything was over and nothing had been set right for them. The women were waiting for Bangabandhu Sheikh

Mujibur Rahman's return to the country. Having been freed from his Pakistani prison, he would personally give permission to the prisoners-of-war to go up to the Indian border. In the middle of all this uncertainty, the baby in Mariam's womb started moving. In the rehabilitation centre the time limit set for termination of pregnancy was four months. After this, it was impossible even for the foreign doctors. Mariam was admitted to the centre under the emergency category. There the schedule was a long serial of, first, medical treatment, then rest, and then abortion. By that time the women had left for Pakistan via India with the prisoners-of-war.

"If they had not left, would you have gone with them?"

"Perhaps I would have."

"Did you have any particular plan regarding this?"

Mariam answers Mukti's professional interview question with another, "Regarding what?"

"Well, regarding going to Pakistan. What would you have done there, where would you have stayed, those kinds of things."

"If I stayed behind in my country, where would I have lived, what would I have done, were all these questions settled then? Are they worked out even now?" Seeing Mariam so perturbed, Mukti keeps quiet. That generation is strange. She may stop talking altogether if she gets annoyed. Then she would have to pack up her tape recorder, leave behind some of her cassettes and batteries and take some along with her and leave quietly.

Mariam's frown deepens. Strange that the pattern of questions doesn't change even if the people change. When these questions were first asked some twenty-eight years ago, Mukti may or may not have been born. These girls have learned the questions while they were in their mothers' wombs. Even now that the political leaders clamber on to a stage and declaim that the country has gained independence in exchange for the honour of two lakhs of our mothers and sisters, where are those two lakh mothers and sisters? Only thirty or forty left for Pakistan, where are the rest? How are they faring? Mariam's question to Mukti is, "What about the trafficking in women to

Pakistan even now. They are being forced into prostitution, why is nobody worried about that?"

Mukti hesitates. She is not quite sure what she should say. But she thinks that there is a great difference between then and now. That was when the war had just ended. The wounds were still raw. The group of women who voluntarily went to Pakistan rubbed salt in that open wound. In Anuradha's words, it was revenge.

At that time, of course, Mariam did not agree with Anuradha. And why should there have been agreement? Before you undertake anything, you need a target, you need support. Behind a big rebellion, there are planned and unplanned incidents. These may take place through the agency of someone else living in another corner of the globe.

XIII

Red Roses, Silk Saris, Snow-White Bed Linen

At that time Pakistani soldiers saw shadows of the Mukti Fauj everywhere. Added to that was the fear of Indian attack. Security arrangements were made much stricter. In the week after Shyamali left, a grenade exploded next to the main door of the large room. The soldier guarding the entrance died. The cleaning woman was absent at the time. It was her only crime. The women in that shut off room were wracked by fits of coughing from the smoke billowing in. So their names were also added to the list of suspects. To this day Mariam does not know if it was because of the coughing or if, during interrogation, the cleaning woman had given them the few names that she knew. After the incident occurred, the women were dragged out of the large room and brought outside. "Kill all the bitches. Then…" Mariam did not hear anything else. The scenes that followed were like faded, torn, scratched film reels.

She is lying flat on the backseat of a running vehicle. Her head is hanging from the seat. She feels the thrusts of a rifle butt between her thighs. Two penises were being rubbed incessantly under her armpits. There is a struggle on to stretch her mouth and push a malodorous penis inside. The vehicle does not stop anywhere. Eventually, it enters a rough, uneven road. It stops the movement of the rifle butt and the genitals. The busy soldiers feel annoyed. They start once again when the vehicle moves onto a smooth road. The only difference is that the men change their positions. Dust clouds rise when there is an interlude. The afternoon sun's golden rays enter the vehicle, seeking escape routes.

In the next scene, a woman wipes away the dried blood and semen stains and drapes Mariam in a new sari. Seeing Mariam's sagging body, a brawny man lifts her limp frame onto his shoulders and starts walking briskly. She sees in the next scene rows of upside down pots of plants arranged against a brick road. There is a two-storied, white-washed house nearby. Behind it the evening sun swings from left to right and right to left like a pendulum.

Her hands are bound tightly with a rope to the arms of the chair on which she is sitting. In front of her is a long face, chewing on a pen and constantly blowing smoke on her face. When Mariam coughs, he bursts into raucous laughter. "Now tell me, what do you think of sovereignty? And how do you explain the concept of freedom?" Instantly, there is a Bengali translation to the questions. The long face appears once again through the smoke. "Do you believe in the two nation theory? Tell me, what is the future of Pakistan?" The invisible translator is heard once again.

"Have you seen Sheikh Mujib? Don't you think that the six-point demand pressed by Mujib is a violation of Article 16 of the Martial Law Proclamation? And that bastard should be hanged for it?" Once more the translation.

It is like being read the kalema, the Muslim profession of faith, just before death. Mariam has entered the maze of the Sundari marshes. There is no exit. There are the flickering lights of the fireflies and in the middle of it there is the long face. "Idiot! Just turn off the flashlight." The invisible translator repeats the instruction in Bengali. Across the table, the long face lifts his neck like a tortoise, "Did you kill Havildar Taj Khan? If you did not, tell me who are the killers?" The translator repeats the question, first in a whisper and then at the top of his voice.

The long face tucks in his long neck between his shoulders and leans back in his chair, "Now, we are very sure that you are a miscreant. If you admit that you will be free." The translator repeats the statement in Bengali in a weak voice.

Then one hears the pulling of chairs in the darkness. There are some clattering sounds. "Achha interview tha." It was a good interview, the translator repeats in Bengali happily. Mariam's hands are untied from the chair and she is helped onto a stretcher. Long face lowers his head over her and says, "Bahut achhi ladki ho tum." You are a good girl, the translator translates in Bengali in an embarrassed voice.

"Good night." The greeting is translated in Bengali.

Besides the snow-white bed there is a red rose. Next to it is the folded yellow silk sari. A two-litre bottle of saline hangs from the stand. Mariam feels a pull at the tube if she tries to turn. But underneath the blanket, her feet are untied. Has the country become free? Where is Anuradha? Were they not supposed to leave for Pakistan? The long face suddenly bends over her and asks, "How do you feel?" Mariam gets ready for another interrogation, but the invisible translator's voice is absent. This is a new disturbance, but it is better than before. From that dirty bedding of blankets spread on the floor in that large prison room, she is now on a camp-cot in a clean, smooth, well-made bed, a red rose near her head, a silk sari. That means, there is scope for promotion everywhere, be the place a prison camp and the time 1971.

"Are you ok?" Mariam nods her heavy head and she hears her voice saying "Yes." The man is pleased like Major Ishtiaque. Mariam does not know if this is because he hears her brief response in English or that he notices an improvement in her condition. With her skinny hands on his lap, his long face transforms into the drunken appearance of Major Ishtiaque. Mariam recalls how that inebriated man's slap sent her reeling to the veranda railing like a dry leaf floating in the air. Despite this, she remembers Anuradha's advice and asks, "Are you Major Ishtiaque?" He shouts, "No, no. How do you know him?" Why should Mariam answer this question? The interrogator must know very well how a Bengali girl could meet a Pakistani army officer during the war. All she remembered was Major Ishtiaque's name. Besides all uniformed men looked alike. Once again there is a change in his looks and his whole appearance sags. Mariam gets confused with such quick changes.

"How did you know him?" The man is persistent. Mariam sidesteps a direct answer and says, "He was kind to me." She wants to see where all this will lead. From the corner of her eyes, she observes the change in his expression. Is this an illusion or does the man have extraordinary powers of changing his appearance? Long face begins to look like Major Ishtiaque even as he says, "He was killed the day before yesterday." How strange that even they get killed. Mariam was supposed to have gone to Pakistan with him—that is what Anuradha had advised.

It is probably against the rules of war to inform the enemy of one's losses. Having broken the rule, the long face instantly becomes angry with Mariam. He gets up from the bed and stands up at attention like a soldier. "Don't try to move. You are still a suspect. You have to answer, who are the killers of that havildar?´

The man marches out of the room. But he has forgotten to pick up the red rose and the silk sari. It is no easy task to secure one's future by exploiting the weakness of the enemy. Would Anuradha have been able to do what Shyamali had done? Other than big talk, she has not yet been able to show any signs of bravery. She wonders: when the man re-enters, will he resemble Major Ishtiaque or come in with his long face.

"She is sick now." Although the voice sounds familiar, Mariam pretends to be asleep. She feels there is no point in working out a new strategy. "Besides I think, if she gets a chance she will join the Mukti Bahini."

An unfamiliar voice says, "Let us see."

This is how Mariam acquires the rights to red roses, silk saris, and fresh white bed linen. All the stuff in the room in which she is kept is now hers. There is no one to stop her from touching them. Perhaps this is the property of some family which has evacuated like the one at Swargadham. Or perhaps it is a recently set up rest and recreation centre. Stacks of liquor bottles and the blood staining the walls like reddish smears of lipstick testify to this possibility. Besides, in the coffee tin, the pickle jar, the sugar bottle, there remain traces of stuff. Mariam dips her finger into the pickle jar and puts a bit of sour mango pickle in her mouth. It had not become bitter and rancid yet. The zing of mustard tickles her nose. Even as she splutters and coughs and sneezes, she looks up to see rows of family photographs. Their looks clearly indicate their non-Bengali origin. They may have left for Pakistan fearing an Indian attack. The moment the mango pickle constricts her throat, she vomits and spoils the carpet. On the floor she sees a tanpura with torn strings surrounded by a pair of sad-looking tablas. On the side wall hang oil paintings which are most distressing. Mariam feels the room is hers if she refrains from looking at the dancing girls in various poses on the walls. Like a caged animal in a zoo, she can pace the room whenever she wants. She has immense freedom here of chatting with her reflection in the mirror, yawning, making faces at it.

The long-faced man says he is Major Ishtiaque. But he calls himself Major Ishtiaque II. The first one has died in war. He enters Mariam's room leaving behind his long serious face and dons the drunken look of the first Major Ishtiaque. And he speaks the same words, "I have to talk to you. If I can't, such a bloody war, I will die."

There is a bit of paradise even in hell. If you rephrase it, you can say heaven at the time is surrounded by the blazing flames of an inferno. Major Ishtiaque II enters the gates of paradise leaving behind his clothes smelling of explosives and wiping his hands clean of the blood stains. His nostrils flare when the locked door opens. He closes his eyes and breathes in deeply the unknown fragrance of paradise.

> *A fairy diffuses the scent of musk*
> *from an escaped lock of hair;*
> *No, she is no doe of the forest*
> *who affrights so upon glimpsing humans.*
> —Hafiz

Mariam steps back a little upon hearing the sweet rhythm of opening doors. This is a moment of preparation. Then it is just a matter of the time it takes for the door between heaven and hell to close and the hunter blindly springs on his prey. No time is lost in ascending to paradise. Outside, there are the shattering sounds of exploding shells and ammunition, sounds which frighten man and confront him with the prospect of death. But here it does not disturb the enjoyment of paradise. Indeed the enjoyment is prolonged. The lacks in both their lives are filled to overflowing.

The world they come back to, after they move away from each other, in that adversarial world Mariam and Major Ishtiaque are each other's enemy. Neither trusts the other. In fact, apart from their sojourn in paradise, they both want to kill each other.

Even so red roses come again. To the accompaniment of wine, Omar Khayyam and Hafiz are recited. Noorjahan's melodious voice weaves an enchantment in the closed room. Love becomes sweetly intense. These hours of war move beyond the rules of war with the help of lovemaking and wine.

Mariam loses her bearings. She completely forgets Anuradha's words that the Indian army, along with the Mukti fighters, is advancing and there will be a big battle. Night and day, she lives in such a trance that emerging from it or not makes no difference. It would be nice if she could spend the rest of her life within that dream. The long-faced major tells her the story of another fairy-tale country and its fairy tale prince. It is the land of the five rivers, well-watered and green Punjab. It would be a mistake to call Lahore, built by the Mughal emperor Jahangir, merely a city. It is a wonder city full of beautiful gardens and elegant buildings. Through it flows a stream of clear water, its banks lined with trees. The heady fragrance of unknown flowers excites travellers. Mariam has seen pictures of the Shalimar Bagh in textbooks. Girls in tight churidars and kameezes strut like pigeons beside the fountain surrounded by rows of cypresses. A strip of dupatta barely covers their heads and is lovingly entwined round their necks. But printed in black and white on newsprint, their faces are blurred. Mariam thinks that one of these hazy faces is Major Ishtiaque's wife. The major says that the woman now lives in a beautiful mansion surrounded by a flower garden where once her husband, a happy prince, lived. After the war started, the husband had to go away to the kingdom of Bengal. There live a rare of species of women with enchanting eyes and long black tresses. They are enchantresses. Their hypnotic beauty had lured Major Ishtiaque's ancestors in the distant past. Those men never returned to the rugged women of the west. The rejected women never forgot the pain of loss of their husbands and the story of betrayal was handed down through generations and is still remembered.

From Major Ishstiaque's pocket pops out the picture of a fearful woman with pink lipstick and thinly pencilled eyebrows. In her letter, she appeals to her husband to be chaste and threatens him with consequences if he strays. To uphold the honour of the family, she is prepared to commit suicide if she learns that her husband is not concentrating on fighting the war and instead has fallen under the magical spell of these dark Bengali women and is taking shelter under the ends of their saris. The major's wife looks on with contempt and suspicion, through her transparent georgette dupatta, at Mariam, who is twelve hundred miles away. The enchantress is not disturbed. She is beyond all these reckonings. Besides, where human life is a lie, how valuable can a photograph be? But the photograph causes an ebb between the lovers. The rising tide recedes from the sandy beach of their relationship. How odd! Mariam suddenly wonders how could she have become so involved with a murderer and a rapist? Especially, one who has a wife and children at home? One who does not even trust her? He keeps her locked up all the time. Red roses, silk sari, ghazals, all these are false and love is a cunning stratagem. The truth is that this man does not love her, he is her foe through generations.

Major Ishtiaque, on the other hand, thinks that Bengalis are not human beings. They are more in the nature of pet cats. They will mew around you the whole day. They will sit on your lap with eyes closed and sway with pleasure. But the moment they get the opportunity, they claw and scratch. The major regrets that they have not been able to administer the country as well as the British. That is why, instead of two hundred years, they have got into deep trouble in twenty-four years. This is the perspective from which Major Ishtiaque conducts self-assessment. Not surprisingly, among friends he is known as a liberal. But in spite of that, Major Ishtiaque suddenly asks Mariam, "Are you a Hindu also?" How do you answer such a question? Will the major kill her if she says that she is Hindu? Just as they killed Malina Gupta's husband, father-in-law, brother-in-law or Shobha Rani's husband?

Major Ishtiaque does not cool down even after hearing Mariam is a Muslim. How can one consider Bengali Muslims as Muslims? Hindus have turned them into kafirs. The accursed people have slyly run a knife through the Muslim brotherhood. The major thinks that one of the blessings of this bloody war is that they have been able to exterminate Hindus from East Pakistan even if it took time to do so. The remaining ones have now gone to the refugee camps in India and will have a lingering death there. The infidels will not be able to return from those hell-holes.

But the truth is that the major is no longer interested in fighting a war. He is exhausted. There is victory or defeat in battling enemy soldiers. But fighting unarmed civilians, he thinks, is like battling shadows. It has a beginning but no end.

Finally, the real war is announced. Enemies from birth, Pakistan and India are confronting each other once again. The arena is no longer Kashmir or the Rann of Kutch but Bangla. While there is an ongoing game of attack and counter-attack in the western borders, in the east the war takes the form of a gathering storm. A sudden storm that lasts only twelve days. The seat of power of General Niazi aka the Tiger gets shaken; his growls subside; he restlessly paces his underground bunker. There is no reason to feel safe there. All the arrows on the battle plans indicate the retreat of the Pakistani army and the advance of Indians. On the telephone and over the wireless, he continuously gets news of his subordinate officers losing their way, surrendering or drowning. But the central government in West Pakistan remains undisturbed.

Here, Major Ishtiaque and his compatriots are surrounded by the enemy. In this state come instructions from the underground bunker of the Eastern Command that no one can retreat from their defensive positions unless they suffer a seventy-five per cent casualty. The order is really a death warrant. But it is not devoid of promise although it is indirect. Because those who are martyrs in a holy war are representatives of heavenly souls. They will continue to enjoy all the facilities they have plus have a bonus of the security of heaven plus many extra incentives.

Major Ishtiaque judges the order from underground in the light of the reality above it. The enemy is present everywhere – land, water, sky. Fighting is meaningless in this condition, but running away is cowardice. What remains is death. "Please forgive me," he says and walks out of the room into the thick of battle. Mariam is astounded. Before she can grasp what is happening, she hears the clang of the key turning in the lock in the door outside. She runs to the door and shouts, "What is happening? Please let me free, I beg of you." The reply that comes from the door outside is a mixture of Bengali and English, "No order."

XIV

Rescue Phase

It took four more days for those who broke open the lock and rescued Mariam to reach the spot. Pakistani tanks and the tanks of the allied forces were confronting each other at the time. The Mukti Bahini were throwing grenades at the open, vulnerable spots on top of the tanks. A guerrilla fighter Rafiqul Islam laughs and tells Mukti, "The first time the grenade entered the tank and burst, we were very happy." Then he shakes his head and adds, "You could not predict what would happen. It was like volunteering for death." During the tank war mentioned above, six or seven of their boys died. Rafiqul cannot even say if the next grenade burst or not because the whole operation was being conducted so stealthily. But on the second day, they advanced quite far. The third day they advanced even further. The commanding officer was just giving the order, "Advance." And they were going forward amid a shower of bullets without caring for their lives. But the Mukti fighters received a report that the "Pakistani army is retreating. Their soldiers are running away." Meanwhile the firing continued. Behind the Mukti forces was the artillery. The artillery was giving cover to the Mukti forces by firing shells. The Mukti fighters were advancing. They could see villages all around them. They could see people walking to the villages with their families on bullock carts. And ahead of them were Punjabi soldiers running away.

On the fourth day, Rafiqul Islam's party entered the town in an open jeep. One side of their jeep was fitted with a machine gun and the other side with an LMG. The town was deserted. The Pakistani soldiers had fled and there was no one on the streets. Some stray dogs wandered about. Shouts of 'Joi Bangla' and blank rifle shots could be heard. The young man who drove the vehicle of Rafiqul's group was from the Sixth Bengal Regiment. His name was Swapan. Next to him and on the seat behind him sat the five of them armed with Sten guns. One of them was Rustam Ali, who would be shot dead during Muharram in 1973. He would become an activist in the Gono Bahini militia of Jasod, Jatiyo Samajtantrik Dal. Another was Shiraz, who was dark and thin. He married the daughter of the Commissioner. He makes a living now as a contractor. Then there was Sudhir, the martyr Sudhir Pal. He was killed the next day in an encounter at Narkel Baria. The one-storied, white house on the way to the jail belonged to the station master. Later he left the railways and worked for an insurance agency. His second son, who is now the director of some bank, was the fourth in Rafiqul's group. And Rafiqul himself is a former businessman. When the business went bust, he sold the roadside store, built a small shed in the lowland at the rear and lived there. According to him, he cannot sleep if he does not take a drink. "I take just a drop or two," he says.

That day, the group of five rode an open jeep and set about rescuing prisoners. Shouting 'Joi Bangla' they proceeded towards the jail. After breaking open the prison gates, they rushed towards the cantonment. Mariam says, "Since morning, I could hear the slogan 'Joi Bangla'. The whole day I heard the same slogan. But from a distance, I could also hear the sound of gunshots."

Mariam had been without food ever since Major Ishtiaque left. She had not eaten a morsel for four days. For two days, she drank water from the bathroom tap. After that the taps ran dry. Everything—water, electricity—was shut off. Her tongue felt leaden when she tried to wet her lips with it. Gradually, she felt a deadening of hunger and thirst. This could possibly be the end. She would die of starvation. In this state, when the 'Joi Bangla' slogan was nearing, Mariam says, "I just cannot express what I was feeling then. Thank Allah, we are saved. We do not have to die in gunfire or of starvation." The strength of demons possessed her body then. Mariam began kicking the door shouting, "Oh! Baba! Oh, brothers!" She could hear their response from outside, "Oh, Mother! Oh, Sister! We are coming, we are coming. "

Mariam wipes her eyes with the end of her sari and says, "Even now I feel like crying when I remember that time. I can still hear their shouts addressing me as Mother." Mariam, who never gave birth to a child, feels grief surging within her when she recalls them addressing her as mother. And yet at that time, there was such hope. Major Ishtiaque had fled, the country had been liberated, the Mukti forces were advancing to rescue them.

"We were madly breaking open one lock after another," says Rafiqul. "Some horrible looking women trooped out of the rooms. They had sores all over their bodies. These were bayonet wounds. There was not an ounce of flesh on their bodies. Each one of them looked like a skeleton. They did not look like humans. They were half-mad. You cannot describe what they wore. They barely covered their genitals."

But what about silk saris? Red roses in the hair? Oil paintings on the wall? Harmonium and tablas on the floor? Something was wrong somewhere. Those whom Rafiqul saw after breaking the locks were some other women. Perhaps Mariam was not among them. When Mukti voices her suspicion, Mariam yanks her sari above her knees and shows her the scars on her right leg. Mukti stops her when Mariam is about to open her blouse saying, "You want to see? Let me show you." Mariam shakes with anger, "Those who told you all this, lied to you. Why should they look at us? They had their eyes elsewhere. We were shop-soiled. The military had robbed us of our chastity. We had scars all over our bodies, we were bloodied, we smelled. Why should they recognize us?" Although she spews out this rush of angry words, Mariam keeps strangely mum about silk saris, red roses, oil paintings, harmonium and tabla. She turns her face away. When she is asked for a photograph to show Rafiqul, she dismisses Mukti after giving her a recent passport size, black and white photo. But the man who had seen her when she was twenty-two, would he recognize her from a photograph taken at fifty-two?

Rafiqul holds up the black and white photograph in the dim light of the kerosene lantern. "This woman is an old hag. Those whom we had rescued were young women of sixteen or seventeen. But they were repulsive to look at."

Mukti stretches her hand out to take back the picture saying, "You're old as well." Rafiqul pushes aside her stretched hand and looks at the photograph intently, turning it this way and that. All the women they had rescued in a state of emotional turmoil, who knows what happened to them? Are they alive or dead? So many years have passed, no one bothered to find out. He is also one of them, as the girl said – old. His liver has packed up. He is alive today, but may not be there tomorrow. Several images float by on the screen of his mind. One face stands out. She had a pinkish mole in the middle of her cheek which cannot be seen in this black and white photograph – but could she be the same woman? When Mukti answers in the positive, he laughs. "The girl with the mole on her cheek came out and asked for a drink of water. We gave her some water. She did not reveal her address. Just said that she had been on her way home from Dhaka when she was captured. At the time, she was very thin. Now I see that she has fleshed out. Heh, heh!"

"What was she wearing? A silk sari?"

"No sari or anything. They were all the same. All of them half-mad. Years later, when I would wake suddenly in the middle of the night, I could see them in my mind's eye."

"Were there a harmonium and tablas in the room and oil paintings on the wall?"

"Says who? It was a dirty, messy room in the barrack where they were kept captive. It had not been mopped or cleaned for nine months. Inside sat this half-mad, demented girl."

"So where did you take them first? To the hospital, or to the Ispahani School in front?"

"Who was taken to the hospital and who was not...?"

"And to the school house?"

"Who was taken there and who was not...?"

Rafiqul's glass is empty. He interrupts the conversation and pleads with the boy-servant for some more liquor. Then he resumes his conversation. "The thing is, a soldier thinks on two levels. One focuses on rescuing people, the other concentrates on killing the enemy. Man does not get drunk only on alcohol. Those who shoot down living humans are also drunk. Hey, pour me a little more. You son of a gun, you want to act as a guardian to a Mukti fighter? It's either you or me tonight. Oh, oh! That's fine. Thank you. The more I burn myself up, the better I feel. Ha, ha!"

The Pakistani military was retreating. The war had not ended. Rafiqul and his friends were only breaking open the locks. It was not their job to see who was being taken to hospital and who was not, who was being taken to the school and who was not. They were punch-drunk with the idea of fighting. At that very moment, instructions came from the commander, "Advance! Onwards!"

XV

Surrender, Surrender: An Important Announcement

Major Ishtiaque's company was fleeing, they were being chased by the enemy. Flight was cowardice but preferable to death and escape was not part of their strategy.

Before leaving the barrack, Major Ishtiaque and his men waited for two days for their white and yellow allies. They looked up at the sky, scanned the sea. The sky was blue, the sea was also blue. There were no signs of the advance of Americans or Chinese. The colours created illusions and unnecessarily wasted time. At last, like buzzing flies caught in a spider's web, they escaped in search of a river under the dark cover of night. From the sky could be seen a sinuous, silvery stream of water. Near its banks were anchored rows of gunboats which would sail over the Padma and reach them to the immeasurably vast mouth of the Meghna. There they would embark on ships flying white flags and sail over turbulent maritime waters till they reached a safe haven where their wives and children would be waiting for them with tears in their eyes and handkerchiefs in their hands. But night fell at the end of day. They saw nothing but the dried-up beds of lakes and canals. The rivers seemed to be like war-ravaged people, vanishing at the sound of their boots. And so the plan of escaping by sea had to be discarded. But it was difficult to survive with the enemy at your back, especially in an area where the local people could not be depended upon for help. If they came face to face with you, they would lynch you. While training at the staff college they had learnt how to survive in an isolated spot surrounded by the enemy. But reality was something else. There was no deserted landscape where they could take cover during the day as specified in the course. Nights were spent stealing food from the fields and in dreaded wakefulness. They fingered their triggers as they listened to the rustle of leaves, the croak of frogs and the cackling laughter of jackals. One night, a terrible incident occurred when they went to steal produce from the fields. It would be remembered many years after the war by the villagers as a moment of pride and grief. It would be described in great detail to the visitors of the village. And a village elder, whose age is beyond reckoning, would narrate the story along with the lamentation-songs for Karbala.

The incident began with Ibrahim Biswas, who now runs a grocery.

Ibrahim was then ten years old. Because of some problems, he had to get up before dawn and go to the slope behind the house. "Problems? What problems?" There is a roar of laughter at Mukti's question. Ibrahim Biswas, father of two sons and three daughters, is now really embarrassed. It is difficult for him to say that having drunk date palm juice at an odd time, his stomach started rumbling like the clouds and heaved as if struck by a teta used to spear fish. He barely had time to call out to his father or take the water pot for ablutions when he rushed to the low-lying land at the rear. Having relieved himself, he lazily looked toward the distant fields. "I was very small, like this one," Ibrahim says pointing to a small naked boy, "I thought there were jackals in the radish fields, scores of jackals." Earlier in Ibrahim's village, jackals would howl when people died. It was wartime and people were dying every moment. Throughout the night, one could hear their continuous howling and scrabbling. Ibrahim thought in astonishment, "Why are they playing hide and seek in the vegetable patches?"

Beside the radish fields, there were rows of chilli plants. There were jackals there also. They were big and there seemed to be several of them. Ibrahim was puzzled. These were no jackals. They were humans munching radishes with chillies with a crunching noise. He could not go to the pond to wash himself. He picked up his shorts, and twirling them like a flag over his head, he called his father Baapjan at the top of his voice. He yelled also to dispel his own fear. When his father came out, he said, "There are jackals in the radish fields." He does not mention that they were humans because he felt a little nervous to say the word. Naturally, during war, people kept their ears alert even while asleep. The neighbours woke up from all the noise made by father and son. They came out in large groups armed with sticks. By that time the early haze of dawn had cleared. It was almost morning. Still, when they see the Pakistani soldiers scurrying in the fields, they thought that they were jackals and not humans. They thought this because just a couple of days earlier, the Pakistani army camp in town had broken up and the soldiers had fled. The Biharis and their families had also followed them. The Razakars had also vanished. So what could they be but jackals? And in the shadowy light of dawn, their appearance and mannerisms seemed like those of jackals. "And seeing the villagers, those people seemed to dance like jackals swinging their tails." The man who interrupted Ibrahim's narration was another eyewitness called Osman Ghani. Of course, by that time the adults had taken over. It was no longer Ibrahim's discovery. The grown-ups leapt upon the Pakistani soldiers with their sticks and rods. It seems that there was no end to this battle. The vegetable fields were transformed into the fields of Karbala. Osman Ghani stops his narration at this point. The moment he stops, an old man begins to sing Karbala's lament. It seems almost a rehearsed piece – singing starts when words come to a halt. The old man sings with eyes closed:

The heart breaks to speak of Karbala,
The mother cries with the child on her lap,
The Prophet's line is destroyed for want of water,
The mother cries with her child on her lap.

The gathering hardens like steel. The air does not move. Mukti sees that the old man's body is bent and wedged between his knees. He is beside himself with grief. After his singing is over, his head with its few wisps of hair, droops to the ground. When she wants to know his age, no one can say for sure. But they think that he is older than another earlier war that took place in the world. Because he knows what occurs when war happens. But they don't know when and where that war experienced by the old man took place. Osman Ghani, the seniormost village leader, thinks that it could have happened during the British rule. Then after the tidal wave of 1970, he arrived destitute from a village near the sea. When he came here, he was wearing a loin cloth, a patched vest and he carried under his arms some old manuscripts. On arrival, he said that he had no one in the world. Everyone had been sucked into the sea. Salt water had wasted away his flesh and he had sores from salt on his skin. When he came he drank huge pots of sweet water from the tanks back then, and he appeared to be as old as he is today. He was supposed to leave at the end of winter. But the war began in the cities. At the time, the old man sang from the lamentations of Karbala and prepared the people of Kamalganj for the forthcoming war. He told each person that war is like a turbulent sea. It destroys, kills one's kith and kin, damages property. War is blind, it makes no difference between the rich and the poor, it denudes and dishonours women. After the war is over, clean, smart, citified foreigners arrive with food and cameras. They bring their own bottles of water, open them and drink. They don't let anyone share the water. Then they distribute the food, shoot photographs and return to their own countries.

Each one of the old man's predictions was coming true. But the old man, bereft of family, did not know how to cope with the sadness of so many senseless deaths, deaths which had occurred not because of the angry sea, but because of the machinations of men. So even after the liberation of the country, the villagers did not let him leave. Since then he has lived here. And he sings only one song—of the Karbala. Whenever the topic of 1971 arises, he sings to them the tale of the Karbala. His duty is irregular, but in return he gets two meals a day from the villagers. He eats very little. Therefore, feeding him even during droughts and famines was no burden to the villagers. Once the villagers finish speaking, the old man lets out a deep sigh. He says, "Alas! Duldul," and falls silent. To Mukti it seems like a part of a rehearsal.

Osman Ghani informs her that on that day, before the afternoon was over, four people had been killed on either side. The ratio was something like this, for each dead soldier, three villagers died. Because the soldiers had modern, sophisticated weapons. The villagers were armed with only sticks and rods and loads of hatred and they continued to fight with these. By afternoon, there was a change in battle strategy. The soldiers fighting in the fields retreated a little. Meanwhile, villagers from several neighbouring villages joined the attack and surrounded the army with country-made tetas and spears. On the second day, the encirclement got tighter, but even then it was as large as Rani Bhanumati's lake and the shape was round. The soldiers kept firing and managed to break out through the circle. Ibrahim's father Ismail became a martyr in that shooting. Another person who died in the firing that day was Afazuddin.

"Who is Afazuddin?" Mukti asks. The answer comes briefly, "The son of Kamal Gazi of Narkelbari Union." That was it. The speakers are more interested in the flight of Pakistani soldiers. That day they could not advance very far as they continued to fire. No matter how well-armed they were, their numbers were limited, perhaps just twenty or twenty-five. On the other hand, the number of villagers had swelled to thousands. Seeing no alternative, Pakistani soldiers entered the bazaar mosque and closed the doors. The villagers were afraid to break down the door in the face of gunshots, but they did not move away either. They besieged the place. By this time, people of half a dozen surrounding villages—men, women, young, old—had become participants in the battle. They brought food for the villagers who were fighting—puffed and pressed rice and earthen vessels filled with jaggery. Thirst was slaked by water from the tank adjoining the mosque. "Alas! The battle of Karbala," the old man's voice can be heard among the crowd. "Forat's water flows with blood but the fighting does not stop." He draws everyone's attention to himself and withdraws into his world of manuscripts. But his head does not droop between his knees as much. His frail body swings like a snake to the rhythm of some unseen snake-charmer's flute.

> *Hearing this Kashem flared up,*
> *Like a tiger leaping on a herd of goats,*
> *Like an elephant trampling banana plants,*
> *He slashes everyone with swords in both hands, oh brothers!*

Mukti looks at the faces around her with a puzzled expression. No one notices. They have all become history's warriors, fighting the enemy with all their might.

The old man tells them through his songs, don't waste time. The water in the tank has dried up and has reached the very bottom. Whatever you have to do, do it quickly. And then suddenly his face is shadowed with grief. There is only mourning there, grief for the boy-warrior Kashem of the distant past. Kashem, who has left behind his newly-wed girl-bride, Sakhina. The warrior has been struck with an arrow and is dying of thirst. He has fallen to the ground and is thrashing about. The old man's voice is tinged with melancholy like the soft whisper of a running stream.

Ibrahim's mother Madina Bibi and the other widows were already standing near the pond. There was no one near the dead bodies fallen in the fields. The women appeared to think that once the enemy inside the mosque was killed, their husbands would come alive and would walk back to their homes just as they returned at dusk with their ploughs and bullocks after furrowing the fields the whole day. Meanwhile, the besiegers found no alternative to breaking down the mosque to destroy the enemy. There was a difference of opinion among them over this. One lot was for breaking down the mosque, the other opposed it. Just at that moment, school student Mahibul could be seen running across the fields and shouting like mad, "Surrender, surrender." He had heard General Manekshaw's orders to surrender over the radio and did not waste a moment in relaying the instructions. Coming closer to the crowd, he parroted the order breathlessly. His face was turned towards the mosque and he shouted without a megaphone. "Brothers, you are surrounded. All air and sea routes have been sealed off. There is no escape. Please surrender, or death is inevitable. If you surrender, you will be treated as prisoners of war under the Geneva Convention."

In spite of all the excitement, the battling men listened attentively to Mahibul repeating General Manekshaw's orders. After this nine-month war, they have learnt that surrender meant raising your hands over your head. "But what is Geneva, Mahibul?" Osman Ghani wanted to know. He kept the circle intact, stretching his neck to ask the question. "Geneva is a country, a country that is independent." Then Mahibul took a breath and said after deep thought, "If they surrender then they will be sent to Geneva."

They were shattered when they heard the news. What kind of justice was this from India? "For nine months, they burned, looted, killed, raped, and yet they will go unpunished? They will be sent off to Geneva?"

Mahibul said, "Ji! Yes," in a soft voice, as if he was an Indian soldier admitting his mistake.

Osman Ghani broke the circle and ran to the high embankment of the pond. His face was red from anger and humiliation like the embers of a wood fire. Wagging his index finger, he started speaking. "Oh my brothers! Have you not killed jackals in the past? So let us smoke these jackals out of their hiding." Instantly, they were ready for action. They brought sacks full of red chilli powder. Quickly, they collected dried water hyacinths, straw, jute stalks, kerosene. One man climbed a ladder to the top of the dome of the mosque. With hammer, chisel, pick-axe, they made a hole in the dome. Through the hole, they pushed in the flammable stuff and the chilli powder. Huge clouds of smoke billowed out and covered the sky. That day the sun was screened by smoke in the Kamalganj sky and noon became night.

The drums of war had set the old man's cold blood on the boil. Grief was replaced by a fierce frenzy. He leans forward and sings in a resonant voice emerging from the depths of his body.

> *Shields and swords are arranged on the horse Duldul,*
> *Husain leaps onto Duldul's back,*
> *Husain disappears with the speed of wind.*
> *Like a tiger, he pounces on Karbala.*
> *There is no record of how many he kills or slashes.*
> *Oh brother! Duldul bites and kills so many soldiers.*

In the smoke and darkness, the men waited outside the door of the mosque, watchful like cats. When each soldier emerged with hands raised in surrender, he was beaten to death like a jackal, ignoring Manekshaw's announcement. In this orgy of slaughter, they did not see the rescuers arriving in tanks.

The man who saw the arrival was Majid Bihari who was a mile away from the incident. He was an eccentric. His head was filled with fantastic notions. While the other Biharis followed the retreat of the Pakistani army, this one stayed behind expecting the return of Pakistanis. He could not believe that the world's greatest fighters would slink away like thieves even though he was seeing it with his own eyes. Then the world became an illusion. No difference remained between the sun and the moon. His prayers were answered on the third day. Majid Bihari had witnessed Partition, seen direct confrontation between followers of the slogans Bande Mataram and Allaho Akbar, watched conflagrations and the flash of daggers. He had had the terrible experience of crossing at night Bihar's hilly terrain and thorny scrubland as well as half of Bengal to come here. And then there was this nine-month long war, but surprisingly enough, through all of this he had never seen a tank. Seeing the tank, he thought that the world's finest army was returning victorious, riding this powerful vehicle with its raised gun turrets. Their arrival reverberated like the coming of an earthquake. His body trembled with emotion. He did not wait a moment longer. "Wait, wait, brother. I am a Bihari, your friend." Shouting these words, Majid Bihari tottered like a toddler towards the monster vehicle moving over the trembling ground.

The scene was observed from the top of the tank by Ata Mian, husband of Marjina, Ibrahim's older sister. Mukti pushes the microphone towards him over other heads, "Can you introduce yourself?" Having asked the question, she realizes immediately that she herself cannot hear what she has said. There was so much noise all around like a fish market. She now raises her volume, "Please speak loudly and introduce yourself." From a sitting position, Ata Mian stands up straight and says, "I am a Mukti fighter, trained in India."

"What were you doing that day on top of the tank?" Ata Mian is stunned hearing Mukti's question. He is deflated. He had no idea that someone could ask such a question, so many years after the war. His mind is jolted. True, that day he was neither the tank commandant nor crew or driver. Nor was he meant to be. Their group showed the way to the tanks of the allied forces. They had returned to their own country like heroes, pummelling the enemy before them. But the heroism could not be expressed either in body language or in countenance. The body of the tank was slippery and the front sloped forward. Their bodies kept slipping towards the conveyor belt under the tank. It was quite difficult for the guides to balance themselves on the palms of their hands. But all that was in the past. After that whenever Ata Mian thinks of the days of his glory, a tank with its snout up in the air rumbles into his memory. Then he is no longer the owner of two katthas of land, nor is he an office clerk at the girls' school or the resident son-in-law of Ibrahim's family. He becomes a rider in the tank, a brave guerrilla fighter who marches forward sowing the seeds of freedom. Mukti's question, therefore, is a threat to his memory. It is even more painful than having your name scratched off from the list of freedom fighters with a stroke of the pen during the final selection. Both old humiliations and pride rise gurgling in his chest like salty sea water rising in a tide. Ata Mian cannot stop the upheavals that he experiences.

At the time the tenor and tempo of war had suddenly changed. The Mukti fighters did not know that guerrilla fighting was over. Now it was going to be real war, a direct confrontation with the enemy with leadership being given by the allied army and people like Ata Mian would have minor parts to play. Before they could catch on to what was happening, they saw in front half a dozen armoured tanks. Binoculars hung from the tank commander's neck and he was wearing a helmet. The tank crew was garbed in dungarees, ensconced in the safe interior of the tank. The poorly-clad Ata Mians of the world were placed atop the elite vehicles to show the way. This way, they would be the first targets of enemy attack. Ata Mian was trembling with fear. They thought that the allies were using them as shields against enemy fire. More than apprehension, the situation was humiliating. But when a shower of shots rained from the opposite side, Ata Mian says, "The Marathi tank commander shouted, 'Please get down, please get off. And then he went inside the tank and closed the hatch. Then the real battle was conducted by the tanks firing ammunition, 'Ka-boom, Ka-boom'." The Ata Mians stayed at the rear and were lying down. Then came the order, the Pakistani army had fled. Advance and take possession of the camp. Possession meant scorched earth, heaps of rubble, abandoned bunkers, vessels of half-eaten biryani, plates and glasses, a few fresh corpses. But the tanks do not stop, because in the New York offices of the United Nations, there is a huge uproar over the Indo-Pak war. The resolutions of cease-fire and withdrawal

of forces from East Pakistan had 104 votes for the resolution
and eleven against. The eleven votes against the resolution came
from nations who supported the Indian and Soviet lobbies.
Meanwhile, the future Prime Minister of Pakistan, Z.A. Bhutto
was leading a seven-member group of representatives and had
left Rawalpindi for New York. The situation was critical. The
Indian tank corps had to quickly reach Dhaka before the cease-
fire resolution was passed at the United Nations. That is why
they chased the enemy relentlessly. The Indian infantry was
marching alongside. Not to speak of the Ata Mians, who were
there anyway.

The news of the fray between the Kamalganj mob and the
Pakistani soldiers came to them over the wireless while they
were on the march. Kamalganj was familiar to Ata Mian. It was
only a few miles from his village. That is why he was welcomed
back to the top of the tank as he had been on the first day. The
tank commander was in seventh heaven with joy. He said to Ata
Mian, "Dost, friend, let us move fast. We have the opportunity
of a lifetime." No longer dead soldiers, now they need live
prisoners-of-war. When the commander glanced at Ata Mian,
he gestured ahead. He signalled that there was no cause for
worry, Kamalganj was just ahead. Just at that moment, Majid
Bihari's appearance in front of the tank was an unexpected
problem. Ata Mian did not realize his presence at first. He was
busy holding on to his position on the slippery tank surface. By
the time he heard the words, "Stop! Stop!", Majid Bihari had
swirled away from the road hit by the infantry bullets. The scene
overwhelmed him so much that he felt no emotion when he
saw smoke curling out of the mosque. But when he saw the
angry mob continuing to fight ignoring the presence of the half
dozen tanks, he jumped off the tank in delight and shouted at
the top of his voice, 'Joi Bangla!'

By the time the infantry soldiers took charge of the mosque
door, some five Pakistani soldiers had been killed. Even then
the people's anger had not subsided. They were determined to
stop the move of sending the attackers to Geneva and giving

them VIP treatment. Manekshaw's "Surrender! Surrender!" announcement was the root of all evil. For the last nine months, they had listened to the radio endlessly, but no news item had been such a slap in the face as this one. Hearing the curt orders of the allied army, Osman Ghani once again jumped on to the banks of the pond. He shouted, "Listen my brothers! Just listen to me once. When these scoundrels shot Ibrahim's father Ismail, where were these minions of Manik-Shah? Where was Afiluddin when…?"

Osman Ghani's shrill metallic shouting and Ata Mian's continuous cries of Joi Bangla were suppressed by the blank firing of the allies. The turbulent mob began to retreat. Running helter-skelter, they reached the two-day-old corpses lying rotting. There the reality was somewhat different…

The bodies were lying bloated wherever they had fallen. Crows, vultures, dogs were fighting over their flesh. There was no difference between the Bengali and Pakistani corpses. The village women forgot about friends and foes and lamented over all the bodies, throwing themselves on the ground and rolling in grief. The men were annoyed at the lack of sense among these apolitical women. They buried the bodies of the Pakistani soldiers in a slipshod fashion and carried the half-eaten bodies of their relations and neighbours on bamboo constructions back to the village.

When the village homes were steeped in grief and the air was heavy with tears and sighs, a real pack of jackals came to the vegetable patches. Ibrahim saw the scene from his house but he did not shout, nor was he afraid. In the middle of his sorrow, the thought of jackals eating radishes with chillies brought a smile to his lips. He thought what a child he had been just two days ago. He had been unaware that jackals are carnivorous. They eat flesh and not radishes with chillies. His father's death had turned him into a grown up.

While the pack of jackals was busy with the bodies of the dead soldiers, the living prisoners-of-war were snoring in their sleep in a small chamber in a nearby town, a mile away. The

Geneva Convention was like warmth on a winter night. Even if
it did not provide them food for their empty stomachs, it gave
them the security of sleep. Under its protection, the prisoners
of war could even dream, although the dreams may have been
nightmares. Ata Mian, at that time, had made a bonfire with
wood and straw found in the abandoned bunkers and was
enjoying its warmth in the open field. Next to him sat the old
man who sang of the Karbala battle. The old man's head, with
hardly any hair on it, was drooping between his knees and it
shone in the reddish glow of the fire. Now that they had the
heroes of the old tales in their midst, the people had forgotten
all about the old man. They did not remember to call him when
a meal was being served. He lost the place where he slept at
night. Now the Mukti fighters were honoured guests in the
homes of villagers. The wheel of history had turned full circle.
Now the guerrilla fighters were the new rulers of the liberated
land. The doors, which were closed to them even yesterday
for fear that they would have to be given shelter, were now
wide open. There was a festive air of welcome in the town
and surrounding areas. Beef and khichari were being cooked in
huge copper vessels under an awning. In order to serve them,
china dishes, glasses, bell-metal wash basins had been borrowed
from neighbouring homes. After the lavish meal, the guerrilla
fighters were happily asleep in warm beds after a long time. But
Ata Mian could not sleep.

During the day, when Osman Ghani's band of followers ran
towards the cultivated fields after being chased by the allies,
Ata Mian discovered himself in their midst. And then floating
like a water hyacinth, he reached the yard of Ibrahim's house.
There he saw two dead bodies. One was Ismail's and the other
was Abdur Rab's. It was only a week before that Ismail Biswas
had married his elder daughter Marjina to Abdur Rab. Sadly,
once again, it was the story of Karbala. Marjina's state was
like that of Bibi Sakhina. She had lost her father, she had lost
her newly-married husband. She fainted every now and then.
Despite the deep sorrow, her mother Madina's common sense

was sharp. There were two dead bodies in her yard, but there was also a living guerrilla soldier there. When Marjina opened her eyes after a splash of water on her face, her mother rushed her to make sherbet for the guerrilla fighter. After repeated instructions of this kind, the mother's words finally pierced Marjina's consciousness. But Marjina Bibi could not stand for long with the glass of sherbet in her hand. She collapsed like a banana plant before the feet of the Mukti fighter. Ata Mian was not at all prepared for such a great honour. He jumped away as if his foot was about to land on a mine planted by the enemy. But the moment he left the Ismail home, he was filled with regret. He dismissed the thought. Whatever had to happen, happened. There was no way that he could return now. The day was over. Ata Mian had to report to his group leader. Otherwise, he would be consigned to the list of casualties. Before going into town, he fixed the directions to Marjina's house in his memory so that he would have no trouble recognizing it a second time.

Meanwhile, there was a big upheaval in town. The allies had forged ahead with their tanks. They had left behind the prisoners-of-war like trash. But heavily guarded. The Indian sentry disarmed Ata Mian in accordance with the Geneva Convention and only then did they grant him permission to meet the esteemed guests. Ata Mian tells Mukti that although he had other thoughts in his mind then, he entered the prison camp in order to see the Pakistani soldiers. About eight or ten of the invaders were lying half-dead, severely wounded on the bare floor in the main room of the Board office. They looked helpless and bewildered like caged animals in a zoo. So this was the powerful, invincible enemy against whom Ata Mians had been fighting without a break for the last six months. Now both the opponents were confronting each other but no one was killing anyone. Ata Mian was puzzled. He could not quite believe the developments. He gaped at them open-mouthed. It would have been nice if Marjina Bibi had been with him. He did not know what would have happened. He could not remember any details of her appearance. What surfaced in his mind was

a glass etched with a design of flowers and leaves in which a
few drops of salty tears and pain were mixed with the sweet
sherbet. He had made his hurried escape from the house after
that. Standing uncomfortably, Ata Mian rubbed his left leg with
his right foot. The Indian sentry did not approve of his posture.
He hurried him out saying. "Your time is over."

Any other time, the blood would have rushed to Ata Mian's
head, but today something else was bothering him. He did not
want to leave this place but if he wanted to remain here, he had
to do something else besides scratching his legs. What could
he do now? While he was thinking all this, Ata Mian spotted
a high-ranking officer among them. He saw that the other
man was also staring at him. Bubbling within him were words
that he could have spoken to Marjina but had not. He asked
the soldier, "How are you Bhaishaheb?" The officer did not
reply. A trace of emotion shivered in the air. The question was
harmless, but a little strange. The sentry had watched various
people coming in and abusing the prisoners, but no one else
had asked such a question. Ata Mian's desire to chat increased
when he saw the sentry smile under his moustache. He asked
his preferred officer, "Why have you turned so tame? Have you
become 'fraidy cats now?" The officer was very smart. Without
answering the question, he glanced sideways at the sentry. As
if the confrontation was only between Pakistan and India.
The East Pakistani Bengalis in the middle were mere pests like
mosquitoes and flies. They were still subjects. Ata Mian's hands
moved restlessly. At the zoo one had the chance to throw peanut
shells and banana peels in the cage. There was no chance of that
here. But he still had within him the words he was not able to say
to Marjina. He asked politely, "When did you people come from
Pakistan?" This time the soldier's dry lips moved but no words
came. Ata Mian went forward, a step at a time, "My name is Ata
Mian. Freedom fighter. Your name, brother?"

"Major Ishtiaque."

Ata Mian returns to the present and tells Mukti with a wide
grin, "It is because you want to know that I am telling you."

Otherwise, at the time, he felt no excitement or joy in the knowledge that a big officer had been captured as a prisoner of war. Instead, he was more eager to talk to the old man who was luxuriating in the warmth of the open fire on a winter's night.

There was heavy dewfall as the night progressed. They were not so well-covered. The heat of the fire warmed their fronts but their backs were almost frozen. It was very difficult. And yet the bunkers of the Pakistani army were standing empty before them. One could easily have gone inside for a night's shelter. But the old man refused to enter a hole while he was still alive. Ata Mian ran around gathering wood and straw, but the old man sat still. From the time he lowered his head between his knees, showing no signs of straightening up even if the world was destroyed. What kind of a man was he? Ata Mian the Mukti fighter felt like scaring him. He said, "Old man, what did you do living here for the last nine months? I know that you did not join the guerrilla forces. Were you a Razakar?"

"Me?" The old man was startled and raised his neck like an egret. "Son, am I of that age where I can fight or be a Razakar?"

"If you were of the right age, would you have been a Razakar?"

The old man was stubborn. He did not answer Ata Mian's deadly questions. He sank his head lower between his two knees. When young was he a dacoit or what? He seemed to feel no fear. The current punishment for Razakars was death. In Kamalganj, a dozen Razakars had been killed in a day. But what would be the punishment for a man who had been a Razakar in his youth? At that moment, of course, one could do anything that one wished. No one was trying a case by the law book. Everyone was crazy with the thought of revenge. They had sufficient weapons. Every time a charge came up, the punishment was decided instantly. There was no need for witnesses or evidence. Ata Mian, of course, did not want to resort to that. His interest was elsewhere. He wanted the old man's support. Should he follow the allies tomorrow and advance towards Dhaka or should he stay back at Kamalganj where Bibi Marjina fainted constantly with grief for her dead husband. "Old man, what is more important, war or friendship and love between people?"

The question, which was uncharacteristic of a fighter, shot from Ata Mian like a sharp arrow. Its impact made the old man raise his head. The old man answered dismissively, "War does not make a king into a subject, nor a subject into a king. The ultimate truth is Karbala."

The next day some bits of news, fresh or stale, floated in.

Some microbuses had been camouflaged with leaves and branches, their bodies smeared with clay. They were buzzing around the lanes of Dhaka. The Al Badr forces were very alert. They were picking up the country's choicest men and after blindfolding them, they were being taken in the micros to unknown destinations.

The American aircraft carrier Enterprise had sailed away from Vietnam and was now in the Indian Ocean.

The Indian air force attack set the Government House on fire. The attackers set their target after studying a Dhaka tourist guide. The Governor got scared and resigned. He and his followers had now taken refuge in the international zone at the Hotel Intercontinental.

The allies had nearly reached Dhaka. A section of their forces reached Demra via Bhairab. Another group marched on the Manikganj Road and was now near the Mirpur Bridge. With them was a company of paratroopers who had landed at Tangail. According to foreign sources, the paratroopers were 5000 in number.

From the underground shelter, a poisonous cobra slithered up the wall onto the map. Then it coiled and raised its hood over Dhaka. General Tiger growled in fear but no sound emerged. By that time, a temptation buzzed round his ears, "Surrender, surrender! An important announcement." He allowed it to buzz, instead of swatting it away.

At that very moment, Z. A. Bhutto was shouting himself hoarse on the floor of the packed United Nations General Assembly, "We will fight, we will fight for a thousand years."

And then in Hollywood style, the paper he tore up, having read it or not, was a resolution for ceasefire from Poland, a Soviet lobby country.

General Tiger ordered the removal of the map from the wall and entered his dressing room. He did not don battledress but dressed for surrender.

Ata Mian lied to his commander, "Please give me two days' leave. I don't feel right. I want to go home." It was a historic moment. At any moment the news of the Pakistani army's surrender might have come. After having fought the whole year, who would want to miss this momentous sight? Although Ata Mian's request sounded mad, the commander was happy to grant it. At the crossroads, Ata Mian felt pulled in different directions. There were four roads. One went to Marjina's house; in the clear light of day he thought that it would not be correct to visit the house of mourning straight away. He would visit after the fourth day ritual was over. The next road led to Dhaka but Dhaka was far away. The third road would take him to his home a couple of miles away. His father was at home with his second wife and children from that marriage. When the unemployed son went to war, he was relieved that there would be some saving on expenses. Now Ata Mian could not go to him empty-handed with a Sten gun slung on his shoulder. The fourth road led to the district town where his aunt, his father's sister, lives. She had been like a mother to him, bringing him up as if he was the son she never had. The district town had been liberated three days ago. It was true that Ata Mian did not wish to fight. But nor did he want to deprive himself of the opportunity of witnessing the victory celebrations directly. If he could reach the district town, he could have his cake and eat it too.

XVI

Buli, We Have Not Forgotten You, Even Today

At the time that Ata Mian entered the district town from the north-east, seven or eight miles to the south, a battle raged between the Pakistani and allied forces in the Nayarhat subdivision. On the way, he saw a Mukti fighter, a boy from his neighbourhood. The young man had lost his weapons in a battle and fled. His appearance was untidy. For the last couple of days and nights, he had been fighting continuously. He said that the Pakistani army was unwilling to cede even an inch of land. The fields were filled with corpses. One could hear the noise of bursting ammunition but the condition of the town was normal. Some people were busy in the streets, looting. No one had the time to look at anyone else. One man, fleeing with a bundle of vermicelli, crossed Ata Mian and his friend. Nearby, some men were dismantling the doors and windows of a house and piling them into a van. One fellow sat atop a stack of quilts and mattresses in a rickshaw with a pistol at his waist. He was coming towards them. The friend said, "Make the dog put his hands up and take his pistol. I need a weapon." Instantly, the idea was translated into action. The man handed over the pistol and ran off abandoning the quilts and mattresses. There were no bullets in the pistol. "The dog picked it up because he got it for free! Never mind, in wartime it's good to have a weapon." They resumed their walking. On the way they heard that an acquaintance of theirs had had his leg blown off by a bomb. He had been brought wounded to the district hospital. Another incident had occurred on the way to the hospital. Some Punjabis had been separated from their group and come onto the street. The public shouted "Joi Bangla" when they saw them. The Punjabis panicked and fired blanks from their Chinese Sten guns. The people thought the Pakistanis had returned. So they fled after destroying the roadside shops. Ata Mian saw no reason to stand around. Both of them were armed but between them they had only two bullets. The bullets were tied round Ata Mian's waist with a gamchha. He had entered the liberated town because he did not want to fight any more. So he was not prepared.

The hospital was in a sad state. There was no doctor there. The civil surgeon was a non-Bengali. He was running for his life, and could hardly manage to dispense any medical treatment. The nurses were running around and doing whatever they could. Ata Mian tells Mukti, "Back then these weren't two hundred or two-fifty bed hospitals. There weren't too many doctors either. Today, there is a doctor for the nose, another for the ears. One hospital has twenty different doctors. It wasn't like that then. Those who were there in the district hospitals had fled."

Meanwhile, the wounded were being brought to the hospital. The freedom fighters had brought in a doctor from somewhere. What could he do alone? The one who had a bullet in his stomach needed emergency surgery, but he was being drugged to sleep. There was no water and no electricity. At night, there used to be a blackout for fear of a Pakistani air attack. Ata Mian got stuck when he came to visit at the hospital. The friend who had come back from war needed rest. He had vanished at some point. Ata Mian also wanted to escape. Suddenly, he heard the rat-tat-tat of guns. One could make out it was blank fire. Had the

Pakistani soldiers come back? Ata Mian did not know that these were the victory celebrations. He descended into the darkened corridor of the hospital. The sound of gunfire sent the patients running helter skelter. From the opposite side strode the doctor who had been commandeered to help the hospital. He came and embraced the bandaged patient and held him aloft. He did this to four patients. He did not lift up the fifth. Instead, he embraced Ata Mian, Sten gun and all. He said, "Brother freedom fighter, the country is free. We are all free, independent. We are all citizens of a free country."

The doctor's jubilant shouts crossed the corridor, the male ward, passed through the closed doors of the female ward and reached the ears of Mariam, the only patient there. It made no difference to her. Yesterday, she was brought to the hospital from Ispahani School. The previous two days, Mariam had been like a caged animal in a zoo. Crowds of people came to see her. The other women were somewhere else. She was alone. She did not eat, or bathe. Her condition worsened in the face of people teasing and making fun of her. She could not stop vomiting. After she was brought to the hospital, a nurse bathed her and then gave her medicine to stop the vomiting. She'd been sleeping since then.

The evening General Niazi was signing the surrender document, Mariam was in a drugged daze. She entered a space which contained Shalimar Bagh and the city was named Lahore. She walked barefoot on the green grass of Lahore spread out like a carpet under her feet, stood a moment near a fountain, appreciated the beauty of rows of cypress trees. But she did not see a single woman wearing a tight churidar-kurta and a dupatta coiled round the neck like a noose. The scene comforted her and opening a door to the future, she went back to sleep.

Freed from the doctor's embrace, Ata Mian ran out. He wanted to get out of the hospital irrespective of whether he participated in the victory celebrations or not. But conditions outside were even more despairing. The morning had been lively, its atmosphere animated with robbery, looting and blank firing by Pakistani soldiers. Now the city seemed dead. And Ata Mian was the only pedestrian. He walked to the Town Hall. There were some eateries in front of it. People were thronging the only sweetmeat shop. Before the shop, a man sitting on a rickshaw was speaking into a loudspeaker exhorting people to observe victory celebrations peacefully. No victory celebrations were being held anyway, with or without peace. Ata Mian wanted very much to celebrate a little. Before that he wanted to eat a few sweets. He may not have had money in his pocket but he had a Sten gun on his shoulder. Ata Mian says to Mukti, "Those days people fed freedom fighters for free. They would drag them home and offer them comfortable beds and say, 'Brother, sleep.'" But Ata Mian's craving for sweets was not satisfied that day. Before he had even entered the shop, the glass-fronted showcases were all empty. The shopkeeper kept wringing his hands and saying, "Sir, there is flour. May I make you a couple of *parathas*?" Before the parathas could be fried, freedom fighter Shahjahan Siddiq descended from the rickshaw and stopped the announcements. They were meeting after a long time. At first they did not recognize each other's unshaven faces. When they did, they embraced each other and Siddiq said, "Friend, there is trouble in the suburbs. This is not the time to eat parathas. Later, I will treat you to rice and meat. Now, come with me."

The Biharis lived in the suburbs. Ata Mian and Shahjahan Siddiq went there and raised slogans "Bengali Bihari Bhai Bhai. Bengalis and Biharis are brothers. We eat from the same plate. Who are you? Who am I? We are citizens of independent Bangla." It did not seem that Biharis had heard their slogans of reassurance and even if they had, they probably did not understand. They needed a secure refuge at that time. Meanwhile, the night was deepening. They returned to Shahjahan Siddiq's shelter. There, a huge gathering of freedom fighters had collected. It did not matter who knew whom, or who was rich and who was poor. All of them were brave freedom fighters and the country had been liberated through their collective efforts. There was no end to their talk. The night was spent talking of their heroism, their sorrows, their hardships, their joys. In between, the Ratan Hotel had twice supplied them with rice and meat curry. When they went to sleep, the first rays of sun of an independent country crawled near their legs.

The next evening Ata Mian discovered himself going down a narrow alley to the outskirts of the city. It led him to a grief-stricken house with its tin roof and a border of bamboo railings standing behind a twin toddy palm. The toddy palms had become taller and had grown in girth. Otherwise, the exterior of the house was unchanged. But the interior had a sorrowful air. Phupu's plump figure had thinned down to a point where her body was as flat as a board. Her oily black hair had become white and dry. The happy housewife's neat coiffure had become untidy and tangled. His aunt sobbed her heart out when she saw her freedom fighter nephew. He could not make out what she was saying through her tears. From his cousin Duli, he heard in detail about his uncle becoming a martyr. The Pakistani soldiers shot him beneath the toddy palms for no good reason. For two days and two nights, the corpse lay at the foot of the palms. It is the duty of a Muslim to bury a Muslim, but people were afraid to come out and perform that task. The whole neighbourhood was disturbed by the onslaught of dogs and crows. The stench was unbearable. Then Duli's husband Amjad risked his life and dug a grave next to the corpse. Duli helped to lower the rotting body of her father into the grave. Overnight they planted grass to cover the grave. The grave was only two months old. When crossing the palms, he did not recognize it. When he later formally visited it, he thought, was it really his uncle Abdul Karim, who was a head clerk at the court for forty years, lying here, or was he praying for the souls of the twin palms.

"It was not written in my fate that I will mourn for your uncle. For thirty years, we have made a home, lived under the same roof. The man was shot right before my eyes and died flailing and thrashing, but I could not shed a tear for him. Is there any end to my troubles?"

Suddenly his aunt stopped speaking. Duli and Amjad were

hesitant. Ata Mian recalled with a jolt, "Where is Buli, Phupu? I've been here for awhile but I haven't seen her?" The little girl of the house was staring at the gun all this time. The five-year-old got an opportunity to speak. She did not waste a moment, "Mama, o Mama." She tugged at the strap of the gun, "The military have taken Aunt Buli away." Immediately, Phupu began wailing and Duli's daughter got spanked by her mother for speaking out of turn.

Was there not an iota of peace anywhere in independent Bangladesh? What had the sons of bitches done to the country? Ata Mian could not bear it anymore. As he made ready to step out, his aunt quickly grabbed the strap of his gun, "Where are you going son? Before you leave, why don't you shoot your aunt?" How was he to handle this one? Behind her the wick of the oil lamp trembled with Phupu's sobbing. Ata Mian stood stock still. Looking out at the ghostly palms, he thought that there was another war beyond the war that had taken place. Did a freedom fighter have the responsibility of bearing its burden? He did not know Marjina Bibi of Kamalganj village previously. He had not even seen her before and yet her mother Madina Bibi wanted to give away her daughter to him even as her husband's corpse lay in the yard. A part of his heart belonged there. But his aunt was also close to him. Only two months earlier, the soldiers had carried away his cousin Buli. There had once been a marriage proposal between Buli and Ata Mian, but the idea did not take off because the boy had little education. The proposal sank even as it had surfaced. Who can say what happens to a man's life? But the area had been rid of the enemy four days ago. What had Amjad Hossein done for his sister-in-law these last few days? Or had his responsibility ended with the burial of his father-in-law?

Now his questions were answered by Buli's older sister Duli, "What can Munni's father do single-handed? Now that you have come, why don't you make enquires?" Phupu went even further. She embraced her nephew and said, "Son, the country has become independent but where is my daughter? Go and bring her to me. Let me douse the fire in my heart." Although for two months, Phupu had imposed a stony silence on herself, now she could bear it no more. She began beating her chest. Meanwhile, Amjad Hossein had donned a sweater and was ready to go out in search of his sister-in-law along with freedom fighter Ata Mian.

When Shahjahan Siddiq heard all this, he listed four or five places where they could enquire. But he said, "Do you think you will be able to find her? If she were alive, she should have come home by now. But it also could be that she is hiding in shame. Try and see if you can find her."

After talking to Shahjahan Siddiq, Ata Mian and Amjad Hossein went straight to the trash heap by the river bank where the unclaimed dead bodies had been thrown. The place later became known as the Kalitala Badhya Bhumi, the Kalitala Slaughter Grounds. They went there first because it was nearby and because Shahjahan Siddiq had said that the chances of her being alive were slim indeed. They saw hundreds of kerosene lamps there. People had gone there with lanterns to search for the bodies of their loved ones. The corpses were many days old and were rotting. Many were just skeletons. People were merely guessing and carrying away the bodies. Ata Mian and his companion had no light with them. From the death grounds on the river bank, they went to the suburb where the Biharis lived. Along with the Pakistani army the Biharis had slaughtered Bengalis for the last nine months and they'd pushed the bodies down manholes. Now was the time for revenge. As many of the decaying Bengali corpses were pulled out of the manholes that night, Bihari corpses were being pushed into the empty spaces left by them. This orgy of killing went on till dawn. Towards morning, they recalled Shahjahan Siddiq's words, "It could be that she is ashamed to show her face." Instantly, Ata Mian and Amjad Hossein ran towards the bunker at Naya Bazar. They took with them a nylon sari which Buli could drape round herself. Ata Mian managed to get it from a wholesaler by pointing his Sten gun. Nothing was gained by taking the sari. No one was being allowed to enter the bunker that day. A freedom fighter's hands

and legs had been blown off when he stepped on a Pakistani
land mine. He was struggling for his life. On the second day,
they could enter one of the Naya Bazar bunkers which had been
searched by the allied army. There they found bangles, saris, long
tresses, but no human beings. Next they went to Ayub School
which was later renamed as A K Fazlul Haque School. Entering
the school, they found some women sitting in a room without
benches and blackboards. Their faces were veiled like those of
new brides.

Curious people peered into the room. An armed sentry stood
on guard. Some freedom fighters were struggling to cope with
the situation. Boys and young men who were pulled down from
the window ledges perched themselves on the boundary walls.
Or leaped like monkeys onto treetops. Two men had fallen from
the trees and broken their legs. Hearing their story, one freedom
fighter known to Ata Mian led him and his relative into a room.
There, like a roll call in a school, they called out Buli's name, her
father's name and the name of her school just as the freedom
fighter had instructed. But none of the women with covered
heads responded. Only one of them, at the last call, brought
out a thin hand and scratched her back. Thinking she was Buli,
Ata Mian made a move towards her but he was stopped by the
freedom fighter. He was told, "It's not what you think. Living
in a hole, they have got lice on their bodies. That's why she's
scratching herself." Then scratching his own body with the rifle
butt, the young fighter informed them that these women would
be transferred to the hospital as soon as beds were available.
Ata Mian continued to be suspicious. If everyone was infested
with lice, why should only one scratch herself when they were
calling out Buli's name? "But there are rules for everything," the
freedom fighter told them, "If someone does not want to show
her face, you cannot force her." Besides, Ata Mian was a freedom
fighter himself and he should be the first to observe rules.

Then they started walking towards the hospital. Although
the women would not be transferred there till the beds were
empty. Between Ayub School and the hospital there was the

open compound of the Town Hall. There, the prisoners of war who'd been kept in that area were being disarmed. The allied army had kept the place surrounded. The people were raising slogans outside the grounds. "Catch hold of a soldier, eat him with breakfast and tea. We want justice, we want justice, we want Yahya tried. We want justice, we want justice, we want justice for the genocide. Yahya-Bhutto, sons of bitches, dogs." Ata Mian's fellow fighters were very busy there. They had, in one way or another got involved with the disarming, a cause which seemed more noble and worthy than searching for Buli. Ata Mian joined in the disarming. Amjad Hossein became separated from him and after two days and two nights of searching, the mission of finding Buli came to an end before the grounds of Town Hall.

But Ata Mian was unable to forget Buli. Even though he was a freedom fighter and had roamed the streets in search of her, he had been unable to find out whether the girl was dead or alive. How was he to show his face to his aunt? So without saying anything to anyone, he left town. He went to Kamalganj. Marjina Bibi's prescribed period of widowhood was not yet over. But he still married her. The country had just become free. There was no strict enforcement of religious law at the time. The mullahs and maulvis of the area, irrespective of whether or not they had been Razakars, had fled the village. Ata Mian tells Mukti, "If it was now then we would have been whipped." Because the thing was almost the same as committing adultery. The three months of Iddat had not passed after Marjina Bibi's husband's death. In less than a month Ata Mian had fixed the date of the wedding. The mother Madina had her wits about her. She did not wait a second to give her permission, because her daughter had cohabited with her husband for five or six days only. Even then, they had to leave their bed and go into hiding because of harassment by soldiers. Ata Mian tells Mukti, "You cannot fully narrate the sad history. You are an educated woman. You will understand." Villagers ribbed him about the marriage after they returned home, having handed over their arms in Dhaka and getting blankets in return. People said anything that came into their minds, even what they shouldn't. He would pretend that he had not heard anything because he lived with his in-laws in a different village. The old man stood by him in those unhappy times. He was a stranger to the village and so was Ata Mian. They had become friends since the day before the victory when they enjoyed the warmth of the fire in the open field. He began addressing Marjina Bibi as Bibi Sakhina. The old man had also been in big trouble once. When the mullahs and maulvis had fled the village post liberation, the old man was commandeered to take on the mantle of the Imam of the mosque. It was the month of Ramzan. During prostration at the time of namaz, the old man had dozed off. Then he had to atone before the masjid committee and only then was he given a meal in this village. It was a sad sight.

In the village, the old man lived with his Karbala, Ata Mian and Marjina Bibi lived with their children and his job as assistant at the girls' school. Both continued to live in Kamalganj because of the war. That they do not forget. But Ata Mian did not also forget the thin hand that had scratched a back when he had called out Buli's name. If she was Buli, would she not have returned home by now?

But not everyone who was alive had gone home. When Ata Mian was playing an 'important' role in the disarming of the prisoners-of-war at the Town Hall grounds, a clutch of women had gathered in the female ward of the district hospital. None of them had given the rescuers their names and addresses. The next day they joined the Indian army convoy going to Dhaka. With them were the Pakistani prisoners-of-war. On Major Ishtiaque's forehead and arms, there were open wounds, the result of the mass anger at Kamalganj. The wounds were untreated, without bandages. During the ferry crossing, watching the turbulent waves of the Padma, the Major, who was an admirer of the poet Hafiz, was absentmindedly flicking off a fly buzzing around his face. Seeing the gesture, the young boy who sold water at the ferry thought the murderous soldier was saluting him. In return, he abused him, "Damn sisterfucker!" When nobody said anything, the boy decided to show his courage and summoned his friend who sold peanuts. Now their target was Mariam and the women with her, none of whom had given the rescuers their addresses. The peanut vendor told the water-seller, "Look at these women following the military. Where are these whores going?"

The fly that Major Ishtiaque flicked off began buzzing inside Mariam's head. They were surrounded by young hawkers. This was an unusual reception in an independent country. The Indian soldiers, who did not understand what was being said, were laughing and bending down and shaking outstretched hands. Whose country was this? They were the heroes and the Mariams were the trash. The Indian military convoy left the ferry and climbed the slope onto the river bank. Mariam silently bid farewell to the Padma. She addressed the twilit golden sky and muttered, "I do not know what the evenings of other countries are like. But what has my own country given me?" Was twenty-two years a long time? Life is longer.

XVII

The Birangana Office

"Don't you have any pictures of the Biranganas?" Mukti is interviewing a former social worker in her drawing room. On the walls hang a number of group photographs showing the hostess with Mother Teresa, Sarojini Naidu, Aruna Asaf Ali, Madame Tito, as well as many other unfamiliar foreign women – valuable testimony at once to her youth as well as her life as a social worker. Mariam, a.k.a. Mary, had not till then been seen in photographs or in the flesh. The only Birangana photograph that Mukti has seen so far was a black and white photograph by Kishore Parekh. It showed two anonymous women, one whose face was covered with the drape of her sari and the other whose face was only partially visible. The social worker says, "Where will you get photographs? The moment they saw a camera, the girls would pull the ends of their saris over their heads to hide their faces in either shame or repugnance."

Even if it was possible to hide their faces with their saris, they had time bombs in their bellies, the babies ticking away in their wombs. They could destroy the future of the new country by exploding at any time. The social worker said, "The country had only just become free. Destruction and loss on all sides. There were not enough people to do the work. There was a lack of training. Everyone was confused. How should one prioritize the work? Everything needed to be done and done right then and there."

A special ordinance was passed in 1972 to arrange for the women to have abortions. Medical experts arrived from foreign countries. The babies of those who had crossed the fourth month of pregnancy were allowed to be born. Mother Teresa was happy. An independent country was partially absolved of the guilt of foeticide. Six nurses from her charity home had gone with incubators and announced on landing at Kurmitola Airport, "We have come to save the war-babies." Under instructions from the nurses or with their help, the mothers-to-be combed their hair, braiding it tightly, washed themselves and wore clean clothes before the night of the delivery. They then spent a sleepless night that was different and nuanced from the nights during the war. The next day, because of the physical torture, hunger and malnutrition they'd lived through, the fear and anxiety about the future, it was not surprising if they had prolonged and complicated labour. After delivery, even before their tight braids had a chance to become loosened, the babies were packed off abroad for adoption. Perhaps the next day the newspaper readers would see a photograph of a nurse with a baby in her arms and an airplane about to take off. That was all.

The former social worker tells Mukti, "It wasn't as easy as you think. The girls would cry and scream. Sometimes we'd have to drug the mother to get the babies away from them. These infants could not be kept in the country – they were Pakistani bastards. If some foreign country offered, then we would give the babies to them for adoption. So most of the babies have gone to Canada. Many have also gone to Scandinavian countries." She brings her lips close to Mukti's ears and confides, "Those mullahs, they would phone and say that those babies cannot be sent abroad. They'll all be converted to Christianity. Those mullahs weren't part of anything good. Maybe they'd spent the nine months as Razakars."

This social worker had warned the Razakars by sending

them anonymous letters and leaflets. The boys of the Mukti Bahini would send her notes by hand, "Khalamma, winter is around the corner. Please send us fifty black pullovers." She would immediately begin knitting pullovers suitable for guerrilla warfare. During the war, the military would come suddenly, they would take away someone, kill someone else. In spite of such disruptions, she managed to finish a dozen pullovers. But not one could be used. The war was suddenly over by the time winter came.

These young men from the Mukti Bahini brought information about the women kept in bunkers, in army recreation centres, in storehouses. The women were weak, sickly, and helpless. To rescue them one needed cars, houses to keep them, hospitals to treat them. Slowly, all the arrangements were made. But there was confusion and one did not know what the other was doing. Another social worker tells Mukti, "The work was being done on an ad hoc basis then. We were the ones doing it but none of us knew what the others were doing." And that is why, twenty-eight years after the war, despite extensive interviews with several social workers and substantial cut and paste jobs with the interviews, Mukti was still unable to construct a full length chapter under the heading 'The Birangana Office'. The long process from rescuing the women to rehabilitating them was encapsulated in some people's minds, some paper cuttings, and some disconnected incidents.

Till just before the abortion, Mariam retained control over herself. But she couldn't afterwards, because then the matter became clinical. By that time, the foreign doctors, nurses, and volunteers had arrived in Dhaka and started their work. In the white house on Road No. 3 in Dhanmondi, which became quite well-known in those days as the Birangana Office, an average of a hundred abortions and deliveries would take place daily along with the necessary treatment. The women had two destinations after their hospital stay was over. Either they would return to their former addresses or they would take shelter at New Eskaton Road. There were two houses there facing each other – one was for training, the other was a hostel. Only women whose former addresses had not been found stayed in the hostel. Or even if their address had been found, the father would come and say, "Please wait a couple of days, my girl. I will come back later to take you home." Later no father or brother came to take the girl back. After some time, it wasn't only the war-affected women or Biranganas who stayed in the hostel, but also needy women and orphaned children.

"Those who could not feed their children, those who had too many children, would come to the rehabilitation centre in the darkness of night and abandon the child." Mukti was told this by Bokul Begum, the then resident of the rehabilitation centre and now a minor actress in the Bangla film industry. From 1972 to 1974, for two years she has taken turns to cook at the rehabilitation centre for one week and bathe the orphaned children the next week. Mukti will listen to Bokul's story another day. She gives interviews for two days running for a fee of fifty taka per day, the same rate as wages at the Film Development Corporation.

A month after the news about Montu being missing was printed, Mariam volunteered her address to the authorities. Father: Kafiluddin Ahmed, Village: Fultali, P.O.: Saharpar. And she added that this was Montu's address, not hers. Montu, who had been missing since April, 1971 and whom the parents and the two younger sisters eagerly awaited.

The delayed case history of Mariam began to be documented then for the first time. The work was done by Baby, who was the same age as Mariam and whose husband was killed in the war. Baby remembers Mariam because her statement was unprecedented. That is why she spoiled many forms while writing it down. And she was used to filling in hundreds of forms every day without having to scratch out any information. She does not remember the names and addresses of those women, let alone their appearance. "It was a cruel time," Baby tells Mukti sitting on the opposite side of the glass-topped desk, "I used to be afraid to look at my own reflection in the mirror."

This was her desk in her office. The wrinkled skin of Baby, now over fifty, is reflected in the glass of the table where the passport size photograph of a young man can be seen. "Whose photo is this?" The moment Mukti asks the question, she feels that she has made a mistake, has put a dollop of ghee on a flaming fire. Baby sings a line from a Bangla song, 'Remembrance is painful.' Although a little tuneless, her singing is touched with melancholy. Her second husband does not want a single memento of the first husband lingering in any corner of their home. So the first husband has taken shelter under the glass of her office table. Baby chirps like a bird, "My feelings are like caged birds so I have to hide them here." In the office, there is the first husband, the moment she enters home she is in the clutches of her second husband. "This country and I are in the same shoes. Our histories have to be hidden in two places." Baby supports the fight for freedom. She votes for the Awami League. She believes in the Bengali heritage of a thousand years. That is why her conversation has traces of poetry. When she explains hard reality in softened cadences, it is like water from a running stream that splashes out of the water pot. But she got the job at the rehabilitation centre because she had suffered losses in the war. She confesses this frankly to Mukti. And she has done whatever had been assigned to her, never shirked her duty.

A major campaign it was. The babies were being sent abroad. From outside came money, strange-looking people, and all kinds of foodstuff. Sewing machines arrived, as did blankets, milk, porridge and clothes. Rejected by husbands, driven out by fathers and brothers, with no future prospects, these empty-wombed women ran laundries, bakeries, sewed clothes, embroidered handkerchiefs and pillowcases. This was a rehabilitation project for a poor country. That was why the first thought was about how to fill empty stomachs. The hapless women left signs of their talent in whatever work they did. The paper flowers they created carried an extra brightness. The baby clothes they sewed were large – suitable for both thin and plump infants. They made things from easily available and inexpensive

material like bamboo and jute, products of everyday use that
helped the war-ravaged economy. Through their fine sewing
and handicrafts, they wanted to decorate the pride of Bengali
nationhood. On the first anniversary of the victory celebrations,
an exhibition was mounted with these priceless gift items, and
a glass thresher was displayed. A relic of their lost lives. An
image showed women threshing paddy and close by a few men
stood holding sheaves of rice. The delicacies they had cooked
increased business for the shops in Dhaka. On this day, whatever
was on offer at the local confectioners—homemade pickles,
jams, jellies, cakes, biscuits, sweetmeats, powdered spices and
other items of daily need, behind these were the Biranganas, the
brave women who survived the war, and their heart-rending toil.
Baby tells Mukti, "They gave a great deal to the nation, wringing
themselves out to the last drop. But history has not remembered
their contribution."

Mukti is stunned to hear all this from a salaried social worker.
It is a cruel irony of history that the sacrifice of Biranganas
that has remained largely obscured from the public gaze was
expressed in a few glass jars, some plastic packets and colourful
paper blossoms. The accomplished women of the city would
come in their cars, teach the women whatever special dishes they
knew in a very short time and immediately leave in the same cars.
This way the women became superb cooks free of cost. Food
cooked by them was even sent in lunch packets to the Secretariat
for the bureaucrats. Baby regrets, "The best housewife does not
get a home, the best cook does not get a husband." Otherwise,
why were they not able to make good matches, in spite of all the
governmental and non-governmental efforts?

At first, when they saw the advertisements in the papers, men
swooped down like kites and vultures. Baby herself opened
many applications. The time was April 1972. The girls were still
terrified of men. They were intensely reluctant even to talk, let
alone get married. They had been turned into stones devoid of
all emotion. And so another advertisement was issued to deter
the men who were applying to marry these girls.

"They had sad lives, born to misfortune," Baby laments. "As far as I can recall, one time ten girls were married and ten thousand taka spent on each. Bangabandhu's wife herself gave them household goods and appliances like sewing machines. The men who married for the dowry took the money but did not take the wife. Those who took home the wives, took them in order to humiliate them at every step."

Another social worker, whose obsession and profession was making women self-sufficient, says, "One girl, who was named after a flower, was married off by us. She has been happy in her marriage." Between 1972 and 1976, she arranged marriages for the girls or jobs for them with equal efficiency. If the girls faced any problems, they immediately rushed to her. "Aunty, what did you put as my age at the time of appointment? They say my time of retirement has come." She cannot remember what she had put down then in haste. Actually, worry and anxiety had made them look older than they were. A sixteen-year-old girl would look like a twenty-six-year old. During the silver jubilee of freedom, she tried enquiring about the girls. One woman said right at the gate, "Please don't come. Your arrival reminds me of too many things. It increases the pain in my heart." But she is doing all right with her two children. When she went to another house, she found that the woman had committed suicide ten years earlier. The husband had learned later on that the wife had lived in the enemy camp during wartime.

Baby tells Mukti, "This could have happened to me as well. It could have happened to my sister or my mother. We escaped that fate." But Baby had always felt a sense of bonding with the women who faced such humiliation that they made her forget the sorrow of her untimely widowhood. Even now, she tries to cover for them. At that time, Baby and her fellow social workers would write down the case histories and then tear off and burn the portions where the addresses were noted. They would do this so that the girls could settle down in their new homes without hassle and no one could harass them by raking up the past.

This was how people who supported the fight for freedom

thought. The people who came to power afterwards doused those bundles of case histories in petrol and torched them. "But was it right to burn such valuable records, such rich historical resource material?" Baby's opinion is that it had not been right to burn the case histories, but neither is it right to search for the women with a fine tooth comb in the name of history. Baby says, "They are not waiting to see what you'll do or won't do. They have accepted their fate and there is no space for experiments and investigation."

Mukti still wants Mariam's address from Baby. The address was burned. Yet Baby is filled with wonder how she remembered the address after so many years. But then no one has control over one's mind. She swears Mukti to secrecy and poses tough conditions. And then they enter into an unwritten agreement.

B: The address has to be kept secret.
M: Yes, even her name will not be disclosed.
B: You cannot turn her into an object of ridicule.
M: No, and there will be no distortion of the facts.
B: You will not write sensational articles about her in newspapers or journals.
M: No, that will not be done. Neither will there be any news reports or columns on her.
B: You cannot produce a TV play.
M: Nor will I produce full length or short feature films.
B: You cannot reproduce photographs.
M: Neither black and white nor coloured photographs.
B: It's a difficult job.
M: Yes, very difficult.

The conditions are verbal. So, Mukti is communicating them to Mariam orally. Mariam pooh-poohs them straightaway. Someone whom she has not met for the last twenty-eight years and whose face she cannot remember is in no position to make such conditions on her behalf. But like Baby, Mariam says, "That was a time when I was scared of looking at my own face in the mirror." Besides, Mariam felt like swapping her face and her body with someone else. But who would agree to it? Even a needy woman like Baby, who lost her husband during the war, even she would not agree to it. Not only is a widow's garb white, her body has no blot, something which Mariam did not possess. One day, when a rickshaw puller called the Dhanmondi house the Birangana Office, the sky fell on the social workers. They tried to escape whichever way they could. Then they set about trying to prove that they were not Biranganas. But how could that be done? The Biranganas had not been awarded any medals, so they could not push aside the sari ends and show their bare necks saying, "Look at my neck, it's bare. There is no medal. I am no Birangana." But for the sake of employment, they had to come to this office everyday. The rickshaw is the only vehicle if one does not have a car. Mariam tells Mukti with unbearable bitterness, "The title Birangana was like a venomous insect or some communicable disease. As if its touch will cause deadly sores, as if limbs will rot and fall off." But people would say effusively, "You are Biranganas. You are the pride of the nation. You are noble women." People like Baby wanted to be noble, some of them had even become the pride of the nation, but no one wanted to be a Birangana. It made Mariam sick.

The bit-part player Bokul has no such complaints like Mariam. Instead, someone who was a social worker at the time complains about Bokul. She is now retired. After the Bokul incident, she crossed her heart and vowed not to let Allah do good in this world through her hands. Because Bokul had almost taken away her all. Her marriage would have broken up had not her colleagues come forward to help. "One should not help people. Once their troubles are over, they strike back," the old lady says to Mukti from her own experience.

Bokul had no place to go. Her heart was not in the sewing and embroidery at the rehabilitation centre. Once, on her younger son's birthday, she had invited Bokul to help out a bit at the party. Bokul had a marvellous time, as if the birthday was hers, not of the son of this house. She said, "Auntie, you have such a lovely home. I wish I could stay here." The hostess smiled at the praise, "You silly girl. Can one have everything one wants?" But in her own heart, she thought of other possibilities. Her cook was getting old. His eyesight was failing. He added dead cockroaches to the curry mistaking them for cinnamon. It might not be such a bad idea for Bokul to stay on. So Bokul came to stay. She cooked rather well. The master of the house was full of praise for her cooking. When he returned from work every day, he would bring for her powder, cream, or perfume. When the wife expressed resentment, he would say, "If we had a daughter, would you not have given her this stuff? Let us think of her as our daughter." There was no reply to this.

Actually, Bokul was like their daughter. When they had guests, both husband and wife would introduce her as their daughter. The girl would also chirp like a bird, calling them Abba and Amma. But not even a year had passed before Bokul got pregnant. "Tell me who has brought this calamity on you? I'll make him marry you this very moment." She thought of her drivers Matin or Sadiq. When she forced her, Bokul said, "Abba." Fortunately when she was grilled by her colleagues at the rehabilitation centre, she had fingered the driver Sadiq. They dismissed the old driver and appointed a new one. But if her husband's name was besmirched in public, what would she have done? This happened four years after the war. The foreign doctors had left much earlier. The term for the special ordinance was over by then. They had a lot of trouble in arranging an abortion for Bokul.

Mukti is surprised. Such a big incident and yet Bokul Begum remembers none of it. She says, "Are you talking of the film *Pita Putri?*" In that film, she had a similar role. The film ended with the scene of her being driven out of the Bibi Sahiba's house after the abortion. In her youth, Bokul had played many such minor characters. Today, she doesn't remember many of them. If she thinks of one story, she remembers another. Back then was a high time for her. She had good looks, a slim figure. Once while acting the part of the best friend of the actress Shabana, the major share of dancing and running around fell on her. In the film, Bokul introduced the heroine to cigarettes, she taught her judo and karate so she could be on an equal footing with men. And then who got to marry the rich hero in the film? Why, cigarette-smoking Shabana, of course, and not unlucky Bokul, who had a miserable life from birth. This saddened her. She could not sleep well at night after the acting was over. Her pillow would be wet with her tears. She would think films were the most unjust place in the world. When the stomach is full, people think about many things, worry about them. At that time, she had youth and money. Now, she gets a call very rarely and that too for a grandmother's part. She sits the whole day at the studio, her back aching. At the end of the day, the young manager comes over and says, "Hey, Bokuli, nothing doing today. Swing by tomorrow." These days it's all work for daily wages. So she has to return home empty-handed. Empty hands mean an empty stomach.

"Why don't you find some other work?" Mukti's question annoys Bokul. She snaps back, "Everyone says do some work, find work. Is there a dearth of work? I can put on a torn blouse and petticoat and beg in the streets. I have no problem with that. The issue is honour. If a Birangana's honour is not protected, what will happen to the nation's honour?"

"So which film were you playing the Birangana bit in?"

Bokul smiles and shoots back, "It's the film called Life."

"And you haven't forgotten this one?"

"Silly girl, can one forget even if one wants to? Some memories remain. All is not wiped out."

The scene that was not from a film but which Bokul Begum has been unable to forget for the last 29 years took only fifteen minutes to happen. She no longer remembers the date. It was a Monday. The military entered the house around ten in the morning. The moment she saw them in the yard, she covered her head down to her nose and ran inside. They kept saying in Urdu, "Don't be afraid, nothing will happen." They leapt on to the veranda in front of the cottage. One soldier stood guard in front of the room with raised bayonet. The other grabbed her and pulled her to the bed.

"What did the man look like?" Mukti sounds like a lawyer interrogating a raped woman. It jars on her ears. But she has no alternative. It's better to pose questions than to listen to lurid descriptions of the rape. Bokul twists her lips and says, "He was dark and skinny." She herself was delicate and slim with a dusky complexion. "Even now if I'm all dressed up, you won't be able to recognize me," Bokul tells Mukti proudly. In fifteen minutes, her world ended. In the next room, her mother-in-law sat on the prayer-mat with her two granddaughters. She did not even get the time to come to her help. The sentry at the door entered the room and broke the lock of the trunk and took her gold earrings. From the shelf on the wall, he removed the table-clock with the picture of a rooster. It was a gift to her eldest daughter from her grandfather on her birth. After pocketing the clock, the monster ripped the leather suitcase in two. He spat on her face before he left but did nothing else.

When her husband returned home, he started breaking and smashing things. His behaviour was no different from the soldiers'. Her parents-in-law would not eat food cooked by her. Lying on her lonely bed in the kitchen, she had nightmares that she was fleeing the soldiers, from this neighbourhood to that to somewhere else. No one was giving her shelter. Then somehow the country became free. A distant uncle heard about her and rushed to her side. Appeals to her in-laws did not help. They kept her two daughters. Bakul asked the forgiveness of her parents-in-law and left her husband's home forever to come to Dhaka. It was towards the end of March, 1972 that her abortion took place in the Road No. 3 house in Dhanmondi.

Mariam was still there. She was all right if you discounted some minor ailments. But she was not interested in learning sewing, typing or cooking. In justification, she tells Mukti, "These skills needs concentration and patience like a housewife." At the time she did not possess these. Her past was a horror, her future uncertain. Montu's existence was limited to an illustrated news item in the papers. There was no response from Kafiluddin Ahmed in spite of a letter. In this time of trouble, her only acquaintance from the past was Shobha Rani, her companion from the military camp. Shobha Rani was to become mother of a child of the invaders. The night before delivery, Mariam parted her hair in two and plaited it neatly. A widow's first child. It was also probably her last chance. Mariam was only twenty-two years old. When she would marry and have a baby, someone, if not Shobha Rani then someone else, would be by her side, would comb and plait her hair. Shobha Rani said excitedly, "Oh! Mary Di, how hot it is." Mariam tenderly patted her neck and face with talcum powder. In the labour room, she bore down on the doctor's orders and her moans were all mixed up with tears and sweat, turning the powder on her skin into mud. The mother-to-be laughed sometimes, sometimes she cried. The whole night she fought against a conspiracy. At pre-dawn, her high stomach slowly collapsed and from between her legs emerged the lamp to light Bimal Das's family lineage. In the Hindu home, a lamp would once again be lit.

Four days before Kafiluddin Ahmed and his family arrived in Dhaka, Shobha Rani's mother-in-law Surabala made enquiries and reached the Birangana office. She could not wait a minute longer after receiving the letter from the rehabilitation centre. She made a bundle of some pressed rice and jaggery and came to Dhaka. What Shobha Rani had dreamed of had come true. But where was Anuradha? She had disappeared at the time the grenade had exploded. The attackers had not sent her back to the women's prison room. Shobha Rani was there till independence. What had happened to the girl? Perhaps, like Mariam, some other officer had marked her 'dangerous' on her report and confined her. Had Anuradha been able to leave for Pakistan? Mariam suddenly remembered Major Ishtiaque. She lacked self-confidence. That is why she thought it was not befitting to go to Lahore with a baby in her womb. She would have lost out to the Punjabi lady with her lips painted pink and her eyebrows finely drawn. Alluring eyes and enchanting beauty are the special treasures of Bengal. It evolves and declines within this land itself. Elsewhere, it does not reach its target. If Anuradha had gone there with her myopic, fish-like eyes, what was she doing there now?

Mariam felt bereft when Shobha Rani left with her mother-in-law Surabala and her son in her lap. The emptiness of her womb engulfed her. In response to letters dispatched the same day, Surabala had come and fetched her daughter-in-law and grandson, but Kafiluddin Ahmed had not turned up. The heir to the family was all, a daughter alive was nothing, even after such a major war. Millions of people had died, how many babies had been born of the Biranganas in the various medical facilities? Had it been so necessary to pack them off abroad, couldn't the liberated country have functioned without having done this? Were they only children of the treacherous Pakistanis, not of Bengali mothers as well? All the poking and the prodding had injured Mariam's womb, Major Ishtiaque had returned with the same unscathed body with which he had come. There was not even a small bruise anywhere. Only his route had changed between his coming and going. Arrival: Pakistan-Bangladesh via Sri Lanka. Exit: Bangladesh-Pakistan via India. In between, how many people were killed, how many women were tortured and oppressed, how many homes were burned, how many bridges and culverts were blown up, Mariam would ask everyone and count the numbers on her fingers. In the mornings, she had no problems counting, but by afternoon she lost track. The night was spent in a morphine-haze. The next day, the numbers turned into wriggling snakes. On the third day, the doctor diagnosed her illness – epilepsy psychosis. The symptoms were loss of sleep, lack of appetite, fainting fits, running around and restlessness. On the fourth day, Kafiluddin identified his daughter. He told the authorities that insanity was their family illness. It had no connection to the war. Mary's grandmother had also been temperamental and the granddaughter had once left home for no good reason saying that she was going to a movie. Before March 25, when everyone was fleeing to the villages, she had sent her brother home to Fultali and stayed back alone in the house at Rayer Bazar. Were these not signs of mental instability?

The only reason that Kafiluddin aired these family secrets was that he wanted to take his daughter away from this place as soon as possible, attaching her with a shady reputation — as per Golam Mostofa's suggestion. Even so, Mariam had to remain for a week under the doctor's treatment.

TWO

XVIII

An Ideal Museum

The reason for the delay in Mariam's parents' arrival in Dhaka was Kafiluddin Ahmed's deliberations. It would not be right to bring her to the village, nor would it be judicious to leave her at the Birangana office. The house at Rayer Bazar, he had heard, was not habitable. Where then? He sought the help of his regular adviser Golam Mostofa. Although the state of his cunning brother-in-law's affairs was not as sound as before. According to the newspapers, some four thousand Pakistani agents had been arrested within eight weeks of victory. The Mukti Bahini would capture Golam Mostofa one day and release him the next. He was about to lose his assets and property. Out of his three houses in Dhaka, two were in the possession of alleged freedom fighters. He was lying low in the three-roomed house at Maghbazar, having sent his sons and daughters elsewhere. It was at this time that he received a letter from Kafiluddin Ahmed saying, "Dear Mostofa, My friend in need. I don't know if you know but my disobedient daughter is now at the rehabilitation centre. What do I do with her, where can I take her?"

Biranganas! Pride of the nation. There was a lot of hoopla about them. Not only were Bangladeshis making a song and dance about them, but the foreigners were making much of them as well. If his freedom fighter nephew had been alive, Golam Mostofa would not have been in such dire straits. Since he had not returned four months after freedom, would he return at all? If one had a freedom fighter in the family, then one could achieve the impossible these days. He had fathered three bastards. Not one of them was of any use. For nine months, they lazed around in their beds roosting on the eggs of bed bugs and helping to increase their numbers. During interludes, they bet on cards. Would Pakistan lose, would India win? As if it was a cricket match and offered the same kind of fun. If at least one of them had joined the war and been martyred, he could have been the lucky father of a Bir Bikram (BB), the mighty brave, or Bir Pratik (BP), symbol of bravery. Who would then dare to take over his property? Anyway, at least the niece was still left. She was a Birangana, nation's pride. Golam Mostofa hatched a plan. He wrote to Kafiluddin Ahmed, "Dulabhai, your luck is bad. I do not know for what sin Allah has displayed His annoyance. All is His graciousness, we are just here to carry out His orders. But He who sends us problems also sends solutions. Please immediately come to Dhaka with my sister. No matter what my situation, my door is always open to your children. Your servant, Golam Mostofa."

Kafiluddin Ahmed folded the letter and placed it in a trunk. He asked his wife to prepare for travel. Monowara Begum was completely unaware of what was happening. The correspondence between the brothers-in-law had been kept a secret from her. She thought it was some news of Montu, which could only be bad. If he was well, he would have returned home on his own. Montu, her son. For the last one year he had only appeared in her dreams. The moment she woke up, he vanished. During the day, he was submerged within the sea of her eyes, only to float in distant waters at night. He swam, flailing his arms and legs but he could not be touched. He had no definite form. Every day he was different, just as it had been when he was in her womb. This way through her dreams, Montu returned once more to her womb.

After Montu was conceived, Monowara Begum desperately wanted a son. Having delivered two stillborn sons, she gave birth to Mary after ten years of marriage. The girl was a happy, healthy baby. But that pleased no one. The way everyone behaved, it seemed as if it was better to be the mother of stillborn sons. Before Montu came she wore many amulets and made offerings before the graves of holy men. The only boy in the family. She brought him up with such tender care, as if he would be bitten by ants if put on the ground or bitten by snakes if she took him in the water. Compared to Mary's obstinacy, he was quiet and well-behaved even though he was a boy. He would not cry if he was not fed. He did everything he was told. Was it this same boy who nurtured such fire within? That he went off to war without telling his mother? More than the loss of her son, the pain caused by the betrayal of trust seemed more terrible. It was as if a part of her own body had broken faith with the rest of her body. Monowara Begum burst into loud sobs.

Kafiluddin Ahmed could no longer bear such scenes. During the whole period of war, a brick wall had risen between husband and wife because of his efforts to shield the son for fear of Pak soldiers and to hide the daughter for fear of society. The plaster of that wall had now begun to crumble and the ugly brickwork revealed. What would happen to them? How would they spend the rest of their lives? Did Allah have anything more to offer from which they would find sustenance? The only son was gone. It would have been better if the daughter had not lived, instead of surviving like this. But he could not give her up either. After all, Kafiluddin Ahmed was her father. He believed like other fathers that because he had brought the children into the world, he would protect them with all his might and to the last of his ability. Such a big war and he so helpless. He could not save his children. People forget that a person who they have not seen weeping can weep. Their heartbroken wails sound like satiric laughter. Monowara Begum did not realize at first what was happening and was startled. The brick wall between them was breaking down. This man of stone, who had not approved of his wife's shedding tears in secret for the last year, could be seen melting before Monowara Begum's very eyes. Oh God! Was there anyone so hard-hearted in the world who would not want to die rather than see the face of a dead child? Her husband was really a living corpse. He had been acting the role of a living being in fear of Pakistani soldiers. Monowara Begum's secret tears no longer remained hidden. Loud cries rise from both their throats in public.

Holding on to the door, the younger twin daughters, Ratna and Chhanda were sobbing spasmodically. Their cheeks and chins were smeared with tears and dirt from their hands. Fultali villagers thronged their yard. A whole flock of crows flew over Sundari's wetlands and came cawing. It had been four months since the country had been liberated. The reckoning of who was alive and who was dead was over. Although Montu's act had been kept hidden for nine months for fear of the Pakistani soldiers, it had now been revealed. The missing announcement printed in the newspapers had made it known all over. Only Mary remained veiled behind a mysterious curtain. But her story was not unknown to villagers. Now they gathered in the yard to simply verify what had been a rumour till now. The joint mourning by husband and wife confirmed what they had known. When Kafiluddin Ahmed left for Dhaka with his family, he was like a beggar on the streets having lost the veil of secrecy. He was impoverished, stripped of his self-respect. In this state, he crossed the Sundari marshlands with his family, boarded the bus pushing through the crowds, then crossed the river on a ferry under a broken bridge, then taking a rickshaw, a ferry and a bus again, they finally reached Dhaka. There lived Golam Mostofa, his friend till death, who could return his self-respect.

Golam Mostofa was ready for him.

Although the Maghbazar house did not have the earlier spit and polish, although the curtains were torn, the table cloths and pillowcases soiled, and in the kitchen foul-smelling ration rice was cooking, Golam Mostofa welcomed them with his ever-smiling face. Monowara Begum clung to her brother and cried till she had no more tears left. She had sent the son and daughter to study in Dhaka on his advice. Sometimes she was blaming fate for her misfortune, at other times she was holding Golam Mostofa responsible. Kafiluddin's behaviour was different. It was as if he had re-entered the safety of his mother's womb. Kafiluddin needed just such a calm, steadfast man who stood before him and who was not shaken one bit by all the accusations and embarrassments. But it did seem that his earlier enterprise and alertness had ebbed a little. He was not seen to go out of the house even once during the day. He appeared to have no friends. His only guide seemed to be the printed words on the newspaper. He pulled out a few sheets from the piles of newspapers to show Kafiluddin Ahmed. Money and people were arriving from abroad for the rehabilitation and treatment of girls like Mary. After the girls recovered their health, they would be trained for jobs. There was no dearth of money. They would be given employment. If they wanted, they could start a business. But was that all in life? One had also to think of marriage. Even the government was thinking of it. Marriage advertisements were being published in newspapers. Golam Mostofa held the sheet before his brother-in-law, "Dulabhai, look at this."

Kafiluddin Ahmed almost fainted. Such praise for the government, had his brother-in-law changed sides once again? Should he look at the newspaper or at his brother-in-law? He concentrated on the newspaper since it concerned the future of his daughter. Golam Mostofa felt that all those who were coming forward to marry the Biranganas were not good people, they were motivated by self-interest. No matter how much the government claimed that they were patriots, they were not marrying for their ideals. Everyone had some kind of a family, a society. Society would not keep quiet and even if it did, then for how long? Even before the tragedies of war were forgotten, society would voice its protests. Golam Mostofa glanced around to see if his wife or older sister were anywhere near, "Besides, Dulabhai, you are a man and so am I. Would you marry one of them or would I?" Seeing Kafiluddin Ahmed embarrassed and sorrowful, he cackled. A fine high-pitched sound also emerged. Laughing by himself double-voiced, Golam Mostofa told his older sister's husband, "Yesterday, Dulabhai, I showed the paper to Saju and asked him whether he wanted to marry one of them. Immediately, the boy's face became pale."

On hearing his brother-in-law, Kafiluddin Ahmed's face also turned ashen. He had come to Dhaka with such hopes. He had not come to take his daughter back home. What would he do if he took her back? Use her as a doorpost? He had come to settle her properly. If even the idiot Saju was averse to marrying a Birangana, then what about others?

This is exactly what Golam Mostofa wanted. He pushed Kafiluddin Ahmed into deep waters, and threw out the bait of a marriage between Mary and Saju in order to bring him back to firm ground. Dulabhai now had no alternative but to bite the bait in order to come to land. If a man who married a Birangana was recognized by the state as a patriot, then could the groom's father be treated as a Razakar? He was a patriot as well. But aloud what he said was that he had no requirements, no demands from this marriage. He wanted none of the sewing machines, the vessels and utensils announced as gifts by the government. He may be in an uncomfortable position at the moment but he could still afford to buy Mary ten sewing machines. It was the infinite grace of the All Merciful that Saju loved Mary from childhood. He may have been mentally challenged but there was no dearth of love. He would have no objections to the marriage.

A drooling face floats before Kafiluddin Ahmed's eyes, an idiotic appearance, brainless. A marriage proposal for his graduate daughter with this abnormal creature? At any other time, he would have flattened his brother-in-law's big mouth with a resounding slap. But Allah had destroyed him. If his son had been alive, he would have taken revenge for this, if not today, then some other time. But Kafiluddin no longer had a future. The girl was also star-crossed. What would he do with her? How would he face Fultali village on his return? That was his biggest fear. Finally, exhausted by his brother-in-law's insistence, he said, "Let me talk to your older sister. After all, Mary's also her daughter. Isn't she?"

Goodness gracious! The excuse sounded so strange. It was most unlikely that Kafiluddin Ahmed had consulted his wife on any matter ever before. Who knows when he'd claim that even the daughter's consent was needed along with the mother's! In which book had it been written that along with the country's independence, women would also be liberated? It was Golam Mostofa who scanned through three or four newspapers daily. Carefully, he read between the lines. All these bastard children of the soldiers who were being shipped abroad in instalments, had anyone taken their mothers' consent? Even when the mothers were Biranganas, they were mothers after all. Which mother would agree to her infant being snatched away from her arms to be sent abroad forever? Kafiluddin Ahmed was no greenhorn that he would need to consult his wife. He was just looking for an excuse because he could not swallow Saju's name as the groom. He was buying time. Just in case, by a stroke of good luck, a groom from a good family appeared. Golam Mostofa knew his brother-in-law well. On the surface, he was simple and straightforward but inside he was convoluted like the curls of a jalebi. However, what was important was that such decisions should not be delayed. So Golam Mostofa said, "Leave it to me to get my sister to agree. After all, Saju is her nephew also, isn't he?"

This was not merely a war of words. The reality was very hard, especially for parents whose only son was missing and whose daughter was a Birangana. Through the whole night Monowara Begum shared with her husband a soiled pillow, tears and thoughts like these. After a long time, the man was openly sharing her grief. They were crying together, sighing together, talking with each other. Besides her brother was sleeping in the next room. There was something comforting about his loud snores. Monowara Begum thought that no matter how painful life was, she was not a lonely unfortunate person. That night, under the same roof, she had her husband and her brother.

The next day, she would be able to see her daughter who had been lost. In the midst of all the grief, something remained with people – a night of tears, a night of sharing a pillow and pain, a night of waiting, a sleepless night. A mere three months later Monowara Begum would think that such a night had never come in her life. And if it had, it had been a dream. She had never had a husband or a brother. The only truth was that she had lost her son. And she was not capable of bearing another son.

The mishaps started occurring from the next morning. Golam Mostofa dismissed the idea of his sister's going to the Birangana office. His excuse was that people suspected any woman seen on Road No. 3 of Dhanmondi. They took her to be a Birangana no matter what age she was. So in the end Kafiluddin went by himself. Golam Mostofa kept in the background, hiding in the paan kiosk behind the Science laboratory. But from there he was controlling each and every move. The first time that he saw Kafiluddin coming back alone to the head of the Dhanmondi Road, he went into a flaming rage. The father had gone to bring home his daughter. Who were they, in-laws or what, to say no? Who were they to keep her back? He was not even moved to hear of Mary's mental breakdown. He told his brother-in-law, "Why blame the war if there was insanity in the family?" What can the doctors do in this condition? Whatever had to be done, had to be done by the parents. The second time around Kafiluddin Ahmed returned to say that Mary would be released after a week or so. Golam Mostofa's bag of tricks was empty. He could think of no new ruse. He needed some privacy to think out a new strategy. It was not possible to do this standing on the road. Who knew who would spot them there. The Hindus were returning from India in droves. Golam Mostofa had drawn a blank in his activities during wartime. Whatever he had done, he had done in the countryside. Like looting and pillaging the homes of the Hindus, threatening and forcing them to leave Pakistan and go to Hindustan with their entire family. His nervousness was not about the Hindus themselves, but their land and property. He would not be free of danger unless he could drive out the accursed infidel Hindus entirely. Meanwhile, he had not touched a Muslim even with a stick for the last nine months. In fact, he had cleverly saved a few from being shot. That is why if one group of Mukti fighters arrested him, another group would get him released. This game had been going on for the last four months. But even then ill-luck never came with prior warning. So when Kafiluddin Ahmed wanted to check out his house at Rayer Bazar, he left him on the road and hurried home.

Kafiluddin Ahmed paced up and down on the lane in front of the house and yet he could not recognize his own house. The clump of bamboos that could have been a signpost had disappeared. The address in white lettering on the black gate had also been wiped out. The head of the tubewell in the yard was broken. The fence of bamboo strips had been razed to the ground. When a man's sole assets in life, his children and land, go, then what remains of his life? While he was in the village, he had heard from various people about the condition of his establishment in the city. But he had not thought that he would not be able to find the house, that it would vanish. Just as he was cursing his luck, thinking of returning to his brother-in-law's home, a man quickly came out of the house next door. He was a well-wisher. He was acquainted with Kafiluddin Ahmed from the time that the house was being built but they had not met for a while after that. The war had changed people's appearance so much that even one's near and dear ones seemed to have become strangers. But the man was neighbourly. He guided Kafiluddin Ahmed to his gate. But he stood outside for fear of mines. So the owner of the house also felt nervous about entering. He too stood by his neighbour on the road.

The house had been transformed into a recreation centre for the Pakistani army almost the entire duration of the war. The bamboos were slashed down at that time for fear of the Mukti Fauj. The address written in Bengali was also erased at the time and in its place a new signboard was put up on which was written in Urdu – Harem. All this was thanks to Haji Shaheb's wonderful achievements. But the neighbour was deeply grateful that he had saved the lives and properties of people in the neighbourhood. Kafiluddin Ahmed was annoyed that in the process his property was damaged. If everyone made excuses for Razakars in this way, then no matter how many agents and Razakars the government arrested, how would they be tried? One needed witnesses and evidence to prove guilt, didn't one? The neighbour was sympathetic to Kafiluddin Ahmed but did not share the same opinion on the damages to his property. Because Haji Shaheb had done nothing wrong in clearing the bamboo grove. Such wilderness was not befitting a city. Kafiluddin Ahmed hung down his head in embarrassment as if he had committed a worse crime than the Razakars by allowing the bamboo to grow in an unsuitable place. The neighbour's eagerness increased at his reaction. Besides, he said, the Haji had spent money to make proper sanitary arrangements for his latrine. One must also take that into account. But the soldiers had planted mines before leaving and the head of the tubewell disappeared after liberation. Then the house became a camp for the guerrilla fighters. They pulled out the Urdu signboard and burned it. The military broke up the doors and windows and burned the wood to cook biryani. One of the Haji's camp followers took away the beds, chairs, tables, clothes rack and the tin roofing in broad daylight. At night, a petty burglar stole the utensils, books and notebooks to sell by weight. A guerrilla fighter's leg was injured when a mine blew off. A foreign doctor amputated his leg when he was taken to the hospital. The well was filled up and sealed because it was full of the hair and bones of women. The Indian army came to remove the mines and took them away.

The neighbour paused for rest. Kafiluddin Ahmed had lost track of what damage had been done by whom. Even if some one had itemized it ten times like this, he would not remember. Before them stood a skeleton of a house, a country, a subcontinent. It could be a solid witness to the Partition and destructions of 1971 as well as the shifts in power balances. In fact it could become an ideal museum, a wonderful sight-seeing spot for tourists, curious populace from the countryside and lovers. For a low-priced ticket, they could enter the museum where a signboard of the archaeological department would hang. On it would be written: This house belonged to Kafiluddin Ahmed, Village: Fultali, P.O.: Saharpar. He bought the five cottahs of land dirt cheap from a Hindu called Nikhil Chandra Saha in the year of the India-Pakistan war and built a house like the one he had in his village. In it lived his son Montu and daughter Mary. They were both college students. Montu became a martyr in the 1971 war. Mary, a.k.a. Mariam, became a Birangana. The house was occupied by the Pakistani invaders and the Mukti Bahini and finally returned to the possession of the original owner Kafiluddin Ahmed in April, 1972. The museum authorities had preserved the house, without any change whatsoever, in the state that he handed it over.

Mariam was the first visitor. She entered the house in a trance. She went in through the black gate and stepped on the scattered bricks to avoid the muddy path. She pressed the hand pump and gulped down water from the tubewell. She rested for a while in the shade of the bamboo grove and then walked to her room passing by Montu's room. She then lay down on the same bed from which she had left with the people of the neighbourhood on the morning of March 27 when the curfew was lifted. After a very long time, she was in her own bed, in her own room. The moment she rested her head on the pillow, accumulated sleep consumed her.

What had been happening for the last two days at the Maghbazar house had prevented Mariam from sleeping even after she took sleeping pills. In the next room, several rounds of discussions took place between Kafiluddin Ahmed and Golam Mostofa and mostly they broke down in anger. Mariam did not know the topic of discussion. Neither had anybody informed her of it. But even through the coils of sleep she sensed that a conspiracy was going on, an old conspiracy. They would force her into a marriage. The man who appeared dressed as a groom was no other than Saju. She woke up and sat up on bed with a start. Monowara Begum helped her to lie down again. Golam Mostofa's reticent wife Zulekha Bibi ran in with a glass of water. On the last occasion, the strength of demons filled Mariam's body. She rose from her bed, pushed Monowara Begum roughly aside, upset Zulekha Bibi's glass of water and threw open the door before walking out. Kafiluddin Ahmed tried to scare her by shouting of the land mines that were buried in the house at Rayer Bazar. It did not work. So what else could he do? He jumped onto another rickshaw and chased after his daughter.

The sight of the house filled Kafiluddin with spiritual thoughts. This residence was in space, a vast, floating space. It was just like his life. The sky and air could move freely through the open door frames and windows. The birds flew in and out. The sun's rays and rain fell directly from the sky. Mariam had spent all her strength and spirit in her short journey from Maghbazar to Rayer Bazar. When Kafiluddin Ahmed arrived, he saw his daughter lying curled up on the bare floor and sleeping in the roofless house open to the sky. Had his daughter gone mad? Could anyone but a lunatic sleep so soundly in a house which had neither roof, doors, gate nor boundary wall?

On one side, there was his daughter, on the other, his brother-in-law. Both of them were his near ones; both of them his enemy. In the tug of war between them, he was ready to hang himself. He could not look at the girl's eyes these days. As long as she was awake, her pupils moved restlessly like a top or burned like glowing coals. If you took a piece of paper or a bit of wood near it they would catch fire. They were the exact replica of Kafiluddin's beloved mother's eyes. Barring two or three months, she would remain mad for the rest of the year. During those times, she had countless accusations against the world. For instance she spent a whole afternoon blaming and abusing her father. Because on some occasion long ago, Kafiluddin Ahmed's grandfather had not allowed her to go out of the house to hear the lay of the Gazi. The rest of the day was spent in accusing and cursing her dead mother-in-law. The reason: the summer that the Gurkha soldiers arrived in the village to capture an accused murderer, she had not been allowed to visit her father's house. But it served them right: unable to find the accused, the Gurkha soldiers entered each home and mixed up all the stores of rice and dal. For the next six months, every villager had to eat khichari. The year of the famine in 1943, all the members of the family had eaten rice and left only the rice water for her. That sorrow surfaced at least once in the nine months of insanity in Kafiluddin Ahmed's Ammajan. She would go hungry that day. None of her children or grandchildren could coax or cajole her into eating that day. Her husband was a one-eyed mild-mannered man. He had had small pox and although the disease left him on his bed of banana leaves, it took away his vision from one eye. The vision in the other eye was also weakening. In this condition, all that Kafiluddin Ahmed's father, Salimuddin could do was tolerate his wife. But who would tolerate Mary except Saju?

Golam Mostofa could not quite believe that his brother-in-law Kafiluddin Ahmed was agreeable to the marriage. He wanted to call a Maulavi and get her to say the marriage vows while she was still in this drugged state. Later, they could erect awnings and play music through loudspeakers and celebrate the wedding. The chief guests would be Bangabandhu and his wife. If he could not make it because of his busy schedule, then his wife, Begum Mujib would certainly come. She was the foremost organizer of the Birangana weddings. This way, Golam Mostofa would let his countrymen know that he could still work wonders and was not ready to be written off. There would be photographs in the paper captioned 'Yet another Birangana wedding'. Begum Mujib would be seen personally handing over the bride. The groom was Sajed Mostofa, a.k.a., Saju. Father: Golam Mostofa. The bride was Mosammet Mariam Begum, daughter of Kafiluddin Ahmed.

Kafiluddin Ahmed had objections to the last sentence. He also deeply disagreed with all this drum-beating publicity. This way Golam Mostofa would inform everyone, even those who did not know so far what had happened. He disapproved of these plans. Golam Mostofa was also not prepared to budge.

How could the girl sleep in the next room when there was such a rumpus in the house?

The situation was such that no one agreed with the other, no one trusted anyone else. But on the surface, a sense of truce prevailed. Because Golam Mostofa quickly needed to be transformed from a Pakistani agent to a Bengali patriot. This way he could repossess the titles of the two houses that he had lost. And Kafiluddin Ahmed wanted quickly to be relieved from the responsibility of his daughter. So it was decided, that the wedding would be arranged only after Mary was fully conscious from the effects of her medicine. The news of the wedding could be published in the papers but no pictures could be printed. The meetings in the Maghbazar house would stop. And both sides would cease from creating a furore, at least for a while.

In such an apparently peaceful environment, Mary was brought from the Rayer Bazar house to the Maghbazar house and she was kept in a room locked from outside. But Golam Mostofa could not be trusted, especially in the matter of getting pictures published. Anyway, a news item was bad enough. People would connect the name and address with the appearance of the person. Kafiluddin Ahmed was not happy with the idea. But he did not express his reservations. Marriages involved bargaining. One needed a certain amount of secrecy and cover-ups which would not be possible if he continued to stay in Golam Mostofa's house. So, in order to consolidate his position, he quickly started on the repairs of the Rayer Bazar house.

Man proposes, but God disposes. Golam Mostofa was more correct in his assessment of the situation than Kafiluddin Ahmed. When Mariam came out of her drugged spell, all the plans and preparations for a wedding came to naught. The reason why Kafiluddin's blind father could not control his wife, was the very same reason the son could not control his daughter. Because, both of these women were mad.

XIX

Slashed Midriffs and Awakened Youth

Mariam walked out of the house and went straight to S.M. Hall. Everything looked the same as before, only the bullet holes in the walls were new. And Abed was no longer around. Suman was brushing his teeth. Seeing Mariam, he swallowed a mouthful of toothpaste. Someone wolf-whistled from the next room. Mariam laughed freely, the first time in quite a while. That surprised Suman even more. As he wiped his face with a dirty towel and buttoned up his shirt, he thought, how Abed Bhai had changed – like night turning into day. What should he tell this girl now – the truth or a lie? Why begin the day with a lie? Abed Bhai did not even recognize his roommate Suman any longer. And yet on the night of March 25, if he had not pushed up Abed's heavy body, he would not have been able to cross the boundary wall and escape. The military had entered the hall by then. Just one year and two months ago when all this happened. People forget everything so quickly, especially leaders. As a rank and file worker, he had a right to rebel.

Abed was now the head of a mercantile firm previously owned by a non-Bengali. In return for helping the former owner flee to Pakistan through India, he had married the man's exquisitely beautiful daughter. Meaning that after the war had been won, he had a whole kingdom and a princess as his share. Instant reward for liberating the country. But Suman and Montu had also gone to war. One of them was wiping his face with an unclean towel and the other had not returned. They had both been younger than Abed and had been his devoted disciples. Mariam startled Suman even further when she said that their relationship had been finished and done with even before the war. So she was not interested in Abed's personal life. She only wanted his address. She herself was now a Birangana. She gestured with her hand before Suman's gaping face and said, "I hope you know the meaning of Birangana. She is the pride of the nation, the pure and chaste woman of independent Bangladesh."

When she entered the tracery of shadows under the rain trees, she remembered a story from long ago. It was the story of a wonderful city of gardens and palaces. In that city lived a prince. He had a wife and a son but whether he enjoyed a happy life with them was not known. He had to go to war to such a land where lived women with long black hair and mesmerizing eyes. He fell in love with one of them but kept her imprisoned. He spoke to her of all that lay deep in his heart but when the war was done he went back to his own country. The story ended there. But some stories never end.

Abed's wife was a Pakistani. Could she be a Punjabi and was she from Lahore?

Mariam stood at the Palashi crossing waiting for a rickshaw. Suman walked her to the spot. He was more composed and sincere now. The cobbler that they had encountered on the first and last day of her meeting with Abed was not there. His spot was empty. The nearby slum was also gone. It had been burnt to ashes with all its sleeping residents on the night of March 25. Suman pointed towards the scorched land and said, "The cobbler lived there."

Accompanying her on the street was Suman not Abed. The cobbler and his slum had been burned down. Only Mariam was like the mythical phoenix who was indestructible. She had risen with a new body from the ashes and returned to her former life, her past address. This was the story of all people in all countries after a war. This story has the same title and had been written again and again, but still wars happened. As long as wars continued, such stories would continue to be written. But the time and the situation was not favourable to Mariam, she could not spare a moment to grieve for herself or mourn others.

Kafiluddin Ahmed awaited his daughter, a sharp boti in his hand. He was standing next to the black gate on which now his name and address had been painted with fresh ink. Only the clump of bamboos could not be grown overnight. The well near which bunches of wild flowers had blossomed after the first showers of the season was still filled up. Otherwise everything else was working. He was ready to kill his daughter with a single swipe if he saw her coming. Call it what you will: the qurbani of the Muslims or the animal sacrifice of the Hindus. Monowara Begum's words of warning – find your own way. If you survive, you will live, if you do not, you will die. We will not be there by your side or support you. Like the phoenix, Mariam was fending for herself. Even though she had a new lease of life, she was treading on familiar ground where old acquaintances were gone and those who remained had changed their positions. She was young for such a rebirth after a death – she was just twenty-two.

Although she had Abed's address, it took her till noon to locate his office. It was lunch break. Mariam sat by the gate and waited. Next to her was the smartly attired guard. But beneath his uniform, he was simply another man without a job. He offered his stool to Mariam and informed her that he had come from Abed's village and was a distant uncle. He had to address his nephew as Sir, as was the custom of the office. "The previous guard was a Bihari." The new guard conveyed that he had been killed by making a slicing movement across his throat with his index. Sir was a very good man and very helpful and he was saying this not just because he was a nephew. He ate the packed lunches that came from the Birangana office. He said, "Don't be contemptuous of them. They are your mothers and sisters. They have sacrificed their honour for the country." Not just because he is a nephew, but "Sir has no disgust. Otherwise could anyone eat meals cooked by those sluts?" Then Abed's distant uncle wanted to confide in her. He glanced toward the office, then turned towards Mariam, "The wife is a non-Bengali. He married her because of the war, but she can't cook rice and fish." He felt hot as he saw someone coming out of the office. He took off his cap and muttered to himself, "After all, it's new and therefore still warm." He then admired his own uniform, "The dress was personally bought by nephew, sorry, Sir." There seemed to be some similarities between Abed's distant uncle and Rameez Sheikh. If he were alive could he have been the guard at this office and she the Sahib's private secretary-cum-telephone operator? A war made many impossible things possible. Mariam's turn had come to be summoned to Sir's office. The guard put on his cap and saluted amateurishly, "Come again, Lady. I have no one to talk to. I feel suffocated." Rameez Sheikh used to say the same thing because of the thirty years of his life, ten had been spent in prison.

Mariam knew where she had come and to meet whom. Abed probably had not known who his visitor was. He sat down as quickly as he had risen to greet the visitor. He took a fraction of a minute to collect himself, but that time seemed to be an hour, a day, a whole year plus two more months. From the Palashi crossing to March 25, the training camp in India, the Liberation War, the surrender at the Race Course, a kingdom along with a princess, he had to run desperately to cover all of these incidents. When he stopped, Mariam was still standing, he had not yet asked her to sit. After she sat down, there was a loud explosion. If it were filled with explosives, instead of words, the well-decorated office would have been blown up. But Mariam was immovable. Day after day, she had seen clever, powerful, armed men stripping themselves naked, murdering, enjoying themselves sensually, loathing, loving—the past romance made no difference to her. She thought of her former lover as a callow young man. She felt his love and betrayal was like a light spring shower that after the summer months was washed away by the torrential monsoon rains. It was immaterial whether she forgave him or not. But Mariam needed a job now, and barring Abed, she did not know anyone in this big city who could give her a job. If Abed said that Mariam would be given a job in exchange for her pardon, she would happily forgive him. So in her identity of a Birangana, she had asked Abed for a job. To prove that she needed a job urgently, she described how Kafiluddin Ahmed had hid behind the black gate with a boti in his hand and how Monowara Begum had told her to fend for herself. She then told him that she would have applied for the post of gatekeeper for someone else but that was no longer necessary. The man had already died. And, of course, she saw that the post was no longer vacant. Apart from this, Abed did not ask about Montu, nor did Mariam volunteer any information. Her status as a Birangana should have been enough to secure her a job, what was the necessity of mentioning that she was the sister of a martyred freedom fighter? Abed himself was a freedom fighter. Moreover, he occupied a chair which had once belonged to thick-headed non-Bengalis who, in turn, had inspired him to fight. His side had won the war. He had managed to take possession of the chair. If Mariam did not get a job, should she fight against Abed?

Abed absorbed some of the words, some he did not grasp. After his initial surprise, he felt a sense of let-down, the girl seemed to feel no sorrow at having lost him. Instead of requesting him for a job, if she had slapped him twice, he would have felt better. His new-found power would have been worthwhile. It was not enough for a man to have money, assets, house, a beautiful wife – he needed more. One such thing was the person who had been treated and discarded like a bundle of rags on the street, for her to come like a bitch repeatedly to lick the feet of the man. This girl had not come like that. She had come on her own self-serving mission. But she wasn't like this before the war. The woman who talked of nothing but marriage in those days, how many men had she lain under that she now no longer sought a man, but looked desperately for a job? There was a certain whorishness even in her appearance. As if she had won the whole world. Birangana connoted a helpless, oppressed woman, whom people despised under the cover of pity. How had she acquired such courage that she'd been able to come to her ex-lover not to plead for his love, but to demand a job? And that not only for herself, but also for a dead man, who if he had been alive would have been the gate-keeper at Abed's office? There had to be a catch somewhere. But identifying it needed time and thought. Abed packed her off soon with the promise of a job.

Mariam did not get up from her chair immediately. She was overwhelmed by a host of doubts about getting a job. Abed could not be trusted. She continued sitting on the chair and said that Mariam was his ex-lover whom he had not married. It did not matter, but now that she needed a job so badly he could easily give her one. She would not bring up the topic of the dead man who, had he been alive, could easily have been a guard in his office. It was his duty to help a Birangana and a martyr, he who sat in the throne of power. If he did not do this, was Abed sure that this would not trigger off another war?

It would not be strange for Abed to have a pistol in his drawer. Some of the freedom fighters had surrendered their arms, but many had not. He could shoot her. He could call the police and tell them that the woman was an extortionist, a Pakistani spy or a CIA agent, who had been paid to take the life of a well-known Mukti Joddha. Before any of this could happen, Mariam got up from her chair and left the room unimpeded. The guard saluted and opened the gate for her – the same man in whose place she could have applied for Rameez Sheikh had he been alive.

The thrill of adventure did not last very long; just from Segunbagicha to Hatirpool. A one page leaflet, issued by the Newly Awakened Youth of Bangladesh, blew into Mariam's rickshaw. It carried the hair-raising headline 'Slashed Midriffs.' It gave women fifteen days' notice to discard shameless clothes. After that if women were seen on the streets wearing such clothes, unfortunate and unpleasant incidents could take place.

The Awakened Youth thought that "wearing blouses with slashed midriffs and without sleeves as well as wearing saris below the navel was vulgar." In an independent country, women would not be allowed to wear such clothes. Mariam was garbed in a long-sleeved blouse and a mill-made sari of unbleached cotton with a red border. They were clothes suited to a Birangana. At the rehabilitation centre, she had seen a few women wearing the kind of clothes that had been described. They had been the ones who had returned from India. The fashion must have originated there which five months after independence, the awakened youth of Bangladesh could not tolerate. Who were these awakened people really?

"Who else but wicked people. People who have nothing else to do but meddle in the business of others." Rina, Mariam's friend from college, was annoyed when she saw the leaflet. Only last month, she had had the tailor stitch half a dozen such blouses for her. All of them had not even been worn yet. Where could she wear them to? Her college term was over. The family had firmly spelled out that she would not be sent to university. If she wanted to study further, she could do so after her marriage. While crumpling the leaflet into a ball, her eyes went to the big bag that Mariam was carrying. This was not a new phenomenon. The gates of this house had been open to Rina's friends even before the war. Mariam had gone to her in this hope. It was only for a couple of nights or so. The moment she got a job she would leave. But she had to make up stories to tell each one.

For instance, she told a story to Rina. She had to repeat it when Rina's mother came out of the kitchen. The third time she had to recount it was when Rina's father returned from work. What was more was that next to Rina's home was an open space used for public meetings and speeches. Since evening, a public rally called by a leftist group had been going on. And so bits from the speeches got mixed up with Mary's concocted stories: *Comrade Lenin/* Her parents had spent an anxious time these nine months worrying about her. There was a military camp right next door/ *This is a golden opportunity for establishing socialism/*

They had not worried about Montu. If he had remained home, the military would have killed him. At least, he had been fighting for the country/ *If India was the midwife in the birth of a new nation, then its father was the Soviet Union. The new nation's identity should be known by the father's name*/ Montu did not return from the war. She had no other alternative but to search for a job. Her parents were shattered. They did not want her to come to Dhaka. She had practically to force her departure from Fultali/ *We will help the Mujib government wholeheartedly in building a socialist state. (Loud slogans and applause from the public who had lost all) Inquilab Zindabad. Your leader, our leader. Mujib-Indira-Kosygin. Long live the revolution.*

After the speeches had ended, Mariam went to sleep in Rina's room. The whole day she had talked and talked like a mad woman. She thought she would fall asleep counting how much of it was full of lies and how much true. Rina's whining complaints denied her that opportunity. The war, although it lasted only nine months, had seemed very long. And it was boring. Rina had taken to playing Ludo and Snakes and Ladders. Her two teen-aged brothers had taken to smoking bidi and hukkah. They were in their maternal uncle's house at Chandina where there were more Razakars than freedom fighters.

Again, the war! Mariam's head began booming with the noise of explosions. Culverts, school houses, buildings were breaking down there. By then, Rina had left the war and gone straight on to love. While her parents were going mad worrying about when the military would enter the village and take away the women, Rina was getting adept at how to cheat at the games. She was helped in this by a young boy who lived in the house next to her uncle's. In the beginning, he objected but later came forward to help. The boy was on her opposite side in the game. Even so he saved Rina's counters from snake bites and saw to it that she scaled the top of the ladder. This made the game lose its bite, but it deepened a love between them. They became engaged in a risky love affair and discarded the war within a war that they played out on a rectangular piece of cardboard with snakes and ladders. It created an uproar. Sometimes the snake swallowed them, sometimes they scaled the ladder and from there slid down and fell. But they did not stop and rushed towards the ladder again. Next to its crest, a huge snake awaited them with its gaping maw. Their points gained or decreased with such rises and downfalls. But they stood firm in their promises of love. Even after their relationship became public knowledge.

The boy was a good match if you considered that it was wartime. But he came from a low-born family. No one knew where his ancestors had come from, or anything about them. After settling in this village, they became *ryots* of Rina's maternal uncle's great grandfather. So Rina's parents, uncles, everyone objected vehemently to this marriage. They threw away the Ludo and Snakes and Ladders boards into the pond and confined Rina to her room. Strange! In the time of war, where could the young pair have run to? There was no place to go to other than the refugee camps in India. Her problems were not over even when she was confined. The day she placed the Holy Quran on her head and formally repented, she felt she was teetering on a ladder and was filled with fear. She felt that she would fall off. Then the boy's older sister threw a crumpled sheet of paper in her room through the window on which was drawn a strong ladder and asked her to take an oath on it. She also said that her earlier atonement was like a snake. Through his sister, the boy was promising to save her from the venom of the snake and reach her to the top of the ladder. Rina swore an oath once again. On one side there was the snake, on the other the ladder. The war between India and Pakistan had started by then. It took just twelve days. Rina's parents had heard about the exchange of notes across the windows through her cousin Pichki. But they also were reassured when they heard that the note contained, merely the picture of a ladder, there was nothing written on it. Rina could not decide. There was no way that she could communicate with him. Because she did not know where the boy was. She constantly thought that she had been put up a tree and then the ladder removed from under her. It was a bad situation.

In their dreams that night, Rina kept being bitten by a snake and Mariam kept falling off the ladder. The next night it was the opposite. The third night was a repetition of the first night's dreams. Mariam's sleeping pills were finished. There was also no news about a job. She would dress herself in Rina's sleeveless blouses that had truncated midriffs and kept visiting Abed's office. She would sit face to face with Abed for a while and tell him all the things that she kept secret at Rina's home. At the Hatirpool house, she was the sister of a martyred Muktijoddha looking for a job. In Abed's office, she was a Birangana who claimed employment as her due. Abed had to give her work because he was in a position of power. Abed would repeat the promise he had made on the first day and send her off every time. The next day, she would again put on a sleeveless, skimpy blouse that belonged to Rina, who did not have the opportunity of wearing them outside, and go out. She would sit opposite Abed. On the table in front was an invisible square of a board on which was marked snakes and ladders. Both of them moved their counters. The possibility of being bitten by a snake or climbing the ladder – the risk of profit or loss – was equal. In the midst of all this, a careless move by Mariam moved the counter to the square belonging to Major Ishtiaque. Abed, as a result, felt he had been set on fire by a snake bite. He threatened Mariam saying that now he understood what made her so bold and brazen. Mary was actually an agent, a pseudo Birangana. She was the mistress of the military during wartime. If she came one more time to demand a job, he would hand her over to the police. There were many women agents who were rotting in the central jail. Mariam overturned the board then and told him that there were many real and fake freedom fighters to be found in the market as well. People were ready to lynch the pseudo freedom fighters whenever they found one. She had known from before that he was not the real thing, but now she would tell everyone. If Mariam was the mistress of an army man, then what was Abed? He was the bought slave of a non-Bengali businessman and his daughter.

That night Mariam was bitten by a snake and she also fell off the ladder.

The next day, the gate-keeper was waiting for Mariam on the main road before the entrance. He was sweating profusely under his new uniform and instead of looking at his watch for the time, he was constantly looking upwards at the sky. Even though Abed was his nephew, he was newly rich and ready to flaunt the power of his wealth. Otherwise how could anyone call the police to the office to get a woman nabbed? He would not make excuses for his nephew but how would Abed Mian feel if the women of his family were rounded up by the police? He had a mother and sisters at home too! The fault lay in his blood. Abed's father and uncles were great ones for lawsuits. They may not have been able to improve their own position but they had harmed others. Abed may be a nephew, but Abed's own grandfather had taken over land belonging to the gate-keeper's father by forging the title deeds. That is why, Abed Mian was today Sir, and he was a gate-keeper. To hell with such a job. He stood on the road and took off his uniform. He was no longer the slave of the grandson of a crafty litigant. He was the citizen of a free country.

Mariam did not recognize him at first when he leapt forward to stop her rickshaw. She thought he was one of those 'wicked people' whom Rina had mentioned. Perhaps a member of the 'awakened youth' who were distributing leaflets against women who wore their saris below their navels and short sleeveless blouses that displayed their bellies was now attacking her rickshaw clad only in a loin cloth. But he did not appear to be one of them. He was polite and well-spoken. With joined palms, he was begging her not to move forward. Why? By Allah, Abed's distantly related uncle clad in a loin cloth told Mariam, not just that he was his nephew. But there was police in the office. Mariam must not go one step ahead. Allah was his witness; she would be sent to the central jail. Abed was entertaining them with tea and snacks on the office lawn.

The rickshaw turned back towards the house at Hatirpool. A

platform for speeches was being erected in the field beside the house. Flapping in the air were red flags with hammer and sickle and countless placards with a list of demands. The freedom of the proletariat was coming soon. Raising wages wasn't enough, what was wanted was socialism. The nationalization of industry and business should be quickened.

The door was opened by Khalamma, Rina's mother. Mariam's early return raised her hopes regarding finding a job. These days there was no talk of war, torture by the Pakistani army was not talked about in the house. The main topics of discussion were the rising prices and thefts and burglaries. Whatever sympathy they had had for Montu had evaporated after reading about lootings and killings by the freedom fighters in the newspapers. If he had been alive he would have been a dacoit like the others. It was good that he had been martyred and saved his parents from the prospect of such infamy. Mariam choked on her food. The meal bought at steep prices and the people around the table seem to her to be part of a distant banquet. Where she has no right. Rina was oblivious to it all. She just needed a ladder to climb down from the tree, which she soon found.

The day Abed arranged prison for Mariam instead of a job, a letter arrived for Rina with a ladder drawn on it. Ladder and snake, snake and ladder. Ill-luck and good fortune, both lived side by side in the squares. Rina's young man had been posted in Chittagong and had been lobbying for a transfer to Dhaka. That had come through. He had not participated in the war. This was his reward for not working through the nine months. Rina was delighted. In a rush of happiness, she gave Mariam half a dozen of her sleeveless, skimpy blouses saying that Mariam needn't return any of them. But she had a question – what was Mariam so busy with during the nine months of war that she had had no time to play Snakes and Ladders? If she had, would she have to roam the streets today begging for a job? Rina castigated Mariam in her mind – what a silly girl she was! Didn't she know that wherever there was a snake, a woman's fortune was to be found there?

That night the snake swallowed Mariam and Rina effortlessly climbed up the ladder.

The next day Mariam packed her bags. What was the point of staying on in Dhaka when there was no chance of a job? She told Rina's parents that she was returning to her village, Fultali. They were glad. Rina helped her dress in a sleeveless, short blouse and a matching Rubia Voile sari with large sunflowers printed on it worn below the navel. She gave Mariam a long-handled black umbrella which she might need to hit the awakened youth on their heads. Rina's parents laughed together, although it was only Rina and Mariam who had seen the leaflet. Mariam stepped on the street leaving behind a happy, affluent family. She was not going back to Fultali, but to the women's rehabilitation centre. Her first task, when she reached there would be to discard the clothes she was wearing and put on a long-sleeved blouse with a free mill-made sari.

XX

Father and Son

Every night, Monowara Begum heard someone crying in Mariam's voice. The sound came from the well that had been filled up. What was there in this well that once held clear water that it had to be filled? She asked her husband again and again but got no satisfactory answer. Her only consolation was that wherever Mary was, at least she was alive. The sound of weeping was only her imagination. Such a big war, so many people had died; there must have been wailing and keening by so many people who had lost their near ones. Had not a trace of it lingered in the wind? Her own heart wept in silence. She was often startled by the sound of her own crying. No one else in the world but a mother could hear it. Where had her son gone? Could the well be his grave and the fact was being hidden from her? At Monowara Begum's urging, the missing person advertisement for Montu was repeated in the newspaper.

When he read the advertisement, Montu's fellow fighter Sarfaraj Hossein did not waste a moment. He folded the paper and set out. During their stint at the training camp, Montu had told him that in case they needed to find him, they should search Dhaka and not look for him at Fultali or its neighbouring villages. Accordingly, Sarfaraj crossed the river. There was a potter's colony on the banks. There, on the revolving potter's wheel lumps of clay were being transformed into vessels. Elephants, horses, *tepa* dolls were being shaped by the potter's fingers. Incredible animals were emerging from the kiln. It was Montu, who led Sarfaraj through the piles of broken pots and mounds of flower pots. It was through Montu's nose that he smelled the stink from the nearby tannery. But when he neared the house described by Montu, he could not find the clump of bamboos. Moreover, instead of Mary'bu, who was supposed to come out of the house, it was Montu's parents who emerged. When he followed them into the house, Montu vanished, leaving him behind. What should he do now, all by himself? Before him sat the couple, looking anxious. Sarfaraj felt annoyed with himself They had been so carried away with their own victory celebrations that they had completely forgotten to convey to the family the news of their fellow-fighter's death. Like the crumpled newspaper in his hands, the news of the death formed a lump in his throat. Before he could say anything, Montu's mother began crying. His father was silent. He was like the still, oppressive moment before the storm broke. In olden days, the emperors and the badshahs would execute the messenger who brought news of death from distant places.

When Sarfaraj walked out of Montu's house with his head still intact, the day was not yet over. But he did not linger. Montu had been alive all this time. He died today, when his parents heard the news. Sarfaraj took long strides, because he would have to return alone through the broken vessels, flower-pots, incredible animals with the stench of the tannery in his nostrils.

That night, Monowara Begum did not hear herself crying. But the wail rising from the depths of the filled-up well curled and billowed in the air till it spread through the whole neighbourhood. It woke the neighbours. The boy whose mother's laments they would hear through the night, was the boy who had painted slogans on the walls in red and black before the war. His calligraphy had been neat and beautiful like the printed word. They had whitewashed the walls during the war for fear of the army. Now had come the news of his death. The neighbours, whose sleep had been interrupted, recalled his neat script. But they could not remember the slogans.

The next day Golam Mostofa, forgetting the past bitterness, rushed with his family to visit them. The younger daughters, Ratna and Chhanda were summoned from the village. The whole day they clung to Monowara Begum like breast-fed babies. Arrangements for Montu's qulkhani were made in the very house where Montu had been sent, to guard his older sister. No one mentioned Mary's name even once. Only Golam Mostofa suggested that the Quran should be recited in memory of both the boy and the girl. Monowara Begum broke out in loud sobs. Her daughter was yet alive. How cruel was her brother! Thirty maulanas performed their ozu with water from the water-pot on the wild grass covering the well. They sat in a circle on a white sheet and chanted the holy Quran. But the times were not good. So they finished their recitations so fast that it seemed that they had entered through one door and gone out through the other. Their sacred chanting floated in the air for a little while over the scent of attar and incense smoke, injecting a fear of the afterlife.

The arrival of Sarfaraj from Dhaka's western borders was fixed as the date of Montu's death. Because, although the boy had mentioned more than once when and where Montu had died, Kafiluddin Ahmed and Monowara Begum had not been in the right frame of mind to register the information. The messenger who had delivered the information had not left his name and address and had left the way he had come. On the fourth day of his departure, the Milaad was performed in the house and the poor were fed. By the side of the walls where Montu had written slogans in his neat handwriting, the beggars and destitute sat down, spreading out banana leaves. As they raised each mouthful of rice mixed with buffalo meat and bottle gourd curry, the blank white wall obstructed their view. This disturbed some people. They kept crossing and recrossing the paved road with curry spilling from their banana leaves. The country may have become independent but they still remained beggars. They had come for a good meal. How could the city's white walls remain blank when people had so many grievances and needs? After a few days, the walls were no longer white. They were filled with demands of the beggars and with other kinds of accusations and warnings. Instead of Montu, another boy of the same age copied them in a neat handwriting.

Kafiluddin Ahmed had emptied his pockets and spent lavishly. The only son, he had just sat for the intermediate examination. There had been a lot of expenses ahead for him. Compared to that, feeding hundreds of the poor or some fifty or more maulanas was nothing. Besides, when the son was no longer there, for whom were the house and property, land and money? Golam Mostofa advised, "Dulabhai, rent out the house." Earlier Dhaka had been merely a provincial capital, now it was the heart of a new nation. Even foreigners who had come to help noticed the city. Like the prices of food grain, rentals would also skyrocket. Dhaka's land would become as valuable as precious metals. But Mary? Even though nobody mentioned her, the name stirred in everyone's mind. Golam Mostofa had something to say in this matter as well. Let the girl stand on her own feet. The way a human being is born – alone and without a thing. Whether anybody wanted it or not, the war had left her in such a position. She had died at the age of twenty-two and been born anew. The people responsible for her second birth were not her parents. During Montu's qulkhani the Quran had been read in Mary's name as well. Let it be thought that the well was Mary's grave. Her mother and father had interred her there. She was a closed chapter. The responsibility for her new life was hers – or independent Bangladesh's. Golam Mostofa was an ordinary person. He had not bothered much with education in his life. But even so, he had been brave enough to attempt to rebuild his educated niece's broken life. Whatever Allah did was for the benefit of man. "Dulabhai, just think of me once. On one side it is my own son, on the other, the daughter of my elder sister, who is the same as a mother. Whose interests did I consider, or didn't I?" Kafiluddin Ahmed was uneasy before his glaring gaze. Why rake up the past in a house of mourning and insult them? But Golam Mostofa did not give up easily. He never let go of an opportunity. "If the boy has a defect, so has the girl. You have understood everything Dulabhai, now tell me whose defect is greater – your daughter's or my son's?"

Kafiluddin Ahmed stared blankly at his brother-in-law. Allah had given him the opportunity, he could say what he wanted. Monowara Begum could not stand his words. She picked up the prayer rug and went into the other room. Her exit brought some sense into Golam Mostofa. He turned the conversation carefully. In a sudden cheerful outburst, he slapped Kafiluddin Ahmed's knee and said, "Dulabhai, you will soon see the Razakars and the freedom fighters drinking at the same waterhole. The situation is not as bad as you think. No matter what enmity we harbour in our hearts, all Muslims are brothers. And Pakistan and Hindustan are two different countries. Bangladesh has come as a bonus. It is here today, but may not be there tomorrow."

The reason for Golam Mostofa's garrulity became clear, albeit a little later. During the forthcoming Bakr Eid, he was going to congratulate Bangabandhu. Someone close to the government had arranged the meeting. "Dulabhai, the struggle now is not just between Hindustan and Pakistan. The whole world has got involved. By Khoda, it is absolute inside information." Golam Mostofa's lips and Kafiluddin Ahmed's ear drew close to each other. Although what they were saying could not be heard, their subject was the split within the Awami League. One faction tilted towards India and Russia, while the other was a supporter of America. There were equal numbers on both sides. Bangabandhu was trying to maintain a balance between the two, occupying a central position. An enemy of India since birth, Golam Mostofa would penetrate the Awami League and fight for America. His activities would start from the day after the holy celebration of Ed ul Azha.

Kafiluddin Ahmed woke up in the middle of the night with a deep sense of desolation. He could not recall the dream from which he had awoken. But the fact of the matter was that he was without a son and that is how he would have to leave this world one day. But why? Who had he harmed that he would have to accept such harsh punishment? He had distributed sweets at the milaad with his own hands, counted out the cash for the maulanas from his own pocket – but all these acts were formalities performed during the day. At midnight, he felt tormented. Instead of asking forgiveness for the soul of his departed son, he wanted a living son – a son who would throw earth on his grave, a son in whose veins his blood would flow when he was not there, a son who would breathe through his nostrils and circulate air through his lungs when his own nose and lungs would be gone. Kafiluddin Ahmed must have a son. Accordingly, he advanced in full vigour. Both his mind and body were prepared. But another anger flared as he mounted her. The siren call of night deluded him into forgetting that his wife had reached menopause. The act was unpardonable. Torture for a bereaved mother. For the father yearning for a son, the frustration of failure was even more distressing. And in this way, as the night progressed one rage led to another. Monowara Begum watched the man leaving the room like a shadow as she wept in humiliation and sorrow. In one hand he held a shovel and in the other a basket.

Kafiluddin Ahmed was digging in the light of the setting moon. The muscles, over sixty years old, moved up and down with the movement of the shovel faster and faster. And yet there was no rhythm to the movement. This unbalanced condition had been with him since he had left the bed. At the crack of dawn, he dug four holes in the four corners of the house. He unearthed the four holy bottles, but they were all broken. He smashed them even further and placed the pieces in the basket. Now he was ready for his second project. The place: the well. In the light of day, the blood-smeared man took on frightening dimensions. Monowara Begum rushed to him with her two daughters in an attempt to stop him. Hearing their shouts, a neighbour came out. He said that Kafiluddin Ahmed did not have the right to dig up this well, although it was on his land

and built with his money. Those who had filled up the well were the only people authorized to dig it up again, after obtaining permission from the government. Besides, the leader of the neighbourhood, the Haji Saheb had returned home on the night of Montu's qulkhani. His permission was necessary from now on to do any such thing.

When he heard the Haji Shaheb's name, Kafiluddin Ahmed abandoned the shovel. The basket was upturned. A full-grown adult suddenly appeared nervous like a child. Those who were supposed to remain hidden were crawling out. Like a snake crawling out of its hole. The Haji Shaheb had not delayed his return for a moment after hearing about Montu's death. The obstacle in his path had been removed permanently. This was a golden opportunity. Now, like Golam Mostofa, would he too take a pro-American stance and fight? What had happened to the country? The war was not over yet. Last night the man who had behaved insanely driven by his desire for a son was now crying loudly for the children he had lost in the war. Ratna and Chhanda were shaken. They were unable to understand the significance of the Haji Shaheb's return on the night of Montu's qulkhani. They were unaware of the history of this house. Thus, the bottles and the well seemed mysterious to them. These mysteries were best displayed in an ideal museum. Even so, before returning to Fultali with their parents, they carefully filled up the holes with their small hands. And they cleaned up the weeds growing above the well and planted a Queen of the Night shrub there. It was the twins' own idea: the scent of the flowers would attract snakes at night. Their only brother had died in the war. Their eldest sister had left home. Till they grew up, the house would be guarded by the poisonous snakes, instead of the bottles with the spells in them.

XXI

Home Instead of the Park, Mattress Instead of Grass

Even though the house was built for the son, Mariam had been the first to inhabit it. In some ways, she continued to have a right to it, although she had left and been changing her address frequently. But now it was not in a group like in wartime. Now she was alone. She was in a working woman's hostel after having stayed at Rina's house, then the rehabilitation centre and the house at New Eskaton Road. There were a few other Biranganas like her there. They all worked at different jobs. The women who were raped during the war of independence had no role in either the looting and extortion or the reconstruction of the new nation apart from their jobs. They did not respond to the home minister's call to citizens to "come forward with a revolutionary mindset and put a stop to smuggling". They played no role in the nationalization of factories and industries. They had nothing to do with either the constant setting of the jute storehouses on fire or with putting the fires out. They had neither killed, snatched, plundered nor had they resisted these acts. They took a back seat when the new Constitution was being framed and new laws enacted. They did not worry about the loopholes in the "Collaborators Act 1972". They listened quietly to Bangabandhu's announcement of general amnesty. They did not once condemn the cruelties perpetrated by the security forces. They did not participate in the movement of eradicating class enemies by the Sharbahara Party. They did not applaud the law minister when the International Crimes Tribunal Act, 1973 was passed, although under Section 2(A) of the Act, rape was designated as a crime against humanity. They did not raise their voices when the Constitution was amended and the President was given the power to declare Emergency. They did not join the single party BAKSAL either. Actually, they were engaged in a struggle themselves. They had a single agenda – the social rehabilitation of the Biranganas. While the government had failed in this through advertising in the papers and offering dowry as bait, they decided to do it by taking a leap in the dark.

The working women's hostel was next to the National Theatre, a stone's throw from Ramna Park. After dusk, the roads around were desolate. In the shadows of the trees broken intermittently by street lamps, Mariam and other inmates of the hostel moved around wearing nice clothes. They munched on *jhalmuri, chanachur* and such savouries from paper bags, sharing them with each other. They didn't waste money on theatre tickets. They refrained from sitting or standing below the lights. Like blind people, they went round and round in the lonely, dark streets.

After sunset, Ramna Park becomes a marketplace for the buying and selling of the bodies of prostitutes. One day a group of customers left the flock and came out of the park. They were bored of screwing prostitutes on the grass day after day. On top of which there was police harassment. They entered the deserted streets where Mariam and others were already walking around in their best clothes. Then the chanachur and the jhalmuri got shared. They entered the theatre with their male escorts to watch plays. In the darkened auditorium, they sat in pairs – a Birangana and a former Ramna Park client – munching on savouries and watching plays. Those who had trouble appreciating intellectual theatre would leave in pairs and go to the cinema halls, Balaka, Naz, Madhumita. There shows like *Bodhu-Mata-Kanya, Kancher Swarga, Jiban Sangeet* were running to full houses for the second week. But the film *Gopal Bhanrh* wasn't doing so well. Bengalis had forgotten how to laugh. And if the former Ramna Park clients wanted to see such farcical fare, the women raised objections. They said, "One feels like laughing when one hears Gopal Bhanrh's name. Oh Lord, the man is so odd!" But that was only talk. For them, this pairing off was no light-hearted matter, nor was it the luxury of a new experience or avoiding the humdrum. The problem that the nation had failed to solve – the social rehabilitation of the Biranganas – they had now to bear its heavy responsibility on their shoulders. Mariam and others like her had fallen on the streets through the cracks in the smug statements made by the leaders, "We have overcome such a major crisis." Whatever had to be done, they had to do themselves. Newspapers and magazines helped them in this. They repeatedly printed the picture of a Birangana whose face was covered with her hair thus rendering all of them faceless. And they had always been voiceless because they had never chanted slogans either for or against the government or called press conferences. So not only in the darkened auditoriums, they couldn't be identified even in broad daylight. Thus as they watched movies and plays and munched on snacks, their faces screened by a cascade of flowing black hair, they moved ahead to solve the national problem.

So far, Mariam had thought Momtaj was a woman's name. But he was a man. He had proudly announced at their first meeting that he was a former customer of the Ramna Park whores. He was a businessman. Although he had not actually taken up arms, he was one with the freedom fighters heart and soul. Thus he had acquired a certificate affirming that he was a freedom fighter. Using that, he had managed to procure a trade licence. It was later that Mariam found out that his business was siphoning off rice, wheat, blankets meant for relief work through underground channels and then selling it in the open market. Presently, though, the groom-to-be wanted to leave his bed on the grass and return to the security of a comfortable bed at home. For Mariam also, it was important to return to a home. First a home and then society – the Biranganas could be socially rehabilitated through marriage.

In between watching plays and movies and snacking on jhalmuri and chanachur, Momtaj proposed marriage to her one day. Mariam heard in that proposal the sharp whistle of the referee in a game of musical chairs. And the marriage ceremony was carried out as quickly as sitting down on the first available chair. She had competitors among both the Biranganas and non-Biranganas. Furthermore, according to the rules of the game, there was one chair less. But her fears lay elsewhere. Abed had also proposed marriage to her when they were at the stage of sharing peanuts under the shady canopy of the rain trees. But once he had taken her to bed, the proposal kept on getting postponed until finally it disappeared. No one made the same mistake twice. Especially when the person had the experience of nine months of war. However, she rejected the advice of her friends from the hostel and moved her hair from her face like lifting a veil. Momtaj was a liberal man. If he got a Birangana as a life partner then his existence as a man would be fulfilled. After all this time, he was going to do something that was worth the glory of fighting in ten wars of liberation. He did not want sewing machines or cooking utensils. There was no need to put up an awning or mikes. The Birangana would be married without any news reports or photographs. Mariam informed her parents in two separate letters in the same envelope. Finally, after all the humiliation, Kafiluddin Ahmed could stand up straight once more. His Birangana daughter was not getting married to a slobbering, mentally-challenged, subhuman being. The groom was well-to-do, liberal and educated. Kafiluddin Ahmed sent the good news to Golam Mostofa by return post. Mariam left behind nine months of war, countless corpses, broken bridges and culverts, burnt homes and shops and one death and entered a new life at the age of twenty-four.

The newly-weds had set up their home in a house abandoned

by a non-Bengali family. Even before Momtaj had taken possession of the property, the doors, the windows, the electric and sanitary fittings had vanished. The furniture must have been taken away even earlier. He spent a great deal of money to get the house repaired. In competition with the invisible owner, he bought expensive furniture, fittings and decorative items matching the style of the mansion. Then he brought the bride. The house was a substitute for the park and the bed for grass.

After Fultali village, all the places that Mariam had lived in had belonged to people evicted from their homes in one way or another. They had all been political refugees. With the birth of a new nation each time, they had been ousted from their homesteads. It was only force of circumstance that made Mariam an occupier. She left her job (which was a condition of marriage) and decorated someone else's home as her own. She laid down a thick mattress. Over it she spread a soft mattress stuffed with cotton wool. She covered it with a sheet on which she had skilfully embroidered flowers, leaves and vines with coloured threads. She had started it at the rehabilitation centre but had not finished it till after her marriage. On the pillow covers, she embroidered delicate couplets on love. These lines had remained strung like a garland in her mind from the time she had been in her teens at Fultali village. Although they had later been pulled apart and scattered by Abed's betrayal and the strains of war, now at the mention of marriage, they revived and played in her mind like some eternal song.

A marriage was a marriage, it brought peace even if it was with someone of no consequence. Under the splendid shelter of marriage, the afternoons were Mariam's own. She enjoyed incomparable affluence and limitless security. But only for a few days. After that she no longer remained alone in the afternoons. During the solitary afternoons, Montu, Anuradha and all the people who had disappeared from her life appeared as guests in turn. They looked through Mariam's well-appointed home, admired her needlework, and occasionally gave her peculiar advice. Montu said, "Well, Mary Bu, aren't you a Birangana? Why

isn't the flag of Bangladesh flying from your roof?" Anuradha
constantly criticized the house. She tapped the concrete walls and
smoothly polished teakwood doors with her index finger. She
predicted, "The house is a house of cards. You just wait Mary,
it'll fall apart while you sleep and you won't even know." Shobha
Rani giggled, "Money, money, money, it's money that makes the
world go round." Major Ishtiaque peeked in and skulked away
like a thief. He did not dare enter. Rameez Sheikh was an extra.
It would have been better perhaps if he had not existed. Yet he
had parted the shower of bullets as one parts water hyacinths
with both hands and had appeared to be swimming towards
Mariam. In the end, he couldn't manage it anymore and flew off
into the void. Even in the sunny, airy afternoons in Mariam's
new home, the claustrophobic atmosphere of that hall room
of 1971 settled in. If she opened the doors and windows,
the people from her lost past entered. One by one, they took
possession of the bed, the chairs, the sofa set, the carpet, the
threshold – everything.

When Momtaj returned home in the evening, Mariam
complained that she found it difficult to while away the lonely
afternoons. She had finished arranging the house. What could
she do now? It would be different if they had had servants in the
house. She could spend her time giving instructions and making
them run errands. Momtaj was against employing any servants
because he thought that after they found out that Mariam was a
Birangana, they would not remain home in the afternoons. They
would visit every house in the mohalla. The word would spread
from one servant to another, from one ear to another. "The
Bibishaheb of that house with a mango tree was dishonoured
by the military. It's trying to forget that sorrow that makes the
Shaheb spend every evening with his bottle." After the spread
of such gossip, the house would not remain a home. Scores of
visitors every morning and evening would transform it into a
museum of the war of liberation.

Should Mariam return to her job then? Her husband didn't
agree. Her identity in the office would not be an employee but

a Birangana. Everyone from the peon to the boss would know. They wouldn't care if she had a husband at home or not. They would demand extras. "If you could give your body to the Khans, then why not us? You could offer us a taste here and there."

That left only her in-laws who, claimed her husband, lived in the village. "It's such a big house. They could easily come and live here."

"Yes, they could," said Momtaj controlling his anger and spitting out each word, "but some people are not happy unless they ask for trouble. Would you like it if your mother-in-law or sister-in-law yank you by the hair? If they call you a whore of 1971, what would you do then?"

The final description was always whore or Birangana. Momtaj did not directly address her as such. But again and again he made her aware of her 'real' identity through words he put in the mouths of invisible people. Apart from that, there was no other mention of the war. Where had he been those nine months? Had he been at Ramna Park? When the Kali temple at Ramna was being ravaged, where had he been then? Had he been absent from there as well? What was this man's past, where was his future? Now he was raking in money and spending it. Why had Mariam married him? For the social rehabilitation of the Biranganas? Or was it that she wanted a baby? Not a baby from the Pakistani army, but a baby by a Bengali. Momtaj said, "What's the hurry about having a baby? We've just got married. Let's enjoy life and then we shall see."

This business of enjoyment was even more confusing. When Momtaj embraced her, Mariam's eyes bulged like the eyes of a dead fish. Her body gave way instantly. She began breathing through her mouth and her heart thrashed like a trapped rat. At first, Momtaj did not think this unnatural. Because the prostitutes at the park took money with one hand and lifted their clothes with the other before lying down on the grass. Tender lovemaking and foreplay were irrelevant there. It was better for both parties to get it over with before the police arrived. But the bedroom was a substitute for the park and the bed replaced grass. So why did his wife behave like a prostitute? She never said 'no' to going to bed with her husband at any time. Actually, she never took any part in it. The whole time she just lay there, as if submitting in the face of a gun. In an effort to make his wife a more active partner, Momtaj slowly took on the role of a rapist – like the Pakistani army four years ago.

Momtaj bit into Mariam's wounds of 1971. He would swear at her in filthy language. Momtaj had always been a habitual drinker. Now that he had a fat wallet, he was drinking even more. One day, when he was drunk, he poured a bottle of whisky on his wife's genitals. He was scared the next day of going to work, leaving his wounded wife at home in bed. She could run away. Even if she didn't, if any of the neighbours saw her in this state, there could be a hassle with the police. To avoid unnecessary trouble, he did what the Pakistani army would do to Mariam and the girls. He nailed down the windows, locked the door from the outside and left with the keys. But this time the freedom fighters did not come to rescue Mariam. Their shouts of "Ma, Ma" came and receded again and again like the distant waves of the sea. Niazi's surrender had happened a very long time ago. The allied forces had returned to their own country as victors. In accordance with the terms of the Delhi Pact, the Bengalis who had been in Pakistan had come back. The accused generals had served out their sentences in India and had returned to a fractured Pakistan. How many times did a nation need to be liberated?

On such days, Momtaj returned home very early. Panic did not allow him to remain outside the house for very long. When he arrived home he would go about nursing his wife without even changing out of his clothes. He would shed tears and plead with her to forgive him. This was new – the Pakistani army had not done this. Mariam forgave him instantly. She thought that their married life would start afresh through forgiveness. Otherwise, it would once again be the working women's hostel – munching jhalmuri, chanachur in the twilight, pacing the streets laced with light and shade, receiving another fragile proposal of marriage while watching a movie or play.

There had been many women with her who had not yet been rehabilitated in society. So there still were rivals. Besides, the rules of the game said that there would be one chair less. Mariam did not want to take that risk a second time. She had a few good days with Momtaj. The husband returned home from work with saris, bangles, purses. Although he had presented her with silk saris, he had never brought her red roses. He did not have the habit of either listening to or reciting ghazals. Even so Mariam did not think of Major Ishtiaque. When things were good between them, Momtaj would take his wife to a movie. *Deep Jele Jai* or *Harano Sur*. When the show was over, they would climb onto a rickshaw in a romantic frame of mind like Uttam and Suchitra. Momtaj whistled the famous tune, "The night belongs to you and me/ just the two of us." At night, he lay his head on Mariam's lap and dreamt of the patter of paper flowers falling on the bed from the painted shiuli tree on the studio backdrop. The doe-eyed Suchitra Sen had spread out her lap for him. The voice of the enchantress sang "You are my direction in the endless darkness." Mariam was speechless. Coaxed and urged, she uttered meaningless sounds. Instead of shiuli flowers, tears dripped from her eyes and Momtaj's dream vanished from her lap like a little child. In the light of the dim night lamp, a pair of dead fish eyes bulged out. The enchantress's head lolled back. A storm raged within the dead eyes, echoing the tremors of the roof beams in that dreaded hall room. The walls of her home rattled in that storm. The roof kept shifting. Momtaj could no longer keep his cool. He, who had no memories, no stories of war, started behaving like the Pakistani army.

Mariam reproached herself – stupid, idiot. How could she not know what marriage was? If the man had to go back to the park, then why would he keep a wife at home? Mariam figured out that the truth was that a loveless physical relationship was a kind of rape even if the man was a husband. But the question was, what was love? Was there any difference between sex and rape? Like the men in that hall room, Momtaj returned again and again with the smell of liquor on his breath. His whisky smelled awful.

It stirred up memories of her prison life. If Mariam tried to ask him not to drink, Momtaj would say that he knew that drinking was bad. But prostitution was bad as well. To him Mariam was a prostitute. Except that she was polite, educated, cultured. And she did not work in the park, but slept at home.

The choice was limited – a home or a park, a park or a home.

Although slightly delayed, Anuradha's predictions had begun to come true. So why should Mariam take the place of a whore and live with one man? What was the benefit? The advantage was that she did not have to stand around the whole day and return home with rations at night. She did not want for clothes. And she was used to being imprisoned at home. It was an extension of the concentration camp of 1971. The war had fragmented and bits of it had spread throughout her life. But rape and torture could not be carried out on someone throughout her life. Should she change her home then? How many times could she return to the rehabilitation centre? If she did not want to go there or could find no other place, then all that remained would be a whorehouse. What sort of a place was it? Once women entered those gates, they could never come back. Perhaps what she needed now was an address as permanent as a grave.

In the lonely afternoons, when the formless idea of the whorehouse dogged her steps, lured her like a pimp, she received a letter written jointly by her sisters, Ratna and Chhanda from Fultali. Mariam and their Dulabhai, her husband, had been invited to the village. P.S. a dirt road had been built from the Sundari wetlands to the village as part of the food-for-work programme. So Dulabhai would not have to walk to the in-law's house. They could get off the bus from Dhaka, hire a van or cycle rickshaw and directly reach the yard in front of the house. However, during the monsoon no one knew what the condition would be of this dirt road built by hungry people tempted by the promise of wheat. So Mary and her husband should visit as quickly as possible.

Although the letter had been written by the twin sisters, Mariam knew that it had the approval of her parents. They had merely not demeaned themselves by writing directly to the daughter who had voluntarily left home. Mariam sat up. Her relationship with Momtaj had deteriorated even further. At that point in time, he had substituted his wife for a whore and his house for a park. In this state, she stopped thinking of becoming a prostitute and decided to return to her parents.

XXII

The Return

As she stood by the kitchen door, Monowara Begum watched Mariam descend from a rickshaw by herself. Her head throbbed from the heat of the stove. Suddenly, the cooking ladle fell from her hands. Mariam stood in the yard, grinning like a witch. The mother was troubled. The whole day, she had been wiping her tears with one hand and cooking with the other. The last time Mary had returned home, Montu had been with her. This time it was not her own son who was supposed to come with her, but someone else's. But, after all, he was *her* son-in-law. So, she was cooking up some special dishes. He had said that he would come but hadn't. She leaned on the mud and wattle boundary fences, picked the ladle up and asked, "Where is my son-in-law Mariam? Why are you on your own?" Mary was prepared. Momtaj was the reason that she had been allowed to come home. That Mariam knew. But the man had not come. Nor would he ever come. What everyone would know anyway in a few days, she could not tell her mother now. Ratna and Chhanda, the two who had invited them, ran to her and took her suitcase out of the rickshaw. The last time Mariam had seen them they had been wearing short pants, their torsos bare. Now clad in bellbottom trousers, short kameezes, their hair done up in ponytails, they were asking, "So where's Dulabhai, Mary Bu? What's the deal, the big Shaheb didn't approve of this poor man's hut?"

The twin teenagers were competing to show the older sister how smart they were. A vast wetland had kept them distant not only from just the city but even a properly tarred road. The connecting link was recent – a dirt road built by hungry people. The connection had been enough to influence their clothes – bellbottom pants and short kurtas, all the latest fashion. All the dressing up was done for the arrival of the elder sister who was more a stranger to them than family. They had not met too often. Mariam had moved to Dhaka even before the twins had become conscious of their surroundings. They had grown up hearing all kinds of stories about the unfamiliar older sister – some of them good, some not. Mother: "You're just like your older sister. Throwing tantrums without reason, making impossible demands." Eldest Aunt: "The dupatta never covers your bosom. You've got the same habits as Mary." Playmates: "Oh! Sisters of the one who has run away. The military's your Dulabhai. Where would you go? Pakistan (chorus)." The Maulvi Sir, who had come from Noakhali: "Why aren't you like your sister? She always stood first in every class." Villagers: "The twins go to school without covering their heads. They will make a mess of everything like the sister."

After the news of Mariam's marriage had spread, there had been a stillness in the air during the last six months. From time to time, Mother recounted stories from the eldest daughter's childhood – how she lost her milk teeth and got her new set of teeth, how she would splash water when you tried to bathe her, how she dimpled when she smiled since she was very small. Oh! Allah! And my mother-in-law was mad. She would take the child in her lap and tease – Ah! Kafi! Your daughter dimples when she smiles. She will grow up to be quite a tease! And Father would smile. The twins did not possess even a smidgen of the eldest daughter's beauty and talent. Husband and wife harboured regret because of this. But what now? The son-in-law, for whose welcome such elaborate arrangements had been made, had not come.

Mariam left the twins and ran towards the kitchen, "Ma, oh Ma! Look, here I am! Oh! How long it's been. Your son-in-law is such a busy man. All he knows is work and more work. He has no time at all." Monowara Begum's body trembled like a fledgling that has fallen out of its safe hole in a tree. Mariam took her in her arms and hugged her like a child to stop her trembling.

Kafiluddin Ahmed had seen Mary in the distance, coming in a rickshaw over the Sundari wetlands. The son-in-law was not with her. He slipped away from the veranda of the outer quarters and quietly went and lay down on his bed. He did not utter a word. Mariam entered the room after chatting with her mother and shedding a few tears. Abba was lying down at an odd time and pretending not to have heard what had been going on outside. But his bare feet poked out from his lungi. When Mary touched his feet and salaamed, he sat up with a deep sigh. The daughter held on to a bedpost and stood beside it. The father was seated on the bed. Both looked out of the window into the distance. The stormy onslaught of war had played havoc with their lives. Neither of them spoke. In the fading light of dusk, they looked out as if searching for something.

Kafiluddin Ahmed had a strange relationship with his children. Even in happier times, he never knew what to say to them. The silence was interrupted when Ratna came into the room with a hurricane lantern. Abba bellowed, "Why have you lit the lamp before nightfall? Put it out, put it out. Kerosene is so costly!." Then, till the call to evening prayers, he chatted with Mariam about the rising prices and what an incapable administrator Sheikh Shaheb was. Then he put on his skullcap and went to the mosque.

None of the five members of the family talked to each other about the war. The villagers stood around and stared at Mariam and then went away. Some sat on their haunches in the middle of the yard and stared. Whatever food Monowara Begum offered them – whether fresh or stale – they refused, shaking their heads. The objects of their curiosity were the cut of Mariam's blouse, her citified way of wearing a sari, the way she moved, her well-groomed hands and feet. They could not gauge the torture she'd suffered at the hands of the military even after scrutinising her closely. But there was the scandal – well there was no smoke without fire.

Monowara Begum often shed tears. Everyone thought that the sight of Mary had reminded her of Montu. But no one in the house uttered his name. The tin-roofed primary school in the village had been renamed the Shaheed Saifuddin Ahmed Fultali Prathamik Vidyalaya – the name had vanished from their tongues and positioned itself on a signboard. A State Minister came for the naming ceremony. The men in Mujib jackets, who accompanied the minister, gave slogans all the way for the Minister, forgetting all about Montu. Kafiluddin Ahmed was livid. When the martyr's father was called to the dais to say a few words, he kept shaking. The strangers from town thought the trembling was grief for the son. The chief guest himself held him by the shoulder and sat him down in the next chair. There was loud applause then like the spluttering of popping rice. The slogans that rose from the crowd mentioned only two names: Bangabandhu's and the minister's. Ratna and Chhanda sang a patriotic song to the accompaniment of a harmonium – *Amay gethe deona mago ekta palash fuler mala/ Ami janam janam rakhbo dhare bhai haranor jwala* (Mother please string me a garland of crimson palash blossoms/ I will hold on throughout my life to the pain of losing my brother). But they could not finish the song. After singing the line *Tari shokey kokil dakey/ phote baner phool* (From the same grief does the kokil call/ the wild flowers bloom), they came down from the dais with their dupattas covering their mouths. They had only been able to sing that much during the rehearsals as well. The State Minister sat on the stage and dabbed his eyes with his handkerchief. The men wearing black Mujib jackets and looking like penguins were stunned. Although a little late, they followed their leader's example and took out their handkerchiefs. Only Kafiluddin Ahmed's eyes were dry. He returned home and lay down on his grandfather's bed. For two days, he did not touch a morsel of food or a drop of water. Monowara Begum was worried. If she went near him, he turned his face away. When his anger subsided, he began to talk a little. "Mariam's mother, the whole country is riddled with Razakars. Men are no longer human beings. When the government declared the General Amnesty, did they ask us? Did Sheikh Mujibur Rahman take our permission?" Monowara Begum stared wordlessly at her husband. She had no connection with newspapers. "What are you saying? Who should ask whom? Do kings ever seek permission from their subjects? This is mad, silly talk." Kafiluddin Ahmed was annoyed, "You won't understand. I am trying to get something into your silly head. Illiterate female."

One day after school was over, Mariam went with Ratna and Chhanda to look at the signboard. Sitting on the grass in the school grounds, the two sisters told Mary that their father was donating money every month for the improvement of the school. He went from house to house and told everyone, "Send your children to school. It is a virtuous act. It'll bear fruit in the end." But everyone was more interested in the present outcome rather than with the end results. If the children worked as day labourers alongside their fathers, they got instant cash returns. Who had time to think about the next life? Some listened to the advice of the old man who had lost his son, others did not. At Abba's urging, some adults had attended night school illuminated by burning torches made with straw. Abba would directly supervise. He arranged for proper illumination and bought them a light with a gas mantle. But the tongues of the adult students had become thick from chewing paan with tobacco. They were also thick-headed and could not remember the next day what was taught the day before. The lessons slipped out through some invisible hole. If asked, they would give a big yawn. Some snored to the rhythm of the lamp's buzz. The teacher was in a quandary. He could not cane the students as they were old enough to be his fathers. The teacher got no salary. Finally he just gave up.

Ratna and Chhanda chatterd away. They wanted to become intimate with the sister whose fame or infamy they could never hope to match. Mariam kept a distance. Her attention was elsewhere. She had realized that Kafiluddin Ahmed went into town everyday to check whether a letter had come from Momtaj. He returned home even more tired and stooping. Mariam should leave before anybody at home raised the issue. It would not be too long before they began to ask questions. But where would she go in Dhaka – to the rehabilitation centre or to a whorehouse?

Mariam could not sleep for worry about her future. She had nightmares. She felt that somebody was sitting on her chest and crushing her heart. The man's face could not be seen. But his eyes glinted like a cat's. From her chest two hairy hands moved up to her throat. The fingers were like coppery claws. He was trying to strangle her. Mariam screamed – but the tortured sound that came out was like a cow being slaughtered. Kafiluddin Ahmed tried to break open the door with an axe and a chopper. She continued to scream in a strangled voice. Monowara Begum held up the hurricane lantern. Ratna and Chhanda scrambled on to her bed. Mariam foamed at the mouth. The pupils of her eyes had turned upwards like those of a dead fish.

It was difficult to call a doctor in the middle of the night. The news would spread like wildfire the next day. For the time being, Kafiluddin Ahmed gave his daughter a sleeping pill from the ones prescribed for him. The same treatment was continued in the morning. Mariam was also running a temperature of 104 degrees. At night, a darbesh came and performed spells and charms. Mariam's eldest chachi Tahura Begum also knew a spell or two. When the darbesh left, she came down to tend to the patient. She kept praying and blowing on the patient's feverish body. The cold compresses on the patient's forehead had to be changed constantly. The hairy hands shook in the dim light of the oil lamp and moved up from her throat towards her forehead. Mariam quickly grasped the hand with the wet rag and would not let go. On one side her aunt was screaming, on the other Mariam. But what she said was not clear, although it was understood that she would not let go even if she had to give up

her life. Chachi's face had turned white as a sheet. The moment
the grip loosened, she fled the room. Ratna and Chhanda smiled
with pursed lips – so how was the punishment? Just let their
aunt tell them off again about their dupattas slipping from their
chests, they would sic their eldest sister on to her. There was not
a trace of mercy or pity in the girls. Perhaps it was their age.

Mariam's fever subsided. But the weakness had not left her.
One early morning, she was woken from her light sleep by a clap
of thunder. It rained incessantly from the morning onwards. In
keeping with her heart's desire it rained the whole day without
stopping. It rained through the night, and the next day, and the
day after that. A deluge was at hand. Let the world be washed
away. Even if the prophet Noah appeared with his ark, Mariam
would not leave land. This was a golden opportunity to get
washed away with everyone else. Kafiluddin Ahmed's journeys
into town had stopped. Gone was the humiliation of receiving
no letters from the son-in-law. The peon, after all, was a man
of flesh and blood. Till the rains stopped, let the letters which
had not been sent remain safe in the post box. After days of
insomnia and fever, Mariam was sleeping through night and day.
Sleep and rain. Rain and sleep. On her numbed consciousness,
the rain poured blessings.

Finally, one day Mariam really awoke, shaken out of her sleep
by Monowara Begum. She had lost count of how many days
and nights had passed in between. Opening the window near
her head, Monowara Begum happily showed her daughter the
Sundari marsh. It had turned into a sea with the flood waters.
There was no sign of the road. She laughed and said, "See how
silly the son-in-law is. When it was dry, he did not come. Now
that the area is flooded, how will he come?" Ratna and Chhanda
had come home with their books and notebooks sodden. They
hadn't even be able to reach the school. They were also very
happy. "Mary Bu, what fun! Dulabhai cannot come unless the
water subsides. Neither can you go back to Dhaka." Kafiluddin
Ahmed smiled a little and joined in the cheerful mood. Everyone,
except Mary, now believed that the son-in-law could not come

from Dhaka because all roads to Fultali were submerged in water. This belief they had constructed. It was by the strength of such a belief that Montu had continued to live in their hearts even a year after his death.

Kafiluddin's homestead rose like a ship at sea amid the vast expanse of water. One could easily see, as if from a ship's deck, the endless stretch of water. The *aus* paddy had drowned even before the grains had matured. Famine was imminent. It was something that this family also had to think about. Ever since the war, Kafiluddin Ahmed did not like to store things in the house. He had his own logic for this. Man saved for his sons – the daughters would marry and leave for another home, if not today, then tomorrow. His giving away to charities now exceeded all limits. At present, all they had was an urn of rice for their meals and varieties of seed rice for the coming season stored neatly in wattle baskets layered with cow dung. Monowara Begum wanted to share her anxiety with her eldest daughter. Because there was no use discussing all this with her husband. The man had become detached from worldly affairs after Montu had gone missing. Kafiluddin Ahmed looked pleased at the submergence of all the land which he was finding difficult to manage. One day, he called Mary to the edge of the deck and pointed out with his index finger the boundaries of his land. It was a kind of madness, accounting for this land under water. She became worried and began to notice the creases on the slack skin of his arm. The raised finger trembled like that of an arthritic patient. In the thundering voice of an unvanquished sailor, he announced, "All mine." The waves of the sea became turbulent. As if after a long sea voyage, the old sailor was returning home having lost the ship with its hold full of treasures. What awaited him there was death.

That night the mother silently left her bed. "Mariam, wake up, get up. This girl sleeps like the dead. My Judgment Day is at hand, child. I can't cope anymore." Monowara Begum's voice was harsh and jarring as she sat in front of her daughter and spoke. In the next room, the two younger daughters slept.

The thin darkness enveloped them like a fine mosquito net. Although blurred, everything could be seen in the dimness. Mother suddenly peered around carefully. "Your father will not survive long, child." Mother's voice descended to a whisper, "He is going towards his end, aching for a son. I want him to marry again and father a son." Mariam was startled and stopped her mother, "No, Amma, no. What are you saying? Why don't you go and sleep?" But Mother went on, "Let me speak. Why do you interrupt when I am speaking? Either way my life is over. I will raise no objections Mariam, if he wants to marry."

The darkness of night settled on them like the overcast sky. Thunder rumbled signalling turmoil in the heavens. All joy was leached out of life, everything was distasteful. Mother and daughter sat facing each other. Monowara Begum continued to pour out her words, "Even if you don't say anything, I am your mother. I understand your pain. Once fate has dealt a cruel blow, life cannot be patched up again. Don't cry Mariam. Once the water subsides, leave. Go take possession of the Dhaka house. Your father will go to his grave only after he has run through all the land and property."

In the morning, when she looked at her mother she thought that her conversation last night had been mere delirium. Covering her head with a banana leaf to protect herself from the rain, her mother moved from one hut to another. Her shouts and calls muted the monotonous sound of rain and pierced the ear. Half the day, she cooked with damp jute stalks and firewood. Mariam thought that she was competing to pass a breathing test, the way she blew on the chula to kindle the fire. Apart from Ratna and Chhanda, the other three in their home were practically dead. They were only enacting the roles of living people in public. But whether as actors or real life, people had to eat to survive. The baskets of seed paddy were becoming empty one by one. So, in the end, the two labourers tied water pots to their chests and swam in the water to pluck sheaves of rice from beneath the surface. They beat the paddy with clubs to separate the rice from the chaff. Mary and Monowara Begum spread the not-yet-mature grain on a tin sheet and placed it on the fire to dry. Then they threshed it for a good long time. Finally, what appeared were not whole grains of rice but broken bits. This was cooked into thick gruel for all meals. Every day, a few hungry villagers would grope their way through neck-deep waters to share the meal. The supply of firewood and fuel had been exhausted by cooking meals this way. Mother and daughter then pulled out the wooden posts of the cookhouse and brought down some of the straw from the roof. They even chopped up the big wooden thresher for firewood. The two women came very close to each other as they lit the kitchen fire by pulling down the roofing and destroying objects of everyday use, cooking rice by converting the seed paddy into grain. Their needs and desires were the same. Their strategy for survival did not differ. What was the point of guarding against the inevitable? Mariam thought that for the first time after the war that she had found a friend in the true sense of the word. A person whose condition was the same as hers. Both of them had no future. To have to stretch out one's hand to beg for a favour was a shame, false reassurances were even more terrible – the mother was giving practical lessons to the daughter.

The floodwaters were receding fast, leaving behind a layer of silt. Famine advanced, stepping silently on the soft soil. Hordes of men and women, driven by hunger, roamed around blindly, looking for food with dented bowls and earthen platters in their hands. Throughout the day, they walked in and out of Kafiluddin's house. You could hear the continuous din of people asking for rice or rice-water. Even as the food was ladled out into one person's bowl, there was a scuffle for it between men and dogs. Kafiluddin either went to town, protecting himself with an umbrella in order to read a newspaper, or he sat at home cursing independence. His son was an ass. Should anyone go to war, sacrifice their life for such independence? His eyes smarted remembering the famine of 1943. That year his crazy mother had sent him down to the bottomless waters to gather snails and mussels. That was his first encounter with death, under water.

Even as he bobbed up empty-handed after long submergence, his mother would hit him on the head with a stick as she stood on dry ground and send him down again. Two famines in a lifetime. One engineered by the British government, and the other by the Americans by stopping rice exports. What ruthless revenge by rich countries over poor, hungry people. Meanwhile, Monowara Begum was going off her head. When she sat down to a meal with her husband and children, skeletal hands stretched their plates silently through open doors and windows. Their eyes were dead. Their stomachs had shrivelled and stuck to their backs. They did not have the strength to utter a sound. At night, one could not step out onto the yard or the veranda for the huddles of people.

During such a night, in a house filled with people, Monowara Begum left her bed stealthily. Mary was asleep. She was shaken awake by her mother and sat up. "Don't stay here anymore. Just leave tomorrow."

"Why, Ma?"

"Don't waste words, Mariam. Here, take this." In the darkness, the little bundle in her hand that she pushed towards Mariam clinked. It was heavy. All Monowara Begum's gold ornaments were in it. The daughter did not even have the chance to feel surprised. Ma changed the subject. "I knew that your marriage was not a real one. It was play-acting. Your father started dancing when he got the news. He would not listen to me. Oh! the unfortunate man."

The ornaments, which were due to Montu's would-be wife, which could have been part of the dowry for Ratna and Chhanda, were now the capital for Mariam's survival. Handing over the bundle to Mariam, she said, "Be careful how you spend it. I have deprived the two younger ones and given these to you. I don't regret that. They will live their own lives."

Like Ma, Mary also understood that the twins possessed a hundred percent potential for survival. Although they were extremely talkative, they were also very cautious. Instead of going to Mahua cinema hall to watch a movie, they bought film magazines and guzzled all the titillating gossip about film stars. They cut out pictures of the stars and decorated their study. Floods, famine, their father's dotty behaviour, mother's mission of destruction, elder sister's misfortunes – none of it moved them. They did not have much to say about the war of liberation. As if they had known that their only brother would become a martyr in the war. They avoided the pitfalls on their elder sister's former way of life. No matter how crumbly the path was, it was still a path. There were mileposts on that road, like a letter mark in mathematics. So they would not need Jashimul Haques's inspiration to learn the algebra formulas. To study in college, they didn't need the kind of scandal that meant they could not find husbands. Their elder sister was already a graduate. It was quite natural that they would also graduate. If a person made a mistake, another was made to rectify it. Since, there was no Jashimul Haque in their lives, there was no scope for the arrival of an opportunistic man like Abed. And wars did not happen every year. There was a seventeen-year gap between the First and the Second World Wars.

The twins were in no way dependent on their elder sister. Just as they had welcomed her, they possessed the astonishing capacity to send her off with equal ease. The day Mariam left, there was no tussle between them to put her luggage on the rickshaw. They just stood side by side holding on to the door. By then they had become aware that the elder sister was bankrupt, her marriage had broken up. The next stage of Mariam's life could not be an example for anyone. Her sisters would remember all her failures. They would not allow her failures to come near them. Standing at a distance, Ratna and Chhanda bade Mariam farewell by waving their hands.

After the floodwaters had receded, Kafiluddin Ahmed spent most of his time in town. The tea stalls at the market withstood such a big famine because of the depth of his pocket. He sat there, bargaining with brokers dealing with the buying and selling of land. Cups of steaming tea were consumed, accompanied by crisp, hot snacks like nimki, and jalebi. Hearing that his daughter and her husband had separated, he adopted a silence which he did not break even on the day she left. Picking up his discoloured umbrella and putting it under his arm, he left for town even on the morning of that day.

Without any previous intimation, Monowara Begum decided, at the very last moment, to accompany her daughter. All the weak, gasping dependents at home smelt trouble. If the dispenser of food was not there, then there would be no food. The twins were of no use to them except for watching the fun. They quickly collected their bundles and followed mother and daughter on their open van rickshaw in a long, hungry procession. As if Monowara Begum was leading the procession that was going to besiege Dhaka. Left behind were two stunned girls and three rooms with tin roofs. The mud and wattle rooms were broken up and used as fuel for the hearth by mother and daughter who had left no trace of them.

XXIII

The Golden Years

Monowara Begum's self-confidence took a hit the moment she entered the city. She couldn't take even a single step unless she held on to her daughter's hand. The woman who would stride through the pitch darkness at Kafiluddin's homestead was constantly stumbling in the well-lit streets of Dhaka. "Ah! Mariam, take my shoes off and carry them in your hands. How do people walk wearing these deathly things?" Walking out of the bus stand, Mariam quickly hired a rickshaw. But where would they go now? Golam Mostofa had rented out the house at Rayer Bazar two years ago. During those days of looting and squatters, they would have lost possession of the house had it not been rented out. Earlier, when they had come to Dhaka, they had gone directly to the Maghbazar house. Now they were two women separated from their husbands. Was the hospitality of a tenant, who was a stranger, better for them or the house of a relative? No response was forthcoming from Monowara Begum even when the question was asked. Sitting comfortably in the rickshaw, she looked around her with interest. Like a child, she had endless curiosity. She also had a lot of questions. She had come to Dhaka after a long time. The city was somehow worthless. So many imposing buildings and ordinary homes, so many cars and other modes of transport, such dazzling flashes of light – and yet the darkness would not go away. Where did they all go, these groups of people with their bundles, their little kids? All these starving, skeletal, rootless people? The rickshawallah said, "To the free kitchen. The government has started free kitchens. That is where they go to eat." Monowara Begum immediately recalled the hungry procession at Fultali village. If they could come into the city, they would survive by getting some food in their bellies. She had not been able to bring them with her because she did not have the fare. She would have had to reserve a whole bus for the dozens of people. That would have cost at least a thousand taka. Where would Monowara Begum have gotten so much money? The fare for her daughter and herself, she had quietly removed from Kafiluddin's pocket the previous night. Both of them had somehow jumped into the bus with that money. The hungry procession stood at the edge of the road stupidly. She had led them all the way, clapping like a snake charmer and then deserted them at the bus stand. The people felt betrayed and angry. The bus conductor would not wait. Before the crowd could strike, just like a snake raising its hood, the conductor smacked his hand on the bus and the driver drove off.

The road came to an end before Monowara Begum's regrets were done with. Their rickshaw stopped in the dark lane before the black gate on which were written Kafiluddin Ahmed's name and address. The two women silently entered the open gate like a couple of robbers. Outside there was the wonderful perfume of the thriving Queen of the Night shrub, inside lived a poor clerk with his clutch of children. He was a harmless man. Golam Mostofa had taken into consideration the fact that even if he could not keep up with the rent regularly, he was a quiet, humble man who would not react easily. His trusting nature proved useful for the mother and daughter. He believed Mariam and Monowara Begum instantly even though he had never directly seen his landlord or knew anything about him and his family. He gave them a share of their rotis made from ration-shop flour. He vacated the larger room for the use of the mother and daughter and drove the half-a-dozen hungry children to the smaller room next door. As if the new arrivals were his cherished kin. He looked after their needs with utmost care. On the other hand, the clerk's wife did not utter a word from the very beginning. Her face, white like paper, became paler with panic. The added burden of two persons in these times of want! Besides, they had arrived with a notice for vacating the house like the appearance of Azrael, the angel of death. They had not said anything as yet, but it was clear that the mother and daughter were not the kind of people to share hardships with a whole lot of people in a crowded home. They were the kind used to spreading out and living life on their own terms. The clerk's wife's thoughts became a reality the next day.

In the morning, Monowara Begum woke from her sleep and began finding countless faults with everything. She drove the couple deaf by shouting and screaming, pointing out where dirt had accumulated, asking why the trees and plants had not been cleared of weeds, why the paved area near the tubewell had been allowed to become slippery with algae – "Oh dear! If I slip and fall, my old bones will not be whole." The children, if they dared to make a sound, would get a scolding from her. It reminded Mariam of her own life as a dependant. Her mother had no idea in what hell she had lived the last five years. This the daughter realized as she witnessed the humiliation of the clerk's family. This was a new facet of mother's personality. She was completely copying Kafiluddin Ahmed. Although she had left home without telling anyone, her husband's shadow had trailed her to the city. Mariam said nothing. If her mother became annoyed and changed her mind, she would be left with nothing. Instead, let the clerk's family be driven out onto the streets.

Monowara Begum ruled over the family for one whole month without hindrance. But she suddenly softened the day they left. Impulsively, she gave the eldest daughter of the tenant a pair of gold earrings as an advance gift for her wedding. She made the younger children sit on her lap and petted them. The whole family and their luggage filled a single handcart. Mariam had always found shelter in the abandoned properties of ousted people. All of them had been political refugees. She had never witnessed their departures. This time Mariam broke down in tears when she saw the cartload of eight people with all their belongings move on. She cried for all the refugees in the world, for her own repeatedly uprooted life. When Monowara Begum wanted to know the reason for her tears, she could say no more than "Ma, we will not be happy" to explain her feelings. "Happiness," Monowara Begum spluttered with rage on hearing her daughter use the word, "Does happiness grow on a tree, Mariam, that you can pluck it and it will be yours? You have ruined your own life and you have finished mine. Such a daughter you are."

What was Ma saying? Mariam's tears dried up at once. What happened then between them could be called a spat, an argument. Each accused the other. For the next eight months, they did the same thing every now and then. The phase ended with the predictions of an astrologer at Bahadur Shah Park. The man's tame parrot picked out an envelope with its beak which held the secret of Monowara Begum's future. Mariam never got to know what was written inside. But Monowara Begum packed her bags the very next day and went home to the village. And Monowara Begum's undying achievement was that, defying the predictions made by Anuradha, she had saved Mariam from turning into a whore. To do so, was a mother's difficult responsibility on behalf of her daughter, and what was more, it was a nation's unfinished task, the partial rehabilitation of a Birangana in society.

It was a golden period for Mariam. Mother and daughter earned their livelihood from the sale of gold. The first thing they did was to sell a pair of thick gold bangles and buy a sewing machine. They survived by buying the exorbitantly priced supplies with money from selling jewellery, before they managed to earn anything from the sewing machine. They took some gold in a pouch and went to the market. It was exchanged there for half its price. The money once again changed hands for rice, fish, vegetables. Monowara Begum could not stand the smell of ration-shop rice. She couldn't bear to taste powdered milk. And yet the price of rice was climbing every hour. Even when the price of rice had doubled within a month, mother and daughter could be seen bringing a sack from the shop. Every morning, an old milkman from Kamrangir Char brought a jug of fresh, frothy milk. For breakfast, they would have parathas fried in oil instead of dry rotis. Monowara Begum's view was that if you had to live in the city, you must live like proper city people. There could be no short cuts. Meanwhile, she had become quite accustomed to tripping through the streets in high heels. There was hardly any trace of the Fultali village accent in her speech. Her stock of English words was increasing as fast as the price of rice. Golam Mostofa came occasionally and was full of admiration at his sister's manners and conversation. He would take Mariam aside and gave her some advice in a low voice. He'd say, "It should not be forgotten that the fulfilment of a woman's life is in marriage and motherhood. A woman's youth is like a banana plant. It dries up faster than it grows. Then the woman is worse than a street dog."

Golam Mostofa's words were sharp but the way he spoke was somewhat detached. It was as if he was giving some valuable advice to his niece because it was his duty to do so as an elder. He was still a busy man as he had been earlier. The government of an independent country had kept the Enemy Property Act intact but changed its name. But Golam Mostofa was no longer interested in property belonging to Hindus. The political conditions were so confused at the moment. It was as if one could land fish even if spreading a torn fishing net. He was now engaged in politics full time. His opinion of Kafiluddin Ahmed was stated in a forthright fashion. There was nothing roundabout in it. In a loud voice, he told Monowara Begum, "Dulabhai is continuing to lop the branch that he is sitting on. I am telling you, Bubu, he is completely mad." Monowara Begum immediately agreed to the words spoken by her understanding brother, "Does a woman leave her home unless there is unbearable suffering? The man lost his mind before my very eyes. Whom can I share this sorrow with?" For a while the brother and sister discussed how Kafiluddin Ahmed was destroying their family by selling off all the land. The only disagreement cropped up when suddenly Golam Mostofa said, "Bubu, first let me finish what I have to say. A man whose son's a martyr, does he need to do anything else, these days? Dulabhai is a fool. He hasn't the sense to make the most of this opportunity."

Even before Golam Mostofa could finish what he had to say, Monowara Begum pulled away the unfinished plate of snacks from in front of her brother and strode into the kitchen. When she came out, her eyes were blood-red and dry. If they rubbed against gunpowder, it would probably catch fire and explode. Golam Mostofa did not wait any further. When he got up saying, "I have an urgent meeting," Monowara Begum roared, "Where are you off to, Mostofa. Wait." Her high-pitched voice deepened. Taking long deep breaths, she spat out, "You'll see me dead if you take Montu's name once again in this house."

Golam Mostofa stomped out of the house. But Monowara Begum's curses and rantings did not stop. "My brother's a low-down scrooge. He's inhuman. I hope Khoda lets him burn in the same fire in which I am burning. I swear to you Mostofa, you will witness the death of your son."

Even if they did not reach Golam Mostofa's ears, the outpourings lightened Monowara Begum's heart. After her brother left, she took out a nicely folded sari from her trunk and wore it carefully. She powdered her creased cheeks, stuffed a paan in her mouth and trotted off in her high-heels. Monowara Begum was the marketing manager of Mariam's readymade clothes. She went from door to door and said, "My eldest daughter has golden hands. Her stitching is not shoddy like the stuff in the market. She will sew petticoats, blouses with or without sleeves, bell bottoms, kurtas at half the price. Do come to the house with the clump of bamboos, now, of course, there is a Queen of the Night bush."

The bamboo clump was still fresh in the memory of the older women residents of the neighbourhood. But they came to the house following the scented trail of the Queen of the Night. The boy from this house died in the war. The girl was a Birangana. Having been invited by the mother, they actually came to see the daughter. The mother was also worth a look. But they did not think that Monowara Begum felt any grief for her lost son. All they could see was the show she put on. These women did not have the empathy to understand that the mother was slowly being pulverized inside, her inner self being eaten away by sorrow just as a woodworm eats into wood. Monowara Begum sensed their thoughts and their covert glances and felt very let down. They didn't even bother to look at the new sewing machine. They had no time for Mary's golden hands. They pushed aside the clothes with attractive new designs and closely scanned the body ravished by the military. Then they left, having partaken of refreshments and tea made with condensed milk. Monowara Begum escorted the guests to the gate, as was her habit. They talked more while they stood outside than when they were inside. After some trivial comments, they said, "Can you live on your daughter's income? Won't you get her married?" Or they said, "Why don't you get her married? Don't you get proposals?" The women of the neighbourhood went off to their own homes having had their say. Monowara Begum re-entered her home, grumbling away and sat with her accounts. Tea and refreshments, eight annas per head. Total: one taka. One paan: two paisa. "Oh Mariam. Will these people only eat and leave? Will they never place an order? You've sunk yourself and now you're sinking me."

After this, could there be anything pleasant to say? They wrangled about who was ruining whom. The more their store of gold diminished, the more they quarrelled. Fed up, one day Mariam left the house. She was angry with herself more than with her mother. What was wrong with her that she could not adjust to life with her own mother? Where could such a woman find shelter? Right from the beginning, whenever she had faced a crisis, the avenues of rain trees on Fuller Road had drawn her. One day, Mariam's dreams had taken wing under the interlaced shadows of the trees. This time, when she ran out of the house, she went to that source of her dreams. The area was busy as before. But there were no processions and no slogan-shouting that had earlier disturbed even the crows. The various slogans and demands painted on the walls had been whitewashed away. Everyone's needs and charges had been buried under a layer of white. The prolonged struggle and the movement were at last over. Or was it that the participants were tired? Mariam was still in her Golden Age. She did not know that there was an Emergency in the country. Meetings, processions, strikes and lockouts were prohibited.

Mariam walked by the blank walls, along streets without slogans. When she felt tired, she sat on the dusty pavement. Over her head was a richly ornamented regal canopy of rain trees. Under it, a new pair of lovers were shelling peanuts and feeding each other. Their dreams were unreal, their eyes misty. They saw Mariam sitting nearby but her presence did not really register. Towards evening the number of couples grew and the place became quite crowded and noisy like a fish market. There were not many places to sit. When Mariam would come and remain sitting there, the couples would make rude comments and push her out. For one thing, she was without a partner, for another they were quite strict about age limits. That Mariam was getting older, she realized from their comments. Even then she would not give up her right to the source of her dreams. At home, there was Ma's irritable temper and the stench of hides rotting for lack of salt at the tannery. From the moment Mariam woke every morning, she began her preparations for going out. But she never left home before afternoon. When the lovers of the rain tree grove were looking at their watches impatiently as they sat in classrooms listening to the professor's lectures, Mariam would be spending her time taking care of her skin and hair. Monowara Begum was amazed at her daughter's sudden attention to dressing up. Then she realized it was her age that drove her to it. But if her daughter set up a new home, then what would be her fate? Or, what if she became a whore?

But suppose the girl did not turn into a whore and got married to someone instead, and then had a baby? Monowara Begum knew that Mary's child would only serve to intensify her grief for her lost son and not lessen it. In despair, she kept throwing household objects onto the floor. She would pick them up only to hurl them down again. She could find no words to articulate her feelings. She remained silent even when Mariam went out of the house trailing a scent of cosmetics in the air and letting the end of her sari float by. She stood on the threshold and repeated like a chant the slogan which Mariam had told her about had been coined for International Women's Year : "Won't be a Mother in 1975". Monowara Begum's fear-frozen face slowly broke into a mischievous smile. She planned to write a small note to Kafiluddin Ahmed. The only words to be written on it would be "Won't be a Mother in 1975." This would be an apt lesson for the man who had gone crazy about a son. The idea was highly amusing for Monowara Begum.

In the grove of rain trees, Mariam experienced the dreams of others through her own eyes. Although these dreams are like expensive clothes seen through the plate glass windows of shops and completely beyond her reach, her vicarious dreaming did not stop. She walked down the misty path of her dreams which led her to a lost city from five years ago. There were meetings, processions and speeches all around like scintillating sparklers. The people galloped like horses. They all shouted the same slogan. Their aspirations were also the same. Hungry men or well-fed, paunchy men, naked men or men who were suited and booted – all were united in their demand for freedom. In that unified, uncomplicated, animated city, the army marched in one day. Her dreams flew away like a flock of birds does from the din of gunshots, the smell of explosives and the sound of marching boots. Leaving behind the paper bags of peanuts, the men went off to war. Their beloveds were left floating, vulnerable. The enemy soldiers chased them and dragged them to camp from behind hedges, pond sides, under the shelter of the trees. Death or pregnancy was their inevitable fate. When the war ended, the lovers who were still alive returned to the city. But they did not get back together again. In search of old dreams at the grove of rain trees, the afternoons and early evenings slid away like droplets of water from yam leaves.

Time was a great betrayer. No new dreams were spun for Mariam during those afternoons and evenings. But whether through sitting rooted at the same spot each day, or her overly done makeup, she finally attracted the attention of passers-by. This was a first step towards dreaming new dreams. It meant bringing down her age level to that of these young lovers. But the gestures and suggestions that men made at her had only one meaning. They wanted quickie sex for a paltry ten or twenty taka. And for this they would signal with a flick of the finger that she should go to Ramna Park or the client's hostel room. If one scratched out the park option for its lack of privacy, then what remained was the hostel room – bachelor's quarters. There three or four persons lived in a single room. Dirty, soapy water collected in their bathrooms. A stale, fuggy smell of tobacco clung to the cobwebs in the room. The signallers, their teeth stained with paan juice, their looks leering, could arouse no response in Mariam's loveless body. When they would move to one side of the rickshaw and indicate the vacant seat to her with their eyes, Mariam would turn her face away and look at the young lovers sitting next to her. For she wanted dreams, not lust, even if she had to see the dreams through the solid plate glass windows of shops. But even that glance was frustrating. She was forced to turn her gaze away from the intimacy of the lovers and look once again at the road. Some days, at that precise moment, the droppings of a crow flying overhead fell on her head. Mariam glanced around her and began rubbing her hair and plait with her handkerchief. Then there was no sense in her continuing to sit there. Before she could be driven away by the sarcastic comments of the lovers, she left her place on the kerb and quickly started walking towards the crossing of Palashi for a rickshaw. There was a new cobbler where the old one had been seen on the first day. He had his head bent in the same way, mending shoes. When he heard Mariam's tired feet shuffling by, he raised his head and looked. But he did not see her. Peering through the eyes of the earlier cobbler, his gaze searched for Abed. Mariam thought that like the cobbler of old, he could be living in the newly-repaired slum next door and if there was a war again, like the previous cobbler he too would be burned down with his entire family at midnight.

The cobbler, who might be burnt to cinders in another war, had his eyes glued to the road. There were two men on a rickshaw who had followed Mariam from the rain tree grove to the Palashi intersection. One of them wore bell-bottom pants, a brightly printed shirt and sunglasses. The other man wore ordinary clothes but had a headful of long hair. When the cobbler suddenly stood up, his eyes fixed on someone, Mariam turned and looked over her shoulder. The man wearing sunglasses got off the rickshaw and stretched his long arm towards her. Surprisingly, he wore a smile. Mariam stood stock still with her back to the white wall beside the kerb and till he took off his sunglasses, she did not recognize Abed's one-time good-natured roommate, Suman. Apart from the cobbler, all three of them broke into peals of laughter. Once again, the cobbler bent his head and began repairing shoes.

Suman was a young man with an income. Not having secured a job, he had become a contractor. He had a place in Azimpur. It was walking distance from where they were. The young man with him did not do anything for a living. But he had a flair for writing. Suman was an admirer of his talents. Suman's respect for the youth was quite obvious. Mariam agreed instantly when they invited her to their home. But the new cobbler was not happy with the idea. The woman had drawn his attention by dragging her feet homewards daily. The new cobbler had felt reassured by that. Today, as he watched Mariam leave with the two young men, a deep sigh fluttered out of his chest for the Abed and Mary known to the earlier cobbler.

Their destination was a two-roomed bachelor's quarter next to the Azimpur graveyard. Overhead on a length of string hung a huddle of lungis, underwear, gamchhas. The bathroom was damp with scummy soap water. The smell of stale tobacco hung in the air. The rooms were exactly like those that could have belonged to the men in the rickshaw who had gestured to her to share their seat. Mariam felt disturbed – the setting was a copy of something she had seen in a bad dream. But she could not leave even if she had wanted to. After all, she had come voluntarily. The men were not behaving badly. They had invited her to sit on the only chair in the room. Suman changed swiftly into a lungi and went into the kitchen to make tea. From there he ran to the head of the lane and bought biscuits, bananas and chanachur from the local grocery store. In comparison to him, the genius was more lethargic. In the absence of Suman, she did not know how to start a conversation with him. The man was also silent. From time to time, he moved his fingers through his long hair. As much as Suman sang praises of the poet, the poet himself was equally reticent, as if he was forced to tolerate his admirer. After setting out the tea and snacks, Suman pulled out a pile of published and unpublished writings as well as drafts from under the pillow. As he was doing this, he got a scolding from the writer in a low voice. But it didn't make him less eager. Poor Suman! From 1969 to 1971 student leader Abed had been his guru, from 1975 it was a writer. So how had people's attention been diverted from politics to literature? Were the heroes of the day those who wrote? Mariam tried to understand the present through Suman's fascination. Turning the pages she saw that the writer's name was also Abed. But there was no Jahangir attached to it. It was Samir. Abed Samir – a fitting name for a literateur.

XXIV

Mother-Daughter Tailoring

From what courage, Woman,
Do you navigate this world of agony?
Lightning flashes from the sky
The wind brings freezing chill,
You are resolute, holding aloft to the left,
The Sword of Allah.

Al-Mahmud

The day Abed Samir accompanied Suman to Mariam's home, he was actually quite loquacious. He did not give anyone much of a chance to talk. In his opinion, the house with Kafiluddin Ahmed's name and address on it was a valuable relic of history. It deserved to be conserved from top to bottom. Writers and artists should be living in such houses. But sadly, those who were living in this one may have had artistic temperaments but felt no urge to express their talents. Suman was very proud of his writer friend's enigmatic comments. He expressed his agreement by nodding furiously. Monowara Begum took Mary aside and said, "Hey Mariam! The boy seems a little mad to me. See how he has kept his hair long like a woman. You have set up a salon in your home; will these men give you some orders for clothes?"

By then, their joint venture in readymade clothes had dipped in the red. The sewing machine was about to get rusty. The pot of gold was also empty. Monowara Begum was losing her head. Her daughter, instead of replying, made a face and went back to her friends.

Monowara Begum stood outside while random thoughts raced through her mind. Her daughter had gone astray. She was the one who would now have to take over the running of the household. It did not matter what price she would have to pay. As her rage subsided, her thoughts turned towards practical business matters. Like a professional actor, she assumed a different persona and entered the stage. It was now time for her to occupy centre stage with a cool head. Very soon the topic of the *adda* veered from abstraction in literature to conditions in the country. She said, "I don't see any way that a person can make an honest living and enjoy a simple meal of rice and dal. What on earth has come over the country?" After that she directed the conversation to a point where she slipped in the information of their financial distress. The audience felt a little uneasy. She got up and brought out some dresses in eye-catching designs, and she took the sewing machine as well and placed them right in the middle of the gathering. Monowara Begum spoke in a measured tone. The deep resonance of her voice cast a spell on the two men but made Mariam very anxious. She said, "You know, my dears, my only son laid down his life in the war of liberation. Did he go to war for this wretched country? Who does this country belong to nowadays – some frauds, hoarders, blackmarketeers." Had there been a public meeting there would have been applause at the end of such a speech. Mariam and Abed Samir sat quietly. Suman got up and examined the clothes. He looked worried. He was a helpful person. He was the one who took the initiative to ease the financial hardship of the mother and daughter.

That evening, Abed Samir's literary language skill brought forth the name 'Ma-Meye Tailoring' (Mother-Daughter Tailoring) and posters for the venture. Monowara Begum went to the kitchen and made a paste with flour and water. Then they went and stuck the posters made with coloured paper on walls, lamp-posts and tree trunks at Jigatola, Rayer Bazar, Tannery Crossing. The initiative held novelty. The posters were attractive. They inspired people to get new clothes even during this inflation. People bought coloured, printed cloth by the yard and tucked it under their arms or wrapped it in old newspaper and arrived at the house that had Kafiluddin Ahmed's name on it. Monowara Begum had placed a long bench on the veranda for customers to sit. Mariam measured their bodies, cut the material with the click-clack of the scissors, filled the bobbin with thread and spun the handle with a loud whir. Scraps of coloured cloth grew into mounds around her. A web of threads surrounded her. And around her neck a measuring tape was wound day and night like a striped snake.

Monowara Begum delivered the ordered clothes and took the payment. She would make out the receipts and keep accounts. Both mother and daughter remained very busy with their enterprise. As long as the handle of the machine turned, the wheels of the household would run smoothly. Their livelihood was now entwined with a machine. Monowara Begum liked to repeat this to neighbours and customers whenever she got the chance. It was difficult to know whether she said it with regret or with pride. It was Mariam who first rebelled at the routine. She felt as if she was continuing to do what she had done at the rehabilitation centre. She was a refugee from life. How could a mere sewing machine rehabilitate her? Was it possible? These blisters between her fingers, this aching spine, the constant tingling of pins and needles in her legs – what were they for? She was after all a single person and had only to feed herself. Besides the stomach there were other organs. And a human being was not only a body. To be hunched over a machine the whole day was a waste of life. She began to make more and more mistakes in cutting and stitching. One day, she stitched the sleeves of a blouse the wrong way round, kicked at the mound of cloth scraps, tore the web of threads, pushed away her sewing machine and rose from her work station at the wrong time. Monowara Begum shouted a warning, "Mariam, what you're doing is not right. We're supposed to deliver a dozen blouses today. People will come and wait. One cannot play jokes with one's livelihood, my daughter." In response, Mariam threw down a pile of plates and utensils on the kitchen floor and went out of the house.

The lovers of the rain tree grove were still in their classes, surreptitiously looking at their watches while listening to the lectures. Till the sun set in the western sky, the new cobbler would not shift from his place on the left pavement to the right. Mariam avoided that side and went to Azimpur. Suman was not at home. Abed Samir sat with reddened eyes amid a heap of unsatisfactory, rejected drafts crumpled into balls. His hair was dishevelled, his mood irritable. The moment he opened the door, he greeted Mariam with the question, "What do you want?" Mary's mood was equally sour. "Whatever I may want it is not you. Where is Suman?" Without waiting for an answer, she strode towards Suman's room. She hesitated a bit before sitting on the bed spread with a dirty sheet. Was the hesitation because of the unclean sheet or the absence of the room's owner? Mariam thought it could be both. Having lived through nine months of war in indescribably filthy conditions, she had not become used to dirt but had become even more finicky. The absence of the room's occupant gave her a bit of relief. At least she could be alone for a while. She had lost her temper and left home. Over and above that there was the rude behaviour of Abed Samir. What did these men think of themselves? If they could not write themselves, was it the women's fault? Would it have been better for her to sit at the pavement near the grove of the rain trees, instead of coming here? Yanking off the oil-stained pillow cover and stuffing the pillow under her head, she thought that would have been no better. All those dreams and such were stuff and nonsense. Especially when they were old.

Still, as she lay on Suman's bed, Mariam dreamt a dream of the old days. Armed with a rifle, Major Ishtiaque was controlling traffic in Dhaka city. He climbed down from his signal box and marched towards her blowing his whistle. Why had that man come again? Because of those people, Montu was dead, she was left to roam the streets – what need had they to come here? The Major was garrulous. He said that it was attraction, that he could not wipe out the soft spot he had for her. Mariam thought that such talk about attraction and soft spots was all rubbish. Golam Mostofa was her guardian and he had informed the Major and brought him here. When the man had come, they would certainly get married. Mary was not able to get married because of the war. Major Ishtiaque side-stepped the question of marriage and said with a shy smile that this was the land of his birth. Mariam was amazed – birthplace? The Major said, Wasn't it though! Just hear how well I sing Rabindra Sangeet *sahena jatana, dibas rajani* (cannot bear the pain day and night)…

Right in the middle of the song, Mariam understood that the possibility of marriage would hover in the air but would not happen. She was lying on the dirty bed of Suman's Azimpur residence and dreaming. The song was being sung by Debabrata Biswas, on a record player next door. But despite understanding all this, she could not awaken from her sleep. A dream wound around her lightly like golden vines and raised a serpentine hood towards the sky. The sun was in the western sky. Major Ishtiaque lit a cigarette at the Palashi crossing. But he looked like a clerk returning from office. He was carrying a briefcase and Mariam was his wife. The Major held up his hand and gestured to his wife not to go to the grove of rain trees. Why? Why? Mariam was not prepared to obey his ban. The Major said that curfew had been imposed there. No entry. Mariam was determined to go there, the man would not let her. The cobbler from the first day came forward to settle the dispute and was shot in the chest. No-o-o-o! Mariam broke through the knots of the golden vines and sat up on the bed with a start. She was streaming with sweat. The bed warmed by the afternoon sun, the lungis and vests on the clotheshorse disoriented her about where she was. More than the dream, her falling asleep in such a place struck a discordant note.

The door between the two rooms was ajar. There was at least an inch of space in the opening. One could hear from this room the murmur of conversation in the other room. Suman had returned. The two friends were talking to each other. Mariam thought that the talk was about her. Although the people in the dream seemed more real to her than the people around her, she could not quite ignore the men in the next room. Was it Suman who said, "Gosh! How hot it is." This would then be Abed Samir's voice, "Sleeping like a buffalo in this heat." "No, no. I had left the room and gone to the terrace." "It seems like there was some trouble at home." "Maybe, but did you have to escape to the terrace?"

The words made no sense. Was Mariam still dreaming? She forced herself to get up from the bed, rearranged her sari and dragged her feet towards the door. Half of Suman's body was hidden behind the newspaper. Abed Samir was snoring. "Why were you both saying nasty things about me?" Hearing Mariam's words, Suman lowered the paper and looked at her with surprise. At the same time, he managed a pleasant expression with difficulty. "How do people sleep in this heat?" Mariam smiled and replied in a voice heavy with troubled sleep, "Sleeping like a buffalo."

"Oh! No. Last night, unable to bear the heat, I had gone up to the terrace to sleep." Traces of the dream-state vanished from Mariam's mind instantly. Suman quickly enquired, "Has there been some trouble at home?" Strange, that a dream could converge on reality so completely. Or could it be that when they saw her enter the room, one of them stopped talking and faked sleep and the other covered himself with a newspaper? It didn't seem to be like that from Suman's words. He had come in from the burning sun and seen two people asleep in the two rooms. He had been ousted from his own house. Although Suman smiled as he talked, Mariam felt that he was hinting at some link between her and Abed Samir. So let him. Mariam was still caught like a fly in the web of her dreams and did not want to think of irrelevancies. But Suman would not let go. Out of the blue, he introduced the name of Abed Jahangir into the conversation. Abed had slipped badly in trying to continue his father-in-law's business. His wife had gone to visit her father's place in Lahore and was not coming back. They were not even exchanging letters. "Abed Bhai is close to going mad." Suman continued happily, "Now he wants to join BAKSAL and become a leader. So lowly Suman has been summoned suddenly at an odd time."

Mariam thought that it would have been better if he had pulled out Abed Samir's manuscripts from under the pillow than telling her all these things. Her temper would have remained equable. But Suman had no time for that today. It was clear that he had just returned from his former mentor in the blazing sun. After belching loudly Suman said, "Abed Bhai was so insistent. Otherwise, does anyone eat biryani in this heat? And kachchi biryani no less." Mariam suddenly remembered that she had not eaten lunch. Had Abed Samir eaten? Poor fellow! His days here would soon come to an end. The way Suman was racing towards his former Guru, the roof over the gifted writer's head was bound to shift soon enough. He may be out on the streets. But why was Mariam thinking about someone who had only a couple of hours earlier behaved so badly with her? Or could it be that she expected such ill-treatment from men, as if they did not think of her as a human being but as a stray dog. Otherwise, how could she have lived with a brute like Momtaj or a killer like Major Ishtiaque? Mariam felt restless. She wanted to slap Suman's belching face and walk out of the room. Who was the real street-dog—she or Suman? The person who ran to taste biryani the moment a beckoning whistle was blown, was not her but Suman.

Suman was deep in his own thoughts. He suddenly asked her, "Do you want to join politics?"

What audacity! Mariam gnashed her teeth and asked, "Why?"

"No, I mean instead of tailoring, if you took up politics as a career, what's the harm? After all it is the age of politics."

"Or is it that since Abed Jahangir is now entering politics, I have to take it up also?"

"No, no. What's your connection with Abed Bhai? He is a married man and you…"

"What am I?"

Suman was annoyed.

"And what am I?" Mariam was raging. She had to know from Suman, who was she? Abed Samir awoke from his nap and looked at both of them in a dazed way. His mute eyes queried when the room had turned into a battleground. Mariam didn't care. She repeated the same question again and again, shaking like someone with hysteria. Her questions ended when Suman roared, "Why pretend you're a decent woman? We all know what you are. Trash left behind by the army. And you're talking big."

When Mariam came down to the street, it seemed the burning fever within had been sweated out of her. Everyone who spoke to her wore a mask of goodness and said nice things. How long would she have to go through it? She could only find peace when she tore off one mask after another. Like a mad woman, she muttered as she walked, "Yes, yes. I am trash left behind by the army. What's that to you? Am I your wedded wife or the mother of your child?" Behind her followed Abed Samir. He was trying to say something. Maybe he wanted to apologise on Suman's behalf. Mariam was not ready to give him that chance. She knew all of them. Suman also had escorted her once from S.M. Hall to the Palashi crossing. That day his eyes had been moist with sympathy for this army trash.

Mariam boarded a rickshaw without mentioning the destination or settling the fare. She did not look back. Ahead was the Palashi crossing. There stood Major Ishtiaque, briefcase in hand, like a clerk returning from work. The cobbler of old was repairing shoes single-mindedly. There was curfew in the rain tree grove. One could not go that way. From now on, she had to keep her dreams in check. How many who were so close to her had disappeared from her life forever within a short time. She had no way of reclaiming them except through dreams. If she did not keep this pathway open, then the mainstream that nurtured her life would get dammed up and create an aridity in her. Like the desolation of the grave's darkness. Mariam instructed the rickshawallah to take her quickly to Rayer Bazar.

Monowara Begum opened the door in silence and stood aside. Mariam was now a defeated soul. She who had stormed out of the house a few hours ago was now entering her room with the silent steps of a cat. The room was at least a refuge. Did her mother know of the thorny, barbed world outside?

In those few hours, all of Monowara Begum's strength had been exhausted. In the afternoon, when she was collecting the scraps of cloth and stuffing them into a sack, a thought suddenly hit her that she was living on the earnings of Mary. Would her daughter have to spend the rest of her life whirling the sewing machine with bandaged fingers? With the revolutions of the machine, days, months, years were passing by. Who could stop this passage of time? Let Mary find her own direction, if there was any. She would not stop her.

Mother and daughter sat down when the evening lamp was lit to eat the cold rice made for lunch which had become a bit watery in the heat of noon. There was pin-drop silence in the room. Each was absorbed in her own thoughts. How quickly a day could become different from all other days. Monowara Begum had stopped counting the marketing expenses on her fingers. She was no longer concerned about the profit and loss of 'Ma-Meye Tailoring' or its future. Life was a great betrayer. Its big account was being reckoned by someone, invisible to man and beyond counts kept on fingers. The mouthful of rice stuck in Monowara Begum's throat. She put down her glass of water and said to her daughter in a soft voice, "I know one kind of life. Husband-children. Allah did not allow me to keep them. But I think life is not just of a single sort. You have time ahead of you. You find your own life, my daughter."

A son's death, loss of daughter's honour, did it make a mother grow up? Otherwise, it was unbelievable that she was saying these things. Following the incident of Mohua cinema and the slur on Mariam's reputation, her mother's life had been ruined. She would constantly pray for her own death. She would also tell her daughter, "Die, die, take poison and kill yourself. Oh Ma! What is this black serpent that I carried in my womb. Khoda, please take this servant of yours, please take me. Dear God!"

Now Monowara Begum was defeated by the complexity of life. The city streets were flooded by rains. But she remained immobile. After her morning ablutions, she would sit herself down somewhere and remain there for the rest of the day. Mariam ran the machine intermittently. The coloured posters of 'Ma-Meye Tailoring' had been washed out by the rains. There was no point in putting up new posters during the monsoon. Besides, the people at Rayer Bazar, Tannery Morh and Jigatola knew about 'Ma-Meye Tailoring'. They had got clothes stitched from them according to their needs. The demands of this lower middle class neighbourhood had been taken care of during the last three months. The bench outside, where the customers sat, remained empty. According to the rules of capital growth, what was needed now were new markets and new customers. That needed new, well-designed attractive, smart posters. The ebb in the mother and daughter enterprise prevented that possibility. Mariam stitched together bits of cloth and made shifts for babies, pillow covers, cushions, tea cosies. From time to time, she came and stood at the door and stretched herself to ease her joints. Monowara Begum continued to sit by the window. Her eyes and her mind were focused on the pouring rain outside indefinitely. Now, who would take the stitched products to the market to sell?

One day, drenched in the rains like a wet crow, Abed Samir came to Mariam's house, Monowara Begum did not know anything about Suman and Mary's quarrel. She got up from her window seat to welcome him and made him sit in the veranda. Mariam was in the sewing room stitching baby clothes. Hearing Monowara Begum's cries, she looked up as if she was coming out of a trance and closed the machine. "Mariam, come, come. Get up. Look who is here."

Stitching was not just a means of livelihood for Mariam these days. With the revolving of the machine her life spun in reverse and went back to the past. She lined up the little coloured dresses on the bed – this one was for Shobha Rani's baby, this one was for Bindubala's and this for Tuki's. Mariam did not deprive the infants of the rehabilitation centre who were flown off to foreign lands in airplanes. At the very edge of the bed, she kept a few clothes for the expatriate war babies. At home, other than her mute mother, there was no one else to disturb her private activities. So Monowara Begum's excited calls today felt like they were jolting her out of sleep. "Get up and come quickly. Mariam, see who has come."

Who has come Ma, Montu? Has Montu come, my Mother? Mariam's thoughts, deep in reverie, screamed the question in silence and she jumped off the bed just as she used to as a child. It was now the turn of Monowara Begum to be surprised. "Wait, Mariam. Arrange your sari properly. I have made Abed sit in the veranda." Abed! The name causes a tremor in Mariam like a landslide on the mountain. But prodded by her mother she was on the veranda by then. The duplication of names was a constant in her life. Major Ishtiaque, number one, number two. Abed Jahangir, Abed Samir.

Samir became a little nervous when he saw the deep scowl on Mariam's brows,. He quickly rose from the bench, "I was going this way. Suddenly there was such a downpour." Monowara Begum echoed him, "Yes, Son! What rotten rain. There is no way that one can go out. We're very happy that you came."

What was up with Mother? She had no interest left in the business. Why was she eager to make Abed Samir sit for a while? Then she said, "You two sit and chat." Then getting wet in the rain, she went to the kitchen to make tea. Oh! So this was Mother's second project. Mariam woke up from her long slumber. Mother was giving her the chance to discover whether there was a life beyond husband and children. There had never been any match between what her parents desired and what she wanted and attained. When she had resigned from her search for a different life, here was her mother urging her to resume the research. Who was right – Mother or she?

Abed was bewildered by the contradictory signals sent by mother and daughter. But he could understand Mariam's behaviour – her anger had not subsided. And it was not expected that it would subside. But the girl would surely be pleased with the news that he had landed two tuitions and was now self-sufficient. But Mariam was unmoved even by this information. So he wanted to see the clothes she had made. But that was a secret, even more of a secret than Abed Samir's crossed-out drafts of poems. It was Mariam's private pleasure to make clothes for infants and stack them in neat piles. Those were not for exhibition or for sale. So only pillow covers, cushions and tea cosies could be shown. The first thing that Abed Samir looked at when he entered the room was those objects of Mariam's private joy. "Let's see" he said and picked up a bunch of those tiny shifts. When Mariam snatched at them, they fell from his hands and scattered. These were mere clothes. What was so secret about them and why did the girl let out a sob when they had fallen to the ground? Samir's curiosity was aroused. A pile of clothes for new-borns was lying forlorn on the floor of a childless home. The scene was enough to perk up a man's filial affections and a woman's maternal instincts. Looking at Mariam's embarrassed face, Abed Samir thought for the first time that behind the rough appearance, this girl's face was tragic. It demanded attention rather than sympathy.

Monowara Begum's new project 'A different life for her daughter beyond husband and children' progressed towards fruition. But it moved forward at a slow pace like a tortoise leaving imprints of its steps on dry ground. Towards evening Abed Samir would come with his shoulder bag. Sitting on the veranda, he would bring out some new poems from his bag. Not more than a couple of customers came here through the day. Most of the requirements were for alterations of blouses, stitching falls on a sari, patching up an untimely tear, just repair and maintenance. The exchange of clothes and material were done by day's end. In the evening, the place was ideal for literary readings. Mariam had a bath, changed into fresh clothes and sat outside to listen to poetry. She could not, however, concentrate on it for very long. She remembered Anuradha very often. If the girl had been alive she would have been a well-known writer. She had had a very sharp brain. The way the listener's attention shifted eluded Abed Samir. Because his focus was more on himself than on Mariam. Monowara Begum cooked various delicacies for him. Dreaming of becoming a famous writer, he would have his meal, wash his hands, pick up his shoulder bag and leave.

There was no dynamism in such a life. It was like a still, algae-covered pond where one had to push away the water hyacinths to proceed. Monowara Begum's restlessness grew even as her energy abated. What kind of a man was her husband? She had lived with him for thirty-five years; she had been away in Dhaka for eight months, he hadn't even bothered to write a one-line letter. The man had not even replied to her note that said, "Will not become a mother in 1975". He was a total country bumpkin. The subtleties of city life did not touch him. Some of her annoyance with her husband was directed towards Mariam. She pretended anger and told her, "What kind of a daughter are you – you don't even enquire about your father. Would it harm you to write him a couple of lines asking after his health?"

It would not harm Mariam for sure but she did not write the couple of lines. She gave her mother the newspaper and told her to read it to pass the time. That led to a major crisis one day. Monowara Begum became depressed when she saw a photograph of a smiling Bangabandhu with his daughter-in-law wearing a golden coronet. If Montu had been alive, he would have been of an age to marry. She would have got him married with whatever they could afford. She may not have been able to afford a coronet but she could have got something smaller, say like a *tikli,* for the head of her daughter-in-law. The man, who had asked for every home to be turned into a fortress, for everyone to fight with whatever they had, had not suffered any

loss as far as his son and daughter went. How cruel! Now, he
had got his own son married and brought home a daughter-in-
law. Monowara Begum's regrets and laments did not stop. From
time to time she said, "What is this Mariam? The same path
leads to different places. Who had died and who was reaping
the harvest of the war? Let the rains stop. I will go to No.32 and
question that son of a Sheikh."

Mariam thought that mother had completely lost her mind.
Otherwise, how could she harbour such bizarre thoughts?
Could rulers and subjects ever be the same? One day, Monowara
Begum went out in the pouring rain although she told her not
to. Let her go, Mariam grumbled, when the gate-keeper would
throw her out, then she'd learn her lesson. In fact, it wouldn't be
surprising if she got arrested by the President's bodyguards. In
the evening, before she could tell Abed Samir the details, he told
her that he had seen her earlier at the Bahadur Shah Park getting
her fortune told by a man with a parrot. He had not greeted her
thinking that she would feel embarrassed.

Bahadur Shah Park. That was very far. Would she be able
to find her way back? Mariam was stunned. That day, Abed
Samir, instead of reading poetry, started reading loudly from
the newspaper.

"Sadarghat, Bahadur Shah Park, Bangabandhu Avenue,
Gulistan, Farm Gate. Fortune-tellers are sitting on the pavements
with signboards for fortune-telling and palmistry. They have
with them old manuscripts and a parrot. They read palms and
horoscopes and advise the wearing of amulets and rings of
coloured stones to overcome crises. To have fortunes read by
a parrot is even easier. Four tame parrots pick out an envelope
from a row of arranged envelopes. In that cover is a piece of
paper in which one's fortune is printed. The wheel of fortune
does not find direction in this round maze."

Monowara Begum returned home even before Abed Samir
had finished reading. But she did not bother to look at them.
Instead of cooking goodies as on other days, she shut the door
of her room and went and lay down on her bed. Abed Samir

slipped away when he saw the tricky turn of events. Mariam had nothing to eat that night. Ma showed no signs of getting up since she had taken to her bed. What had happened to her? What had the fortune-teller predicted that she had taken to bed? Mariam dozed off a bit thinking this and that. Monowara Begum woke her up at midnight. Again the night's drama was about to begin. All her dialogue now would probably be from some jatra seen in her childhood.

Close to Mariam's maternal grandfather's house had been a huge cattle and livestock market. Every year, during winter, jatra troupes would come and put up their tents. Ma said, "I grew up seeing jatras till I reached puberty." After she began menstruating, she was forbidden even to peer outside the house, let alone going to see jatras and plays. Monowara Begum was imprisoned in the enveloping purdah. And the countless dialogue from the jatras that she remembered from the past got stuck forever within her rib cage. If you put your ears to her chest, you could hear her rehearsing the dialogue to the rhythm of her heartbeats. Occasionally, late into the night, the dialogues unheard for a long time surfaced like women in purdah sheltered from the public gaze. At such times Monowara Begum did not like to have lights. That day also in the darkness of night, she sat by Mary in her bed and said with a deep sigh, "Mariam, my situation is worse than a beggar's. Whatever I had, I have given you – given you beyond my limits. The rest is in your hands."

She brought out from under the drapes of her sari the crumpled title deed of the house and gave it to her daughter saying, "Don't do anything foolish, my child. Allah the Holy does not like stupid women. Give your heart to a man but never hand over the deed. This is yours. Only yours, remember that."

Mariam's sleep vanished. Ma had finally decided to go away, but where? From her behaviour it appeared that like the king Harishchandra, she was about to distribute her riches and bid adieu to the material world. Mariam knew that the Rayer Bazar house was deeded in mother's name. But what was the use of giving the deed to the daughter unless it was legally gifted and registered? Mother must have witnessed this in the past in some jatra, some crumpled document changing hands. But she didn't feel like discussing this in the middle of the night. That her mother was leaving was itself a nightmare. Whether it was a nightmare or not, no sound came out of her throat when she tried to speak. She asked in an indistinct voice, "All this fuss, where will you go?"

Perhaps Monowara Begum felt embarrassed to give a direct answer. She said in a roundabout way, "Your father is half-mad. God alone knows what the state of the house is in these last nine months. Besides you, I have two other daughters. Your father may not have answered my letter but Mariam, unless I look after them, who will?"

Oh! So that was it. It was now the mother's responsibility to look after the two daughters who had not bothered to ask once about the mother in all this time. Actually, Ma was quite canny. And Monowara Begum thought that Mary was completely self-centred. She had never thought of the twins as younger sisters but claimants to her share of dues. How could they manage to be self-sufficient when their elder sister, ten years their senior, was barely able to keep her head above water. The endless dark night did not allow them to be more understanding with each other. Mariam shivered with apprehension imagining her future days in this house without her mother. The moonlight entering the unlit room cast a mysterious glow on Ma's flowing hair and one side of her face. Ma was motionless. From tomorrow, this spectral form before Mariam's eyes would not be there. She would be completely alone in this desolate house. When she would lift her eyes from the machine, only the Queen of the Night shrub would stab her vision. The only sounds to be heard would be the buzz of the sewing machine and the clanking of the tubewell handle. The neighbours would get to know immediately from the customers that the house with the clump of bamboos, which mother and daughter had once shared, was now occupied by the daughter alone. It was the same woman who had lived in the house on her own during the war of '71.

Mariam held her mother's hands. "Please Ma, please stay back for a couple of days." Both mother and daughter had trembling, cold hands. Ma withdrew her hands very lightly. The daughter was adamant, "Ma, let me write to Abba. Let him come and take you back."

"Am I a little girl who cannot go home without your father? Is the house his alone? Do I have no rights there?"

So many questions at one go. Mariam failed to understand how else she could plead to make her mother stay. In the darkness, she groped for her mother's cold hands. She kept repeating, "Please Ma, stay for a couple of more days, please." Monowara Begum gathered her loose hair into a knot. "Please don't stop me Mariam. One doesn't have a mother all one's life. It's your own misfortune that you're alone. In the name of Allah, just let me go."

How cruel, how arrogant! With a mother like that, how could one expect anything but sorrow? Mariam spent the rest of the night watching the moon play hide and seek through the clouds. Then for another fortnight, she made the moon her witness and had this imaginary dialogue with her mother, "Yes, I agree that no mother remains all through a daughter's life. But who will restore my luck? Ma, I cannot bear to live alone any more."

XXV

Oh! My Soulmate...

Mariam struck gold unexpectedly when, on a moonless, pitch-dark night, Abed Samir landed at her doorstep. Their relationship, moving at the pace of a tortoise, quickly accelerated into the speed of a racing hare. The woman did not want to know where the man had vanished to, what he had been doing. But she heard the man speak almost in a soliloquy that the road to poetry was very slippery. It takes single-minded dedication. For those engaged in that pursuit one needed also to stray. For two nights, Samir had paid a prostitute twenty taka just to see her naked body unfold from a distance. Knowing that on the third night he would have to touch her, he fled without paying any money. Although it had been only two days ago that the filthy abuse had followed him, now, as he sat beside Mariam, he put his hands on his ears to shut off that memory. One could have asked him: why was he here? Was she a harbour? Was Mariam his excuse for poetry?

In the darkness, Mariam only listened and asked no questions. She knew from experience that such questions were futile and answers would amount to deception in the different kind of life lived outside the orbit of husband and children and in which she enjoyed the support of Monowara Begum. Questions would only aggravate the suffering. At the beginning of their relationship, the poetry sessions that took place every evening on the bench that the customers used were an excuse for a man and woman to spend time together. There was a subtle hint of opening up their bodies to each other. After Mother had left, they moved from the bench to the bed. Four years is a long time especially for the mortal body. After the war, this was the first time that Mariam's heart and body were ready. For the present, leaving the heart aside, they sought to sate the demands of the body.

Abed Samir was an inexperienced man. He was clumsy, awkward, but at least like Momtaj and the Pakistani soldiers he did not come to her smelling of whiskey. It was that stink that forced Mariam to surrender even without a revolver being brandished. Momtaj used to be unhappy about this. In his opinion, any woman who surrendered herself so quickly, who opened up the moment you so much as held her hand could be nothing else but a whore. Mariam's marriage broke down very quickly because she behaved like the prostitutes that Momtaj had known. Now Abed Samir stretched out on the bed and pleaded, "Mariam, please teach me, I want to learn."

Four years after the war, the dead fish eyes regained their sight. And that sight can penetrate deep inside. Mariam saw that the young man wanted lessons in sex from a woman who had been raped day after day. He could have gone to a professional prostitute for this. Indeed, he did go to many. But those places were unsafe, dirty, unhealthy. There was the threat of police raids. There was also the risk of filthy diseases. So instead of going there, Abed Samir had come to Mariam. With the same twenty taka in his pocket he would buy food before coming to her house or bring inexpensive cosmetics or accessories for Mariam. The 'Ma-Meye Tailoring' business was not doing so well. When Abed Samir opened the packet of food and said, "I didn't have time for lunch today. Come Mary, let's share this," Mary would wash her hands and sit down to eat. The person who gifted the soap, powder and hair oil and the person who received them—both knew what the truth was but kept it under wraps.

Mariam did not bother with these things now. What she thought about were things whose range and depth she could not comprehend. This different kind of life without husband and children was Mariam's alone. Abed Samir was only marking time there. The moment he could afford to set up home and have a wife and children, he would run away from her. This interlude would then be counted as past experience which was essential for his literary activity. The point was: how long would the garnering of experience continue? Could it be gauged by the measuring tape wound around her neck? One day for want of something to do, she tried to measure time. Abed Samir got annoyed at this and said, "This is the trouble with you women. You want to measure even love with a measuring tape."

"Oh! So this is love?"

"Yes, of course, it is love."

"What about the food packets, the hair oil, soap and powder?"

"Gifts."

Whither gifts or not, in straitened circumstances, one had need of these. Mariam became depressed and said, "Forget about it."

Even if Abed Samir did forget about it, Mariam was unable to. If she did not have happiness written in her fate, why should she be the instrument for someone else's pleasure and that too for some paltry things in exchange? She was not an incense stick but a log of firewood. She was the sort that would light a crackling fire and emit billowing smoke. Her function was not to distribute cheap pleasure. As long as one could stay in this smoky atmosphere, sneezing and spluttering all the while, that was fine, and if not, then they could just leave. Nobody came to her to stay permanently. Even her own mother hadn't been able to stay with her, so why blame others?

Monowara Begum had left almost a month ago. When she was leaving, she would not even allow her daughter to take her to the bus stand. "Mariam, am I a little girl that you need to see me off? Stay at home, child. Customers may go away if they don't see you here." Mariam stood on the half-brick near the tubewell. She clutched the clothesline with her right hand and with the left she wiped her eyes with the corner of her sari. Like Montu, her mother stepped onto the scattered bricks and left home. Montu had had a terrible war ahead of him. He had not returned. Would Ma return?

Every morning, Mariam sat on the veranda and thought that Ma had not written her a letter since she went away. Rather today Mariam would write one. "You have freed me, Ma. I am well." Would she write about Abed Samir in that letter? The man was still sleeping comfortably on her bed. Mariam became tense if he stayed back at night. If an impatient customer arrived the first thing in the morning with some new material to place an order, she'd have to make sure they were kept outside the gate. If necessary, Mariam would make her stand outside and take measurements with her measuring tape in the lane. She would make out the receipt and send her off from out there. Often, Mariam came and sat on the veranda with the measuring tape wound round her neck, her receipt book and notebook, her chalk and pencil in hand even before dawn had lightened the sky. The wooden bench was not comfortable but at least it was a relief. From writing a letter to her mother to all her other unfinished chores, Mariam did it all in her mind as she sat there. The exercise was sometimes a bit strenuous, and she fell asleep while she sat there with the measuring tape around her neck like a noose. In the light morning breeze, the leaves of her notebook ruffled like the sheets of a calendar.

How quickly time flew. Four years filled with good and bad happenings had gone by. Sarfaraj was now married. His daughter had just crossed her sixth month and a couple of days later would reach the seventh. Montu remained where he was—he grew no older. There was no question of marriage for him. Yesterday, Sarfaraj had come to Dhaka and gone to meet Sharif Bhai. It was he who brought up the topic of erecting a permanent gravestone for Montu. He also said that there would be a reunion in Dhaka of all the guerrilla fighters who had fought side by side in next year's Victory Day celebrations. The work on the souvenir should be started right now. They needed a passport size photograph of Montu for it. Sarfaraj was given the responsibility to get it.

Although the Victory Day celebrations were five months away, he arrived early in the morning at Kafiluddin Ahmed's house for a photograph of Montu. He was nervous. The last time Sarfaraj had hoped that Montu's Mary Bu would open the door. But she had not been there at the time. He had been forced to give the news of the son's death to Kafiluddin Shaheb and his wife. Now, when he expected the old couple, the gate was opened by a shrewish woman in dishevelled clothes.

Mariam's customers were all women. If they were males, they were young boys who had yet to sprout hair on their faces. They came, holding on to their mother's hands, to get short pants stitched. Or, they wanted to wear trousers but were too young for them. So the parents weren't buying them any. They would appear with their fathers' old-fashioned khaki pants and say, "Please chop off the length and narrow the waist. Please put an elastic band around the waist." They also came with their mothers. But this was an adult male, unaccompanied by a mother. He had presented himself at her gate so early that even though he repeatedly mentioned Montu's name, it took a while for Mariam to comprehend what he was saying. When she understood, she remembered that Abed Samir was still sleeping under the mosquito net. She could not take the man inside. Standing at the gate, and keeping an eye on the inner room, Mariam spoke haltingly of how it would take another month to have the photograph brought from the village because "you know we have no other brother and Abba's health is not too good." Surprised, Sarfaraj heard some of it and missed some. When the tailor's design book was extended to him, impetuously he wrote down the name of Montu's last battleground. The martyred freedom fighter Saifuddin Ahmed's grave was there. He said disjointedly that the grave had been submerged in the floods of last year and collapsed. It now needed to be repaired.

He said all this very fast because he felt that this woman was not really paying attention to his words. He was asked to come a month later and sent off from the gate. Neither knew then that Montu's photographs would never be needed. Just ten days later, on August 15, there would be an assassination which would snatch from Sharif Bhai the responsibility of producing the souvenir for Victory Day.

Seeing Sarfaraj walk away, Mariam suddenly remembered that he was Montu's fellow fighter and she had a lot of questions for him. How her brother had died, had he said anything before he died, did Montu have any last wish, how could his grave be repaired – she ran after him on her bare feet for a bit. "Hey! Hey! Listen!" She shouted and realized that she did not even know the name of the man. Had he left his address? Standing on the road, she turned the pages of the design book and deciphered a few words under the design of puffed sleeves – Aillarganj Kather Pool, Village Madhyamtala, Post Office: Chanderhat. A little below that was written – Montu's last battleground. Next to it was written the man's name – Sarfaraj Hossein. There was no address anywhere. She lost sight of him at the bend of the lane. It was not possible to find out any more about Montu for the moment. The man, for whose sake this opportunity to hear more about Montu after four years had been given up, was sleeping happily under the mosquito net.

From the courtyard, the scene of Abed Samir sleeping inside the room struck Mariam as bizarre and unpleasant. Who slept peacefully in exchange of whose heartrending sorrow? The man took no part in her happiness or her sorrow. As she took the tea-kettle off the stove, the rag she was using caught fire. Mariam thought – should she throw the flaming rag on the mosquito net? All her problems would be solved at once. A few days later, drinking tea together, she told Abed Samir about the impulse to set the mosquito net on fire. The moment he heard this, the young man was beside himself with fear. He saw before him an unbalanced woman who could torch him at any moment with a smile. This particular experience he didn't need for his writing. Life was more important. Literature came only if one was alive. Abed Samir put down his half-finished cup of tea, pulled on his trousers, took his shoulder bag and went out. He was seen no more.

The imagined scene of burning the mosquito net with a flaming rag amused Mariam the whole day. She kept smiling to herself. Anyone who saw her would think that she was a conspirator–one of those who would let loose tanks in the streets before the night was over and by whose hands the President of the country along with his family would be killed. The only differences would be that she would not be directly present, she held no army wireless in her hands, she had not left the house for one whole week and most importantly, there was not a single woman, let alone a Birangana, involved in the group of assassins.

Towards dawn, Mariam awoke to the noise of gunshots and explosives. The sound seemed to be coming from the BDR Camp at Pilkhana. The next moment the noise of firing seemed to be coming from the university area. It felt like the night of March 25. As if she had gone back four and a half years in time without even a single revolution of the sewing machine handle. In front of her was a copse of rain trees. On the pavement nearby, the cobbler who'd been burnt to ashes in the Operation Searchlight fire. Mariam found this running back in time unbearable. She left her bed and went into the sewing room, switched on the light and sat in front of the machine in meditation. Now, when she would turn the machine handle, it would take her back at most as far as the rehabilitation centre but not to the war.

Mariam was still in the sewing room when one of her customers came and informed her about the early dawn slaughter. Her machine stopped. There was pin-drop silence in the room. When Montu went away, he had taken the radio with him and a new one had not been bought since then. Radio broadcasts could be heard from the next house. Mariam crawled to the plank bed and opened the window next to it. She heard,

"This is Major Dalim speaking. The dictator Sheikh Mujib has been put to death."

"Who is this Major Dalim?" Mariam asked her informant without even offering her a seat. The customer was a hospital nurse. She had seen the tanks on the street as she was on her way home from night duty. She had heard about the assassination of Bangabandhu from the people on the street. She didn't know anything more than this. Mariam mumbled to herself, "Since he is a major, the army must be involved."

"Oh heavens! Speak softly."

"Why? What has happened?"

"They're deadly. If they hear, they will roll the tanks in here." The girl's horror of tanks had not left her. In the short distance from Dhaka Medical via New Market she had seen three tanks with their guns aloft moving around. What an alarming sight, the guns looked like raised elephant trunks. "Mary Apa, just wait, there will be another war." If war started, everyone would get scattered. No one would have a fixed address. This was a still-fresh experience for them from about four years ago. So the girl had come to take back the material for the blouses she had ordered just a couple of days ago. Mariam closed the window, covered the machine completely with black cloth and got up. It was odd. But the informant had no time to notice. She had to rush home after collecting the material. A curfew had been declared in the city.

Mariam's life seemed to be tied by an invisible thread to the lifetime of that man who had been killed last night with his entire family. If she could think of herself as a wooden or cloth puppet, then he had been the puppeteer.

> *"Puppet, the one who knows how you were made,*
> *is the one who pulls the strings made of light."*
> Selim al Deen (*Jaibati Kanyar Man*)

In the last five years, she had experienced intensely every pull of the puppeteer's strings. Ripping away the string again and again had not freed her. This Singer sewing machine that was used by the girls at the rehabilitation centre was now Mariam's livelihood. It was the puppeteer's string pulling that led to the sale of Monowara Begum's jewellery to buy the sewing machine, the naming of 'Ma-Meye Tailoring' by Abed Samir and Suman, the postering at Jigatola, Rayer Bazar, Tannery Crossing. Now his bullet-ridden body was lying on the stairs in a heap. The buzz of the sewing machine had also ceased. Mariam had been liberated from the puppeteer's control forever. Although, she had seen the man only once in her life.

Mariam was then at the New Eskaton Road rehabilitation centre. Bangabandhu was supposed to inspect the centre. The girls were rehearsing "*O Amar Darad-i/Agey Janle, Agey Janle Tor Bhanga Naukay Chartam Na*" (Oh my soulmate, if I had known, if I had known, I wouldn't have got into your leaking boat.) He smiled slightly under his moustache. The song stopped midway. Forgetting their day-long rehearsal, the girls stood in disarray, silent. He got stuck in that disorderly group. As she stood nearby, Mariam saw a tall man wearing black-rimmed glasses and a desperate girl standing before him. Her head, looking up at him, did not even come up to his chest. Tears were flowing down her face. She did not know what her future would be. He raised his hand and addressed everyone, "You are my mothers. You are Biranganas."

XXVI

Radharani is More or Less all Right

An elderly social worker tells Mukti sadly, "With Bangabandhu's assassination, the rehabilitation centre was closed down. I heard that they hurled everything out onto the streets. The women were thrown out as if a brothel was being shut down."

"So what did the women do, where did they go? Did you try and find out?"

"I had become aloof from everything then. People were being arrested right and left. All my thoughts were on when I would be imprisoned, how I would be tortured."

The woman mentions some addresses where the Biranganas can be traced – all of them are addresses of brothels. But Mukti is searching for Biranganas! "So what? The Biranganas became Baranganas, prostitutes," the social worker says. "They're the ones who will open up and talk to you. You can make a mega-story out of it."

"But did the tortured women of 1971 really enter prostitution?"

"What else could they do? Nobody cares for Biranganas. Forget society as a whole, not a single individual was bothered about them."

Then she gives Mukti a long list of invisible Biranganas. Those who had fallen into the clutches of traffickers and had gone abroad were lost forever. Some had committed suicide. There were those who had voluntarily emigrated and settled abroad, for nobody cared about these kinds of things in those lands. If multiple marriages were not a problem, then this was merely an accident. No one bothered with what had happened in the past. But it is not as if these abused women did not have a settled life in their own country. They are now fifty plus or sixty and have family lives, their past a secret. Now reaching the end of their lives, would they risk the loss of husbands and sons by recounting their 1971 experiences? No one has the right to ask this of them. Still, if you want to go and talk to them, go ahead – but no one will respond.

The social worker gives Mukti the whereabouts of Baby, a salaried worker at the rehabilitation centre. Baby remembers Mariam's name and address twenty-eight years after the war even though she had burned the records herself. By now, Baby is a senior official in the department for women. When the rehabilitation board was merged with the department of women, Baby was transferred to the new department. She has remained there ever since. Mukti decides to go to the red light area before she gets in touch with Baby. The social worker gives her directions.

She says, "You can go to Banishanta." The Banishanta red light area was on the west bank of the Pashur river, south of Mongla port. The Sunderbans lay further south. Mukti was more afraid of the pimps and madams of the brothels than the Royal Bengal tigers of the Sunderban. What if she couldn't come out once she entered the red light district? A whorehouse dogs the footsteps of every woman. Besides Banishanta is quite far and she is afraid to go there alone. "Then there's English Road, right here in Dhaka. The name of the red light area is Kandupatti." Kandupatti was demolished a couple of years ago, in May 1997. Those women now solicit customers on streets, in parks and the religious *dargahs*. The social worker will turn eighty in 2000.

If she has heard about the demolition of Kandupatti, she does not remember. Then she tells Mukti to go to Tanbazar. "Before you enter the Tanbazar brothel area, you will see the Hangsa Theatre. It's a beautiful old building." In the sixties, she had watched *Anarkali* in the Hangsa Theatre. Madhubala was cast in the role of *Anarkali* and Dilip Kumar was Shahzada Selim, who later became the fourth Mughal emperor Jahangir.

Tanbazar was a brothel dating back a hundred and fifty or two hundred years. It was located in the ancient port town of Narayanganj on the banks of the River Sitalakshya. The brothel had sprung up in some distant past for the entertainment of visiting sailors and merchants. Today, no foreign ships anchor at Sitalakshya; there is no booming trade in jute and cotton, but even so the number of women is rising like the flood waters in this red light district. At present, the count is three thousand. The profile of their owners and their customers has changed. When the social worker asked Mukti to go to Tanbazar, there were plans to demolish the area. Everyday, there was some news of Tanbazar in the papers. Mukti goes there one day accompanied by some journalists. Once there, she barely manages a glance at the beautiful, old Hangsa Theatre. Her eyes almost pop out at the sight of the women waiting for customers in broad daylight, leaning against staircases or sitting on the verandas fronting the shuttered shops. Their clothes, make-up, the traditional standing posture tell you who they were even if you are visiting the area for the first time. Yet in this lane, unless one is introduced to the cigarette vendors, real estate agents, informers, journalists, lovers present there, one cannot identify them. There are children crawling and toddling beside the adults. In order to cross the lane you have to leap over them. And to cap it all there are uniformed police posted here and there. Mukti thinks that it might have been better not to have come here to search for the 1971 Biranganas at the promptings of an old woman with a fragile memory. At the same time she cannot say anything about her misgivings to her companions. After calming down a bit, she sees that they are surrounded by an angry mob of

women. The journalists are asking them about their demands.
And the women are giving sharp retorts to simple questions.
Some women are not even waiting for questions. "Did we walk
the main roads to solicit custom? Did we beckon your husbands
to our shanties that you're trying to evict us?" Mukti does not
respond but hangs her head in shame, although she has not
married yet and has no husband. Then the woman asks the male
journalist behind whom Mukti has taken cover, "We have never
asked you whether you have a wife at home or whether you have
left her. You've paid money, enjoyed yourself and gone. Money
changed hands and the game was over."

The women who are providing leadership to the anti-eviction
movement have no paint on their faces and have not bothered
to dress up. Their voices are hoarse from giving speeches at
the capital. Mukti reckons that those who are in their fifties
today must have been young women of twenty or thereabouts
in 1971. In a rasping voice one of them imitates the style of the
Bangabandhu's March 7 speech. "We will see that your meals are
stopped, that you get no water." The Sheikh's party is in power.
They have stopped water and electric supply to Tanbazar and
created all kinds of obstacles so that clients do not visit that
area. They are depriving the prostitutes of food and water. A
Bihari woman asks, "What did I gain out of this? I was a Bihari,
I became a Bengali. The Sheikh's people are trying to oust even
me." The Bihari woman is named Nasim Banu. A victim of
gang rape by Bengalis, she came to Tanbazar in 1972. There was
no trace of her parents or brothers and sisters. She doesn't even
know whether they are dead or alive.

So there's trouble right at the beginning. Mukti sees that she is
entering a dark road in history. Seeking a Bengali, she has found
a Bihari woman. Leaving behind a Birangana rehabilitation
centre, she has arrived at a brothel. Many years have elapsed in
between a story of ups and downs. And history too has turned
cartwheels in that time. After Bangabandhu's assassination, the
rehabilitation centre was demolished. Now his party men are
waiting to demolish the prostitutes' quarters where, according

to the social worker, women from the rehabilitation centre are also staying. If they are, then where are they? It would be difficult to identify them from among the thousands of women caught in the upheaval of eviction. If asked about themselves, they answer, "My mother was a whore, I'm a whore." No one is concerned about the past, their only thoughts are for the future. They are lamenting off and on about their impending fortune, "Oh sister, even if we are bad women, aren't we human beings? We are one of Allah's finest creatures. We have not killed anyone for gain, we have not attacked and looted anyone's possessions. Why should they treat us like this?"

Mukti reports when she gets back. When the social worker hears her, she says, "I am an ancient banyan tree, a witness to passing time. I find all this intolerable." But she tells Mukti to continue her search and enquiries in those areas. Mukti, however, cannot go there again because Tanbazar is demolished. The women are arrested and taken to the Kashimpur and Pubail centres for homeless destitutes, although the Tanbazar women were not beggars according to the criterion of the 1943 Vagrancy Act of Bengal. Neither could their postures or gestures in streets and crowded areas be said to indicate that they were asking for alms. The imprisoned women climb trees at the destitute centre and give interviews to journalists who wait outside the walls. Those from the Tanbazar-Nimtoli brothels who managed to escape by scaling down pipes on the night of the eviction could not remain in Narayanganj. There were continuous announcements over microphones the next day around Gymkhana, Bagan, Deobhog, Bandar: "Respected local residents, Respected local residents, the prostitutes of Tanbazar-Nimtali brothels are tying to flee whichever way they can. If new tenants have come into anyone's house, please drive them away. Otherwise, you will be punished."

Under these conditions some of the women come away to Dhaka. The state minister for social welfare has released some of the women from the vagrants' home to fake guardians with a sewing machine and 5,000 takas each. These women sell off the sewing machines and join the prostitutes who went to Dhaka.

With the help of women's organizations, during the day, they hold press conferences, send memoranda to various places, participate in sit-down strikes and shout slogans before various UN agencies. Then when night falls, they solicit custom at the Osmani Gardens, the Suhrawardy Gardens, the Outer Stadium, the Doel roundabout, the Mirzapur Mazar and the surrounding areas of Parliament House. Mukti's feet have broken out in blisters after walking around with them but she had still not managed to trace the 1971 Biranganas. The 50 plus Bihari lady also seems to have disappeared.

The only remaining place nearby is Daulatdia, the brothel on the banks of the Padma. This time Mukti does not follow the social worker's advice but chalks out her own plan of action. She may be a banyan tree and time's witness, but she has no idea that today NGO activities are spreading like wildfire in the red light areas and in addition to pimps, recruiters and customers, outside women are also moving about freely in the localities albeit wearing aprons to show that they are not prostitutes. The old woman had never heard of all these developments or even if she had, she has forgotten. She has only one piece of advice, "Go to Kandupatti." Kandupatti has been demolished two years ago. "Then go to Tanbazar." The Tanbazar women are up in the trees. Every Friday, during jumma, milaads are held at Tanbazar. "Strange! How will your work get done if you keep sitting in Dhaka city! Why don't you go to Daulatdia before all the women climb trees?"

Before Mukti goes to Daulatdia, she seeks help from the women social activists in aprons working in that area. They run an education project for adults and children, explain the benefits and the use of condoms and encourage women without a future to save. It is through one of them that Mukti finally meets her first 1971 Birangana–Radharani.

The senior social worker's predictions do not come true. Radharani plays hide and seek with them through the maze of lanes and alleyways of Daulatdia. Let alone opening up to them, Radharani does not even come close. Once they come face to face in a narrow lane. Radharani says, "I am a Birangana of 1971, educated, but a prostitute – these are my sins, grievous sins. Don't bother me. Just get out of my way." She twists her body like an eel and makes her way out of the lane. The NGO worker carefully steps over muddy puddles and says, "None of these women speak the truth. Please be careful of where you step. Or you'll take a toss, I tell you." On the veranda of the room opposite, a prostitute sits with her legs stretched out. She wears nothing but a petticoat knotted loosely over her chest. She gives a wry smile, "Radharani helps to transfer tenants. Will you be giving her some money, money for her booze?"

Mukti looks nonplussed at the smart-looking prostitute. She cannot answer. The apron-clad NGO worker at her side smiles, "Don't you understand? That's Radharanani's business now. That's how she buys her liquor. Don't you step in the slush, you'll slip."

Mukti and her companions move away from the mire and stand on drier, high ground. It is the main entry gate to the red light area opposite the railway station. Some fifteen or twenty women stand there in varying poses in the middle of the day. Clients are going in and coming out. Bystanders watch with amusement the bargaining and scuffles that go on between the prostitutes and the customers. A cassette player is blaring out a Maiz Bhandari Sufi song. *Dekhe Jare Maiz Bhandari, De-Khe-Ja-Re, Dekhe Jare Maiz Bhandari Haitechche Ranger Khela, Noore Mawla Basaiche Premer Mela, Khaja Baba Basaiche Premer Mela* (Come see the Maiz Bhandari, look at the play of colours, Noore Mawla has set up love's fair, Khwaja Baba has set up love's fair). Mukti grabs the sleeve of the apron that the NGO worker is wearing and asks, "What's Radharani's story? Why don't you tell me about it?" The girl drags her to the head of another narrow, slushy lane. She says, "Bapre baap! The music is playing so loudly that one can hardly hear anything." Mukti is still holding tightly to her apron sleeve. She asks even more loudly, "What's Radharani's story?" That very instant, Radharani appears at the head of the lane. "They're like ghosts, they don't give up haunting you." And once again she crosses the mud and slips away.

"So now you see?" the amazed NGO worker asks.

"See what?" Mukti answers.

"She insulted us and went away."

At that moment, across the road from where they are standing, a door opens a crack and half of Radharani's face pokes out, "I am a woman who is a Birangana. No man has ever loved me. No one has helped me either." The door bangs shut in their faces.

What kind of style is this for giving an interview? As if the son-in-law of the house is coming to take home his bride from his in-law's place, and the bride is playing hide and seek. She's not quite sure whether she'll give herself up or not. Seeing Mukti's annoyance, the NGO field-worker bursts out laughing, "You think it's so easy to catch them? When the woman starts abusing you after getting drunk, then you'll know what's what. Be careful that you don't slip in the slush and go for a header."

The monsoon rain is very mercurial. It suddenly pours from the heavens without any prior notice. The shanty where Mukti and her companion, wet and mud-spattered, take shelter belongs to Radharani's sister. Although they're not really sisters. Her name is Kusumkali. The NGO worker says, "In the 1971 war, Kusumkali participated in guerrilla activities. She would carry grenades in sacks of rice and deliver them from one place to the other." When Kusumkali is asked, she is embarrassed, "Oh dear! I did those things for money." What is she saying? In one stroke, she lets go of her rights. So many people claim that they were guerrilla fighters without even participating in the war. But Kusumkali is eager to talk about Radharani. "No one in Daulatdia has brains like my sister. She is so educated. Speaks English fluently." Kusumkali sprinkles her own speech with distorted English words like 'berein' for brain. Kusumkali says ruefully, "So many young men from well-to-do families left her because she drinks. At one time she was very well-known. She'd been a madam. She'd earned huge sums of money. All of it she has blown on liquor. Now she makes a living from tenants' transfers."

"What is this business about tenant transfers?"

"Say, for instance, someone has money trouble so the madam evicts her. Perhaps, they get fewer customers. Perhaps, they want to buy fancy stuff. So they don't pay their rent on time. Then there's a to-do." Barely has Kusumkali paused when her foster daughter, Anarkali, butts in, "Then Radharani jumps into the fray."

Even though Kusumkali is annoyed at her daughter's interruption, she does not show it. Because she lives on Anarkali's earnings. Whatever she has to show is bought with money earned by her foster-daughter. The girl has entered the business recently. She is still quite young and has a fresh, limpid beauty like dewdrops on a lotus leaf. She gets customers even if she does not stand at the head of the lane. That is why she is arrogant. She has no mercy for those who have passed their prime. There are posters of film stars on the ceiling of her room. One gets a better look at their intimate poses while lying down. It was Kusumkali who had climbed a ladder and pasted these pictures on the ceiling of the shanty. Her only regret is that Anarkali does not like Radharani. Calls her 'cilique-baaz' to her face.

Kusumkali slowly reveals the story. "Actually, Radharani constantly keeps moving through the neighbourhood, wooing one tenant here, one there, helping them rent another room and shift there. She gets five hundred rupees for brokering a deal. That's the end of the story—in one day she spends the money on liquor and hash."

Radharani's seven-year-old daughter lives on the mercy of neighbours. Kusumkali wants to adopt her but Radharani refuses. She says, "I will educate her. I won't turn her into a whore."

The woman who spends her day in a stupor of dope and liquor and cannot look after her daughter, how will she manage to educate her?

Kusumkali says, "I have asked her why she drinks so much and her answer is 'why should I not drink? I have nothing left in life.' When Radharani was young, the military abducted her. She was kept in the camp for a few months and then released."

"Was she accepted back at home?"

"No, she was not taken back at home."

"She was from a Hindu family?"

"You can't tell whether she's Hindu or Muslim from the way she acts. She's firm in her belief in Hinduism as well as well as in Islam. She makes her obeisance when she sees a Hindu deity, she does salaam when she meets a Muslim. So how can you tell what her religion is? You know, she also speaks on religious matters."

"What does she say?"

"For instance, she always remembers Allah. Even when she is drunk, she remembers Him. Some days back, a woman from here was murdered. The body was returned from the police station after four days. After she was brought back, some people said that her dirty clothes should be changed for something better. Radharani was wearing a clean sari. She just took it off and draped it on the corpse and she herself wore the soiled dress of the corpse. After putting it on, she sat down in prayer. She wasn't scared or disgusted. That's what she's like."

"What does Radharani drink?"

"When she was in Sonagachchi, we hear she used to drink Double Tiger rum and gin. Now, here at Duludia Ghat she's drinking Bangla liquor."

"How much does the liquor cost?"

"Here one litre costs two hundred taka."

"Two hundred! When did she go to Sonagachchi?"

"That was in 1972. And then a pimp brought her from there. He told her 'you're a girl from a good family' and promised to get her married. He lured her away and then sold her at Faridpur. From Faridpur, she came here."

"Then?"

"Not much more then. She was pregnant with her eldest daughter when she came to Goalundo. She's got that daughter into the business, but the daughter doesn't take care of the mother. It's that sorrow that's driven her to drink."

"If she drinks that much, doesn't she have any health problems?"

"No, she has no illness. She spikes her drinks with salt. If you mix your drinks with salt your lungs will rot in days. Radharani doesn't read palms but she can predict the future accurately. The other day she said she would live to be a hundred. With all your good wishes, the prayers of the Huzoor of Medinipur and blessings of the Big Pir, Radharani is more or less well."

When Mukti comes out of Kusumkali's room with the NGO worker, it is late afternoon. The sky is clear and bright. Over the river Padma the white clouds are scudding like egrets in search of fish. The NGO worker worries, "Oh dear! Your clothes are covered with mud. How will you go to Dhaka wearing these?" Mukti glances at her clothes. It would have been nice if she could have met Radharani. She cannot accept the fact that she has had no discussions with her. Is it possible to do research by using information given by other people? The NGO worker pushes through the crowd to bring Mukti out of the red light district. She says, "You think Kusumkali is telling you the truth. I don't believe a word they say."

She supplies the prostitutes with condoms, explaining the advantages of their use to these women. Does she know if the clients use the condoms or not? These sex workers keep their doors open during the day while they service their customers. If she wanted to, she could easily check if the clients were using the condoms or not. But they don't check on that. Year after year, they supply the prostitutes with condoms, examine their blood samples, record case histories, working only on blind faith. Or perhaps, they work routinely without believing in what they are doing. Should Mukti trust them or not? There is no doubt that Radharani is a Birangana. She will come back very soon to interview her. The NGO worker waves a farewell to her. She says, "Ta ta, bye, bye, hope to see you again."

That meeting takes place another two years later. The moment she returns from Daulatdia, she goes to meet Baby at the department for women. As a result, she gets caught in a wider net even as she had cast her hook from the other bank of the Padma. The place is a crowded locality on the western edges of Dhaka called Rayer Bazar. There is a house where there no longer remains even a clump of bamboo, let alone a shrub of Queen of the Night. But the nameplate is in place. Like Ali Baba's secret code of 'Open Sesame', the heavy iron-gate swings opens easily. Once Mukti enters, it takes her two years to draw in her net and leave. Because the resident of that house in Rayer Bazar, who had lived there for nearly three decades from when she was in her late teens to when she grew into a young woman and right up to now when she is fifty, had been waiting for Mukti for the past one year.

XXVII

Marriage

"How old are you, girl?"

"Twenty-eight."

"You are the same age as my daughter."

"You have a daughter? Where is she?"

No answer.

"You didn't say where your daughter is."

"She isn't there. She got aborted from an overdose of sleeping pills."

"Oh. But can sleeping pills abort a baby?"

"Yes, possibly. Look, my name's Mariam and I'm called Mary. Mariams and Marys do not have children when they get married; when they have children, they're not married."

Apart from Momtaj, Mariam had been married one more time. She had been forced into marriage by the people of the neighbourhood. And worse, she was married off to the wrong person. One could understand if Abed Samir had been dragged here and the Qazi summoned to read the marriage vows. Had that been the case she would have had a twenty-four year old child now. "But I told you my real name is Mariam and I am called Mary by everyone."

After August 15, 1975, Mariam realized that she was pregnant.

She was completely broke. She had no money for food let alone an abortion. She could not sleep at night from hunger and anxiety. In the darkness of the night, she paced inside and outside the house. It was just like those days before March 25. Montu had gone home. She was waiting for Abed Jahangir. The atmosphere was also similar, tense, ominous. A dog howled all night long beneath a street lamp outside Haji Shaheb's house. Military rule was in place, all meetings and processions were prohibited. Mariam was pacing the yard in her house and waiting. She was waiting and pacing. After four and a half years, in September 1975, Abed Jahangir came and stood at the black gate defying the barking dog. He knocked on the iron gate and called out – Mary. Mariam was awake from hunger and worry. She thought that the person knocking on the gate was Abed Samir. The pursuit of literature followed a slippery path. He had slid down on it, and once again had come to her door. Mariam was happy and relieved. She savoured the happiness. But the one who stood outside the gate was far from happy. A slight delay could be fatal. Impatiently he called out again and again – Mary, Mary. Now she thought that the voice was unknown to her. Who could it be so late at night? "I am Abed, Abed, Mary." When Mary yanked open the gate the man who strode in with long steps and stood beside the Queen of the Night was not Abed Samir but Abed Jahangir. Was this 1971 or 1975? Mariam felt dizzy and fell to the ground.

Abed Jahangir hid in the house day and night. He pulled out cash from his pocket, with which Mariam shopped for food and cooked meals on the stove. There was no greater pleasure than eating. And yet there was another life growing in her womb. Abed paid for her abortion. And he counted the days. October did not seem to end. Around November 3, Abed stirred himself. A coup had taken place under the leadership of Khaled Mosharraf. It was said that he was an Awami League supporter and was pro-India. The assassins of Bangabandhu were packed off to Bangkok the same night by air without even arranging for a trial. After returning from the victory procession on November 4,

Abed Jahangir proposed marriage to Mariam. He held her hands and said, "I have learnt my lessons from history. I know we will be happy." The next day brought the delayed news of the killing of four top leaders in the Central Jail. Even worse news trickled in two days later. The soldiers had revolted in the cantonment. There were slogans—The *Sipahis are brothers, we demand the blood of officers.*" And yet after killing Khaled Mosharraf, they placed Ziaur Rahman, who was not a sipahi, in the seat of power. What was going on? Abed was completely shattered. Although he did not bring up the topic of marriage again, he hid in the house till the end of December. In January and February he began to go out and explore the scene. Some days he came back and said, "The situation is stabilizing in the country, Mary. After all the bloodshed, things are more peaceful now. But no one can say what sudden turn things will take."

The sound of thudding boots beats in Mariam's heart. If one set of boots went out, another entered. Although she does not think very much about the country, nor does she have much faith in Abed's promise of marriage, but the way her provider was rushing around, what guarantee was there that he would return home at the end of the day? So many days after Bangabandhu's death, Mariam suddenly started thinking of herself as an orphan. "You are my mothers, you are Biranganas." In the absence of the puppeteer, her condition was like the grimy, soiled, abandoned puppets. She would never be able to dance in public, not on her own nor at someone else's command. Her life would end in one corner of her house.

"Mary, I went home today and saw that cockroaches and bats were having a field day there. I had to hire two men to make the house habitable." Mariam forgot her regret at not being able to dance in public as she listened to the details of his house cleaning. If this man went away she would have to die of starvation. Were all the army leaders dead? Why wasn't there a counter coup? Abed would then have stayed at home to avoid public appearances. And Mariam would go to the market with money in hand to buy rice, dal, vegetables. Let the country go to the dogs. She had no other thoughts on her mind but a good meal. At that time Mariam had grown so fat that she had to let out her blouses at the seams. When she expressed her anxiety about another coup, Abed said, "No Mary, there is no possibility of that now. Yesterday, at the crack of dawn, Colonel Taher was hanged." Abed became annoyed with Mary. "What do you do the whole day sitting at home? I see that you don't even read the newspapers properly. Ziaur Rahman has established himself in power. Now's the time to make connections and fix on a business."

Having fixed his line of business, Abed was returning home. Mariam clutched at his shirt and asked, "What will happen to me now? How will I spend my life, Abed?" Abed answered, "Let go of my shirt, Mary. Such behaviour only befits bad women. Don't worry. I've asked someone to find a job for you."

After a week Abed came bearing good news and bad news. Mariam had a job almost ready for her in a travel agency. After an interview of a couple of minutes, a mere formality, she would get her appointment letter. The starting salary was twelve hundred takas a month. If the agency established itself, then the next year the salary would be doubled. So much money at month's end. Hope to God, the agency found its feet. When she offered Abed a chair, he did not accept it but stood at the door and talked to her. He seemed to be in a hurry. He would not enter the house even when she tried hard to persuade him. Before leaving he told her quickly that three days later his wife and daughter were returning from Pakistan. It would not be possible for him to visit her regularly. It would also not look right for Mary to visit Abed's house. Because the way relations between Pakistan and Bangladesh were improving, his parents-in-law could come over any time. Abed said modestly, "Actually the house and the business are theirs, I'm merely a caretaker."

After Abed left, Mariam alternately cried and laughed. The farce of history and her private life had become interlinked like the threads of the bobbin in a sewing machine. After her laughter and tears, she thought that a job was more desirable than marriage. She had gone to Abed in 1972 to ask for a job after all. He had not duped her. He had got her a job in 1976 after four years. The office was in Motijheel. Through the swing door you entered a smartly done-up office. There was a thick carpet on the floor, as well as an upholstered sofa, a glass-topped table. There were five staff members. There was another girl younger than Mariam. Both of them had to work in the glass-partitioned room, selling tickets, answering telephones, typing. Abed's friend Zaman Shaheb was the owner-cum-manager of the agency. If Mariam made one mistake, she got ten scoldings from him. But he was never angry at the other woman, instead he would take her out to lunch at Café Jheel or the first floor restaurant at Stadium Market. Why he had been irked at Mariam from day one became clear in a couple of months. By mistake, Mariam had paid a client an extra ten taka. A woman who had got letter marks in Mathematics, how could she make mistakes in calculations? Or if you like to put it another way, if she couldn't miscalculate, who could? So many things had happened in her life that were outside any kind of reckoning that there was a heaven-and-hell difference between the girl who had obtained good academic scores and the woman now. Moreover, her certificate and mark sheet were lost during the war years. Although Abed had explained all this when he had fixed up the job for her, the travel agency chief did not completely believe him. The lurid account of her rape excited him one moment, but also angered him the very next. Because of that mounting anger, he dismissed, along with all her other virtues, her high marks in Mathematics, not supported by any document. "False, bogus." Zaman Shaheb shouted down the office for ten taka. Just because he was a good man, Abed had foisted a raped woman of 1971 on him. "It's impossible, impossible, impossible." Mariam's ears flamed. But the rest of the staff showed no change in their expression even when they heard there was a Birangana present in their office. They bent their heads and clattered on their typewriters, silently balanced their accounts or took this opportunity to make some personal telephone calls.

In 1972, when the rehabilitation centre arranged a job for her and other women at the Red Cross building, there would be people thronging around them all the time. "What's the matter? What do you want?" If the question was asked, the answer would come, "We have come to see Biranganas." Exasperated by people's curiosity, some of the women left their jobs. That was just four years ago. People had already lost interest in Biranganas! Had people also forgotten that there was once a war in this country?

The agency found its feet even before the year was over. Mariam's salary, instead of being doubled, did not increase even by a paisa. Zaman Shaheb constantly reminded her that he continued to pay a raped woman of 1971 because he was truly a good man. Anyone else would have kicked her out a long while ago.

Mariam's days were spent in the glass office. The months stretched into years. People, who bought tickets from her, went off to faraway places. Her college friend Rina, who had fallen in love while playing snakes and ladders during the war, bought a ticket from Mariam and went off with her husband to Qatar. Before leaving, she said, "Mary, I feel sorry for you. How long will you remain unmarried? Here you are sitting the whole day in a marketplace. Find someone and get married." Abed Jahangir came three or four times a year to buy PIA tickets. With him came his wife and children and sometimes his in-laws. They sat in the manager's office and drank Coke and Fanta. He talked of trivial things like his son's school admissions, his daughter's milk teeth and the new teeth that are replacing them, that Bangladesh was a thousand times behind Pakistan and Karachi's dazzling power had to be seen to be believed. Then he went away. There was no sign of Momtaj either in this country or anywhere. None of the Biranganas were ever seen buying plane tickets. They perhaps crossed borders by road with the help of traffickers. The big shots of the rehabilitation centre went abroad either to attend seminar workshops or at the invitation of their children living in foreign lands. When they came to collect their tickets, their glances met. But they pretended that they did not know each other. As if remaining strangers was the best solution to the Birangana problem. But Mariam looked with sidelong glances at those who sat across her for longer periods. Everyone was getting older. Even more than the signs of age, there was a weariness in their expressions which could have been the outcome of being forced to participate in the canal digging movement against their will or being compelled to start things with "Bismillahir Rahmanir Rahim". When they looked at Mariam they were reminded again at how steep a price came freedom. Some experienced pricks of conscience at that. They had an easy life, going abroad three or four times a year; some had been appointed advisers to the departments of education or social welfare, but the lives of these young women were ruined. Before departing they left their phone numbers on small slips of paper, casually depositing them on the table as if a bit of paper fell out of the bag. And their glances said, "Girls, please let us know where you girls are, how you are. Thus will the future one day decide how successful we were in rehabilitating the Biranganas."

Mariam never phoned the social workers, not even by mistake. She just kept changing jobs from one travel agency to another in the Motijheel, Dilkusha, Fakirapul areas. Each one of them had similar glass fronted rooms, typewriters, telephone sets. Neither were there any great differences between the bosses. Apart from one, each one found fault with her work. The one who was different was middle-aged. His wife was insane. She would telephone her husband every hour. If she could not reach him on the phone, she would rush to the office in any old clothes she was wearing at home. This was one of the major signs of her madness. He did not care if Mariam made mistakes in calculations. He had only one demand: that Mariam stay back for some extra time after the office closed. When the Motijheel office area became desolate and the office buildings emptied, he would unzip his trousers and sit with his legs spread wide on top of the secretarial table so that his penis, limp like a dead fish, could be sucked. Some years after Mariam resigned from the job the man died of lung cancer. Despite several messages while he was terminally ill, she had been unable to visit him. But it turned out that Mariam was the first visitor who had lifted his wrist from under the blanket to find that he had no pulse—that he had died.

As she changed offices one after another, Mariam herself did not realize when the stamp of Birangana had fallen from her body. She had moved away very long ago from the well-defined occupation of sewing and tailoring prescribed by the rehabilitation centre. No one now saw her in handloom saris and blouses with long sleeves. Now she dressed like other women who sat like puffed pigeons in glass compartments. They also dressed alike. Their hair was hennaed, the creases of their faces were heavily powdered, their lips were coloured with dark lipstick, a yard of material was not enough to make a proper blouse for them, so lumps of fatty flesh showed under the transparent chiffon or georgette saris. The customers saw no reason to waste their time as they sat across the table from Mariam and women like her to buy tickets. No matter how softly the women spoke through their tinted lips, they were sure that these women were married, their husbands suffered from high blood pressure for the last few years, their sons were going to colleges, and gold ornaments were being bought for their daughter's dowry with the Eid bonus. One buyer was an exception. He had found out, even before he had discovered her Birangana status, that she had no husband with high blood pressure, no son going to college, no daughter for whom she was buying gold. It would be better to describe him as a visitor rather than a customer. Because he did not come to buy tickets but to check on prices after getting his monthly salary. And always his destination for the tickets he never bought was Berlin.

"But you are not going anywhere. Why do you waste my time?" Mariam asked him the question in sham annoyance between explaining to him the details of airport and travel taxes when the other ticket sellers moved away after seeing the young man. He wouldn't accept that he was not going to Germany. Excitedly he fished out a faded photograph from a discoloured shoulder bag. The photo showed a group of people riding up on an escalator. In that lot, the brown man with black hair was his friend. His name was Ashiq Khondkar. And this young man's name was Debashish Datta. Ashiq Khondkar and Debashish Datta had been friends since they had been very young. They had been roommates when they were in university and worked for the same political party. Ashiq had taken political asylum and gone to Germany six years ago. Debashish was waiting for a visa. Debashish Datta told her, "The moment I get a visa I will buy a ticket from you." He said this because there were very few people in this world like Mariam who would listen carefully or understand what others were saying.

Once Debashish had shown the photograph to Mariam, his chatter would not stop. He had one topic – childhood friend, room-mate in the same hall, Comrade Ashiq Khondkar, who had forgotten his dearest friend Debashish after travelling abroad.

"What do you think Mary?"

"About what?"

Well, it's been one year, six months, eight days since I've last received a letter from Ashiq."

"Maybe he's busy. Or maybe he hasn't found a job, he's unemployed. Life abroad is very tough."

"You're right. But!"

"But, what?"

"He's been writing to his mother regularly."

"Everyone writes to their mothers." The moment she said the words, she remembered that she had not written to Monowara Begum for a long while. It had been ten years since Kafiluddin Ahmed had died. His death had come as a relief to everybody. He had been selling off his land till nothing remained. If he had lived a couple more years, the homestead at Fultali and the house at Rayer bazaar would have changed hands as well. In the beginning Monowara Begum had accepted her widowhood, but later she seemed to be changing everyday. Ratna had moved with her husband to Saudi Arabia. Chhanda was the headmistress of the school named after Montu. After her marriage, she would also move away. Ma would be alone then. But she was absolutely unwilling to come to Dhaka and stay with Mariam. Those nine months were still a nightmare for her. She must have gone off her head then. Otherwise, how could she, the wife of a respected man, behave so wildly? How could she have written such shameless words as "Won't be a mother in 1975" to her husband? It was all Mary's fault. What a daughter that even led her mother astray! When she recalled those times, she slapped herself on her cheeks and said, "Tauba" in repentance. She shed tears and prayed to Allah that she should die before Chhanda got married. If Mary wrote her a letter then she would ask Chhanda to reply and write whatever she felt like. She never asked Mary to come home. The mother so loathed her Birangana daughter.

"What is Ashiq's mother like?"

"What do you mean?

"Does the mother love her son?"

Debashish was puzzled at Mariam's question. A mother who did not love her children was a rare occurrence in the world. His own mother, of course had been writing to him repeatedly and irritating him. She had only one plea—either marry a girl of his own choice or let them choose a girl for him. But the bride would most certainly have to be a Hindu Kayastha. Debashish had decided that he would not marry any girl, let alone a Hindu or a Kayastha. But what about Ashiq?

After hearing about Ashiq's marriage in Germany, Debashish lost his head and rushed to the Rayer bazaar house in the middle of the night. Mariam's experience of forty years was that no one dashed to this house, and that too at midnight, unless they were in trouble. But why should a young man break down in such a manner hearing the news of another young man's marriage? Still, with the burglaries going on in the area, she was glad to have someone to sleep in the next room. When Mariam was about to unlock the room where Montu would have stayed had he been alive, the room which had been sublet to a small family for the last five years who had left a month ago after quarrelling with Mariam over some trifling matter, Debashish stepped back in alarm. "Mary, I beg of you, please don't ask me to sleep alone tonight. I will spread a mat on the floor of your room and lie down there, please."

After dillydallying for days, Debashish did not end up leaving Mariam's house. Ashiq's marriage in Germany had vehemently upset him. He had saved bit by bit from his salary to buy a ticket on the flight to Berlin and now when he could afford it, this sudden news of the marriage arrived like a thunderbolt. What was he going to do with that money now? Even working at a job was meaningless. But seeing Mariam, Debashish had come to believe that people could continue to live simply because death did not arrive and people could continue existing for years. So after his office closed, he returned to Mariam.

"Mary, what do you think?"

"About what?"

"You know, this whole marriage thing. Do people marry out of love, or are there other reasons for marriage?"

"I don't know." Mariam had married Momtaj because she had needed to be rehabilitated into society, an act that the state had failed in. Or had she wanted a child? Or a husband? As others had? If she had had that, then she wouldn't have had to live like this, isolated even from her mother and sisters.

"Of course," Mariam added to her previous remark, "Whatever the reasons behind it, marriage is necessary."

"You don't know," Debashish said as he smiled, "but I know."

"What do you know?"

"I know that Ashiq has married in the hopes of becoming a German citizen. He doesn't really love that girl."

Good. It was good to be able to think like that. It made life easier. Debashish was thinking that Ashiq's was a marriage of convenience. But over there, just as many girls married foreign young men in exchange for money, they also married for love. How was Debashish supposed to know what the truth was from so far away. Ashiq hadn't written him even a single line in the past two years. Even the news of the wedding he had found out when he phoned Ashiq's mother.

The days were spent in work and impossible dreams. At night he plotted and planned with Mariam. Lying in the room, where Montu would have lived had he been alive, Debashish dreamt of the world as a map on the globe. He walked along its surface, crossed India, Pakistan and entered Iran. A river of milk flowed from the oil wells of the Middle East. The river of milk soon changed into a glacier. Debashish stood at the foot of the mountaintop from where a cascade of water fell near his feet. The place had a mossy green colour. It was slippery. To reach Ashiq he would have to undertake an arduous task and reach the top. Man was so helpless before nature. Looking up at the crown of the mountain, he thought there was not much difference between man and ant in this instance. He became an ant and climbed into a boat. There were many boats with ants which capsized with all passengers in one swell of water. Scrambling out of his dream, Debashish sat up with a start in the dark and wondered what he was doing there. Was he a man or an ant? He had managed to go quite far but had to return from the threshold of Germany. Now it would be meaningless to fall asleep again and try to retrace his steps in the dream. Ashiq Khondkar was living happily with his wife. Debashish's throat became parched when he recalled the scene of the capsizing boat.

Mariam grumbled about such a grown-up man being unable to sleep alone in a room and dragging his pillows and kantha from one room to another. What would people think? The part-time maid saw Debashish coming out of Mariam's room every morning. A watch was kept on this house from the first floor of the Haji's house. But Mariam was now forty. Her boat had sailed far away from the jetty, there was no possibility of return. She had no household, no husband, no children. Even though she lived in society, she was not a part of it. She was an exile in her own land. Why should she bother with what the neighbours thought? She had wasted many years just worrying and fretting. From Montu's room, the young man had come into her room frightened by a nightmare. Let him sleep in peace. She needed her sleep as well. They both had to go to work the next day.

One morning when she opened the gate, some seven or eight men entered the compound instead of her part-time maid. Debashish was standing near the tubewell brushing his teeth. His mouth was filled with foamy toothpaste. The gang of men did not even give him time to rinse his mouth. They tied his hands behind his back. "What is this? Who are you? He is my guest." A man shouted Mariam down. At that very moment, the Haji's son entered with a maulavi. To Mariam's complaint "Just see Bhaijan...", the adjudicator, the Haji Shaheb's son said in judgment, "There's no place for such shameless behaviour in this locality. Maulavi Shaheb, please get ready."

Was Mariam in a bad dream? She could have understood this if it had occurred ten years earlier. Such a scandal at this age? Or were the men playing a joke on her? What sort of a prank was this when she and Debashish had to leave for office in an hour? The Haji's son said, "Forget office. From now on, the locality will run according to what I say."

Oh! So that was it? So, he was going to be a leader after his father. The Haji Shaheb had passed away at the dawn of another August 15, ten years after Bangabandhu's death. But he had died a natural death. The son, who had been thrown out of the house, had come back to his father's estate. In 1970-71, he had been a supporter of Bengali autonomy. In 1988, Hossain Mohammed Ershad had declared Islam as the state religion. The country was not run according to Sharia law. But the Haji's rebel son stood in Mariam's front yard and stamped his feet, "Dig a hole here, bury this brazen, shameless slut. If she doesn't agree to marriage she'll be stoned to death with 101 stones. Huzoor, are you ready?"

The Haji's old widow rushed in when she heard the fatwa of stoning, "I beg you in Allah's name, child, please agree. My son is mad. Just like his father."

Mariam objected, "But Khalamma what are you saying? Debashish is like a younger brother to me."

"He may be like a brother but he's not your own brother. Daughter, please say yes. This son of mine does whatever he says he will do."

An hour later arrived her maternal uncle Golam Mostofa. The previous month he had had a stroke and his left side was paralysed. He limped along with the help of a stick. "So I hear that you're doing a live-together with a man, niece. *Naujubillah, naujubillah, Astagfirullah,* May Allah be our refuge, may Allah forgive us. Your aunt is coming with a sari. You will get married after mid-day."

Another crisis presented itself before reading the marriage vows. No one, apart from Mariam, had known that Debashish was Hindu. The Maulavi, who had been brought to stone her, performed ablutions and sat down to convert Debashish. It would have been risky to circumcise him at this stage. He could get tetanus. Golam Mostofa said, "It's enough if he reads the kalima five times and affirms his faith in Islam." When the reading of the kalima tyyeb began, Debashish whimpered. Jeering laughter and snide remarks arose from the crowd. "You damned malaun, you could screw her for free, but now you cry because you have to say the kalima? Sobbing, he repeated after the Huzoor, "La Ilaha Illallahu Muhammadur Rasulullah." The foulmouthed men joined in prayer with the Huzoor without performing the ozu, without rinsing their mouths out. They had come to perform one virtuous act but were lucky enough to add another one. They would share in the sawab of converting an accursed Hindu into a Muslim. They'd just made their places in heaven certain for the next seven generations. In Debashish's shirt pocket lay that letter from his mother, "The girl most certainly has to be a Hindu Kayastha."

The name Debashish could not be used after he had converted to Islam. He had to be given a Muslim name. After his stroke, Golam Mostofa's brain did not work. He couldn't even remember the names of his own sons. He spoke loudly toward the women's quarters, "Niece, you are an independent woman. Why don't you suggest a name for your husband?" From the next room came the suggestion – Abed Ishtiaque.

Debashish had no way of knowing that the name had come from Mariam. He was well-acquainted with both the names Abed and Ishtiaque. He had heard of them from Mariam. But separately. Now hearing them together he was in no state to be startled or scared. All he thought was that whatever was happening was worse than his nightmare of the previous night. But it was enough that they were not being killed.

Mariam had overcome another peril. Her destiny seemed to be to return again and again from death's door. Aunt Zulekha Bibi said, "Mariam, thank Khoda that you have been able to get married again at this age. Your Abba would have been very happy had he been alive." She helped to drape Mariam in a Katan Benarasi sari full of holes made by cockroaches. An odour of mothballs arose from the sari. In all the rush, there had been no time to run to the stores to buy saris and ornaments. Zulekha Bibi was using all she had in stock to dress the bride. The part-time maid was scurrying around making arrangements for food. All her tattling had finally been successful. The Haji's son had performed a virtuous act. After all, she did not work in a whorehouse that she would have to watch the scandalous behaviour of some brazen hussy. From the next day, the maid's employers would be a married couple.

After the wedding ceremony, the husband and wife were made to sit on a rug spread on the bench in the veranda where Mariam's customers would wait when she had her tailoring business. Debashish was wearing a sherwani and a turban on his head. After having read the kalima, such a change had come over his appearance that one would think that he wholeheartedly believed that Allah was the only god and Muhammad was Allah's prophet. When it was time to serve sweets, he swallowed a rasagollah whole. He had not eaten anything since last night so he must have been hungry. The mirror that was used for the bride and the groom to see each other was the mirror which

Debashish used for shaving. It was small in size. Only half the face could be seen in it at a time. He couldn't see Mariam in it. But he gazed at the mirror without blinking. Even if the neighbours created a song and dance about the wedding, it was only Mariam who knew that the person Debashish was waiting for was not a woman but a flesh and blood man. Mariam knew that she had to deal with this truth. Night was descending. After the wedding feast, Golam Mostofa and his wife would go back home. The neighbours would leave, having earned heir kudos in this world and securing certificates for paradise in the next. Debashish and Mariam would be alone then. How would they bear the burden of an unreal marriage?

XXVIII

Either a People's Court or a
War of Liberation

When Mukti first comes to the Rayer Bazar house after
searching persistently for the address, ten years after Mariam's
second marriage, Debashish is no longer there. The door is
opened by Tuki. Mukti waits on the bench in the veranda for a
Birangana whose age, in Baby's case history, is written down as
twenty-two. Baby has told her proudly that after her treatment
at the rehabilitation centre, she had looked even younger. Even
though she did not respond to their repeated questions, Baby
and her colleagues saw through her loose, flowing hair that
when she smiled to herself, her cheeks dimpled. Then Mariam's
mental illness was diagnosed. The doctors said it was epilepsy
psychosis. But it was lucky that her guardians came at the right
time and took her home. Otherwise after the foreign specialists
had left, she would have been transferred to the Pabna mental
hospital. Those who went in once never again saw the light of
the outside world. For them the lunatics there became their only
family and the rest of liberated Bangladesh a lunatic asylum.
Finally, using the language of missing persons advertisements,
Baby told Mukti that the girl had a pinkish mole on her left

cheek and her face was round like the moon. Later on, Jaitun Bibi of Notungaon, describing Mariam to Mukti, referred to her moon-like face.

Mukti sits on the unstable bench in the veranda and waits for a woman whose identifying marks are a round face and an age of twenty-two. Tuki moves around as if she is the mistress of the house. She brings in the clothes from the clothesline in the yard. She clucks at the hens, beckoning them to follow her to the kitchen. The only reasons that Mukti does not think of her as Mariam are that she is not twenty-two and her face is not round. When Mariam comes and stands before her, she rises to pay her salaam. She introduces herself and says that she wants to meet Mariam. She has been waiting for a while and it will be nice if she can meet her soon because she lives in Mirpur, night is approaching, and she has to return by bus. Listening to her long speech, Mariam enters the room and switches on the light. She offers her a cane chair and sits on a cane stool herself. "I am Mariam Begum."

No words cross Mukti's lips. She slowly remembers that twenty-eight years have slipped away. Even so the lady must be just fifty years old now. Is it possible that a Birangana could be so ordinary looking? Radharani wasn't like this. In spite of excessive drinking, there is a shine to her appearance. The moonlike glow in Mariam's face has been eclipsed by age. But her appearance should have been like that of the mothers and aunts in cinema and theatre who have been made up to look old but actually aren't.

Mariam does not like her appearance to be thus scrutinized by someone else. Is she a new bride that people would come to take a look at her? She asks Mukti what Baby has said about her. But it seems that she neither has the interest nor the patience to listen to the answer. Suddenly she interjects, "That woman's a scatterbrain." And then listening to her abusive comments, Mukti discovers that her ordinary appearance is disappearing and the pink mole on her cheeks has begun to glow. It would be unnatural for a Birangana not to have anger. What was petulance earlier is now hardened into resentment – but one cannot identify against whom. Whatever it may be, one needs to soften her up before one can talk seriously.

"Without your sacrifice the country could not have gained independence. You were something special, I mean…" Mukti stammers halfway through her words. But it takes the wind out of Mariam's sails. She leaves her stool and flops on a chair next to it. Her eyes glance upward towards the ceiling. After so many years, someone has sought out her house. Anuradha had not lied. There was a value to a person's hardships and suffering. But that they were something special, what exactly did that mean? Can that be measured against esteem, status, love or respect?

After her two marriages, people's respect for Mariam had grown even though it was short lived. Although that had no direct connection with the torture of 1971. Long before her second marriage, her Birangana uniform had slipped away without any effort on her part. Through the agency of her neighbours, she had entered into an unnatural marriage. Their excuse was that they were saving the reputation of the neighbourhood, but actually they were bent on shackling a Birangana who was spending her nights with a man she was not married to..

On the second day after the wedding, the Haji's son invited them for a meal. The Haji Shaheb's widow presented Mariam with a half-silk Jamdani sari. And for Debashish she brought a tussar punjabi with a silk cap. When they met on the streets the youngsters of the neighbourhood greeted the couple with a salaam. The only person who did not relent was Monowara Begum. "Rubbish! Is this a wedding? You've gone mad, Chhanda – dancing with joy at the news of your sister's wedding. Your father also went overboard when she married Momtaj." Not only did she not come to Dhaka but she did not allow Chhanda to come either. In fact, when Chhanda married her schoolmaster colleague later on, Mariam and Debashish were not even invited. The other person who was unhappy at Mariam's marriage was Debashish himself. The natural friendship that he had had with Mariam was destroyed after the marriage.

He remained in the same house for another couple of years because he had nowhere else to go. But he slept in the other room. The nightmare of the sinking boat could not make him enter Mariam's room again. The part-time maid was astounded. What kind of a marriage was this where the husband and wife did not share the same room, the same bed? The maid brought home from her village all kinds of charms, amulets and spells to bring the husband under control. When none of these worked, she left the job.

The maid managed to free herself by resigning. But the failed marriage gave birth to rage within Mariam. She was forty years old then. Nothing barred her from having a child. She had a husband in the next room but she could not sleep with him. The neighbours had sentenced her to a life-long punishment. Perhaps stoning her would have been a better option. At least it would have put an end to everything. At midnight Mariam rose from her bed and knocked on Debashish's door. No response. Sitting outside on the bench in the veranda, she was filled with sky-high loathing towards Debashish. Couldn't he open the door even once and come out? Mariam did not want a physical relationship, she did not want a child, let Debashish just put his hand on her forehead and she would sleep peacefully. The next night, after hearing this, Debashish came out to stroke her head to help her fall asleep. The knots in her body loosened when the man, who was purely attracted to other men, touched her. Her breath became hot. Soft moans escaped her lips. Debashish removed her head from his lap and left. God alone knew why Mariam wanted him in bed even after she knew everything. The whole night Mariam paced the veranda like a tigress in heat. No one was there to see the goings-on. The first floor of the Haji's house was dark. All were asleep in their beds. Mary and Debashish were husband and wife. People had forced them to marry, and then left them to their own devices. Now, no one was concerned about how they spent their nights. Mariam wanted to scream at the top of her voice, "Why does a man who can't do anything come to stroke her head?"

Was this deprivation worse than being raped? One by one, Mariam recalled her rapists of the past. Their long line stretched from the yard of her house to the head of the lane. Was she going mad? She no longer wanted Abed Jahangir or Major Ishtiaque. That night she only wanted Debashish, who did not desire her.

During the day Debashish shouted, "You are sick, Mary, I am telling you, you are sick, you should consult a doctor." Mariam was getting ready for work. Look who was calling whom sick. She threw her sandal at Debashish and said, "Get out, you bastard!" She thought that he would be shamed into not returning here. But, sure enough, he came back after two days. He brought with him a younger man. Debashish introduced him, "This is Anupam Sikdar. He's a second year student of Jagannath College." Neither of them was the least bit bothered that it was Mariam's house. Leaving her numb, they entered the room and shut the door. Mariam was silenced by the situation. She was now a stranger in her own home. She would lose her husband if she protested. The environment outside the house had also heated up. A movement had started to bring about the downfall of Ershad. There were strikes, hartals. If there was office one day, then the next two days they would be stuck at home. The two young men were not bothered about stepping out of the house. They had settled down comfortably in their room. They listened to the radio going full blast. In between, they would get up to cook khichari and omelettes. They would eat and give some to Mariam too.

Monowara Begum was very happy with this arrangement. She had come to Dhaka to consult a doctor. Instead of coming to Rayer Bazar, she had gone straight to Maghbazar, to Golam Mostofa's house from the bus stand. She came to meet her daughter the next day, "Mariam you've got a good husband. The boy is cute." She was annoyed to see the daughter's glum face. "What kind of a mindless woman are you? You've got married at a late age. It's for you to take care of your husband and serve him. Instead, you're lolling about and eating meals prepared by him."

Mothers were supposed to understand the sorrows of their daughters. But Ma had got hold of the wrong end of the stick. Mariam wanted very much to tell Ma the real story. Let at least one person in the world know what kind of a hell she was living in. But Monowara Begum's attitude seemed to say that she had no time to waste on such trivial matters. The days passed quickly. The compound was filled with weeds. What purpose did the Queen of the Night bush serve anymore? There was no need for a pair of snakes, now there were two men to guard the house. She gave Debashish and Anupam axes and choppers to cut down the shrubs and trees. They cut down the trees with great enthusiasm. Monowara Begum stood outside in the burning midday sun and supervised the whole exercise removing the chopped branches. Mariam felt restless. Ma, she thought, was becoming a little girl as she grew older. Could she stand that kind of labour at her age? Her heart wasn't in very good shape and she had diabetes. Monowara Begum paid no attention to her daughter's words of caution.

Monowara Begum denuded the house, shoved Mariam into an abyss of despair and left for her brother's house before nightfall. She had nothing to hold her back. The mother, who in '74-75 was beside herself in her thoughts of rehabilitating her daughter, had changed so much by '90!

The year ended with many signs. A riot broke out in Dhaka because there were rumours of an attack on the Babri Mosque. Mariam and Anupam were both anxious for Debashish. The government permitted the destruction, looting and torching of Hindu property–homes and commercial establishments–the whole day. Then in the evening curfew was declared. Anupam went out to inspect what was happening. He came back and said, "All this is because of Ershad's dictatorship. He's inciting a riot just to divert the anti-government movement." Debashish did not reply. He had pins and needles in his legs from sitting at home all day. When he wanted to step out, Anupam clutched his shirt like a devoted wife. "Debashish, please stop. I'm telling you, don't you go out in this turmoil." Mariam stood leaning on a veranda post. Debashish, glanced toward her and smiled at Anupam in an embarrassed manner. "Ah, let go. I'm not Debashish, I'm Abed Ishtiaque." He was right. It had slipped Mariam's mind that Debashish had converted to Islam. Anupam said, stubborn as a mule, "Abed Ishtiaque or whatever you are, fine, but you're not going out just now."

Debashish did not go out but Anupam sat pouting in a huff. He did not like Debashish glancing tenderly at Mariam and talking to her affectionately. He had snapped his moorings when he left the hostel. Whether his friends understood or not they teased and made fun of him. They were suspicious of Mariam. The woman was a Birangana of '71, she was used to many men. One husband was not enough to satisfy her. That was why she used her husband as a decoy to lure him away and rent his services. They thought of Debashish as a hermaphrodite, a blot on the male of the species.

Listening to the charges recounted by Anupam, Debashish called out to Mariam, "Mary, can you hear me? Just come listen to what Anu says. It's most amusing." Mariam came to the door and saw Anupam had clamped Debashish's mouth with his hands and was mimicking him with a distorted face, "Come listen, come listen…" Debashish had brought home a boy half his age, day by day he'd find out what it really meant. Mariam was about to move away from the door. Loosening Anupam's grip on his mouth, Debashish said loudly, "Mary, do you know what the students of Jagannath College call me…?"

The time for such sweet nothings was soon over. The environment both at home and the world outside was erupting violently. The police mowed down a procession in Dhaka by driving a truck into it, America was about to attack Iraq, the fall of Iron Lady Thatcher was imminent, Benazir was losing the elections. Debashish could not fall asleep unless he listened to the BBC news. Anupam got irritated with this and one night he broke the radio by hurling it on the floor. Mariam was reading a magazine while she lay in her room. She frowned slightly when she heard the crash and then went back to her magazine.

The seriousness displayed by the Mumbai film star Rekha in the picture was incomparable. Dilip Kumar, who had a strong personality, had got entangled in the problem by trying to help Rekha. Even after Rekha was conceived, her father Gemini Ganesan did not marry her mother Pushparani. After Mukesh committed suicide, not only Rekha but her mother also became embroiled in controversy. After so many years, Pushparani could not evade the pressure from journalists. A probe into the past had begun.

How strange the world was. It was fortunate that Mariam had no daughter. But, what would have happened if she had had one? So she would have had a daughter. Debashish entered the room with a sulky expression. He had come to say something to her but when he saw her with the magazine, he left without speaking. Debashish was probably not liking the fact that Mariam was warming her hands as she sat at the edge of an inferno. He wanted to involve her also in the Anupam business. But how could he? Their paths were different. They were husband and wife only in name.

After participating in the victory procession following Ershad's resignation, Debashish and Anupam did not return. Mariam waited a long while, and then, at midnight she went into their room and switched on the light. The clothes rack next to the door was empty. The room was empty of all belongings. There was a small slip of paper weighed down by a pillow on the bed. The handwriting was shaky like a suicide note. Debashish was leaving. Because Anupam couldn't stand Mariam any longer. He was jealous. They were leaving without informing her because Debashish thought that Mariam would not let him go. Debashish said that searching for them would be a waste of time.

With every change of scenario in the country, Mariam lost a boyfriend. Only this time she had not become pregnant. Possibly, the reason for it was that Mary, alias Mariam, did not conceive when she was married and when she got pregnant she was not married. The fact that Debashish could not bed women was only an excuse.

The curiosity and enterprise of the people of the neighbourhood had ebbed. This woman's life was a failure, like the liberation of Bangladesh. Their twin destinies were to stumble time and again into dark pits. Trying to help her turned counter-productive. They were also getting older. They were tired of watching Khoda's plans for them and the hypocrisies of political leaders. To the new generation in the locality who had left behind their short pants and had started wearing trousers, who smoked on the sly, fingered their emerging moustaches, Mariam was the same age as their mothers. But she was nobody's mother and the fathers of her unborn children were here today and gone tomorrow. They had watched all this while they progressed from crawling to walking and then to running. Now they played football morning and evening in the alleyways of the neighbourhood. This woman was as much a part of their lives as the birthmarks on their bodies. They would have been happier if only the woman's manners were more pleasant. If their football zoomed away from the lane and landed on her roof, Mariam began screaming at the top of her voice. Very seldom could one retrieve the ball from her. If the boys took their courage in their hands and jumped across the wall, they had to abase themselves and promise, "Aunty, this is the last time. The ball won't fall on the roof again." The inside of the house fascinated them. They did not know why. To them the war of 1971 was as distant an event from the pages of history books as the battles of Panipath and Palashi. Like words surfacing and getting blown away by the breeze.

Mariam fell into dark pits in her nightmares just as she did in reality. But she also survived miraculously. One night she saw herself falling from a terrace, she was falling, falling and there was nothing below to support her but she suddenly found a ledge to hang onto. Another night, she saw a hanging ladder at the moment of her fall. Another bad dream that Mariam often had was that she was crossing a stream spanned by a wooden bridge which had nothing in the middle. Beset with panic in the middle of her slumber because she had no alternative but to crash into the water, she vaguely saw something to help her cross to the other side. She could not remember what it was after she woke up. But Mariam thought of it as a boat with tarred planks, sail and rudder.

Although she did not know how and where life would end, the sign of the sailboat bore within her the assurance that she would climb out of the abyss into which she had fallen after Debashish had left. That is why on the morning of March 26, 1992 she entered Suhrawardy Park by the western gate. The park was packed with people. After twenty-one years, the sentence on war criminals was to be announced. Mariam was wearing dark glasses and her hair was tied in a knot high on her head. She looked like a film star in disguise. Through her dark glasses, she looked for familiar faces of the past. Would those who had been tortured and humiliated not turn up for this delayed trial? It didn't matter that the trial was only symbolic. If no one else came, Anuradha would most certainly come if she was alive. Like Mariam, a few other women were moving around in dark glasses and top knots. They could also be Biranganas of '71. They had come to hear the outcome of the people's court or, like her, were seeking compatriots of the tortured group. The sun's glare was mounting. Not too far away could be heard Bangabandhu's March 7 speech, "If another shot is fired... Turn each home into a fortress..." It was the same venue, the then Race Course Maidan. But there had been no trees back then–just an empty expanse. Montu had become alarmed at the surging crowds, "Mary Bu, don't look for me if you're lost. Just take a rickshaw and go home directly."

How long ago had it been? Twenty? Or twenty-one? Mary took off her glasses and wiped her eyes and then looked again at the surging crowds. Suddenly, she felt a tug at her sari. "Isn't it Mary Apa?" She turned around to find Tuki. She was holding a tiffin carrier. She was the maid at Notungaon,who had been captured by the military on the same day as Mary. But Tuki had not come to attend the people's court. The park was a short cut on her way to her job at a garment factory. She was late for work because of ulcer pains.

The garment factories remained open even on Victory Day, Independence Day? How strange! Mariam was amazed. Tuki said, "What do you think? It's open all three sixty five days. If you're absent, you get a pay cut." But after she met Mariam, Tuki skipped work and loafed around Suhrawardy Park aimlessly with her. Because of the thronging crowds it was difficult to follow who was being tried and for what. Three Biranganas were supposed to come from Kushtia to appear as witnesses. Mariam wanted to have a glimpse of them. Just in case she knew them. "You'll have to climb a tree then," remarked a kurta-pajama clad man standing next to them. It was true, there were people atop the trees. From one corner of the park, Jahanara Imam read out the sentences of the people's court as she stood in the back of a truck. The people below her could not see her. There was no mike either otherwise they could at least have heard her. "The Police have confiscated all mikes in Dhaka." The man in kurta-pajama continued to speak although no one asked him any questions. Tuki dragged Mariam out of the park saying, "That's a bad man."

Although Golam Azam's sentence of hanging was not carried out, on that memorable day Mariam found Tuki. The house returned to life after Tuki came to stay. Monowara Begum had cleared out the Queen of the Night bush. The clump of bamboos had been eradicated long ago. The paving near the well had been broken. The first thing that Tuki did was to clear the place around the well. Along the wall, she planted banana and papaya trees. Then she started keeping a few poultry and set up a project as a substitute for her job at the garment factory. The capital for the project was Mariam's, the planning and execution Tuki's. "There's so much empty ground around the house. How can anyone live without birds and animals?" This was Tuki's theory. Mariam was irritated and fed up because the rooms were dirty with the birds' droppings, the chicks would clamber up on the bed and cackle at odd times. But she didn't say anything. If Tuki stayed, then the birds would stay, if the chickens were thrown out then Tuki would leave – this was an unwritten rule. It had to be observed. If she did not, she would inevitably stumble into the chasm which she feared more than death.

Mariam was no longer alone at home. When she came home from office in the evenings, there was someone to open the door with a smile. She could open up her heart and talk about trivial and serious matters such as which client did what during the day, how the boss had behaved, what she had for lunch. Tuki petted the poultry, "What nerve the garment factory owner has to exploit us! I am a Birangana, huh! Come, come, cluck! cluck! Mary Apa, I think the white speckled hen's ready to lay eggs. She's been looking for a place the whole day."

Although delayed, Tuki's rehabilitation was achieved in the model of '72. Back then a poultry farm had been opened at Mirpur to generate income for the Biranganas. They would keep chickens. Baskets of eggs would go to the market. To encourage the venture, the organizers of the rehabilitation projects began to buy the eggs. After cooking them at home, the lady of the house would tell everyone, "Enjoy the eggs but don't ask where they've come from." The authorities had instructed everyone that the source of the eggs should be kept secret. What if people really stopped buying the eggs if they knew the truth! Tuki didn't have that problem. Apart from Mariam, not another soul in Dhaka knew that she was a Birangana.

"But Mary Apa, what have I gained?" Tuki asked at night lying in bed next to Mariam. Mariam did not understand at first and asked, "What do you mean by gain?"

"This, that not a soul in Dhaka got to know that I'm a Birangana."

Mariam smiled to herself in the dark. The people's court whipped up Tuki's ambitions. She was no longer content to be an ordinary person and wanted to be a leader. But would the people of her country accept her – a person who didn't even know her letters. They would give her a reception and wash their hands of her, expecting her to fend for herself as before. Boys and girls, young enough to be her children, would photograph her and push a mike before her face, "How many times a day did the Pakistan army rape you?"

Tuki could not gauge Mariam's thoughts in the dark. Neither could she see the sly smile on Mariam's face. "I got no husband, no children, no home in this life." The list of things Tuki did not have was endless. It wouldn't be finished even if she recited them the whole night through. But now she had money in her pocket. If a man had money, then even if he was double her age, he could get a wife, children, a home. Tuki was a woman. Age was a big factor for her. Even if one forgot about the Birangana issue, however one looked at it, as good or bad reputation. In the dark, Tuki changed tack. "Mary Apa, are you sleeping? There's one more thing I want to say." Mariam did not respond. Tuki, of course, would say what she had to even if Mariam slept.

She wanted to talk about the three women from Kushtia who left after giving testimony. Tuki had a grievance, "They also got money I hear. And we didn't get to know anything, or understand what was going on even though we're right here in Dhaka! Mary Apa, how many Biranganas are there in this country? Even today on full moon nights and nights when there is no moon I cannot turn from one side to the other when I'm lying down. The whole body aches. A fever rages inside." Tuki gave a deep sigh in the darkness. Mariam was an educated woman. She worked in an office. How could a people's court take place without her knowledge? Mariam assured her that from now on she would keep her eyes and ears open. So that Tuki did not miss the opportunity of standing in the witness-box on the dais.

Tuki fell asleep, dreaming of another people's court. Now it was Mariam's turn to shift restlessly in her bed. Would she testify if there was another people's court? Who would she testify against? All the Pakistani soldiers who had raped her day after day? She didn't know the names of those rapists, or their ranks. Even their faces were indistinct in her memory. The person whom she remembered after so many years of war was Major Ishtiaque. How would she classify her love affair with

Major Ishtiaque? Would her evidence go for or against the man? And then there were Abed Jahangir, Abed Samir and Momtaj – didn't she have any charges to make against them? Those who destroyed her life? The death of Mariam's younger brother Montu who was martyred in combat could never be brought up for trial. Because he was no civilian, but a guerrilla fighter. But there was no answer to the question why he had to go to war even before he had hair on his face. Mariam's uncle Golam Mostofa was a collaborator with the Pakistan army in 1971. He was a war criminal. The house in which Mariam lived was enemy property. Kafiluddin Ahmed had bought this property, a home abandoned by Hindus, at a rock-bottom price. He was dead now. Mariam inherited this property. Would history exonerate her?

For the two decades of the seventies and eighties, Mariam had been involved with her own problems. The nineties was a time of reckoning, of settling issues. But no one could say who would win and who would lose. If suffering was counted as a yardstick, then Mariam would surely win. Because the amount of torture perpetrated on her by Pakistanis was like an ocean in which her affair with Major Ishtiaque was like a dewdrop. And Mariam had no links with Golam Mostofa's Razakar activities. Besides, she had always disliked him.

The night was spent in alternately playing the roles of plaintiff and defendant. Like Bangladesh, she was bewildered about trying war criminals. Tuki had no such dilemma. She was from the proletariat. In her dreams, she was rushing towards a future that promised happiness and prosperity. Her destination was another people's court .

Years passed but another people's court was not held. Tuki questioned, "Mary Apa, have you scanned the papers carefully? Put on your glasses and concentrate." Tuki could not believe that people were delaying the setting up of another people's court for so long. Mariam now had a new problem with her eyes. Earlier, things at a distance got blurred without glasses. Now she had to take off those glasses to be able to read the newspaper, otherwise the print looked indistinct. She looked at

Tuki with her glasses on and the next moment took them off to read the newspaper. Tuki didn't like any of it. Mary Apa had a detachment about her. She was going through her life as if she was half dead, and she didn't want Tuki to make something out of her life either. God! What kind of a person was she?

While the thought of a people's court was getting erased from Tuki's mind, as Mariam leafed through the newspapers, the name of guerrilla fighter Taraman Bibi surfaced in her clouded vision. Her home was on the eastern side of River Brahmaputra in the riverine tracts. It was an arduous trek. The journalists were crossing the river and rushing over the hot sandy soil of the tracts. Taraman Bibi appeared in person after the news reports and photographs were published. A woman with sunken cheeks, disease ridden appearance. A beggar by profession. She was facing the nation twenty-four years after independence when she had reached the last stages of a life ravaged by tuberculosis. Just open a newspaper and you saw her photograph, a news item, an interview. Taraman wanted a full meal of rice. Taraman wanted to live. Taraman's message to Bangladeshis, "Once upon a time my body was strong, now I am just skin and bones with no strength left. My appeal to you is, hold on to this country, do not let it pass into other hands." Taraman stated, "I think the country has become free once again." The reason Taraman participated in guerrilla warfare, "West Pakistanis were taking away all our best foodstuff, our textiles. We tried to hold on to these, we have fought and liberated our country." Taraman was awed with her experience of Dhaka. "Here people eat such delicious food, have a roof over their head. And I can't even manage to get a meal of rice and salt." Taraman complained to the BBC, "If I was someone accused of murder, surely the government would have hunted me down or locked me up in jail. Yet I've fought, I've shed blood during the war, and today I sit at home. No one even bothers to ask after me."

Tuki also harboured such thoughts. If she could get up on stage and express these thoughts, it would have been nice. But that chance had come only for Taraman. Even if she stood on the street and jumped up and down, the camera would not turn towards Tuki. They were busy capturing Taraman – the prime minister awarding Taraman Bibi a medal, Taraman Bibi inaugurating the Victory Day programme at Shahid Minar, Taraman Bibi offering wreaths at Savar Memorial, artists singing patriotic songs in the presence of Taraman, women leaders holding a mike before Taraman's face.

Tuki heard from Mariam that the government had given Taraman Bibi twenty five thousand taka. "So much money! She's rich now, Apa! What has she done to deserve so much money?"

"Taraman fought with weapons."

"You get money if you fight? Won't there be another war in this country?"

Tuki Begum forgot about waiting for a people's court for war criminals and began to wait for another war. Then she could take up arms and fight. But money and fame arrived only when you got tuberculosis, twenty four years after independence. Did she have all that time in her hands? Tuki sat in sadness amid a clutch of roosters and hens. Her life was not improving because of the lack of opportunity. What could she do by selling eggs for fifty or hundred taka? If she could get twenty-five or fifty thousand taka at one go like Taraman Bibi, that would be another matter.

About a week later, Mariam suddenly realised that the number of chickens was going down rapidly. When she asked Tuki, she snapped back, "A mongoose is getting them, what can I do?" In Dhaka, where even cats are scarce, where could a mongoose come from? After persistent questioning for two or three nights, it came out that Tuki was selling off the birds to hawkers. She was no longer happy with her small-scale business. What would she do then? Mariam became upset – whoever came to live in this house seemed to lose their heads. Whose fault was it – the house or Mary's? Should she once again get bottles with spells in them and plant them in the four corners of the house? Mary would get that done. But before that, to satisfy Tuki, who had such a craving for fame and money, she should phone the newspaper offices and let them know that Tuki was a Birangana.

The journalists may come with cameras although that will not guarantee that she would get money. Besides the newshounds may discover that not one but two Biranganas lived in this house. The second one was educated and had a job. So far, all the Biranganas who had been tracked down were poor. They had humiliated themselves in front of society for the second time by describing their dishonour in 1971 as they were seeking money or jobs for their children. The educated ones are faceless, anonymous. Professional actors played their roles on television. If journalists found her, then it was probable that they would dismiss Tuki and zero in on her.

So much politics centring on Biranganas. When Tuki realized all of it, she lost interest in giving interviews. She once again concentrated on poultry-rearing. She raised the chicks as if they were her own children. She alone was parent to them, their sibling, their uncle and aunt. During her leisure time, she would sit on her prayer mat and count the beads of her tasbih in prayer. Tuki was getting ready for the next life but should Mariam, about to turn fifty, leave this world without telling anyone anything?

A weight lifted from her chest when Golam Mostofa died. He died of illness, without ever being punished for war crimes. The other person who may have rushed to Dhaka to scold her had she read her daughter's story of humiliation in the newspapers, had also passed away. On Monowara Begum's first death anniversary, Mariam decided to tell her story. She felt no need to inform Ratna and Chhanda. They were living happily with their husbands and family—one in Fultali and the other in Saudi Arabia. She had never had any help and support from them in times of crisis. So Mariam felt it better to keep them at a distance in this matter as well. When Mukti knocked on her door, the whole process of decision-making was nearly over and the country had been independent for nearly twenty-eight years. The year was 1999.

XXIX

Where Does Life End?

Two years is a long time – especially for a case study. There was no written evidence or document certifying that Mariam was a Birangana. The Birangana office had been bankrupt on this issue for quite a while. After the 1975 assassinations and riots, a new ruling group had emerged. In a country where the struggle for power is the primary aim, no great project can move in a smooth, straightforward fashion. And travellers are always scarce for a difficult journey. The former social workers wound up their activities. But they could not escape history. Research scholars, journalists, columnists jog their age-weakened memories on December 16, March 26 and some other days in the year. It was almost like plucking fruit from a tree. Then the interviews with social workers are published in newspapers with their photographs. Sometimes they are quoted in publications. But Mukti is empty-handed – Radharani of Daulatdia had slipped from her hands like an eel the moment they met. Baby, a salaried social worker, stayed away from such scenes, but preserved some memories under the glass top of her table. That is how perhaps she remembered Mariam's address which then reached Mukti's hands. Mariam was present and absent there at the same time. For the story of nine months of war had followed her crossing the river Padma and travelling further afield. Mukti had to follow that trail. The new research showed that Rameez Sheikh, who in the third month of war could not differentiate between the slogans 'Pakistan Zindabad' and 'Joi Bangla' was now seen as a patriot. Toothless Jaitun Bibi of Notungaon begins to talk. She still recalls Mariam's moon-like face. But the eighty-year old lady thinks that the girl is ill-omened. The military had sniffed their way after her right to Notungaon village. Mariam had vowed to cement Montu's grave. Aminul, who had been the guide for the company of Muktijoddhas, who had seen Montu leap onto the headlights of the enemy vehicle like an insect, is now a landless farmer. He says, how can you build a grave for someone whose corpse was not found? The thirty-year old dilapidated grave, eroded by rain and floods, belonged to the freedom fighter Majibar, the one with the raised arms. Ata Mian of Kamalganj, the son-in-law who lived with his in-laws and who had led one failed sortie after another but had never lamented the fact, was the only person who claimed to be able to identify Major Ishtiaque. Having locked up Mariam in a room, Major Ishtiaque was trying to escape. Then he encountered the angry villagers and was saved by the skin of his teeth. The Muktijodhha Rafiqul, who was drunk first on war and then on alcohol, is filled with loathing even today when he thinks of Mariam's stinking body, abused by the enemy. Mariam isn't remotely interested in FDC side-actor Bakul Begum. Bakul Begum who made an entrance during the Birangana office episode and exited; who Mariam had never even met; who appeared to be more of a character in a film than in real life. Mary, alias Mariam, has only one request again and again, "Mukti, please arrange a meeting for me with Anuradha. Your office has found so many people. Why don't you try and see if you can find her?"

"Why?"

"I want to hear something from her. I want another prediction."

"What is that?"

"I want to know where my life will end."

Mukti suddenly remembers Radharani of Daulatdia after two years. The woman who had been able to forecast the future without reading palms, who had predicted her own lifespan: a hundred years. Such a clairvoyant could surely foretell where Mariam's life would end. Mukti thinks of going to Daulatdia a second time. Mariam says, "Go if you want to. But I don't believe in fortune tellers. My mother believed in them."

It does not matter if Mariam is a sceptic. Mukti has other business with Radharani. The interview with her would certainly be unique. Mukti has caught Tuki's fever of high ambition. She needs more interviews and testimonies to be able to organize a public trial of war crimes which is the main objective or goal of their research project.

When she sees Mukti, the NGO worker laments loudly. "You've come so late. Radharani's dead."

What is she saying? "How did she die?"

"Of heart failure."

Perhaps Mukti had also believed that Radharani would live to be a hundred. But the NGO worker hadn't believed it. She says, "Rubbish! What are you saying? Crazy talk from someone educated like you!" On the other hand, Kushumkali is still firm in her belief that Radharani was supposed to live till a hundred. No one can budge her. When Mukti asks "How'd Radharani die?" she says, "Somebody'd poisoned her drink. Else would Radharani have died so easily! She would've lived to be a hundred."

"Who did it?"

Is there any lack of enemies in a whorehouse! The brothels are the holy places of love. When love ebbs on the home front, a man peregrinates here seeking love. And he brings with him jealousy, hatred, terror. "You know how many prostitutes have been murdered in the locality in the last one year? Jochhna, Piriobala…" Kushumkali counts the names on her fingers and tries to recall the names of the dead prostitutes. The NGO worker butts in, "Altogether five."

"You're leaving out Radharani," Kushumkali gets angry with the NGO worker. One of them believes that Radharani has been murdered, the other that it's a natural death. Mukti stands between the two. Now she has to mediate, "Are you sure that Radharani was murdered?" Kushumkali bristles, "Of course I'm sure – one hundred percent!"

Because four days before Radharani's death, two middle aged clients had come to Daulatdia. They separated and entered two rooms next to each other. They looked like they were twins but actually they were Azrails, Angels of Death, come to claim the soul of Radharani. When they were leaving, they encountered Radharani in a drunken state. Then one of the twins or Azrails said, "Hey aren't you Anuradha? Daughter of B K Sarkar? The one who was an advocate in the lower courts?"

Mukti trembles. Radharani was jolted out of her drunkenness. She said, "No, you're mistaken, I am Radharani. My father's name was Khedmat Ali. He was a chowkidar. He's dead now." Radharani said these words in a rush and then went to her room and locked herself in. At the time Kushumkali had been coming this way bringing a relish made of dried fish, a savoury to accompany Radharani's drinks. At the head of the lane, she met the twins. They were talking among themselves, "Anuradha Sarkar has joined a whorehouse and turned into Radharani. Did you see her lording it? And she drinks!" Without any idea of what was going on, Kushumkali knocked on Radharani's door. "Oh, my Radhe! Oh, Rani! Open up. I've made your favourite snack." Radharani didn't open the door. The prostitutes in the two adjoining rooms came out. It was then that Kushumkali found out that their twin clients had let the cat out of the bag. The day Radharani died, the twins came in the evening. They had a bottle of foreign liquor with them. This time they ignored the beckoning of the two prostitutes and went directly to Radharani's room. Then there was a lot of shouting in there. Radharani died of heart failure that same night, after the twins left.

Mariam does not believe the story. She had accepted these last thirty years that Anuradha was dead. So the news of the death is nothing new. But would anyone become a whore just to prove her predictions? She says, "An educated woman like her, how could she have turned from a Birangana to a prostitute? She had enough for basic necessities."

"But she'd become a prostitute," Mukti stresses the point. Mariam shakes her head, "No, no. You're making a mistake." Then to check on the truth of the claim, she wants to know if Anuradha wore glasses. Mukti says, "Yes. But the stems were broken. She had tied them to her hair with string." Even then Mariam isn't upset. Anuradha, the woman who had once believed that a group of researchers would come one day and rescue her bones, torn garments, tresses of hair from the torture camps, that they would not let her be forgotten and keep her memory alive eternally. Thirty years after the war, she did not get a burial in independent Bangladesh. Her body was floated on the River Padma. Mariam shakes her head in the same way when she hears these accounts. "What do you think of yourself, my girl? Would you turn into a prostitute if you were angry with your country and your people? Someone who didn't want for food and clothing, who was educated, would she become a prostitute? Can't you have made a mistake! There can be many people in this world who share the same name. This prostitute was someone else."

Mukti does not put into words that once upon a time, when her marriage to Momtaj was breaking up, Mariam had also toyed with the idea of becoming a prostitute. Even though she had been educated and did not want for food and clothing. The attitudes of people change as they grow old.

In the middle of their conversation, Tuki's roosters and hens leap up on the veranda. As if instead of humans, some other creatures have gathered together to mourn Anuradha's death. Dusk descends. In the shadows of the street lamps, the house appears grey, faded and shabby like some city in the history of a forgotten past. Mariam stirs herself and rises. Tuki has gone to her village these last four days. The chore of feeding the poultry at the end of day and locking them up in their shed is now Mariam's.

Tuki has gone to her village after many years, to buy a piece of land. Her plans are: she will have a pond dug in her own land, breed fish in that pond, various trees and shrubs are to be planted on three sides of the pond and a poultry shed for ducks and chickens is to be built on the fourth side. What is more, if the price was right, then Tuki wanted to buy a piece of land for her own grave before she returned to Dhaka this time. She had had to flee from her village in the fourth year of independence. Even her parents hadn't wanted this daughter of theirs to live in their society as a dishonoured woman. Fed up with the cruelties of people, Tuki's father had begun sharpening the boti. But it was not possible for him to take his daughter's life with his own hands. The next time Tuki's mother had mixed poison with water and forced Tuki to drink it. Day and night, Tuki's mother repeated the same words, "There's no use keeping you alive. Why don't you die!" When Tuki was in the throes of death, her aunt held a torn shoe before her nose and her cousin went to get some human excreta on the tip of the machete. The smell and taste of old shoe and excreta made Tuki vomit and spew out the poison. If they had tried to take her to the hospital, she would have died from the poison on the way. That aunt and the cousin started her off on her way to Dhaka two days later.

At present, Tuki's parents are both dead. She believed that she is going home after twenty-six years. The villagers will not recognize her or if they do, they will treat her with the respect due to a Birangana. But her experience is different. "Ah! Tuki Begum, when did you come from the brothel?" Someone shoots her this unwarranted question on the road, even before she enters her home. Even before Tuki can comprehend what is being said, another person responds, "She's growing old so she's had to retire from the business." The villagers demand double the price for selling land to her and nobody wants to sell her a piece of burial land. Tuki returns to Dhaka having failed to acquire land for her farm or for her burial.

Tuki is fated to be unlucky. She wanted a people's court. It did not happen. She wanted another war of liberation and there was no possibility of that. She even failed in her wish to spend the rest of her life as a householder. She could not buy space for her final resting place even in exchange for cash. Since her return to Dhaka, Tuki Begum is always sad. If Mariam calls to her ten times, she replies maybe once. Or sometimes she doesn't respond at all. It is a problem. Will Mariam look after herself or take care of Tuki? The business about Anuradha has disoriented her. Life is stranger than film and theatre. Should she believe or not? If she believes, then what will happen to the ground beneath her feet? In a country where a Birangana couldn't even get a decent burial, there was going to be a trial for war crimes? She was wrong in letting Mukti record her statements for the last two years.

It's not impossible for a person who harbours such thoughts to grow angry. Mariam sees herself getting angry, but with Tuki.

In the end, one day Tuki opens up, "I was called a prostitute even though I wasn't one. What is the purpose of my life? What did I gain by remaining a virgin all my life?"

"Who's a virgin?"

"Why, me? You've married twice. Have I married?"

"But didn't you have a baby in the military camp?"

"So what? Did I have a husband then or had I wanted to have a child? It was just the result of abuse."

Unbidden, Mariam tries to explain to Tuki that a woman no longer remained a virgin when she has had a child, whether she had wanted to or not. But this leads to a spat between the two. They stop talking to each other. When Mukti visits them at home, Tuki points to the closed door. "She's locked herself in. It's forbidden to knock on her door." What's the matter? Was Mariam mourning Anuradha? It wasn't even forty days since the woman had died. "I think she's sitting in prayer," Tuki says. "If she does not serve God at this age, when will she do it? After all, the end is drawing near."

But on her next visit Mukti hears that Mariam has gone to Daulatdia and she has been going there quite often with clothes, books, pens and pencils for Anuradha's young daughter. But that hadn't done any good. Kushumkali had already introduced Anuradha's nine-year old daughter Champabati to the business.

Champabati had not objected. She was keeping her mouth shut and taking cow-fattening injections.

Tuki accompanies Mariam on one or two occasions to Daulatdia. She does not like the place. "Pleasure may be found here but not peace. There is so much hubbub, as if a fairground round the year." Once she enters a brothel, she feels restless and wants to run away. On a signal from Mariam, Kushumkali tells Tuki, "Let me show you a comedy, sister. It'll cheer you up."

They create a stage by removing a trunk, chair and table fan. Kushumkali tightens her sari end round her waist. This is her solo performance with singing and dancing.

"There lives a rich king, with two wives. The king's very old. He has a senior wife, grandchildren, but the king marries again. He lost his head when he saw my beauty. And he proposed marriage to me. I'm the daughter of a poor man, the daughter of a maidservant. My mother married me off to this old king because she's greedy for his wealth. I have no father. The old man's grandson is Chandan Kumar Das. The grandfather's old, I'm young. In spite of being the grandfather's wife, I make love to his grandson. It's a secret affair. Suddenly, one night I go into the garden. The old man comes into my room but doesn't find me. When he can't find me, he picks up a lantern and a walking stick and searches for me. And he finds me."

There's a table on the stage then. It's covered with a long tablecloth. Chandan goes and hides under the table.

"The old man says, 'You're here, my wife, and I am looking for you all over.' I trip the old king so that he falls. I start a song, 'I won't eat the meals given by you. I won't go to your house again. I have toiled in your home, old man. And you did not give me a nice, coloured sari to clothe myself, hai, hai, to clothe myself. I won't go to your house again.' Then the old man's desire wells up once again. The old king says, 'I will now get a job. Oh my beauty! I will take you with me. So much stuff for make-up, ooh! Hai, hai, make-up, what a lot of make-up, alta to colour your feet, why won't you come with me…'

'I won't go to your house again.'

"The old man takes his seat. I sit on another chair. After sitting down the old king pushes his feet under the table. With his feet under the table, he asks, 'My wife, oh my young wife, what is this moving under the table? I want to know what is moving?' I say, 'Oh! I remember what's moving. Ash gourds were being sold near the house. Ripe ash gourds, so I bought some.'

"So he's saying, 'Why are ash gourds moving?' I say, 'Because you are rolling them with your feet. They're pushed against each other, and that's why they're moving.' Then the old man jabs his fingers on Chandan Kumar's body. 'My wife, why is it so soft?' I say, 'I guess rot has set in one of them.'

"Chandan Kumar comes out from the back and runs away."

Tuki likes the story. The woman Kushumkali isn't such a bad person either. But it is getting late. They need to return to Dhaka.

On their next visit to Daulatdia, before boarding the ferry, Mariam takes Tuki in another direction. There she bargains with the boatman. What nerve, she's thinking of crossing the River Padma in a boat. Mariam smiles from the corner of her mouth. During the year of war she had crossed the Padma on a boat carrying labourers to Barisal for harvesting rice. But that was the time of war and the ferry crossing had been closed down. The motorised launches of the inland water transport authority had been removed from the landing stage well in advance, in case the military tried to use them. Now rejecting the ferry and the launches to cross the river, why does Mariam want to hire a country boat and where does she want to go? She does not disclose much to Tuki. When she coaxes and cajoles, Mariam says, "I was trying to reckon the income and expenses of boatmen."

"Why?"

"No particular reason."

When Mukti goes to enquire in her office, she discovers that Mariam has not been to work for several days. She had left a hand-written resignation letter quite a while ago. She hadn't even returned to find out whether it had been accepted or not.

Another day, when Mukti visits Mariam's home, she finds

Tuki packing this and that. Tuki smiles as soon as she sees her, "Sit down and rest a bit. Mary Apa has gone to Daulatdia." Tuki doesn't know when she will return. Mukti sits and waits. Tuki is very busy with lots of chores. At one time, she gets up to help Tuki net the poultry. Both of them tie the birds' legs with strings. Mukti is puzzled. Why is Tuki Begum tying up the roosters and hens in pairs? Has her old craziness of selling off the birds to hawkers secretly resurfaced? Tuki smiles again, "Mary Apa told me to get this done. So I'm doing it." It's not believable that the stubborn-as-a-mule Tuki would blindly follow Mariam's orders without knowing why. In the face of Mukti's cross-examination, Tuki spills the beans reluctantly. No one was willing to hire out a passenger boat for transporting cargo. That is why Mary Apa has gone to Aricha to make a deposit for a new boat with the money she withdrew from her office. Mukti is startled. After all, Mariam often saw in her dreams a new boat that raised its sails, crossed and recrossed the river. But how was that linked to hobbling the legs of the poultry? Tuki is surprised and annoyed, "What do you mean there's no link? After we're gone, will these birds be left behind in this restless world?"

Mukti teases, "You are taking the birds with you and you won't take me?" Tuki is serious. Only Mary Apa can say whether she wishes to take along her biographer or not. But the fact of the matter is that it is not a must that you have to take along your near and dear ones. When the great deluge had begun, the prophet Noah could not take on the ark his son who had disobeyed Allah. Allah had given strict orders not to take him. Rahmanur Rahim, the All-Merciful had said, "Oh Prophet Noah, if you once again plead for your son, the sinner, your prophethood will be taken from you."

The way Tuki is behaving it seems she has no wish to remain in this sinful world a moment longer. She is taking with her only what is essential. The situation is no longer a mystery to Mukti. But where are they going? They had no dearth of food and clothing that they were forced to move to Daulatdia. And even if they do go, what will these over-fifty women do in a brothel? It is no use asking Tuki these questions. She herself probably doesn't know very well where their journey is starting and where it will end. Meanwhile, she has not been able to meet Mariam for over a month. She has been avoiding Mukti. The news of Anuradha's death had turned it all upside down. People are so difficult to understand. It is easier to understand the angels in heaven – the good and the bad were neatly classified. Was a person who had succeeded in punting along her aimless life for over thirty years desperate now to know its end and ready to set sail in search of a dead body? No one but a lunatic would believe it. But it wasn't impossible for Mariam and Tuki to load their possessions in a boat and set off for Daulatdia. Kushumkali would help them. But Mukti is afraid to visualize the possibility. She thinks of other things, only dwelling obliquely on these two future possibilities for the two women. A public trial of war crimes cannot be held in the absence of the complainant herself, irrespective of whether it is real or symbolic. She needs Mariam for a few more days.

Mukti doesn't know that, let alone a public trial of war crimes, Mariam is going to vanish forever leaving the story behind also unfinished. And she, Mukti, to establish her credibility with her readers, has till the end remained true to reality – right from the start of her interviews which she conducted with care and patched together the statements and confessions of several people, even though occasionally she felt hopeless. But one day she will have to console herself by concocting a story of a long boat journey, a story that she herself will cook up.

After about a year of Mariam and Tuki's disappearance, the Rayer Bazar house is demolished and in its place a four-storied apartment building comes up. There is a black gate in front. Kafiluddin Ahmed's name along with the address, Village: Fultali, P. O.: Saharpar has been erased. In its place the names of the twin sisters – Ratna and Chchanda – had been painted separately. Mary, alias Mariam, is nowhere. No evidence remains of the fact that she was ever there. Still, the readers would have believed the story had it ended in the rock-solid ground of this earth instead trailing off into an imaginary boat journey.

XXX

The Search

"Mary Apa, you're not speaking. Where you taking me?"

Mariam slowly walks through the fog. Although what she says to Tuki cannot be heard, the look on Tuki's face indicates that she is agreeable. Only a deep sigh floats in the morning air. Mariam's dream boat has been made up, locked up, and ready even before dawn has broken. When they board with all their belongings, the boat sets sail. The sails catch the wind. The boatman sits on the prow and pulls at the oar. Mariam is silent. Like a shrouded corpse, her spirit has escaped its earthly bonds. Tuki's heart heaves like the swelling waves of water. She does not know what the ocean is like. Neither does she know the nature of the afterworld. On the banks of the river, smoke billows out of the chimneys of the brick kilns. Why do humans build so much? Close by the floating dockyard looks like a giant. On the opposite bank, there are countless skeletons of ships. Lungis and gamchchas have been hung out to dry on the rusty, broken railings of the doors and windows that seem to be agape. The scenes of cattle bathing, of young women splashing in water on their way home, their water pots filled after their dip in the river, belong to a distant past. The images in school drawing books float in Mariam's mind before sinking again into oblivion.

Tuki thinks that it doesn't really matter if the poultry is fed or not fed at the end of the day. Questions of profit and loss have become immaterial. All the enterprise on both the banks is meant to be left behind. Still, when a kingfisher skims over the water with a fish in its beak and takes off skywards, she cannot help smiling. She applauds the competing swimmers silently. When they see the egrets scrabbling in the mud banks, they both recall their childhoods. "Mary Apa, when I was a child, I wanted to be the wife of a fisherman. Once I'd even wanted to be a bird when I was feeling sad." Mariam cannot even glimpse girlhood fantasies. Year in and year out, she had written in her examination papers in Bengali and English, 'I will become a doctor when I grow up. I will not charge for visits to the poor.' By the time she had begun to think about marriage, Jashimul Haque and Abed Jahangir had arrived on the scene. Then came the war. Nothing of one's likes and dislikes, of one's choice and discernment remained.

When the evening lamps are lit in the houses on the riverbanks, Tuki again feels the waves break against her heart. Vines of pumpkins, gourds and broad beans trail across the roof. Blossoms in all colours have flowered in them. Stacks of golden straw lie here and there. The children wash themselves and sit down to study under the light of kerosene lamps. Cutting through the night breeze, birds fly from one place to another. The pitch-dark sky in the distance stands guard over them in their journey, erasing the image of the home and family that Tuki never had. There is a current of myriad stars across its vast expanse.

Banks of clouds have gathered on the north-west sky. The boatman says, "There's a storm gathering." Another day, pulling at the oar, he says, "The water feels heavy. Doesn't seem a good sign." The boatman settles his accounts for six days of rowing and disembarks on a lonely sandbank. As he leaves, in the glimmering darkness of the starry sky, Mariam sees in him the face of the boatman during the '71 crossing. But as he climbs out of the boat, this boatman hums a popular song of the day, which the earlier boatman could not have sung, "I had a river, but no one ever knew…"

On the seventh day, Tuki and Mariam cross the limited boundaries of human predictions. And at that very moment, they see Anuradha standing on a sandy ground, waving a white handkerchief and beckoning to them. Mariam sheds the sombre mien of a corpse and now looks quite cheerful. If they move ahead a little bit, perhaps they will see Rameez Sheikh and Montu. Meanwhile, the unmanned boat skims towards Anuradha. When Mariam catches hold of the outstretched ice-cold hand as it hangs in nothingness, Anuradha climbs onto the deck of the boat. Even then, they do not let go of each other's hands. Oh they've met after so many years! Anuradha's skin is covered with moss and algae from having floated in water for so many days. But both their hands are equally warm now. And Anuradha is once again the same lively young girl. Mariam, of course, cannot see herself. In front of her is Tuki Begum, who is wearing only a sari, without a blouse or petticoat. She is the domestic help of the Choudhury family. She has slipped back to the age when she was captured. She has gathered the end of her sari into a ball and holds it in front of her face. The sun is setting on the world. In Tuki's eyes is reflected the land left behind that floats like hair against the red horizon. Anuradha looks toward it and exults, "How beautiful is our country!"

Tuki removes the sari-end from her face, "The country for which we shed our blood."